Crossing the Blue Line

To Jene,
Stay loyal to those who matter!
— William Mark

William Mark

Published by:
Southern Yellow Pine (SYP) Publishing
4351 Natural Bridge Rd.
Tallahassee, FL 32305

All Rights reserved. No part of this publication may be reproduced, stored in a retrieval system, or transmitted in any form or by any means, electronic, mechanical, photocopying, recording, scanning or otherwise, without the prior written permission of the Publisher. For permission or further information, contact SYP Publishing, LLC. 4351 Natural Bridge Rd., Tallahassee, FL 32305.

www.syppublishing.com

This is a work of fiction. Names, characters, places, and events that occur either are the products of the author's imagination or are used fictitiously. Any resemblance to actual persons, places, or events is purely coincidental.

The contents and opinions expressed in this book do not necessarily reflect the views and opinions of Southern Yellow Pine Publishing, nor does the mention of brands or trade names constitute endorsement.

ISBN-10: 1-940869-72-2 Trade Paperback
ISBN-13: 978-1-940869-72-8 Trade Paperback
ISBN-13: 978-1-940869-73-5 ePub
ISBN-13: 978-1-940869-74-2 Adobe eBook
Library of Congress Control Number: 2016940862

Copyright © 2016 by William Mark
Front Cover Design: James C. Hamer

Printed in the United States of America
First Edition May 2016

Acknowledgements

To my wife, my best content editor and supporter, I can't do this without you, thank you.

Special thanks to Chris, as always, he helps me keep the story on the right path.

Also by William Mark

From Behind the Blue Line

Crusaders of the Lost Series
Lost in the Darkness: Book I

Some sins never wash away. Lurking, haunting every move, they wait for redemption. It's a glimpse into hell because it's hell that is waiting.

Chapter 1

"So, was it worth it?" Beau asked.

Dylan thought about the question for a moment.

"Yes."

A wind swept over the north hill of the cemetery, sending chills through the two men. Beau stood for several more minutes looking down at the tombstone of Caitlin Akers, not knowing what to do next. He looked up, taking in the western horizon. The sun hung low, painting a brilliant mix of purple and orange hues that splashed across the sky. Beau turned to Dylan with a degree of finality and spoke.

"Good-bye, my friend."

Dylan nodded. His eyes were tear-soaked and fixed on his daughter's grave.

Beau turned and walked up the hill to his car. As he cranked the engine, an odd movement caught his eye. He looked in the mirror, but nothing was there. He glanced in the side-view mirror, still nothing. He passed it off as errant paranoia and drove down the cemetery road and out onto the street.

A quest for revenge had been realized. It was over. The two men responsible for the murder of Dylan's daughter had been exterminated like vermin. Beau and Dylan had found, judged, and executed the men, sending them to the afterlife. Beau believed their path was the road to hell as opposed to the one of eternal grace. He wondered which path awaited him.

With his future uncertain, Beau was surprisingly calm as if he had gained control of his life, and as if Caitlin had forgiven him. Maybe his future was unwritten after all. Maybe, he found redemption for removing an evil man from the world in the name of justice.

Stopped by a traffic light, Beau lowered the window of his brand new Ford Mustang and let the cool air fill the car's interior. The sun had dipped down below the tree line, casting grayish shadows upon the earth.

Suddenly, he was jolted forward with a loud crunch. He jumped in his seat. When he checked the rearview mirror, the chrome grill of a large SUV stared back. Blue strobe lights flashed repeatedly, nearly blinding him. Movement redirected his attention forward again. Another black SUV raced from the cross street to block him in, its blue lights also flashing and the air horn blared, overwhelming Beau. He had less than a second to react or he was finished.

Beau stomped on the accelerator and met the front fender of the incoming SUV. The large truck glanced off Beau's car after a loud thump, but the heavier vehicle sent Beau into the oncoming lane. Instead of fighting against the more powerful SUV, he pulled left and spun the nimble car for a U-turn, evading his pursuers.

"Shit. What the hell!"

Beau floored the gas pedal and sped away from the SUVs, a pair of black Chevy Tahoes with government plates. Their sirens kicked on and wailed as they gave chase. Beau headed south through town, hoping to lose them in thicker traffic. He looked back and studied the two SUVs in pursuit. Blue strobe lights, sirens, and they had attempted a tactical pin. It was obvious, Captain Pritchard had sicced the U.S. Marshals on him. His only advantage, before they called in reinforcements, was his Mustang could out-maneuver the bulkier Tahoes.

At nearly seventy miles an hour, he sped down South Monroe Street past unaware motorists. Squeezing between two stopped cars at the turn for Apalachee Parkway, Beau zipped through the intersection in front of the State Capitol like a speeding bullet. As he crested the hill, he hit the brakes and made a quick turn east onto Gaines Street, squealing his tires as they slid across the pavement. He turned north on Suwanee and ignored all of the red lights, looping his way onto Apalachee Parkway. As he merged onto the highway, he glanced in his mirror to see the two SUVs still on his tail. One nearly ran a civilian off the road while trying to keep pace. Beau gunned the accelerator and weaved through traffic, hoping his near-reckless actions would cause the motorists to clog up the road in confusion, blocking his determined hunters.

The black Tahoes repeatedly blared their air horns, parting the traffic behind Beau, keeping him in sight. Beau made it to Blairstone Road and turned north. The unmistakable thump of helicopter blades cutting the air grew louder. Beau looked up to see the Sheriff's chopper hovering about four hundred feet in the sky.

Shit!

The stretch of Blairstone north of Centerville Road was void of other cars. The SUVs managed to gain ground on Beau's speeding Mustang. As one moved within striking distance, it slammed into the back of Beau's car, attempting to spin him out of control. Beau zig-zagged across both lanes and onto the shoulder, spoiling their attempts. A grin creased Beau's lips as he realized that, to a small degree, he was enjoying himself.

Glass shattered somewhere behind Beau, and suddenly, he was covered in small pieces. He reached up and felt trickles of blood running down his neck. A burning sensation followed. He looked to see that his back window had been shot out by the advancing Marshals. He patted his neck, hoping to find only cuts and no holes. After a few dabs and no gushing blood found, he was still in the fight.

Fuck me! They ain't messing around.

Beau traversed his way to the north side of the city with the Marshals in hot pursuit. The Sheriff's helicopter was calling the chase and soon everyone with a badge would converge on his location. No car in the world could escape a dragnet that large.

With one hand on the wheel, Beau reached into the glove box. He found what he was searching for and quickly pulled it out. He fiddled with his gun, one-handed, making sure there was a full magazine and one round loaded in the chamber. He held the pistol tight and stuffed it under his right thigh, and then he gripped the wheel with both hands.

He was going to have to make a run for it, but there was only one place he wanted to go, only one person he wanted to see—especially if this was the end.

The Mustang sped along the small residential road, and he slammed on the brakes. As the Tahoes negotiated the tight corner turn, Beau leapt from the car and ran for the woods. He aimed his gun at the incoming SUVs and squeezed off several rounds, hoping to delay their chase. The Marshals heeded the gunshots and took cover at the end of the street. Beau's move had bought him more time.

Once he reached the back wood line to the Aker's house, he sprinted across the back yard. He didn't want to bring any danger to Wendy, but he needed to say good-bye.

"Wendy!" he shouted as he ran. "Wendy, are you home? Let me in, please."

Beau climbed the stairs of the deck and beat furiously on the back door, checking cautiously behind him, knowing he only had minutes at the most.

"Wendy, please!"

No answer. Beau heard shouts from the woods. The helicopter searched two houses down then headed in his direction. Beau tried the door. It was unlocked. He went inside and quickly shut it.

The house was quiet, unlike the chaos churning outside. Beau crept softly through the living room and called out for Wendy in a whisper. An eerie feeling came over him. He raised his gun up out of instinct. He stepped around the couch and saw a figure standing in the kitchen, holding a baby.

"Hey." Beau said to Wendy. Alluring and transcendent, she was the image of perfection. He smiled seeing her beautiful face looking back at him. With a blank stare, she stood frozen.

"What's wrong?" he asked. "Whose baby is that?"

Beau grew confused. He lowered the gun and asked Wendy again.

"Hey, what's going on? Whose baby is that?"

A pained expression on her face turned confusion into fear. Beau waited for an answer. Wendy looked at the bundle in her arms and then looked up at Beau with sad eyes and spoke.

"Yours, Beau. He's yours."

Incredulous, he struggled to say aloud, "What?"

Wendy's eyes quickly darted to Beau's left, setting off his internal alarm. He turned to see what was there. Captain Reginald Pritchard stood in the living room with an evil grin spread across his face and his eyes burning hot with hatred. He aimed a gun directly at Beau's head.

"I told you I'd get you, you son of a bitch!"

The blast of fire morphed into white light that surrounded and enveloped Beau like a tidal wave crashing down. The loud, sharp crack of the gunshot echoed into a deafening hiss until everything went silent.

***

Beau Rivers's eyes ripped open, and he shot out of bed. He was panting and covered in sweat. He looked around the quiet apartment, bringing himself back to reality. He was not dead. This time in the reoccurring dream, he had been driving a Mustang and Wendy was holding a real baby. Over the last six months, since he had killed George Shelley, he had driven several different vehicles including a tank, a police car, and Chitty-Chitty Bang-Bang. Previously, Wendy had held a doll, a watermelon, and one time, a miniature version of Beau. He remembered seeing a new, bright red Mustang on his way home the night before which instantly triggered a memory of Wendy. He figured that was why it had become incorporated into his never-ending nightmare.

This time, Pritchard was the one who shot him. This sometimes changed, but for the most part, it was the Captain, now Major, who killed him in the end. He hoped that wasn't a foretelling of real life. One time, Dylan had been the person who pulled the trigger. It took Beau nearly a week to shake off that dream as just a dream.

Beau caught his breath and wiped the sweat from his face. He looked around the bedroom and saw his meager existence was still in place. The framed photo of Dylan and Beau from their academy graduation day lay face down on his nightstand. A half-empty bottle of vodka sat on top. He checked the time on the alarm clock. One thirty-seven p.m. He had to be at work in two and half hours. He did some quick math in his head, and satisfied with the result, he grabbed the bottle of Stoli. He twisted off the cap and turned up the vodka, chugging it straight from the bottle. The lukewarm alcohol burned on the way down like liquid fire and violently shook Beau awake, bringing him back to life. He swallowed and coughed until his throat was ready for round two. He took a deep breath and tossed the bottle up for another pull, nearly emptying it. He put the bottle back on the nightstand and he flopped onto the bed.

He lay in bed letting the vodka soak into his bloodstream. He had calculated the amount of alcohol that was just enough to give him the desired buzz before work. The two-hour wait was enough. If tested at work, he'd remain under the limit. It was a careful balance he calculated each and every day.

Work was not work anymore. It was a chore. After Pritchard and the rest of IA failed to sustain Beau on anything but insubordination, his gun and badge were returned to him unceremoniously. Then rather than being put back on the road to work patrol, he was sentenced to the Airport Unit as penance. The sheer boredom of inaction and mundane tasks drove Beau to the brink of collapse. It was a death sentence. However, to preserve his vow of being a constant thorn in the backside of Reginald Pritchard and his beloved Tallahassee Police Department, he was determined to stick it out. He would never give that man the satisfaction of his failure.

Finally dragging himself in to work, Beau took a seat at the customer service desk, positioned just outside of the TSA check-point, between the A and B terminals.

"Beau, can you do a perimeter run, please? Before the five-thirty from Dallas gets in?"

Beau looked up at his sergeant, Leo Mathis. Mathis wore a pleading look on his face as if he was trying not to upset Beau, even though he was his supervisor.

"Sure. No problem," Beau said, flatly.

"Thanks."

The nearly two-thousand-five-hundred-acre airport had a service road, strictly for airport personnel who ran around the perimeter. It took Beau about twenty-five minutes to navigate the track in his patrol car. Many times on the far side of the property, he would stop and get out to watch a plane take off. He couldn't figure out why, but he enjoyed watching a plane lift off the ground and take flight. He thought it was childish fascination of the mechanical wonder, but the more he thought about it, he gave credence to the idea that an airplane taking off was symbolic of escape, something he wished he had the power to do.

Only halfway through the shift, he had already made three perimeter runs, two parking lot checks, and a walk-through of both wings of the regional airport, making sure all the necessary doors were locked. He dealt with the boredom, but the silence was difficult to take. At this point in the day, all of the airline check-ins were closed and only incoming flights remained. The internal businesses were shut down and most of the employees had left for the day. The skeleton night crew, about four cops, the awaiting airline employees, and the janitors were all that occupied the airport. It was always quiet. Beau found himself stepping out the front door to hear the traffic passing on Capital Circle and to remind himself he was still in civilization.

"Easy night, officer?"

Beau had just finished another walk-through of the A wing when Malcolm, the night janitor, spoke.

"Yep, just like all the others."

"That's good, that's good. Better than having trouble find us."

Malcolm was in the middle of cleaning the men's room in the A wing. He wrung out a mop in a bucket and looked at Beau as if he hoped for conversation. It was clear Malcolm hated the silence too.

"You're right about that, buddy. But sometimes we can't hide from it."

Malcolm let out a hardy laugh. "You know that's right."

Beau smiled. The comment wasn't that funny, but he liked Malcolm. He was a simple man, honest and hard-working, never complained and carried a perpetual smile. Beau checked him out after being reassigned to the airport and found that he had done ten years in prison for an armed robbery, but it had been over twenty years since he was released. Malcolm was one of the few who rehabilitated and stayed clean. Cleaning toilets at night for the airport wasn't prestigious any way you looked at it, but it was better than a life in prison.

"Going to make a coffee run before they close. You want anything Malcolm?"

"Uh, yeah. Thank you, officer. That'd be nice."

"Don't worry about it. Just keep an eye out for trouble would you?"

Malcolm grinned ear to ear and let another laugh get out. "Yes, sir. I sure will."

The last flight of the day taxied in just before midnight, and Beau watched the passengers disembark and walk through the terminal. Some were business-like in how they moved, wanting to get out of the tiny airport as quickly as possible. Others walked more slowly, awaiting a long anticipated reunion. From the courtesy desk, Beau could see people waiting on the other side of the checkpoint for a loved one's return. He hated this part, but he forced himself to watch.

Once through the checkpoint exit and into the main hallway, he watched the passengers be greeted with open arms, long hugs, and even longer kisses. Their smiles were genuine and infectious. Sometimes, small children would be kept up late to greet Mom and Dad with indescribable joy and unconditional love. Beau watched in pained agony until they left the airport, returning to a better life with real happiness.

Beau suffered through these moments because it reminded him, excruciatingly, that he had no one to wait for him at the airport.

On the way home, Beau switched his radio to the primary patrol channel. He listened to the chatter of the officers working the midnight shift, but mainly he waited for the day the emergency alert tone would come, and he would have a chance to be a hero again. The fifteen-minute drive from the airport to his apartment was never enough of a window to grant him that wish.

Once home, he went straight to the kitchen, poured himself the rest of the Stoli, and shot it down his throat. He set the bottle aside and got another one from the cabinet above the stove. This one he poured over ice and took back into the living room with him. Another day, he told himself. He had made it another day.

Reclining in the middle of his sofa, Beau worked the glass of vodka. He recalled the earlier conversation with Malcolm. It was easy enough, not many people actually spoke to Beau any more. Malcolm asked if it had been a quiet night.

Better than having trouble find us. He remembered his reply about not being able to hide from it. Beau had caused his fair share of trouble and wondered when it would eventually come looking for him—and whether or not he could hide when it did.

Chapter 2

Detective Chauncey "Chance" Parker waited most of the morning outside of courtroom 3A. His anxiety level rose exponentially the closer he got to being called to the stand. Next to him on the bench was the murder book. A four-inch-thick, black binder stuffed full of paperwork, copies of evidence, and analysis results. If it wasn't in there, it didn't happen.

Chance leaned his head back on the hard wooden pew and closed his eyes, trying to fight his nerves.

"Hey, Chance."

He blinked one eye open, recognizing the voice.

"Hey Brenn," he replied.

Brennan Headley, the forensic specialist who had worked on the murder, wore a dark gray pants suit and matching heels, the opposite of her usual uniform of a black polo and black BDU cargo pants. Also, her hair was down instead of her trademark ponytail, upping her feminine appeal.

"You look nice," he added.

"Whatever. I hate dressing up for court."

Chance smiled and shut his eye. Ever since he had met Brennan, she had been crawling around crime scenes. It was in her blood.

She took a seat next to him and immediately stirred.

"Have you gone yet?"

His eyes still closed, he said, "No. Couple of the initial witnesses have gone. Last one is on the stand now. I think I'm next."

"All right. You ready?"

Chance opened his eyes and leaned forward before answering. He took a deep breath and blew it out. "I hope so."

"You've testified hundreds of times. Why would you be nervous now?"

"This one is different, you know?"

Brennan shook her head.

"It's been six months since the Shelley and McFadden murders." Chance explained. "We've just now been able to get our heads above water with the community, and this is the first real test. All those community partnership programs started by the department in reaction to those murders have rebuilt some trust, but they won't believe it's working until we get some convictions."

"Ahh, right. I see."

"I worked with Durgenhoff on those cases and put in a ton of hours, like you did. I know Rivers and Akers did it. Hell, everyone in the department knows they did it. We just couldn't prove it."

"You did the best you could. I know how you work, Chance. If it was there, you'd have found it."

"Thanks, but the problem is that I'm not the only one who knows they did it. So does the community. Those two are the reason this case is such a big deal. That's why I have to be twice as good on the stand, twice as good in the field, because of the damage they did."

"Why is this case the test?"

"The timing really, but the shooter, Xavier Toombs, is a legitimate threat. He's dangerous and needs to be in prison."

"Don't you have a witness who saw everything?"

"Yes, I do, but if the jury doesn't believe me and the defense plays the dirty-cop, dirty-department angle, it doesn't matter how good a witness we have. We'll lose."

"Detective Chauncey Parker?" a voice called out to the lobby.

"It's Chance," he corrected.

"You're up."

Chance Parker rose from his seat. He buttoned his jacket and gathered the large binder, tucked it under his arm, and nodded to the bailiff that he was ready.

"You know the way, right?"

"Yeah, I've done this a few times." He tried to ignore the nervousness churning in his stomach, but it roiled incessantly.

With the murder book under his arm, Chance made his way through the galley and across the courtroom to take the stand. Passing the jury box, he met each one's eyes with a professional and courteous smile, hoping to impress upon them competence and legitimacy. He was not like those rogue cops they read about in the media.

"Please raise your right hand and repeat after me," ordered the judge.

Chance raised his right hand and was sworn in by the judge. He made sure his response of "I do" was loud and confident for the jury.

"Good morning, Detective Parker. Please introduce yourself, tell us where you work, and spell your name for the record." Catalina "Cat" Collins stood at the lectern a step away from the jury box. She was a fierce prosecutor with a take no prisoner attitude. Her beauty complemented her passion in the courtroom and was feared by many defense attorneys. She was always up for the fight.

"Good morning," Chance replied, and then turned to the jury. "I'm Detective Chance Parker with the Tallahassee Police Department." He added a friendly smile and then leaned toward the court reporter who sat a few feet away from the witness box. He spelled his name for the record.

Chance looked over to the defendant's table. Xavier Toombs was staring back with devilish eyes. Chance didn't respond to the threatening look, not wanting the jury to see anything inappropriate. He noticed that Toombs had a clean haircut, wore a nice suit, and sported an amiable pair of glasses, clearly a ploy by the defense team to give the street thug a more innocent appearance. They were going for the misunderstood and under-privileged angle. When Chance arrested him, he had long dreadlocks, pants hanging off his backside, and a row of gold teeth.

"Thank you." Catalina quickly moved onto the night of the homicide and how Parker came to respond. She had already laid the foundation by putting on the stand the few witnesses who had seen the fight between Toombs and the victim and then, soon after, heard the gunshots. One witness drove up to the scene after the fact and took the victim to the hospital, who died on the way. The early issue was that none of those witnesses actually saw the suspect shoot the victim. Their reluctance left the police attempting to fill in the gaps.

"And did you respond to the scene that night?"

"No, I actually went to the hospital first."

"What did you find once you arrived at the hospital?"

Chance eyed the victim's mother in the gallery. "He was already dead. He had died from his injuries on the way." He could see her wince at the thought of her son, dying needlessly.

"Were you later able to determine the cause of his death?"

"Yes. A gunshot wound that penetrated his lungs and heart." The mother bowed her head, trying to keep it together.

"Did you ever make it to the scene that night?"

"Yes. After the hospital."

"Did you recover any evidence at the scene?"

"Not much. We found some evidence of a struggle in the front yard and some blood on the ground where the victim was shot and had fallen."

Chance went on to explain how the evidence found on-scene corroborated the initial witness statements. The victim had confronted Toombs on the street corner over the pre-existing beef. A fight ensued, but the victim quickly got the better of Toombs, knocking him to the ground, punching him in the face. The victim was pulled off Toombs and separated from him, but Toombs pulled a gun and pointed it at the victim. Unarmed, the victim took off running, but Toombs squeezed off several rounds and one fatally struck him in the side, under his right arm, entering his heart.

"Did you find any evidence of the shooting, other than the projectile found in the victim's body?"

"No." The answer was disappointing to Chance and the jury noticed. However, it was better to admit your shortcomings on direct, than leave them to the defense to exploit during the cross.

"No?"

"No. We believe the casings were picked up by the defendant's friends."

"Objection!" Toombs's lawyer quickly protested. "Hearsay and there is no basis for that."

"Your honor, I will get to that later. But Detective Parker is stating a fact based on his investigation, not specifically what a witness said."

"Overruled."

Catalina Collins continued with the steps Detective Parker took throughout the investigation. She covered the minimal forensic evidence collected, the fruitless but thorough searches for the murder weapon, and the discovery of the main witness, Truman Davis. Davis was the prosecution's ace in the hole. Davis was hanging out with the victim on the day he died. He was actually standing only a few feet away from Toombs when he shot his friend. Matter of fact, Davis was the one who had pulled the victim off Toombs. As far as eyewitnesses were concerned, he was perfect. Davis had come into the police station and talked with Parker for hours about the case. When Chance put a photo line-up of Toombs in front of him, Davis nearly came out of his seat and screamed at the top of his lungs when he identified Toombs as the shooter. Parker knew that level of emotion would play well for the jury. Davis would also provide testimony that he saw Toombs's friends come later and pick up the shell casings so the police would not find them.

"Thank you, Detective. No further questions." Catalina sat down, and Toombs's lawyer took the lectern.

"Good morning, well, now afternoon, Detective."

"Good afternoon." Chance sounded cordial despite the lack of respect for the defense attorney for representing such a dirt bag. He wanted the jury to believe it wasn't personal.

"So, we've heard you provide a lot of testimony here today, but I'd like to ask you about the weapon used."

"Okay."

"Were you able to determine what kind of gun was used?"

"It was narrowed down through tool analysis conducted by the lab at the Florida Department of Law Enforcement."

"Right. And we'll get to that later. But could you tell us what caliber weapon?"

"It was a nine millimeter."

"What brand?"

"Objection," Catalina said as she stood. "Detective Parker is not qualified as a weapon's expert."

"Sustained. Move on counselor."

"Yes, sir. I won't ask you any more specifics, Detective, but what I want to ask you is if you were able to locate the specific weapon used?"

Chance knew this was where the attorney was ultimately headed.

"No. I wasn't."

"No?"

"No."

"Okay. Were you able to find any gun in this case that was handled or possessed by my client?"

"No."

"So, the only evidence offered that my client shot the victim is based on eyewitness testimony?"

"Yes—"

"Objection, your honor!" Catalina tried to cut off Chance before he answered. "The detective isn't trying this case. Counsel is trying to sway the jury by offering an early summary. He needs to wait till closing, as the rules say."

"I withdraw my question, your honor." Toombs's lawyer collected his notes and added, "No further questions."

The judge sent the jury to lunch and excused the attorneys after giving a warning to the defense counsel about trying the summary trick again. He then admonished Catalina for trying to enforce procedure and emphasized that was his job.

Chance Parker waited outside the courtroom, hoping to catch Catalina.

"Cat, got a sec?"

"Hey, Chance. Good job in there."

"Thanks. I hope the whole gun thing went okay."

"It was fine. He was trying to grandstand, and I think the jury saw that. Don't worry about it. The case is fine. We have Davis going first thing in the morning, and then I'll bring in the Medical Examiner to finish out. I like showing all the autopsy pictures at the end. The sad images of the victim lying there dead tend to stick with the jury through deliberation."

"Hey, whatever works."

"So, go home for today. I won't need you again, but be back in the morning, okay?"

"Yes, ma'am."

"Don't ma'am me."

Chance smiled, and Catalina giggled. She went to the stairwell and headed up to her office for a quick debriefing and a bite for lunch. Chance grabbed the hefty murder book and made his way to the elevator. He was going to stop by the station and check in before heading home.

Chapter 3

The metal gate buzzed then clicked. He waited anxiously but didn't let it show. Patience was his mantra now. The gate slid open, and he stepped through. A small counter with safety glass and a small slit was his last stop.

"Name?" asked the guard manning the counter.

"Toombs, Antonio."

"Okay, wait there. I'll be right back."

Wait, he says. I've been waiting ten years. Now, he wants me to wait more.

Antonio Toombs had served his prison sentence. The clock on the wall read four minutes after eight a.m. An hour-and-a-half drive back to Tallahassee waited. His younger brother was on trial for murder, and he needed to get back.

The guard returned and passed a plastic bag through a drawer under the safety glass. Toombs took the bag, signed for it, and left the property room without saying a word.

He was done talking. He realized no one important ever listened, especially in a place full of criminals. His loyalty was wasted and earned him a decade in prison. That lesson taught him true loyalty does not exist, not in his world. Fear earned respect. Fear created the illusion of loyalty. He had a plan. It was time for him to be the boss. First, he had to get home.

Antonio walked out to the roadside and saw his ride waiting. A skinny kid with bright, green shoes and a matching shirt stood next to a rental car, talking on the phone. Antonio recognized the youth as a cousin, now grown into an awkward young adult. The kid noticed Toombs approach and quickly hung up the phone.

"You Chris?"

"Yeah."

Antonio paused, staring at him with a menacing look that demanded respect. Chris read the look and deflated.

"Yes, sir."

Antonio didn't respond. He opened his own door and sat down in the passenger seat. The young man sat in the driver's seat.

Before taking off, Antonio asked with a matter-of-fact tone, "You got anything in here?"

Chris looked at his passenger as he cranked the car and pulled out to the main street.

"Whatchu mean?"

"You know what I mean. You got anything in here?"

"Oh, yeah. I got some weed in the console? You want to burn one? I know it's probably been forever since you got high."

Antonio's face held a look of disappointment. He remained silent and held out his hand. Chris opened the console, fished out a baggie of marijuana, and handed it to his cousin. Antonio studied it for a minute.

"That's some good shit," Chris said. "About an ounce of Hydro. That'll get you fucked up fo' sho'! Papers are in the glove."

Antonio slowly turned his head to his cousin, his hand still displaying the drugs. He pressed the button on the armrest and rolled his window down. Chris looked over, unsure of Antonio. With a quick toss, Antonio sent the baggie out of the window.

"Hey, what the fuck?"

"Need I remind you that I just left prison? I'm not planning on going back because your stupid ass decided to get high on the ride over. It's dumb shit like that that gives away your power. What else is in here?"

Chris sunk in the driver's seat.

"What else is in here?" Antonio demanded.

Chris held the wheel steady and reached under the seat. He pulled out a gun and handed it over.

"This it?"

"Yeah. I mean, yes, sir."

Antonio studied the well-crafted handgun, a Beretta 92F, and held it firm in his hand. This was a tool, and he needed it. He wasn't going to toss it aside like the weed. He removed the magazine and checked the chamber. It wasn't loaded. *Fool*, he thought, and tucked it in his back waistband.

***

Chance Parker walked off the elevator a few minutes after nine a.m. The trial had resumed and the star witness, Truman Davis, was due to be on the stand. As Chance made his way to the south rotunda, he saw the Medical Examiner sitting on the pew bench, reading her iPad.

Under the rule of sequestration, discussing the case with any other listed witnesses was strictly prohibited. He gave the pathologist a nod and snuck up to the courtroom door. He peeked through the tiny crack until he could see the witness stand. Davis was there. Relief set in as Chance knew there had been a possibility Davis would no-show. In Davis's world, testifying, even for a close friend, was no guarantee. Subpoenas were just paper, and the threat of jail time carried little weight. The tag of "snitch" was a possible death sentence.

The case against Xavier Toombs was circumstantial at best without Davis. Putting a live human being on the stand who witnessed the murder brought it all together. There were some holes, like the absence of the murder weapon and shell casings, but it was a senseless murder and, hopefully, Davis would drive that home with the help of Catalina Collins. This was a win the department desperately needed.

Chance considered all that was riding on this case. If the jury still had the bad taste of corrupt cops, their haste could allow Xavier Toombs back on the street. A not-guilty verdict would serve to empower Toombs, allowing him and his crew to perpetuate their crimes, with the mentality that they could get away with it. Building future cases against Toombs would be much harder.

After two hours spent in agony on the hard bench, Chance wondered what was taking so long. Davis was still on the stand. A small man pushed open the courtroom doors, speeding past Chance while dialing a phone. He recognized the man as a local reporter for the *Democrat*. The urgency with which he moved concerned Chance. Something was up. The reporter talked in an excited, but hushed tone.

More rumblings came from within the anteroom and worried the detective. He tried to ignore this as a bad sign, but an ill feeling grew in the pit of his stomach.

A group of the victim's family burst out of the courtroom, upset about something that had been said inside. Chance tried to discern the reason for the excitement, but he couldn't filter out all the emotion. He heard Davis's street name mentioned and knew the issue centered on the witness.

"That mutha-fucker lied up there. They better put his ass in jail," Chance heard a young woman say loud and clear. He didn't understand what had happened but knew it wasn't good. He stood up to question the family.

"Detective?" Cat Collins stepped out of the courtroom and called Chance before he could ask.

"Hey, what the hell happened?"

"Hang on. C'mere." She pulled him to the side and out of earshot from the family. Toombs's family started to leave the courtroom and filled up the waiting area. Chance moved to the side to keep an eye on the crowd.

"Fucking Davis," Cat said.

"What?" Chance's ill feeling worsened.

"He lied on the stand. I mean, flat out perjured his ass off up there." Catalina was steaming. Being duped by a witness on the stand was unrecoverable.

"Uh, okay. Did you play the interview?"

Chance had recorded his interview with Davis, and it captured, in living color, the emotion he had when describing the details of watching his friend get murdered.

"No. When we prepped him, he was fine. He's been fine this entire time, and now he fucks me on the stand. What an asshole!"

"Can we bring it in? Play the interview and try to fix this?"

"Maybe. I have to put you back on. Is that okay?"

"Yeah, sure. Whatever you have to do."

Catalina Collins rarely got flustered. Having a key witness flip his testimony in the middle of a trial would cause the most experienced prosecutor to worry. She bit the corner of her lip, a nervous habit Chance noticed she did when she was lost in thought. She was probably trying to think of a way to minimize the damage.

Unable to wait, Chance asked, "What the hell did he say?"

"Basically that Xavier didn't shoot him. It was some other dipshit with a drug beef with the victim."

"What?" Chance knew this was in direct contrast to what Davis had told him during his interview. "That piece of shit."

"The problem is we've already brought in the victim's past as a drug dealer to define the relationship with the defendant. So we can't backtrack without looking completely incompetent. The defense will definitely piggyback on this and offer up to the jury any other Joe-Schmoe dealer who wanted him dead."

Detective Parker thought hard about whether he could do something in the next few hours to better the case. He searched his memory of the case but drew a blank on any lead he could follow deeper for quick results.

"Shit."

"I know. He screwed us. Bad. Excuse me, Chance. Be ready to go back on."

Catalina stepped over to the Medical Examiner and spoke to her, leaving Chance standing alone. He played right into the defense's hand earlier, establishing that the case's foundation was built on the eyewitness testimony. He cursed himself for not seeing it coming, but then again he had trusted Davis to do the right thing. For all the sympathy and compassion that he had showed the witness while he was grieving his friend, now Chance wanted to punish him for being such a coward.

By late morning, Chance was back on the stand, and Catalina went over his interview with Davis, trying to impeach some of his statements. It was a risky move to impeach their only eyewitness, but they were at the point of needing a Hail Mary.

The prosecutor carefully went over the recorded interview for the jury as Chance narrated. They emphasized the part where Davis said that Xavier had shot the victim after running away. She then moved into another line of questioning to minimize the damage caused by Davis.

"In your experience, Detective, have you ever come across a witness or victim who is reluctant to tell the truth for fear of retaliation?"

"Yes. It's actually a common fear that I have to overcome in many cases."

"What is the main reasoning for that reluctance, in your experience?"

"Fear of being harmed by the parties involved or by relatives of the involved."

"Thank you, Detective. No further questions."

"Cross?" The judge asked.

"Yes, your honor. Briefly." Toombs's lawyer stood up, pressed his tie down to his stomach and remained at his table. "Detective, you were sworn in before testifying yesterday. Do you remember that?"

"Yes." Immediately, Chance knew where the attorney was going.

"And, you're still under oath today. Isn't that correct?"

"Yes."

"And having testified many times in your career, it's something that happens every time. Correct?"

"Yes."

"Objection, your honor." Cat stood up. "Is counsel going to make a point or ask the same thing over and over again?"

"Move it along. Overruled."

The defense continued. "Are there any measures at the Tallahassee Police Department you can take when talking to a key witness in a case you're investigating?"

Chance paused, not wanting to answer.

"Detective? Do you need me to repeat the question?"

"Yes, there are measures we can take."

"Like swearing them under oath, just as you were yesterday?"

"Yes."

"And do you have them sign anything acknowledging they were sworn in?"

It was a repeat kick to the head. He just wanted it over with. He looked at Catalina, and she gave him a look that said her hands were tied.

"Yes. We have an 'Oath of Perjury' form we have witnesses sign after being sworn in. And yes, I had Mr. Davis sign one before he was interviewed. And I'm sure you have a copy over there at your table."

The lawyer smiled, like a cat trapping its prey. He produced a photocopy of the Oath of Perjury form Chance had mentioned and offered it as an exhibit to the court. He asked Chance to point out his and Davis's signatures after reading it verbatim to the jury. He then published it to the jury so they could see it with their own eyes. It was clear he was going to highlight his closing argument with the fact that the State's key witness was a documented liar. Lying to Chance initially, or now on the stand, it didn't matter. He was now a liar.

"No further questions, your honor."

Walking out of the courtroom, Chance felt the likelihood of a guilty verdict evaporate into thin air. He felt like screaming, but he was sure the jury would hear, even from out in the hallway. He stormed off toward the north rotunda to get away.

As Chance made it to the other end, he circled back. He was starting to calm down, but the image of Truman Davis's face would start the anger cycle all over. As he passed by the elevator, it opened. A man stepped off with a cool demeanor and appeared to be on a mission. The man looked familiar, but Chance couldn't quite place it. He sized up the detective, noticed the badge on his belt, and with an air of indifference headed down the hallway.

Chance followed and watched him go inside courtroom 3A. Unable to place why the man looked familiar, Chance pulled out his phone. He found Sergeant Reginald Polk's number and hit send. He needed to update his chain of command.

On the next break, Cat Collins came out and told Chance the State rested.

"Let's hope your testimony swayed the jurors. Hopefully, they see Davis as a scared witness rather than the liar he is."

"That's a tall order."

"I know. I'm not feeling optimistic."

"I've seen you optimistic in more dire situations, so we're pretty much screwed."

The man from the elevator exited the courtroom and intermingled with Toombs's family. Chance watched him closely. His short-cropped haircut, the distance in his stare, the stress on his face, and he way he constantly checked his surroundings gave him the look of an ex-con. They locked eyes from across the hallway, and his name instantly popped in Chance's head. Antonio Toombs, Xavier's older brother.

"Shit. He's out?"

"Who?" Cat turned to see Antonio talking with his and Xavier's mother.

"Antonio Toombs. Xavier's brother. He was a lieutenant for Carlos Figueroa. He was taken down with him but never talked. He received ten years while Figueroa got life."

"Figueroa, wasn't that—"

"Beau Rivers's case?" Chance spat his name, knowing he was responsible for this mess. "Yes, it was."

"Well, if we don't get a conviction on little brother, they're probably going to have one helluva homecoming."

"Ah, shit. Don't say that."

***

The defense rested, and Chance was officially released from trial. It was mid-afternoon, and local reporters awaited the verdict. Chance couldn't leave. He would go crazy until he heard the verdict, too. He decided to stay and sat restless, unable to focus on anything other than this case.

He checked in with his ex-wife who was watching their daughter. His girl was almost eight and he had planned to take her to the beach for the weekend. The trial was cutting into their time away. Another apology would have to suffice for now.

The oversized door clanked open, and the bailiff directed everyone in for the verdict. Deliberation had only lasted two hours. That told Chance they had their minds made up beforehand. He felt nauseous as he filed into the back of the room.

"Have you reached a verdict in the case of the State versus Xavier Toombs?" the judge asked.

"Yes, we have."

"What say you?"

"We, the jury, find the defendant not guilty."

A mixture of abhorrent gasps and joyful cries filled the room. Anger from the victim's side, jubilation from Toombs's. Chance clenched his jaw, holding back his anger. He wanted to yell at the jury for failing to see the truth: Xavier was a murderer and someone threatened or paid Truman Davis to lie on the stand. He looked over and saw Xavier and Antonio hug while the judge quieted the courtroom. The victim's family walked out in frustration and, likely, with a continued distrust for the legal system. The victim's sister looked at Chance with pleading eyes in search of meaning for why this happened and why there was a failure of justice.

"I'm sorry." It was the only thing he could think of to say. She didn't respond. She looked at him in disgust, as if he was the murderer, and left the courtroom.

Chance remained and watched Xavier from the back of the room. During mid-hug, Xavier looked up and stared back at him. With no more need of decorum, Chance gave him a contemptuous look that was countered with a cocky smile and a "Go fuck yourself" wink from Xavier. Antonio stood next to his baby brother and looked over at the detective in a protective manner. Chance was alone, but he resolved not to back down from either one. The judge addressed Xavier and his lawyer, directing them back to the table. Chance's stare moved over to Antonio. The older brother stared back, his eyes black and cold as ice. This battle was over, Chance decided. He had lost and would have to regroup for the next one, no matter how difficult.

Chapter 4

It was a dungeon, Dylan thought, void of life and filled with horrid reminders of crimes from the last half century. The evidence vault was a cavernous room that occupied most of the basement floor of the police department. Dylan had been sent there in exile. His command in the Criminal Investigations Division had been stripped away while he was under suspicion for killing George Shelley and Earnest McFadden, a case that would remain stagnant as long as he and Beau kept their mouths shut. He now oversaw civilian employees who managed the department's evidence.

The chief relegated him away from his beloved investigations to somewhere far removed. Patronized further, he was given the menial task of auditing the entire evidence room.

Busywork was what it was, Dylan thought. Pointless busywork. He checked his watch and picked up his cell phone. He typed a text message to his wife, Wendy.

Everything go okay?

Wendy had a prenatal check-up that afternoon. There had been no signs of complications, but she had complained of not feeling well that morning. Dylan never used to be this cautious, but losing a child had changed things.

A few minutes passed before she responded.

Yep. Everything is fine. Baby Phoenix is doing good.

Dylan smiled. He liked when she used the name. Initially, she had fought him on it, but when he insisted it was a tribute to Caitlin, she warmed up to the idea and eventually gave in.

The small office tucked away in the Property and Evidence section wasn't as glamorous as his corner office on the second floor. It was about an eighth of the size. There were no windows in the entire section, completing the cavernous feel. A framed picture of Dylan holding Caitlin on a sunny day was the only personal touch. It was the only thing that mattered, family. He had slid a picture of Phoenix's sonogram in the corner and stared at both frequently.

The inventory project was nearly half over, and he procrastinated as much as he could for fear of the next pointless job awaiting him. He sat up in his chair and moved the mouse, waking the monitor. He pulled up the local news channel's website, hoping to see an update on the ongoing murder trial of Xavier Toombs. It was one of many cases he followed in the aftermath of his and Beau's destruction. He would never apologize for what he did; the trust of the community was an unintended casualty.

There was an update. The headline read: Not-Guilty Verdict in Murder Trial.

Dylan felt a degree of responsibility. He read the article, which essentially stated that less than adequate police work was the cause. Dylan didn't believe it for a second. Chance Parker was a dogged detective and would have put forth the best case possible. There had to be some other reason leading to a not-guilty verdict. He shook his head and closed the webpage. He stood up and walked around the small unit to stretch his legs before going back into the dungeon.

Chance Parker stood on the other side of the customer counter at the front of the unit. He was returning evidence from the murder trial.

Parker looked up at Dylan but then, ignoring him, looked back at the property tech logging in the evidence.

"Hey, Chance. I saw the verdict on the Toombs case. Can't win them all." Dylan immediately regretted saying anything.

"No, Lieutenant. You can't." Parker was curt and gave him a glaring look. Dylan could sense his frustration and knew he was partly responsible. The formal use of his rank instead of the friendlier "L-T" meant he had lost respect from the detective.

"It's not your fault. I know you did the best job you could."

Dylan hoped the sentiment would ease Parker's frustration, but he quickly shot back.

"I know that. I blame you." Parker finalized the paperwork with a signature and walked off, letting the insult linger. The property tech who stood at the window sheepishly carried the box of evidence from the window past Akers, returning it to the vault. Dylan stood there and let the shame of lost admiration hit him like a well-placed shot.

I deserved that.

Not a day had passed that he didn't think about what he and Beau Rivers had done, killing those men in the name of justice for his slain daughter. He wasn't sorry the men were dead, but he had been lost in anger, wandering in uncertainty, trying to feel whole again. It didn't work.

Chapter 5

Nearly a week after the not-guilty verdict was read aloud, Xavier Toombs finally made it home. Due to his not-guilty verdict and Antonio's release from prison, a celebration was in order. The barbeque was hot with chicken on the grill, cold beer on ice, and hip hop music thumping from the radio. Family, friends, and neighbors all stopped by to extend well wishes to Xavier and Antonio.

Antonio, stoic and methodical, stood back and only participated in the festivities by sipping on a mixed drink. Abstinent from alcohol in prison, he had decided to instill more discipline in his life and especially now that he was out. Discipline would lead his way to the mountaintop, a place he had vowed to be once he left that hellhole of a prison.

Xavier clearly needed a release. He had already had his way with one girl in the back room of the house and was talking to another. His unsteady sway suggested that whatever mix of alcohol and drugs he had consumed was taking effect. Antonio grew angry at his little brother's lack of self-control, but he was letting him have the moment. Things would soon change.

The younger Toombs stumbled over to his big brother who stood on the elevated porch, looking out over the yard. He noticed Cousin Chris was there, a blunt in one hand and a forty-ounce bottle of beer in the other, moving to the music.

"Hey, man. You're not having fun, bro," Xavier said.

"I have my drink. I'm fine."

"C'mon, I want to show you something."

Antonio followed his younger brother to the back yard and to a wooden shed. Xavier pulled the barn-style doors open to reveal a covered vehicle. Antonio grew interested. He remembered Xavier getting a new ride, but he hadn't actually laid eyes on it. Xavier knelt, peeled back the cover, and pulled it off. Staring back was a 1986 Chevy Monte Carlo SS, sleek black with its original, red racing stripe and twenty-four-inch, chrome star rims. It looked show-worthy and was ghetto envy. As a personal touch, a large "X" sprawled across the hood.

Impressed, Antonio let out a whistle.

"That's what I'm talkin' 'bout, bro. Look at her. She's a beaut!"

Antonio nodded and smiled back at his little brother. Clearly, he was trying to show off.

"It's nice, X. Very nice."

"Shit, we gonna wreck shit in this ride."

Concern crossed Antonio's face, and he turned serious. "This is in your name?"

"Yeah. Why?"

"Dumbass."

"Huh? Why you trippin'?"

"You're smart to leave this right where it is. You can't do anything with a flashy car like this. Especially when everyone knows it's yours. Think about it. You get caught with dope, the cops will take it. You blast fire from it and someone sees you, they'll know it's you and take it. Like I said, you'd be better off leaving it in here, dumbass."

Xavier went silent, thinking about the consequences.

"Whatever man. I just got out. You just got out. Let's go party, bro."

"Fine, but I'm serious about the car."

"Yeah, yeah, yeah." Xavier smiled. He covered the Monte Carlo and closed the shed doors. As they walked back to the party, Xavier found another way to try to impress his brother.

"C'mon, don't you wanna get you some? I know you gotta be cravin' some pussy. Being locked up for ten damn years. Shit, I'da gone crazy up in there."

Xavier may have dodged a murder charge, but he had no clue what prison life was really like. It was take or be taken. It was about survival for men like Antonio, and he had done what he had to, things he wasn't proud of or didn't care to talk about. The one thing he held on to that helped him focus was getting out and taking back what was his.

"I'm good," Antonio said.

"What? I know you ain't turn into no fag in there."

Antonio coldly looked at his inebriated brother but decided he would show him patience. For now.

"No, I didn't."

"Well, take your pick of all these hoes out here. They'll suck yo' dick right nah." Xavier let out a lustful cackle that annoyed Antonio.

As if it were planned, two women exited the house. One glanced flirtingly at Antonio as if to validate Xavier's offer. He looked the woman over as if she were a commodity traded on the open market. She wore tight shorts that exposed her voluptuous butt cheeks. The bright neon tube top matched the faux hair interwoven with her real hair and ran down to her shoulders. She acted coy, batted her eyes, and gave him a gold-tooth-filled smile. Impressive tattoos marked her thighs, arms, and above her breasts. Antonio admitted he wanted a woman, and she would do. Her only value was in between her legs, and that was all he cared about.

He nodded for the woman to come over. She pretended to ignore him at first, but like a lion ruling over his lioness, he demanded and flexed his power presence. She gave in, and moments later, she submitted fully, letting him have his way with her.

The party lasted all night and into the morning. Around three a.m., Cousin Chris wanted to gain the attention of a rival gang by firing multiple gunshots into the air in a "come and get it" display. The only attention it gathered was that of several police cars who circled the area in search of a shooter. Antonio sat silently in his room, watching the imbecilic actions of Xavier and his crew as they hid inside from the cops. It was pathetic. They postured and pretended to be "hard" when they were all a bunch of soft cowards. In the morning, Antonio would unleash hell. It was time for them to get on board or get run over.

***

Xavier was passed out with a half-naked girl across his lap. Empty baggies of cocaine littered the floor, along with empty liquor bottles. The odor of stale cannabis hung in the air like an early morning fog. Three of his crewmembers and Cousin Chris were passed out in other parts of the living room. Antonio carefully stepped over them as the mid-morning sun shone through the window.

Early mornings were his time. In prison, he forced himself up before the guards clicked on the lights and sounded the alarm. He used the extra time to meditate and exercise in his cell, gaining clarity and control over his life.

Standing at the door, Antonio looked at the mindless thugs splayed out around the room. He held the nine-millimeter Beretta tight in his hand. He slowly opened the door, letting the sunlight spill into the living room. The comatose idiots didn't bother to move. He moved the pistol around the room, pointing the barrel at each person's head, even Xavier's.

Antonio moved the gun into the intruding light and studied it again. The smooth chrome barrel, the textured grip, and the carefully stamped logo on the side made the gun a thing of beauty. It was magnificent. He rubbed it against his face, embracing its power. He knew he could take every life in the room before they even knew what happened. The feeling was Godlike.

Violently, he ripped back the slide and charged the gun. The unmistakable sound of racking the slide woke up Xavier who flinched and reached for his waistband. He realized it was Antonio and relaxed. The slumbering girl remained unconscious and deadweight.

"What the fuck, bro?" Xavier squinted in the sunlight.

"Wake the FUCK UP!"

Xavier shoved off the sleeping girl. She rolled onto the floor, causing a thud and moaning, but she stayed on the floor. His crew heard the shouting and started to wake up. Cousin Chris was still hard asleep.

"What the fuck, nigga? You trippin'," said one of the hungover crewmembers.

"Excuse me?"

"Tha' fuck, man. Why you yelling?"

"I said, get the fuck up. Now!"

Xavier nodded to his friends and stood up. Antonio looked over at the pathetic sight of his cousin curled on the floor, still clutching the forty-ounce bottle. He shouted again but it had no effect. Antonio stormed over and kicked Chris as hard as he could in the ribs. Chris gasped as the air left his lungs. His eyes shot open wide to see who or what was attacking him. The pain from the kick manifested as he struggled to get his breath back, and he let out a painful cry.

"Get up."

"Hey, man. What the hell is your problem?" Xavier stepped up to his older brother and looked him dead in the eye. Antonio was pleased to see leadership out of Xavier. In Antonio's absence, he had been in charge. He knew what he needed to do now.

Antonio didn't reply. He stared back with fire burning in his eyes, like that of a caged animal finally freed and allowed to hunt.

Antonio backed down and stuffed the gun in his waistband. "I'm sorry, little brother. I'm sorry." One of the crewmembers helped Chris up as he still coughed.

"It's okay, big bro. We're cool, man. Just easy on that drill sergeant shit."

"You're right. I'm cool." Antonio raised his hands, palms forward in a submissive manner.

Xavier, done with the confrontation, looked back at one of his conquests lying on the floor and smiled. "Someone wake this bit—"

Before Xavier could finish his sentence, Antonio grabbed him in a headlock and kicked the back of his knee, throwing him off balance then dragged him outside. With all his strength, Antonio flung Xavier down the stairs. Xavier smashed against one of the porch steps and landed hard on the ground. His younger brother winced and protectively reached for his ribs. Before he could get to his feet and defend himself, Antonio was on top of him, punching him in the face. Chris and the rest of the boys piled out onto the porch, watching the fight, letting out "oohs" and a few "oh, shits" as Antonio inflicted painful blow after painful blow.

From the excessive alcohol and drug use, coupled with the blunt force trauma he now sustained, Xavier tried to get to his feet but they were cut from under him by Antonio moving around like a prizefighter, toying with his wounded opponent. He landed one final blow to the face, and Xavier was nearly unconscious.

Antonio knelt and removed the Beretta from his waistband. The crew protested from the porch but dared not intervene. Antonio picked up Xavier and helped him to his knees. Bloodied and out of breath, Xavier looked up at his older brother, asking why?

"Anyone could have just come through that door and done exactly what I done," Antonio said. "You and your lazy-ass homeboys just don't get it do you? You will never move beyond this shit hole and get real respect without discipline. This ends now, or I end you."

Between labored breaths, Xavier said, "Ain't nobody gunna fuck wit' us."

"You don't know that." Antonio put the gun to his little brother's head. "And that kind of thinking is what makes you vulnerable." The protests from the porch were silenced.

"Don't do it, bro. Please?"

"Are you ready to follow me?"

"Yes." Xavier let out a bloody sob.

"Are you willing to die for me?"

He didn't answer.

Antonio pressed the gun harder against Xavier's temple. "Are you willing to die for me?"

"Yes, man. Fuck, yes."

"What about you pieces of shit?" Antonio waved the gun across each man on the porch, clearly willing to shoot them without reason.

They all agreed to follow Antonio and for him to replace Xavier as the head of the family. The others helped Xavier up and brought him back into the house. Antonio knew the play would instill fear into this crew and the same fear would help him rule the neighborhood. He looked up and down the street and glanced across the road. A set of curtains moved back from a window. He smiled, realizing someone had witnessed the scene.

He walked over and knocked on the door. He didn't bother hiding the gun and held it to his side. He looked behind him and hoped other neighbors were watching as well. It was the fastest way to get the news spread that he was now in charge.

A muffled voice from inside answered, "Yes?" It was an elderly female. Antonio recalled the woman's face, but not her name. She had lived there as long as his family, but that never mattered in this neighborhood.

"Open the door," he said, flatly.

The door cracked and the woman's face appeared through the tiny open space. Antonio smiled but his eyes remained dead cold.

"You didn't see anything did you?"

"No, no I didn't see nothing." Her voice trembled and she shut the door. Antonio could hear her shuffle away from the door.

"Good."

***

Later that day, as his first order of business, Antonio asked to see Xavier's stash house and the rest of the organization. He was unimpressed as each locale was within a ten-block radius of their house. The proximity would make it easier for the cops to track back. The operation was pitifully small and full of sloppy practices. Antonio grew irritated at his inheritance, but like it said in the books he read in prison, Rome wasn't built in a day. Building an empire took calculated moves and strategic strikes against their enemies. That's what helped Rome flourish as one of the most thriving civilizations in history. Antonio would repeat history.

"Do we have anyone or any place that is away from the hood?"

"Huh? Whatchu mean?"

"Too many opportunistic people dwell in the ghetto. We need an isolated location away from here, so we can better protect it. See what I'm saying?"

Xavier blinked his non-swollen eye and nodded. After a minute of thought, Xavier answered.

"I see what you're sayin'. Yeah, we got a place over by all the college kids. Over off Escambia. My boy Dookie's people stay there."

"Okay, let's go check it out."

The house was not a house, but a townhome in a row of six units. Arranged in the shape of a U, a community parking lot sat in the middle. Most of the units were unoccupied and in various states of disrepair. Dookie's mother lived in one of the cleaner units that she kept up and maintained. Sitting in the far corner, it was in an ideal spot, secluded enough to see anyone coming, but conspicuous enough to avoid suspicion.

Antonio stood out front while he sent Xavier and Dookie inside to convince his mother to let them use the residence for their enterprise. She would be allowed to stay if she kept her mouth shut. In addition, Antonio would pay for the rent, but the apartment would be kept in her name.

"It's a start." Antonio said. Xavier relayed the news that the woman agreed to let them use the house.

"But why you want it here?"

"I don't. This is the best we have for now."

"Okay."

"Who's your plug?" Antonio wasted no time in moving on to the next task.

"Gotta guy out of Miami. He steps all over the shit he brings, but it was slim pickin's for a while after Figs went down, you know. We had to take what we could get."

Antonio knew all too well. But Carlos Figueroa had watched *Scarface* too many times and believed that he was the real Tony Montana. He also snorted too much of his product to think straight and allowed some snitch to give him up. Antonio had paid the price for his lack of judgment, and this time he was going to do things differently.

"Okay. Tell him we need another shipment, and if it's not at least seventy-five percent pure, he better look elsewhere."

"Okay, but Antonio..." Xavier looked worried and added, "He's not the kind of guy who takes no for an answer."

Antonio turned to look at Xavier with his black, icy stare. "Neither am I, little brother."

Antonio wanted to hang out at the new apartment for the evening and get a feel for the area. He wanted to know about the people, comings and goings, and any threats that might be out there. This time, he wasn't taking any chances. Xavier was right though. It was amongst college kids and low-income families, far off the radar from the ghetto. Antonio liked it more and more.

He sat outside while the other members started up a game of dice, gambling away what little money they had to begin with. *Childish game*, Antonio thought. A local rap artist played on the system in Xavier's car, but not so loud as to attract unwanted attention.

Over the course of the afternoon, Antonio noticed a few cars come and go from across the street, not staying more than a few minutes at a time. The callers were alone and had a paranoid look on their faces as they walked up to the door and back. It was a look Antonio had seen a thousand times.

"Hey," he called over to Dookie, dice in his hands.

"Yeah?"

"Who's that servin' over there? Bottom right apartment."

Dookie sat up and looked where Antonio indicated. He pointed at the apartment now that no activity was going on.

"Dunno."

"You live here, don't you?"

"This my mom's, dawg."

"I saw a room with all your shit in it. You live here too. Stop lying."

"Sorry, I didn't know dude was servin'. Prolly some college boy sellin' to the white kids."

"Yeah, you're probably right."

Nothing to be threatened by, he surmised.

Not less than ten minutes later, Antonio spotted a white van rolling down the small neighborhood street. An eerie feeling of déjà vu crawled up his spine.

Watching closely, the white van pulled off to the side and parked short of the drug dealer's apartment building. A team of cops, dressed in raid vests with the word NARCOTICS written down the sleeve, piled out and stacked up along the side of the building. They gestured to each other and Antonio watched, enthralled that this was happening in front of him.

The team moved to the front of the apartment and knocked. No answer. They knocked again. The cop up front gave a five count on his fingers and another crushed the door open with a battering ram. The team filed in the house, yelling and screaming as they entered.

Xavier, Dookie, and the others stood next to Antonio, watching the drama unfold. Additional cops, with raid vests over more business-like attire, came from unmarked cars parked behind the van. A few uniformed officers pulled up too. Soon, the drug dealer came out in handcuffs, his head hung low in shame.

"Stupid," Antonio said, shaking his head.

The group looked at him kind of odd, like they were asking what he was supposed to do different.

"He was working alone. One-man operation. No security, and I'm sure he sold to whoever the fuck had money. I saw at least three people walk up and buy like he had a damn sign out front. Bet you one was a damn narc."

Head nods came from the crew as they began to understand.

"Stupid." Antonio turned to his new crew. "You have to be smart in every aspect of this business. You have to think about each move and operate five moves ahead at all times."

"You right, Tony."

"You boys want to be that guy? Keep your bullshit operation."

Antonio looked around and saw most of them bow their heads, ashamed that in their previous operation, they had managed to be lucky over good.

"You want to reach the top?" he asked them. "You follow me."

***

Detective Chance Parker arrived on the scene of a narcotics search warrant. He was helping out in the case because the target's name had come up in a couple of shootings he was working. The narcs executed the search warrant while he waited in his unmarked car for the all clear. Once it was given, he exited and walked up with a squad mate from Homicide.

Out of habit, Parker glanced around the area to see who was watching. Search warrants tend to gather crowds. Within the apartment complex, only a handful of people took notice. Some were grateful residents; happy the local drug dealer was finally caught. Others were indifferent and waited for the police to move their cars so they could leave.

Chance looked over his shoulder across the street to a U-shaped configuration of townhomes. They looked old and rundown. Chance couldn't recall ever dealing with anything at the location. A group of four or five men huddled next to each other in the back corner of a courtyard. Enthralled by the police raid, they watched closely.

"No substitute on television for the real thing, huh?" Chance's squad mate said as he noticed the group.

"Nope."

Chapter 6

The quiet followed Beau everywhere, around the checkpoint, the airport perimeter, and even where the planes taxied to the terminal. He knocked on random objects just to make sure his hearing hadn't suddenly stopped working. He checked the routine doorknobs, each still locked like the hour before, and the hour before that. He was on the swing shift and was due to get off after the six thirty p.m. from Atlanta arrived.

After the plane landed, he watched it empty and the passengers disembark. As they made their way to the luggage pick-up, he paid particular attention to a man, about his age, walking with his arm around the shoulders of a young boy. The boy had a harmonious smile on his face that indicated his life was in balance. The boy instantly reminded him of his own son, Scotty.

His son existed in rare pictures his mother sent only when she felt like sharing. Every so often, a conversation on Skype would take place, but Beau struggled to make a connection with his son, failing to find something meaningful to talk about. He tried, and he hoped Scotty could see that he was trying. After everything that had happened late the year before, Beau knew his time was limited, so he had begun to reach out more.

I'll call when I get home tonight.

Beau passed by Malcolm, who was at the beginning of his shift, and waved at him. "Hey, Malcolm."

"Evenin' officer. Easy night so far?"

"Yes, sir. I'm on the swing shift today, so I'm headed out after the Atlanta return gets in."

"Okay, okay. Well then, have a good one. I'll see you next time."

"Thanks, you do the same. Call me if trouble shows up."

Malcolm smiled and after a brief pause, let out a full-bellied laugh, a continuation from their last conversation. It echoed off the corridor as Beau finished his rounds. The janitor's reaction caused Beau to break into a smile of his own.

On the way home, Beau stopped at Gordo's on Pensacola Street and ordered a Media Noche, a side of maduros, and an extra Gordo sauce to go. While walking past the souvenir shop in the airport, he had seen an ad for the restaurant, and it made him crave Cuban food. He was tired of cold cereal and stale pizza for dinner. After leaving the restaurant, he had one more stop to make.

The early evening sun was hiding behind the treetops, and a long shadow was cast over his car, making him nearly invisible in the hazy, dusk light. Parking in his usual spot offered a clear view of the red brick house with black shutters. As he finished his sandwich, he waited for a glimpse of Wendy Akers. His compulsion to see her, even from afar, was irresistible, as was she, but at the same time, it was foolish.

Just before he was about to leave, a pair of headlights came from the opposite direction and pulled into the driveway. Dylan parked and got out. He strained his neck down the street to look in Beau's direction and continued up to the front door without pause. To Beau's surprise, Wendy greeted him at the door. The light from the interior flooded the front porch, illuminating Wendy in her pregnant form. She was still beautiful, and her protruding belly made her that much more alluring.

They kissed, and Dylan stepped inside, leaving Wendy out on the porch. She too glanced down the street and instinctively rubbed her stomach before turning around and going indoors.

Beau felt satisfied, guilty, and ashamed all at once. He tossed the rest of his sandwich aside, cranked the car and left. A fresh bottle of vodka waited at his apartment.

***

"How long has he been there?" Dylan asked Wendy as he emptied his pockets.

"Not long."

"Still just hangs out down the road?"

"Yeah. Just sits there. Never does anything but watch the house."

Dylan shook his head. "I miss him."

"I know. Me too," she answered.

"I mean, it has to be this way, right? We can't be hanging around each other like it was before."

"No, not if you want to avoid the whole prison thing. It would be only a matter of one of you slipping up. So yes, you have to stay apart from each other."

"So the doctor said everything is good?" Dylan changed the subject.

"Yes. Heartbeat is good. Weight is good. Everything is good."

The life that grew inside of Wendy was fragile enough. Dylan got emotional thinking about all the bad things that could go wrong. He and Wendy had done everything right with Caitlin, but she was still taken away in the most brutal of ways. He was thankful for the second chance at fatherhood, but it also scared the hell out of him.

Wendy saw the pain on her husband's face and sat next to him on the couch.

"It's okay. We just have to pray everything stays normal."

She comforted Dylan, but at the same time hid a terrible secret. It was the not knowing that tortured her from the inside. Was the baby Dylan's or the result of that one night with Beau? Either way, she fought over whether she should tell him or keep the secret. Deep down, she knew she would have to tell him when the time was right. The problem was that there would never be a "good" time.

Dylan broke her from her own torturous thoughts.

"So, that murder trial I was telling you about yesterday? Not guilty."

"I saw."

"I saw Chance at P & E today after the trial, too. He was returning evidence, and I said something about it." Dylan shook his head. "Guess I should've said nothing."

"What did you say?"

"I told him the not guilty wasn't his fault."

"Okay, so?"

"He said he knew, and he blamed me."

Wendy knew that had dug deep into her husband's sense of worth, and she felt bad. However, she didn't share the same sympathy as Dylan about the subsequent fallout from what they had done. She rubbed Dylan's

back and swayed him away from wallowing in his own misery with the promise of a delicious dinner.
"It'll be okay."

Chapter 7

"You got a ride?" asked Antonio. He stared at Dookie, choosing him over Chris. Antonio had made it clear that Xavier's Monte Carlo, although beautiful, was off limits when they conducted business.

"Uh, yeah. Why? You need to take it somewhere?"

"No. You need to take me somewhere."

Not really used to being ordered around, Dookie was slow in responding.

"Got a problem with that?" Antonio asked.

"Nah, man."

"Good. You got a good license?"

"Um, I mean…, yeah. I think so."

Irritated, Antonio shook his head.

Dookie added to his case. "I don't give a fuck. I been driving since I was ten. Don't need a license. I mean, shit. That's a bullshit charge even if I do stop for po-leece."

"That's why you're a fucking idiot," Antonio barked.

"C'mon, man. Don't be like that."

"If you have a bad license and get pulled over, the cops will find a way to get all the other shit in your car and in your pockets and then charge you. That's why you need a good license, dumbass. How do you expect to move product like that? It's like you're inviting them to search your car."

Dookie stood down, deflated in Antonio's disappointment. Undeterred, Antonio turned to Xavier who had stepped outside amidst the lecture and joined the conversation.

"What about you, X? You good to drive?"

"Sorry, bro. My shit's been bad since before I got locked up."

"Okay," Antonio said. "Call one of your girls, one with a good license and have her rent a car from the airport. Tell her to come by here and get us. We need to take care of something."

Xavier pulled out his cell phone and made the call.

"We makin' a delivery, cuz?" Chris asked, eager to start working and make the real money as Antonio had promised.

"No, a withdrawal."

***

Cousin Chris was given the keys to the rental car, and Antonio directed him to where they were going. Xavier and Dookie rode in the back. Antonio made them empty their pockets of everything and made sure they had no weapons before setting out. They wouldn't need them. Plus, where they were going, it was safer.

Antonio kept the destination a secret, and as they neared the location, he told Chris to turn off Alabama Street and onto Richmond. They parked at the dead end of Richmond, in front of a small, green house with modest, but clean adornments around the yard that gave it a comfortable feel. Out front, a wooden ramp for a wheelchair led to the front door.

"What's up, bro?" Xavier spoke up, unfamiliar with the green house. "Who lives here? We hittin' this place or something, because 'member, you made us leave the guns back at the crib."

"No, we're not robbing this house. You can't see it, but it's a bank. I told you we were making a withdrawal."

Furrowed brows of confusion spread through the rental car.

"C'mon. Get out slow and keep y'all's mouths shut." Antonio looked at each one with his dead-eye stare and waited for an acknowledgment. With apprehension on their faces, they each nodded and followed carefully as Antonio slowly moved up the ramp to the front door.

He looked back to make sure the others were accounted for and silent. Then he knocked three times.

No answer. He counted in his head and knocked three more times.

A muffled, but deep voice came from inside. "What do you want?"

"I need to make a withdrawal."

"Door's unlocked."

Antonio slowly turned the doorknob and pushed the door open. The small room was dim; the only light came from a lamp in the corner. Heavy curtains over the windows blocked out the sunlight. Next to the lamp, an elderly man sat in a wheelchair. Antonio could feel his younger brother hovering over his shoulder, straining to look inside the mysterious house. After scanning the living room, Antonio heard Xavier exhale and saw his body relax.

"Damn, man. You got me all fucked up. It's just an old m—"

Antonio wildly flung his left hand backwards, hitting Xavier in the gut, silencing him. Xavier's body quickly tensed, and he took a half step back.

"Who's that? State your name?" the old man demanded.

"It's Antonio Toombs, Mr. Banks. And my dumbass little brother." Antonio gave Xavier a scolding look. "I got my crew with me just to show them the process. I'm here to make a withdrawal."

"Tony Toombs? That you?"

"Yes, sir. It is."

"Finally home from prison, I see?"

"Yes, sir. Ten long years, but now I'm home."

"Welcome home." A nostalgic smile creased his wrinkled face, but it quickly disappeared. "So?"

In a matter of procedure, Antonio spoke, "I danced with the devil and when he wasn't looking, I stole his gold."

Antonio saw Dookie and Chris exchange looks of confusion. Neither had a grasp on what was going on.

"Indeed, Tony Tombs. Indeed. You may enter."

"And he's been chasing me ever since."

The old man let out a hefty laugh and extended his hand outward. Antonio entered the house to greet the old man. As the rest entered, they were immediately greeted by a giant hulk of a man who had stood hidden behind the door. He wielded a double-barreled shotgun. His head scraped the ceiling, and his broad shoulders looked as if he had to enter rooms sideways.

"Holy shit, nigga. You scared the shit out of me." Chris jumped back.

"Chris," Antonio snapped through clenched jaws and pointed to a small chair in the corner. "Y'all sit down. I said, be quiet."

The giant wielding the shotgun eyed the three carefully as they sat, keeping the shotgun at the ready. They hesitated but trusted Antonio as he seemed comfortable.

"Mr. Banks, I don't mean disrespect by bringing my crew. They are unrefined at best but willing to learn. I'm trying to teach them about the business."

He shook his head in agreement. "That's okay, Tony. If they need to learn, it's you who has to teach them."

They spent a few minutes on pleasantries and playing catch-up after a ten-year absence. Antonio then politely asked Mr. Banks for his money.

"I've been faithfully holding on to it for all these years. That, plus the interest I promised, comes out to be a nice chunk of change. You sure you want it all?"

"Yes, sir. I'm making a move, and it has to happen now."

Without consulting a notebook or computer, the old man calculated in his head. After a moment, he said, "So, ten years with interest, that's one hundred thousand dollars."

Antonio smiled at the sound of his total. The crew was wide-eyed at hearing the amount of money. It was a staggering amount that none of them had ever seen at one time.

"Yes, sir. That sounds about right."

"So be it." Mr. Banks looked over at the hulk in the corner and nodded. "Tiny, please excuse our extra guests." Tiny nodded obediently. Antonio expected the next step, but remained silent. The three others grew anxious as they were unaware.

With a low and menacing bark, Tiny ordered the three men up and out of the house, allowing Antonio to stay. He aimed the shotgun at their chests as they slowly moved from the living room and out the door.

"I'm sorry for the need for security, but you know how it is," Banks said.

"Yes, sir. I understand."

Ten minutes later, Antonio Toombs walked out of the small, green house and down the wheelchair ramp. He carried a plastic potted plant. He opened up the car door, sat in the passenger seat and carefully held onto the plant. The crew waited with anticipation.

"Where's the money? Did you really get a hundred Gs from that old man?"

"Yes, but first drive."

"Holy shit, that's a lotta green."

Antonio explained that while working for Carlos Figueroa, he had visions of branching off and running his own crew. Figueroa was talking about retiring, but instead he got sloppy and then got caught. Antonio was anticipating breaking away regardless and had taken most of his earnings and stored it at Mr. Banks's house. He was an old-time gangster but one of the smartest men Antonio had ever known. He came across him by word of mouth, the only way Mr. Banks advertised. After Banks got out of the game himself, he took up money laundering and specialized in security with a guaranteed interest rate and no questions asked. For illegitimate businessmen, it was an ideal set-up. He made his money by loan-sharking, using Tiny as his muscle when deadbeats didn't pay. Tiny was extremely effective, therefore Banks's business ran smoothly and was low-key, staying off the police radar as well as that of other gangsters. This is how he became entrusted with over three million dollars in illegal money.

"That old man has three mil up in that little shack?"

"Yep."

"Fuck. Woulda never known that."

"That's the beauty. Lesson number one, appearances can be deceiving and should be used for your advantage. Chris, take a left and head down Delaware. I want to show you something else about appearances."

The rental car pulled down a small neighborhood street that stretched for one long block. Even in the early afternoon, the street crawled with drug-addicted fiends, prostitutes, and corner boys.

"What? It's just a bunch of hoes and basers," Xavier said.

"But look where they're hanging out," Antonio pointed, as they slowly passed. Four of the people hanging out had zombie-like stares. Two others were in the street, flagging down potential buyers.

Every man in the car knew how life in the ghetto worked. Strung out from continuous crack cocaine use, the basers ambled aimlessly, tethered to the house by their addiction. They waited for a chance to score more dope. With no money to buy, they waited for someone with money to come along. Connecting the buyer to the dealer, they would help facilitate the deal by acting as a middleman, providing insulation and doubling as a lookout. Their price, unbeknownst to the buyer, was a small pinch from their crack rock to smoke later. The more inexperienced the buyer, the more was pinched.

"Yeah, so? We all worked the corners and trap houses, trying to get in the business, Tony."

"Don't you think the cops notice that shit too? They might as well put a sign out front that says 'We're selling dope.' I mean, how long do these places stay open? A month or two maybe before Vice comes shutting it down. And how much money do they really make? It's crumbs, boys, crumbs."

A moment later, they turned the corner and an unmarked sedan with a pair of men inside was situated in the evening shadows.

"See, there's the po-leece now."

Antonio checked the faces of his crew as they left the hood. Their eyes had been opened and minds broadened. He was pleased with today's tutorial, but there was much more to learn in the lesson.

***

Antonio had pressed Xavier to get his drug supplier to agree to a sit-down and renegotiation of their agreement. This made Xavier uncomfortable, having been loyal for years, but he followed his brother's order. The Miami plug was en route to town with their order and agreed to meet later that night.

At the Escambia Drive house, with Dookie's mother paid to leave, the supplier arrived on time and stepped inside with two of his men. He looked around the drab apartment in judgment as if the place was unsuitable for his presence. Antonio waited in the kitchen. He left an empty chair facing him for the supplier.

"Okay, I'm here. Talk," the plug said.

"Have a seat."

The supplier sat on the edge of his seat, not ready to fully commit to the seat as if it was infected with poverty. Antonio liked the fact the Miami man was uncomfortable.

The plug looked up at Xavier. "Other than the drop off, why am I here?"

Antonio spoke up, "I asked you to be here. I'll be assuming all transactions from this point on."

"Whatever." He acted unimpressed and sneered at Xavier. A sudden flash of recognition hit the Miami man. "Tony Toombs? That you, dawg? I heard you was out but didn't believe it until now."

Antonio couldn't place the connection. He had been away from civilization for far too long. Ten years can change anyone's look. His hesitation made way for the dealer to reintroduce himself.

"It's me, Trey Diggs. I used to run for Figs down in Miami."

"Ah, yes." The name registered. "Lil' Trey back then." They slapped hands, shook, hugged, and ended with a slap on the back. "Good to see you all grown up."

"Yeah, yeah you know. We gotta grow up sometime. So, back to business. What's up Tony? X said you wanted to renegotiate."

"Some things need to change now that I'm in charge."

"Oh? Well, I only renegotiate on my terms. But, we go back, Tony Tombs. I'll at least hear you out."

"Okay. First things first. The shit you bring needs to be more pure. Stop stepping the fuck out of it. Second, instead of one kilo a month, I want five."

Diggs's eyes narrowed. Antonio felt all eyes on him, but ignored them. Upping their intake by four kilos was a substantial increase in product, but he knew what he was doing.

A moment longer of consideration, Diggs returned, "I can't do that. I respect you and all, given our history, but this is business. It's good the way it is, so I don't see the need to mess with it. So…, sorry, no deal. I'm not risking my business and taking on more dope. You'll just have to make do with your share."

Diggs made a motion to get up.

"Sit down," Antonio said with an icy tone accentuated by his dead-eye stare. The implication that hell would follow if he didn't comply was understood. Diggs's bodyguards tensed, anticipating a reaction from Antonio. For the sake of listening, the Miami dealer sat back down.

"So let's make a deal," Antonio said.

"What's that?"

"Supply only to me."

"Not happening."

"Why not?"

"Why not? Tony Tombs, what happens when I burn that bridge dealing only with you, you get busted, and my demand dries up? It's called diversity. I'm not bringing more product up just for you. You're just going to have to deal with it. It's that mentality that fucked our boy Figs and why it's taking me so long to build Tallahassee back up."

"But given our history, my history, don't that count for something?"

"I been supplying the same crew for years now with no hiccups. With you just gettin' out, startin' fresh, you ain't proven. You ain't who you used to be, Tony Tombs. No offense. Now, ten years ago, I'd probably be workin' for you, but that wasn't in the cards, was it? I'll stick with my arrangement as it is, unless something changes."

"Okay. Let me say it another way. Xavier, bring me the plant."

Diggs raised his eyebrow in interest. Antonio watched as the bodyguards keyed in on Xavier. He brought back the pot and handed it to Antonio. Antonio uprooted the plant, tossed it in a nearby garbage can and dug in the remaining dirt. He pulled out a round canister that was hidden underneath and wiped away the dirt. He popped open the lid revealing a thick wad of cash.

"A hundred grand, all in hundreds. Let's call it a down payment on that five kilos."

"Impressive," said Diggs. "But, that'll buy you a one-time five kilo deal. Not enough to change our arrangement. I'll make it back in three months with the other crew. What else you got?"

Antonio paused for a minute, dealing with his disappointment. He hid his anger. Xavier made his way behind Antonio and within reach of the gun he stashed in the bread box. Antonio noticed and subtly shook his head.

"I'm sorry I wasted your time. Please, here's a little bit for your trouble. We'll just take what you brought and revisit this later."

Indifferent to Antonio's sincerity, Diggs stood up and shook his hand. Antonio gave him a thousand dollars and said, "I hope you reconsider."

"Not likely. But it was nice seeing you Tony Tombs."

Diggs and his bodyguards left the small apartment.

Antonio and the crew stood by, watching them walk to their car.

"Hey man, that guy made you his little bitch in there," Dookie said brazenly.

Antonio slowly looked over and sloughed off the insult.

"Did he?"

Dookie second-guessed his insubordination. He shrugged. "I don't know."

"Appearances can be deceiving, remember?"

"Oh, shit." Dookie put things together as did Xavier. "You played that mutha-fucker in there, didn't you?"

"Something like that. And you call me a bitch again and I'll put a hole in you."

Dookie nodded and bowed submissively.

Antonio looked over at Chris and nodded for him to come closer. As soon as the Miami men pulled out of the parking lot, he told Chris, "Follow them. Tell me who he's supplying."

"You got it."

"Dookie, you go with him."

"A'ight."

***

Several hours later, well after midnight, Chris and Dookie entered the apartment and provided Antonio with the addresses of the dealers who shared their supplier.

"Well, done. Good work."

"What do we do now?" asked Chris.

"We change the arrangement."

Chapter 8

"Over here!" The patrolman yelled out to his partner as they searched the area.

"Where?"

"Over here, behind the house." The trailing officer ran up to the first officer, hustling with urgency. The light beam from his Maglite illuminated the blood trail on the driveway. The shroud of night made it difficult to see the evidence on the ground. They looked at each other and followed the blood trail further behind the house. It led to a shed in the backyard. As they neared, the distinct pattern of a handprint was stamped on the outside, wet with blood. Both of their guns were out, ready to deal with whoever was hiding in the shed.

In a hushed voice, the first officer relayed over the radio their location and that they believed someone was inside. He supported the lead, mentioning the blood trail and handprint.

"C'mon, let's get him," the trailing officer pleaded.

"Okay, you pull the door, I'll cover."

"Ten-four."

Both officers crept up to the front of the shed, holding their weapons aimed at the door in case of a sudden emergence. A chaotic shots-fired call by multiple callers had brought them to the area. Because of the two dead bodies already found at the first scene, they didn't know if the blood trail led to a suspect or another victim. Either way, whoever was inside the shed could be very dangerous.

The trailing officer poised himself to yank open the door while the first aimed his gun and flashlight at the shed door. Ready to act, they nodded to each other.

As the door flung open and light poured in, a scared man huddled in the stuffed corner of the shed, his bloody hands held up in surrender.

"Please, no. Please, don't kill me!"

"This is the police. Don't move."

"Huh? Police?" The man squinted his eyes, trying to see through the bright beam of light.

The man was the definite source of the blood trail. His hands were covered, and the left side of his shirt was saturated red. He had been shot and was still bleeding.

"Please, help me. I been shot, man. They came out of nowhere, man, like ghosts."

"Okay, okay, sir. Please, stand up and step out slowly. Keep your hands where I can see them."

"Okay, but help me, man. I'm shot." The man started to cry. "Are you sure they gone, man. They killed 'em, man. Shit." His frightened cry turned into a sob.

"We got an ambulance on the way, but you need to come out of there first."

The man slowly pulled himself to his feet, using the lawn equipment by his side. A loud thump came from under him.

"What the hell was that?" The first officer asked.

"Dunno."

Stepping out of the small shed, the man stepped into the back yard, clutching his side. He started to fade. The first officer caught him by the arm, holding him up.

"Hey, man. He's losing a lot of blood."

"I know. Hold on." He stepped inside the shed and looked back to his partner. "Call EMS and have them come here." The officer shone his light around the shed, double-checking that another person wasn't hiding. On the floor, where the man had been sitting, a chrome handgun lay in a pool of fresh blood.

"Gun!"

Without hesitation, the backup officer snatched up the bloody man and wrenched on a pair of handcuffs.

"Ow, fuck, man. C'mon, I been shot. What the fuck?"

"My partner just found a gun in there, so just chill out until we figure things out."

"I need an ambulance, fuck. That hurts." The man tried to pull away from the officer.

"Stop that. The ambulance is just down the street."

"C'mon, let's get him out of here." The first officer secured the gun and grabbed the man's other arm, escorting him onto the street. Once the man saw the ambulance, he seemed to relax.

"What about those ghosts, man?" the officer asked.

"Huh? Oh, you gettin' me to the hospital?"

"Yes, we are, but we can talk, right?" The officers led the handcuffed man down the street, closer to the scene where the ambulance was staged.

"Shit, man. I thought I was dead. There were like four of them. They just appeared in the house and started shooting. No warning, no nothing, man. Didn't even give us a chance. I think they killed my boys. I got hit and barely made it out of there. I just ran and hid, man."

"So, there were four of them?"

"Yeah, man. At least four."

"Did they take anything?"

He hesitated. "I don't know, man. I just ran."

The officer suspected that the man's hesitation meant they took drugs. He just wasn't ready to admit it. There's no way the risk of so much violence was for nothing. There was something in that house worth killing for.

"So what did they look like?"

"Black guys, but they had on masks. Except for one. He stood in the doorway watching, like the leader. I'll never forget the stone-cold look on his face."

"Okay, what did he look like?"

The blue lights of the responding patrol cars bounced off the neighboring houses, creating a strobe light effect. As the officers neared the ambulance with the bloody witness, a crowd of neighbors huddled across the street behind yellow crime scene tape. The news of violence always brought a crowd from the drug-riddled neighborhood. Women stood with arms folded, shower caps on their heads, and no concern for modesty. A few small children looked on, unable to control their curiosity.

Just before reaching the ambulance, the witness scanned the small crowd.

"Hey, man. Tell me what the guy with no mask looked like?" The patrolman probed.

Suddenly, the man tensed and had to be pulled along by the officers.

"Dude, c'mon. We're almost to the ambulance. So, what did he look like?"

"Huh?"

"Dude, c'mon. What did he look like?"

"Who?"

Irritated, the cop paused and studied the noticeable change in his face. "The unmasked suspect. What did he look like?"

"I don't know, man. Just get me to the hospital. I don't feel like talking anymore. Call my lawyer, man. I ain't saying shit."

Incredulous, the officers assisted the EMTs in getting the bloodied witness on a gurney and into the back of the ambulance. The patrolman couldn't believe how quickly the witness's attitude changed to uncooperative. They tried several more times to talk to him as the EMTs prepped him for transport. When he cried for his attorney again, they reminded him that he wasn't under arrest and was a victim.

Sternly, the officer readdressed the witness.

"You don't need a lawyer. You're a victim. Don't you care about your boys shot dead? What the hell, man?"

"I don't give a fuck. They're dead. What the fuck can I do about it? Ain't nothing gonna change that."

The officer was tired of the reluctance that plagued this neighborhood. Even in the face of the most heinous of crimes, no one ever seemed to truly care.

"You're a fucking coward."

"Fuck you, officer."

"Get him out of here." The officer shut the ambulance door and told his partner to follow them to the hospital.

***

Antonio used the shadows to sneak back to the scene. Walking calmly down the hill, he eased up behind a crowd of onlookers. With the buzz of activity on the far side of the street, he watched, trying to gather intelligence. A mistake had been made and someone had escaped. He needed damage control. His plan demanded it.

Several uniformed officers ran from the crime scene and headed up the street. Suddenly, they stopped and pointed to the ambulance. Antonio heard, "The subject hiding is in custody," transmitted over one of the cops' radios. It was the one that got away.

Perfect.

Hearing the need for an ambulance, Antonio marveled at his luck as he saw one idling near where he stood. They would bring the witness to him. Keeping his eyes up the street, he saw two cops escorting a man with a red-stained shirt toward the ambulance. He was talking, a lot. Talking to the police is not good.

Nearing the crowd, Antonio stared at the bloody man, waiting for him to take notice. Finally, as he waited behind the ambulance, they locked eyes. Antonio glared at the loose end, conveying the code of the streets: say nothing or pay the ultimate price. The witness's face changed and instantly tensed, growing scared.

He got the message.

Slipping back away from the crowd, Antonio left with the stealth he used to return to the scene with no one noticing.

***

Chance stood at the doorway, strategically placing himself to scan the macabre scene but also to avoid stepping into blood. Pools and spray were everywhere in the small living room. He knew it was bad from the two a.m. phone call, but seeing it firsthand, bad didn't begin to describe it.

The first victim had been killed instantly, one fatal shot through the heart. His mistake was that he sat closest to the door. Chance leaned his torso to the right to get a better look between the wall and the chair where the victim sat. The dead man's hand was draped over the armrest, but it wasn't because he was relaxed. He had reached for a shotgun.

"Not quick enough, were ya?" Chance spoke in a low tone, not expecting an answer.

With carefully chosen steps, he leaned back and studied the busted doorframe. The heavy deadbolt on the door was to keep would-be intruders or police at bay, giving plenty of warning to those inside to either arm themselves or flush the evidence, depending on the caller. Chance shook his head as he noticed the deadbolt was still extended outward. The wooden doorframe was nearly rotten and would have given way from a strong push, let alone a violent kick.

The second victim was further inside the living room, lying face down in a thick pool of crimson blood. He had attempted some level of defense because his lifeless hand still clutched a gun. Chance could see a few shell casings on the stained carpet that he figured would come back to the victim's gun.

Already a few steps inside, Chance contorted himself in place to study the front wall of the living room, next to the entrance. A few holes from return fire were scattered around the door and the adjacent window. Chance moved closer to inspect the small section of wall by the threshold. There was more blood.

He closed his eyes and imagined what must have happened, recreating the scene in his mind. Weighing the evidence *in situ*, he came to a conclusion.

"Hopefully, this guy managed to wing one of the shooters."

This was good from an investigative standpoint, because amongst all the blood was the blood of a suspect. Fresh blood on a murder scene, with a DNA match, was the new-age smoking gun. It was such a difficult piece of evidence to refute if the forensic science backed it up.

Chance knelt to look from a different viewpoint. Many times, alternate vantages offered answers to questions that would otherwise go unanswered. Satisfied he hadn't missed anything, Chance stood up for another look around. A small table that sat by the first victim's chair had been knocked over. He looked on the floor where it fell to see the remnants of cocaine and some packaging. A digital scale had scooted across the floor, most likely originating from the table.

After replaying the scene, Chance felt comfortable about what happened. He carefully dodged the pool of blood from the second victim and tip-toed down the hall. He followed multiple sets of shoe prints, at least three, to a back bedroom where the window was completely broken out. The lacy curtains were torn and pulled to the outside as if something large had gone out the window.

Through the window, he saw Brennan Headley taking pictures outside the house. Her blonde ponytail was tightly pulled back, and she had already donned a white Tyvek suit.

"Hey, Chance."

"Hey, Bren. That where the third guy bailed from?"

"Yes, between being shot inside and cutting the shit out of himself on the window jumping, he's lucky he didn't bleed out before patrol found him."

"No kidding. I'm ready in here when you are."

The forensic tech came around to the front and met Chance outside. She smiled, cherishing the moment to work amongst the dead. They were easier to work with than live victims, she always said. She was right, in a morbid sort of way.

"So, what are you thinking? These guys majorly pissed someone off?"

"I don't know. They clearly weren't ready like they pissed anyone off."

She looked around him to see the first guy's hand reaching for a shotgun. "Yeah, you're right. He didn't even have time to reach that shotgun."

After getting the late night call from dispatch about the shooting, Chance was not surprised. He had been expecting it. He knew the not-guilty verdict was just the beginning of something dangerous brewing in the streets. He had been stewing about the decision since the jury foreperson had read it aloud.

"Hey, Chance, did you hear me?" Brennan asked.

"Huh? Oh sorry, what?"

"So what are you thinking?"

"I'm thinking things are about to get a lot worse."

***

Xavier winced and let out a groan through clenched teeth. He was fighting the intense pain that came from a searing hot bullet passing through his body. The wound was a through-and-through. The pain was sharp and came in waves. When he moved, even slightly, it grew more intense. The second guy who came from the back of the house had managed to hit him before Dookie flanked him, dropping him in the living room.

"Hold still, nigga," Chris said to Xavier, as he held a towel against the side of his abdomen.

"That fuckin' hurts, dude."

"Which is why you need to stay still."

"Just get some more damn liquor."

Chris stepped away and eyed Antonio who was watching. He wasn't happy his little brother was shot and the third guy escaped, but the message was sent and was loud and clear. They meant business, and now the Miami supplier would know it too. Antonio knelt next to the couch where Xavier lay.

"Let me see." He asked.

Xavier exhaled, knowing it would hurt when he released the towel. He peeled it back, revealing a clean hole where the forty-caliber piece of lead passed through his body. Blood welled up to the edge of the wound and trickled down the side of his stomach. Antonio examined it closely and figured that based on where the exit wound was on his back, it was likely the projectile missed his kidneys and intestines. He would be fine. They could avoid the hospital and all the questions that would follow.

Antonio stood up. "You did good, lil bro."

The plan was moving along nicely.

A moment later, Antonio's phone rang. All the faces in the living room looked on as he answered. They had been waiting for the call. It was the reason for killing two people earlier that night.

"Hello?" Antonio's face remained stoic, cold as he listened to the other end. After a minute of silence, Antonio looked around the room, meeting each person's eye. Dookie and Chris stood by the couch where Xavier lay in pain. A small grin broke at the corner of Antonio's mouth. The crew knew the move to hit their competition had paid off.

"Deal," Antonio said.

Chapter 9

The news anchor carried a stern look as she reported on the upturn in violence.

"With what the police say is a spike in violent crimes, several Tallahassee families are left mourning the loss of loved ones. Over the past week, several local neighborhoods have fallen victim to the violence, and most of it, deadly. It started earlier in the week with what police officials are saying was a home invasion robbery, leaving two men dead."

Images of a crime scene flashed on the screen. Blue strobe lights flickered against the side of a house surrounded by yellow crime scene tape. Several plainclothes officers and uniformed personnel moved busily around the scene while the camera recorded. On duty at the airport, Beau Rivers watched from a mounted television in the A terminal.

The reporter provided the location and the generic specifics for the at-home detectives playing along.

"Following the home invasion on Tuesday was a shooting on Alabama Street that left one man in the hospital with a gunshot wound, and a late night shoot-out on Apalachee Parkway on Wednesday night, resulting in two men critically wounded and one still in intensive care. And just last night, another home invasion occurred only blocks away from Tuesday's incident, leaving one man dead."

A map with each incident plotted with a virtual pin came on the screen, detailing how the proximity of each incident to the others. The reporter inferred they were all related, and Beau's instincts told him she was right. He didn't know much about the crimes, but Beau did recognize the victim's names. They all had something in common. They were all associated somehow with the drug trade. He remembered specifically that some were rivals to the Figueroa Organization.

The news report cut live to the police chief.

"Here's Tallahassee Police Chief Robert Shaw to comment on the recent violence. Chief?"

He chose to do the interview in his Class A uniform, giving the appearance that he was a member of the rank-and-file and not an administrator, something the at-home detectives would miss. Shaw stood in front of headquarters with the department's name prominently displayed in the background.

"Thanks, Samantha. First, I'd like to extend my deepest sympathies to those families who were affected by this senseless violence. I can honestly say we are doing everything we can to bring those who are responsible to justice."

"Justice?" Beau said sarcastically to himself. "What does he know about justice?" Beau didn't know much about the new chief, but Shaw had seen it fit to banish Beau to the airport which didn't sit well. This lowered his already low opinion. Shaw was a politician in cops clothing and not to be trusted.

"We are following all available leads and encourage those out there who have any information about any of these crimes to please come forward. You can remain anonymous if you choose. We just want closure for the families."

"Do you have any leads, Chief?" the reporter asked.

"Yes, Samantha. Rest assured that our detectives are following all leads in each of the cases, and we hope to have a successful resolution very soon."

That means you have dick.

Beau had heard that before. He had worked enough cases in the past to know when the figureheads were spinning something.

"Do you think the community's distrust has become an issue in these crimes?" She alluded to the fallout surrounding the deaths of Earnest McFadden and George Shelley.

Caught off guard, the Chief quickly regained composure. Beau smiled at his hesitation. "It's unfortunate that the actions of a few have affected the perception of an entire department. I can't begin to apologize about that, but I can assure you we're here to protect the community with all our available resources."

"Okay. Thank you, Chief."

"Thank you, Samantha."

The news report ended with her asking the viewers to call Crimestoppers with any information about the cases and then cut to commercial. Beau shook his head. He was disgusted with how the Chief acted as if he cared. Beau wasn't fooled. On the other hand, he felt ashamed because the distrust the reporter mentioned was his fault. On top of the guilt, the burden of causing an entire community to distrust the police was just more to bear. It served as a painful reminder of his reality and made him feel low and worthless. He hung his head and walked out of the terminal.

Beau stepped outside and took a deep breath of the cool night air. The humidity seemed to take the night off, and the air was refreshing. If only for a minute, it helped him escape, letting him feel like he was anywhere but at the airport. A vision of a dock set over calm ocean waters kept coming back to him.

Sergeant Mathis called Beau's number ID over the radio.

Reality returned.

"Go ahead."

"We got a call of a verbal altercation outside in the drop-off lane. Can you respond, please?"

Already outside, Beau looked to his left and then right. At the far end of the terminal building, two taxicab drivers from rival companies were on the sidewalk, standing awkwardly close to each other.

"Ten-four, I got it."

Beau had dealt with this before. He could recite the script of the argument even before hearing what the drivers had to say. It was an ongoing problem. To be fair, the airport instituted a policy allowing the cabs to form a line at the taxi pick-up point for passengers. So, when the customers exited, they took the first cab available and then the next cab in line could take the next person. However, occasionally, some enterprising "new guy" would break in line and all hell would break loose with those who abided. Beau despised the petty arguments and would rather run them both off than work it out.

As he neared the two men, one middle-eastern and the other a very dark-skinned, black man, were arguing loudly. Beau was right. They were yelling about the middle-eastern man taking the front spot when the black man was already parked in the front. Beau rolled his eyes.

"Hey, hey, hey! Y'all calm down. It's just a damn parking spot."

They stopped, turned to Beau, and in their respective broken English, pled their cases. A buzzing in Beau's pocket briefly drew his attention. He didn't get many phone calls, so he placed a finger up to his mouth to put the argument on pause. Both drivers quieted out of confusion. Beau checked the screen and recognized the number. It could wait. He put the phone back and listened to the nonsense of the cabbies.

"Was he there first?"

"No, he was parked back there when I came up." The middle-eastern man pointed to the other end of the drop-off lane.

"No, no, I wasn't. I was pulling up after dropping off a fare. You were speeding around to get in front."

"I was not."

"Was too!"

"Oh, for crying out loud." Beau hated his job at this moment. He wished he could just kick them both off the property, but having tried that before, he had been forced to apologize to the cab drivers.

Beau tried to appeal to each driver's sense of goodwill, but they were apparently as foreign to that concept as they were to America. Soon a wave of passengers came out and one businesswoman walked out to the cab stand, looking for a ride. The drivers turned from Beau and tried to solicit a ride.

"Nope! Stop right there, gentlemen. You guys called us to settle this and we're not done." Beau spoke loud enough so the businesswoman could hear him. She looked confused. Beau addressed her over the two childish drivers. "Ma'am, these two are busy. Please take the next cab in line, over there." Beau pointed to the line of the compliant drivers. Both cabbies deflated at the loss of a fare. Businesswomen normally tipped the best too.

Beau waved the other passengers looking for a cab around the two causing the problem, intentionally keeping them from getting fares. Their frustration with each other soon gave way to the frustration of losing out on money.

"You ready to get along and deal with each other, or shall we stay here and argue while all the customers leave?" This crowd was probably the last one of the night, so the threat was genuine and potentially very costly.

Like scolded children, they bowed their heads, agreeing to act amicably. As Beau walked back inside, he allowed himself a quick smile.

Another buzz came from his pocket. It was a short one, which meant a text message. He checked his phone. The same number that had called earlier sent a text. It read: Come over later, please.

After Beau's shift, he left the airport and headed to the sender of the message. It was nearing midnight, and the surrounding neighborhood was quiet. As he pulled up, a light was still on inside. Beau took the few steps up to the porch and knocked quietly.

Gary Levine answered the door. He was a petite man, skinny, thick gray mustache, and thinning hair that matched. His eyes were tired. They had seen more than most, but Gary had a confidence about him that Beau instantly respected.

"Hey, Beau. Thanks for coming. Goddamn AC is out again." Gary wore a tank top that clung to his small frame and boxer shorts that looked fresh out of the dirty clothes hamper.

"Okay, that all?"

"Yeah. I could use the company, but I ain't ready to kick it just yet if that's what you're concerned about."

Beau stepped inside and began to shed his uniform and duty belt. Gary Levine was dying. Spending a lifetime abusing his liver, cirrhosis had taken hold inside his body and his inaction had led to a lethal prognosis.

Carrying a half-empty bottle, not caring about his condition, he offered one to Beau. "Wanna beer?" Gunna die anyway, might as well have a drink, he'd say. A lit cigarette hung from the corner of his mouth.

"Sure." Beau was not one to judge how people lived their lives.

Gary grabbed another beer and set it on the table for Beau. He walked to the living room and sat down in his recliner, letting out a groan.

After shedding his uniform shirt, vest, and belt, Beau took a sip from the beer.

"What's it doing?"

"Clankin' noise then blowin' warm air. I feel like I'm meltin' in here." Gary's nasally voice, scarred from smoking, carried a southern drawl.

"Okay, I'll take a look, but not promising anything."

Gary tuned into the television program while Beau tinkered with the window AC unit. After a good ten minutes of silence, Gary spoke up.

"How are you on your training?"

"Ehh, decent. Hard to bank left and right without spinning in circles too fast."

"Yeah, gets tricky sometimes. You gotta get a good feel for the bird, first. Like a woman, she responds to the right touch."

Face deep inside the AC unit, Beau smiled. He pictured the smile on the old man's face as he compared flying a helicopter to romancing a woman. He often spoke about flying and said it was the second greatest love of his life. Beau thought of Wendy in that moment, and the smile disappeared.

"I'll keep that in mind."

"Yeah, young stud like you. Prolly ain't got no problem with the ladies, huh?"

Gary had tried to probe into Beau's love life for months. Each time, Beau dismissed it with a non-committal smile and a nod.

"Something like that."

Truth was, Beau had tried to move on from Wendy, but after a few meaningless dates that ended in equally meaningless sex, he had stayed away from women all together. It wasn't the same. Plus, he didn't want to infect them with his worthlessness. He had done enough damage to the one he actually cared about. However, the loneliness allowed thoughts of her to take a stronghold on his heart.

"There, fixed it. A hose came loose which is why it only blew warm air."

"Ugh, thank God."

Beau wiped his hands and grabbed the beer for another long pull. He liked visiting with Gary and didn't mind helping out. He was just repaying a favor, and Gary treasured the company, not having any family still living. His legacy would end with him. Having been a widower for over a decade and with no children, he tried to pass on what knowledge he could to Beau Rivers.

Gary kept a collage of grainy pictures displayed in random order over the mantle. Among them was a much younger Gary, arm-in-arm with other Army soldiers. In one, he sat in the cockpit of a UH-1 "Huey," and another showed him holding a gorgeous Asian brunette on a Korean beach.

Beau marveled at the lifetime of memories. He stared at each picture, placing himself back in time. He was envious. Gary had lived through the worst violence from a contentious war, fallen in love in a foreign land, and carried around deep scars to tell his story. A story rich in history, romance, and intrigue. Beau liked hearing the old man's tales over cold beers, but there was another connection that brought them together, a dark secret that was left unsaid.

In the corner of the living room sat an artifact that Gary managed to smuggle home after his stint in the Army. It was an M1919 Browning machine gun removed from its mount, originally on the side of a UH-1 Huey. It was an impressive piece of hardware that Beau had noticed the first time he came to the house. Gary claimed the gun had mowed down hundreds of Viet Cong hiding in the rice patties of North Vietnam. With the gun came the belt that fed the ammo into the chamber for a sustained hailstorm of gunfire. Beau borrowed it about six months ago for reasons he hadn't specified. Gary let him have it without question.

Paying the secret no attention, Beau joined Gary in the small living room and noticed a tattoo on the old man's right bicep. He'd known him for the last eight months and never knew he had it. Thinking back, the old man had always covered it up with a shirt sleeve. Gary had other tattoos from his time in the military, but this one stood out. It was of a dog, standing proudly in an over-watch position.

"Is that a dog on your arm?"

Gary looked over at Beau, not needing to check what he was talking about. "It's a sheepdog."

"Okay? Is it supposed to have meaning or does it remind you of a favorite pet?"

"Got it in the Army. Hanging out on base with the boys, we came up with it. Somethin' that we could call ourselves, somethin' that represented us. Others wanted to get sharks or some queer ass snake, but I brought up the sheepdog."

"A shark would've been cooler—or a lion."

"That's not what it represents." Gary was serious. "It has meaning, dumbass." Gary sat up straight and turned his arm toward Beau. "Sheep fear the sheepdog, because they don't know what he is. Wolves fear the sheepdog because they do."

Chills ran over Beau. The quote registered somewhere deep inside. He understood the meaning.

"A sheepdog, huh?"

"Yes, sir." Gary smiled. He saw it register in his young friend. "You don't know it yet, my friend, but you're a sheepdog."

Chapter 10

"I told that nigga not to try me, dawg!" Cousin Chris yelled out proudly, waving his gun around the small living room.

Dookie was just as amped. "Now he got smoked. Yo, that shit was wild. You shoulda seen ya boy."

Dookie had been standing next to Chris when the Southside boy shouldered Chris in the nightclub. The boy smiled mockingly trying to start a confrontation. Antonio saw the anger build and the emotion cloud and quickly pulled his young cousin aside. Antonio told him to wait and take the high road, for now.

"That way, we give him a false sense of security. Let him have the moment, because you'll have the last laugh. Remember how we found the other dealers?"

Chris grinned with anticipation. "Yes, sir."

"Good."

Chris walked away under a barrage of verbal threats and posturing from the boy, losing face in the crowd. But, with Tony Toombs standing by, Chris knew he would have his turn and let the taunts go.

After the club let out, Chris and Dookie followed the Southside boy and his two friends from the club to the corner store on Alabama Street. From down the street, they saw the boy go in the store. That's when Chris made his move.

Dookie drove the rental slowly, carefully to time their pass with the boys' exit. Chris sat on the open window ledge, hooked his leg inside and aimed two handguns in their direction. In the first volley, a bullet caught the Southside boy in the leg, and he fell while his two friends scattered in opposite directions. Chris tried to hit them on the run, but they moved too fast for an accurate shot. However, the boy was left crawling slowly after one of the rounds shattered his knee.

"Stop. Stop the car."

"What?" Dookie challenged.

"Stop the mutha-fuckin car, Dook!"

"Whatever."

Dookie stopped just past the store's parking lot, and Chris jumped out. He walked up to the boy who was steadily crawling away.

"Try me now, nigga." Chris aimed the gun at the head of the helpless adversary as he got closer. "Come at me now, fuckboy!"

The Southside boy froze, trapped by Chris.

"Ain't got nothing to say, do ya, boy?" Chris antagonized, holding onto his power.

The rival didn't answer. Chris shot a glance to Dookie. A quick movement from the ground caught his eye. The boy flipped over, and suddenly, fire spit from his extended hand. Chris stumbled back, but didn't fall.

Incredulous at the move, Chris regained his composure, portraying a calm confidence as he stood over his prey. He pulled the trigger, hitting the boy in the hip and leg with another barrage. One round hit the boy's gun and splintered off into his hand, rendering it as useless as his leg. The boy screamed as the gun fell to the ground. Chris walked closer and put one more round into his head, leaving him instantly lifeless. Chris turned and walked back to the car. Dookie had the car revved up to go, and he peeled out, amped up by what he just witnessed.

Antonio listened as he heard Dookie give an eyewitness account. He looked over at Chris, proud that he didn't cave under the pressure, even after being shot at close range. Chris smiled and pulled off his shirt with a hole in the middle of it. Underneath, he peeled away the Velcro straps of a ballistic vest that had caught the slug.

"Good thing you had that, huh?" Antonio asked.

"You right, cuz. Thanks." Chris reached out and hugged his older cousin. Tony Toombs had given him the vest prior to following the boy from the club.

"If we don't get respect, we will take it by any means necessary."

"Damn right."

"But, that don't mean we can't be smart about it, though."

"True, true."

***

After three and half hours of sleep, Chance Parker was awakened by his ringing phone. He contemplated throwing it out the window before answering.

"Hello?"

"Detective Parker, I need to transfer you to the sergeant on scene. We've had another shooting."

"Fuck."

"Excuse me?"

"Sorry. Yeah, that'll be fine. Go ahead and make the transfer."

Over the last week, Chance had gotten little to no sleep each night. He and his squad had been working around the clock because of the recent spike in violence, and he was getting fed up. With shootings, murders, and home invasions, they were getting nowhere and felt as if they were chasing their own tails rather than legit leads. People weren't talking, and it was making life difficult in the world of homicide.

After getting briefed by the sergeant on scene, Chance took a quick shower and dressed for another long day.

There had been another drive-by on Alabama Street at an intersection notorious for drug sales. Chance had driven by the intersection countless times and had made numerous arrests there as a beat cop. Now, it was another crime scene and evidence of senseless violence.

The victims had walked out of the corner store when a car drove by and started shooting, hitting one of the victims in the head. Preliminarily, it was a continued beef that started at a nightclub. Patrol found one of the victim's friends running from the scene, but he wasn't offering up any details. Chance grabbed some caffeine, a snack bar, and headed out the door.

Midnight call-outs were never welcomed, but one of the advantages was that the streets were devoid of life. This allowed for quick and easy travel to the crime scene. Chance rolled through town, taking Bronough Street south and cut west on Seventh Avenue. He passed the house where either Beau Rivers or Dylan Akers had set up an elaborate kidnapping attempt on George Shelley. His gut said it was Beau. Chance had spent the better part of that day combing through the nasty flophouse looking for any usable evidence. Most of it was still being processed. It had been a miserable day for him. When he got home, he learned his wife wanted a divorce. Looking back, it was just coincidence, but it was hard not to think about one without the other.

A midnight construction crew was working ahead on Bronough Street and traffic was getting re-routed.

"Are you kidding me?" Chance yelled out of frustration. For a moment, he thought about activating his blue lights and driving past the barricades. He thought better of it and turned right down Tenth Avenue. He'd hit Seventh a few blocks over.

As he pulled through the quiet Levy Park neighborhood, he saw a patrol car with the designation of the airport parked on the side of the street. Chance wasn't aware of any cops who lived in the neighborhood. Most of the inhabitants were longtime residents, eclectic hipsters, and a racial mix of young families, all teetering on the lower side of the economic scale. It wasn't known for crime, but it wasn't the ideal place for police to reside. All the lights were off inside the car, like it was shut down, not running idle while on a call.

Chance didn't think too much about it, but as he passed by the patrol car, he saw movement on the porch that drew his attention. The light from inside poured outside over a porch and a set of stairs, making it easy to see who was leaving. He locked eyes with Beau Rivers as he passed by.

Speak of the devil, and he shall appear.

He read the address and committed it to memory. He made a note to shoot Russell Trek with Internal Affairs an email when he had a minute.

***

Beau paused at the base of the front steps as headlights approached. He eyed the unmarked car as it rolled slowly past Gary Levine's house. The windows were down and he recognized the scowl on Detective Chauncey Parker's face. He froze, unsure if the homicide detective was coming for him or just passing through by coincidence. It was an unfortunate reaction since taking part in two revenge murders. He watched him continue down the street and make a westbound turn a few blocks away.

He had managed to keep his association with Gary away from the knowledge base of the Tallahassee Police Department and wondered if Chance was going to make trouble. He was a strong-willed and determined detective, and Beau wasn't sure which side of the blue line he was on.

Chapter 11

Chief Shaw settled down the command staff and called the morning meeting to order. He excused the civilian members and the Public Information Officer, keeping just the sworn personnel in the conference room. His demeanor was opposite the persona he used for the television interview the night before. Today, he was upset and mad.

"What the hell, people?" he barked. The rest of the command staff erased their smiles, feeling the responsibility of the senseless violence plaguing the city. They were failing, and they knew it.

"I want a plan in place by close of business today on how we're going to stop this violence. I'm getting my teeth kicked in every hour by City Hall. My balls are being squeezed by all the black church leaders in town asking why we're letting young black men get killed." Shaw scanned the room, meeting each member in the eye. His serious glower let the rest of the room know he meant business.

"I don't need to tell you that I hate having my teeth kicked in and my balls squeezed, so give me solutions, now!"

The head of the Criminal Investigations Division, Captain Inez Carter, leaned forward, taking the first hit. "Street drug ops always seemed to work best in quelling the violence, Chief, if only for a short period until we get more long-term plans in place. I can get Vice to scramble tonight on something. I assume overtime won't be an issue?"

"No, bring in as many as you want. City Hall can pick up the check for all I care. What else?"

"Well, Chief?" Captain Carter asked with trepidation.

"What?"

"We need more people to work these cases. We've been running short before I even took over, and with the impact these cases are having, my people are flat worn out."

"Hmm." Chief Shaw was well aware of the manpower shortage throughout the department. He had no way to suddenly generate more people. He could only squeeze harder from the same dry lemon.

Shaw had an idea and looked toward the Captain over the Crime Prevention Unit.

"Keep two of your officers and ship the rest upstairs to Inez. That'll give you four right there."

Shaw moved around the room and looked at the Captain over Special Operations. He was responsible for the Motor Unit, the Airport, Traffic Investigations, and the Special Events Coordinator.

"How many of your guys have investigative training?"

"Most of the motor guys are traffic homicide certified. You want them?"

"Yes, keep two to put Band-Aids on problems as they come in. Have the rest report to CID by the end of the afternoon."

A few heads nodded around the room. The feeling that something was getting accomplished was shared amongst the members. It was refreshing to get problems addressed without the interference of a bureaucracy.

"If any complaints come in to your departments, you send them up to my office, and I'll take care of them. I'm tired of this shit." Shaw looked at the two patrol captains. "Tell any of the officers if they want to come in to work, shag calls, do directed patrols, follow-up for CID, whatever, consider it done."

They nodded in agreement and took to their cell phones to relay the message via email. It was clear the Chief wanted this done sooner, rather than later.

"We'll go ahead and move both COPPS (Community Oriented Problem Police Squad) squads to the area, effective immediately. Have them do bike patrols all over those neighborhoods."

The Chief nodded that he liked that move as well.

The meeting continued for another hour as they juggled ideas for long-term solutions. The promise of forming a new squad to specifically target street violence came about, but with a quick look at the budget, it was clear that would only happen through grant funding. Chief Shaw tasked that to one of the captains.

Before adjourning the meeting, the Chief opened the floor to any other suggestions. Major Reginald Pritchard spoke up. "I have something, Chief, that I think is worth discussing."

Shaw hid his irritation as he expected something more self-serving to Pritchard than beneficial to the department. "Go ahead, Major."

"First of all, good work today. I think we are headed in the right direction. But I wanted to discuss more of an image issue, kind of a side-angle approach to our problem."

"Such as?"

"Well, let's be honest...." Pritchard stood up and buttoned his jacket, taking command of the room. "There is a direct correlation with what happened six months ago to what is happening now. Because of what Dylan Akers and Beau Rivers did, we are all suffering. We couldn't get them charged, but I feel like we need to keep digging and we'll find what we're looking for. The public flat out does not trust us because we allowed these dirty cops to remain at TPD."

"What do you propose, Reggie?"

"I propose we fire them. We hang them out to dry and use the press to our advantage. We take out the department's trash so the public can trust us again."

Pritchard's proposal made sense, but it was clear he was masking his own vendetta against Akers and Rivers.

The Chief spoke up, "It's more complicated than just getting rid of them, Reggie. If anyone knows that it's you." A snicker broke out in the corner of the room. "We've tried, but there's nothing that will stick. If you have proof, by all means, fire them, prosecute them, do what you have to do so that we can finally move on."

"But, you can fire them. We can then use a good media campaign against them, so by the time they go through the process to get their jobs back, we'll have solved this problem."

Shaw hated this idea. He saw right through the blatant set-up Pritchard was trying to hatch. Breaking down the impact of the move, he figured if he fired Beau and Dylan at this point, it would be baseless. Therefore, they would eventually be able to get their jobs back. Pritchard was proposing they do this because the time frame to successfully argue and get their jobs back was quite long, at least a year or more, through litigation. On the same side, if the Chief agreed to do this, knowingly fire two officers where no basis was established, they could not only sue for their jobs back, but sue the department for a hefty punitive amount which would culminate in a necessary reaction by City Hall. This would cost the Chief his job. Something Pritchard probably wanted to happen for his benefit.

Ambitious asshole, he thought.

"No, Reggie. I don't like that idea even if it does grant us a cleaner image. If we do it, we do it right."

"Okay, Chief. Whatever you say." Pritchard had a sardonic look as he sat back down in his chair.

The meeting adjourned, but Chief Shaw asked Captain Carter to remain. After the room cleared, she leaned close to the Chief.

"Yes, sir?"

"I need a favor, Inez."

"Name it, sir."

"Have Sergeant Polk bring me copies of the files from the McFadden and Shelley case, please? But keep it between us, okay?"

"Sure, no problem."

Chapter 12

A relentless rain poured down, pummeling the roof of the car and blurring the images outside the window. A dark, shadowy blob moved toward the driver's side in a hurry. The blob transformed into the shape of man who reached for the door handle. He pulled it and hopped into the back next to Antonio Toombs.

"They're ready," Xavier reported.

"Everybody down there?"

"Yep."

Antonio had ordered his crew to branch out and recruit additional personnel and have them come to the Fourth Avenue recreational center for a meeting. He was looking for soldiers, true street operators with connections and above all else, loyalty. He was building an empire.

The gathered recruits were huddled around a picnic table under a covering, trying to stay dry. The rain steadily beat down around them as they waited for their host to make his appearance.

Xavier opened the door, popped up an umbrella, and held it for his brother. They walked down the short hill and joined the dozen men and women underneath the shelter.

Antonio studied the crowd, sizing up the recruits.

A young man stepped forward, and addressed Antonio. "Hey man, why the fuck we here in the mutha-fuckin rain, dawg? My shits gettin' all wet."

The crowd went quiet. The downpour provided the only sound. The insolent recruit was a skinny, dark-skinned kid who wore a flat-billed hat, black T-shirt, and matching shorts that hung down under his butt cheeks. His gold belt matched his flashy shoes. The recipient of Antonio's icy stare, the young man stood his ground.

"What they call you?" Antonio asked.

"Gunner D."

"Okay, Gunner D, I tell you what."

"What's that, G?" The disrespect continued with a wide grin across his face.

"You keep talking to me that way, and I'll put a bullet in your head."

"What'd you say, nigga?" Gunner D challenged and stepped forward aggressively.

With a slight head nod from Antonio, Xavier, and Chris stepped to Gunner D's side and snatched him up by each arm. Before he could blink, Tony Toombs had the barrel of his Beretta mere inches from the boy's face. Gunner's eyes went wide with fright as he realized his mouth had gotten him into trouble. His tone changed and he quickly submitted to Antonio.

"I'm sorry, man. I'm sorry. Please…"

Antonio lowered his gun.

"Kick off them Jordans and stand yo' ass out in the rain."

"C'mon, dawg," the boy begged.

Antonio pointed the Beretta back at the boy's head, emphasizing his command. Nothing else needed to be said. Gunner D slid out of his shoes, placed them on the table, and stepped out in the rain. He was instantly soaked.

Antonio turned his back to the pathetic sight outside the shelter and addressed the crowd.

"The reason you are here is I want to offer you a job. A well-paying job where loyalty is required and insubordination will get you killed." Tony Toombs shot a look to Gunner D. "You may have noticed that I've made a few moves in the hood lately. To get noticed, to get re-established. Take that to mean I'm not playing around. I'm here to stay, and if you stand in my way, I'll bury you."

A few heads in the group nodded.

"If you choose to follow, you will be rewarded with wealth your narrow minds have never conceived. All I ask is absolute loyalty. We'll sell the best drugs, take over the best spots, and use whatever force will make our way the only way."

The nods continued, a few grins were added.

"Tony Toombs? You sure we should be talkin' like this out in the open?"

Antonio smiled at a medium-skinned female with pencil-thin dreadlocks pulled on top of her head like a hair bouquet. She carried herself like a man, dressed like a man, and wore black pants that hung low. Several tattoos were visible on her neck, chest, and arms. She had a calculating look on her face.

"Good question." He looked at her, waiting for an introduction.

"They call me Gigi."

"Good question, Gigi. Look around." Antonio paused, allowing her the rest to look around. "It's pouring outside."

"Okay, it's raining. So?"

"So, we've been here almost an hour, hanging out. How many police you seen?"

The group looked amongst themselves, realizing they hadn't seen the first police car drive by. In the heart of the hood, a rogue's gallery congregated in the open, and not the first police car had bothered to pay attention.

"Po-leece don't work in the rain, my niggas." A smile accompanied the comment. The group laughed.

"So, speak freely my friends. I've set the tone. I've laid it down. What I need to know now is who's in?"

A few "Hell yeah's" were shouted. Others got up and shook Antonio's hand, pledging allegiance. They all agreed to join and take positions within his organization.

"In my first order of business, and hear me clearly, I need you all to lay low this week. Take it easy."

"What do you mean 'easy'?" someone asked.

"No sales, no licks, no beefs, no nothing."

"For a whole week. Man, I gotta get paid, man. I can't do that."

"I got you covered." Another head nod from Antonio over to Xavier. He, Chris, and Dookie all removed small wads of cash from their pockets and tossed one to each person.

"That's five thousand dollars cash, each."

The group whooped and hollered at the gift, knowing they were making the right business decision by joining Antonio.

"Now, take care of your people but no sales, no nothing. I mean it. I don't want to hear about any of you involved in some shit. Just chill out this week. Consider it a paid vacation. Send them basers elsewhere, and we'll be up and running after next week."

"Uh, Tony?" Xavier asked, nodding to the sopping wet kid still standing in the rain. He was a pitiful sight, like a puppy wanting in on a cold night, but afraid to ask.

"Toss me a roll." Antonio said to Xavier. His younger brother tossed him a wad of cash, and he peeled off a few hundred dollar bills. He held it out to Gunner. "If you want in, you're in, but you gotta earn respect, boy. It's not just handed out."

"Yes, sir." He cautiously reached for the money, but Antonio retracted it.

"You come by and see me next week. I got a job for you."

Gunner D smiled. "A'ight. Fa-sho! I'll be there."

"Good." Antonio released the money.

Xavier walked Antonio back up the hill to the car as the rain continued its onslaught. Small rivers of runoff were beginning to flood over the curb.

"That's true what you said about po-leece." Xavier mused, "So, why the break, bro? I mean, I'm with you, just curious as to why, ya know. We been on such a tear, rippin' and rollin', I'm not so sure it's a good time to stop."

Antonio turned to his brother. He waved off the irritation of explaining his motives instead of Xavier figuring it out, but the younger Toombs had gone through most of his life shooting from the hip. Antonio needed to introduce him to strategy.

"You see, we created a problem. It's the police's job to fix that problem. So, while they're out looking for the problem, we take a step back and let them find something else to deal with. That will give them the illusion the problem is solved."

"So then what?"

"We let our competition take the fall for our misdeeds."

"Oh, shit. I see. Damn, that's smart."

"That's phase two, lil bro. Just wait till phase three."

Chapter 13

The tiny heartbeat echoed in the small room. The nurse smiled at Wendy as she moved the wand over her stomach, getting the different angles of the life within. She hit a button to freeze the frame and rolled something on the console to measure various points on the screen. Wendy smiled. Dylan strained his eyes, trying to figure out what he was looking at on the ultrasound machine.

"Everything looks good. Healthy baby...." She paused and looked at Wendy. "Do you know the sex already?" Dylan had been trying to see anything that remotely looked like the baby's genitals for verification but gave up and wanted to hear what she had to say.

"We already know. A boy. Hopefully, it's still the same."

"Yes, healthy baby boy. The heartbeat is strong, length is normal, weight is normal. It's all good. Just about two more months to go."

"Yes, that's right. Thank you."

The nurse excused herself to allow Wendy to redress.

Wendy had put up a front. She was happy in one sense with the promise of new life. But, going through this process again reminded her that she'd lost a child already. In addition, as she looked over to her excited husband, anything to do with this child was the only thing that seemed to bring him joy. She had resolved to tell him the truth about Beau, before the baby was born, because it was the right thing to do. She just dreaded the moment she would tell him the child might not be his. It would destroy him and forever change her world. She could only hope he wanted to remain in her life in some fashion.

"What?" Dylan asked. He noticed she was staring at him, lost in thought.

"Oh, nothing. Just thinking about the future."

"Yeah, me too." He smiled and kissed her on the forehead.

Wendy smiled back, but cringed on the inside. As he sat down, she let the urge to tell him what happened between her and Beau surface. She wanted it over with.

Wendy opened her mouth, but nothing came out.

As she reloaded her attempt, the door opened, and the nurse announced they could leave and see the receptionist. Dylan collected Wendy's belongings and thanked the nurse. Wendy let the urge fade into oblivion.

Chapter 14

What was dubbed, unofficially, Operation Kitchen Sink had been in effect for a week. It earned the moniker because many of the involved officers and investigators realized the command staff were literally throwing everything at the violence problem, hoping something would work. Captain Carter updated the Chief on their progress. As promised, the Vice unit was working street operations non-stop, making dozens of arrests for drug sales, prostitution, and weapons possession. They were able to roll a few arrestees into informants on their respective networks but netted no suspect leads on the specific murder cases. The majority of them kept silent, disavowing any degree of knowledge.

At the end of the week, the numerous arrests were something the department could be proud of, but more importantly, and what did get noticed was the fact that no shootings or home invasion robberies occurred. There were some isolated incidents elsewhere in the city, but nothing tied to the earlier wave. The media ran with the story, and the Chief proudly stood in front of the station, again in full dress uniform, and remarked on the hard work and dedication of the police department.

For a moment in time, morale improved among the rank-and-file. There seemed to be a collective sigh of relief throughout the department and the community, as if the terrible storm had passed and the worst was over. Working together from the top down gave the department a sense of pride that had been long dead.

Chance Parker tagged along on a street operation targeting the Frenchtown neighborhood and the Alabama Street corridor. He hung back while the narcs did their thing, waiting for a chance to talk to anyone who got snagged in the dragnet. He was betting at least one enterprising and self-serving drug addict would have valuable information about who was behind all the recent violence.

After the sixth dealer had been stung in the operation, Chance struck out yet a sixth time, failing to get any useful information. Growing frustrated, he needed something to go his way. All the arrests were great and a step in the right direction, but it didn't help him address the murder cases.

It's just a smoke screen. I've seen it before.

Command staff threw manpower at the immediate problem, hoping to satisfy a pissed-off community. It was a clever way to say, "We're doing something about it," without actually addressing the real problem, the violence and murders. Unfortunately, the community didn't know better and believed something was being done.

Either way, Chance was after a killer and had to ignore the illusions from the smoke and mirrors. After all, his mission was to find the truth. An arrest was the byproduct.

The seventh dealer was targeted, an older man, haggard, scrawny, and dirty. Chance pegged him as the typical middleman. As he listened to the narcs making the deal, he held onto optimism. The older dealers had been through the game multiple times, giving them the edge of experience. But, being close to the fire, the older ones also succumbed to the addiction, and going to jail meant parting ways with the siren's deadly call. Being caught and presented with the opportunity to rat on someone held little consequence compared to ignoring the craving. Chance hoped to exploit this once the arrest was made.

When the deal was made, the dealer was snared. He gave no resistance when the takedown team moved in. It was as if he expected it to occur. After the dealer was patted down, searched, and placed in the back of a patrol car, Chance introduced himself. He recognized the man from dealings on the street almost a decade earlier. Sometimes that smoothed things over. Sometimes it was an unexpected hurdle.

"What's up, man?"

"Shit, Parker. I ain't seen you in a minute. I knew y'all was cops. Sheee-it, I just wanted to score that bad."

"Knew it was us and still sold, huh? Well, that's on you, buddy."

"Yeah, I'm hooked on this shit, man. It's bad."

"Well, looks like you need to help yourself out."

"What y'all wanna know, man. I can't go to jail."

"Well, tell me something I don't know."

"Whatchu mean?"

"I mean, don't give me some bullshit, trap house crap. I work homicide, I could give two shits about dope, but here I am. Now…" Chance leaned in close and, with an aggressive tone, demanded, "Tell me something I don't know."

The dealer was cramped in the backseat. Bowing his head, he debated something internally. He closed his eyes and inhaled deeply, resulting in a cough. Chance wondered how much poison his lungs had endured over the years.

"I ain't got all night, dude. You got something or not?" Chance hoped to hide his desperation.

It worked. "You said homicide, right?"

"That's right."

This time the dealer exhaled, willing the information to just come out. "You ever heard of a guy they call Tony Tombs?"

Chapter 15

Antonio sat on a chair, watching from the porch of Xavier's house. The early morning gave an indication the day would be beautiful, the kind that was meant to be spent outside. He turned and spoke behind him, through a window that led into the living room.

"Hey, Soggy? Get out here."

The screen door opened, and Gunner D, renamed Soggy D for his defiance, stepped out onto the porch.

"Yeah?"

Antonio furrowed his brows with a glare.

"Yes, sir?" The boy corrected himself.

"Come out here, boy. I want to show you something."

"Sup, Tony?"

"Sit down. Here he comes."

Antonio stared down the block, toward Alabama Street. Soggy D sat next to him and waited for what was coming. A police cruiser made the turn and did a slow patrol down the street. The officer crept by and eyed both Antonio and Soggy as he passed. Both sat still. Soggy held his breath until the cop was down the street.

"D'you see that?"

Confused, Soggy looked around and down the street where the patrol car continued. "No."

"It was confidence."

"Okay?"

"He feels in control. If he feels it, they all feel it. Like they have a handle on the pulse of the neighborhood."

Soggy nodded, not sure how he was supposed to respond to Antonio's observations.

"You ready?"
"Yeah, I'm straight."
"You earn respect, remember that."
"I got it, Tony Tombs."

Antonio held out his fist for a bump from the young man, a gesture of encouragement. Soggy bumped him back.

"Remember, loyalty is everything. You cross me, I will kill you, your family, and then burn everything you love."

Soggy held a blank stare. The threat was concerning, but it was the ice cold tone carried in his voice. It had a hint of evil.

"I got you, dawg." Soggy got up, cocked his hat, checked the thirty-eight tucked in his waistline, and walked off the porch.

***

Hours later, Gunner was working the Preston Street house, a recent acquisition made by Antonio and his crew to build up the operation. On lookout from the small, dilapidated porch, he watched as a few basers lingered, keeping an eye out for buyers. The action was light, only a few sales throughout the day. He expected business to pick up later in the evening when the labor force workers were finished for the day.

After a hunger pang struck Gunner's stomach, he walked over to the store to grab a soda and chips. He checked the thirty-eight in his waistband and the container of crack cocaine in his sock, then left for the store. It was a short walk, about two blocks away. He passed by a prostitute who offered him a blowjob for a "twenty rock."

"Come see me later, baby. I'm about to hit the store."
"Okay, don't forget." She licked her lips in an attempt to be sexy.
He liked the attention and power he carried. He wanted more.

At the store, he grabbed food and paid at the counter. He stepped outside and stood there for a moment. He looked around to see who was out and who was walking by. A few old-timers hung out in the corner of the parking lot, drinking beers. Across the street, the mechanic shop had a few customers, and a woman he recognized from the neighborhood sat at the bus stop.

"Hi, Miz Davis. How are you?"
"Oh, hi, George. I'm fine, thanks. How's your momma?"

"She's good."

"Good. Tell her hi for me, won't you?"

"Yes, ma'am."

Gunner left the store, his given name of George echoed in his head. Adopting Gunner as a nickname, he wanted to instill fear, figuring George wouldn't have the same effect. He had rolled out on a few drive-bys, firing off his gun but only at the side of a house of a rival dealer he hoped was home. He waited for the day he could add a body to that list, but for now, he had to manage damage control. His reputation had taken a hit from being forced to stand out in the rain.

Just as Gunner made it back to the house, a dark-colored sedan, foreign make, passed. The windows were tinted, but he saw white knuckles gripping the steering wheel. Good chance it was a cop, he thought. Not too many white boys came to the hood looking for drugs in a car like that. He remained calm and casually walked back up on the decrepit porch.

With the gun in his waistband, crack stuffed in his sock, he looked up and down the street. The sedan moved on as a baser strolled down the street his way. Perfect, he thought.

"Yo, dawg. I got the gator. You up?"

The baser walked into the yard and up to the porch.

"Yeah, but shit. I only got ten. You can hook it up, though?"

"C'mon, man. I ain't giving it away."

"Fine, just cut it half then. C'mon."

Gunner contemplated the deal, and figured it was better to make some money than none at all.

"A'ight, dawg. I'ma hook you up."

The buyer looked around, uneasy about conducting business out in the open. Gunner knelt down as if he was tying his shoe and slipped a small piece of crack from a tiny tube hidden in his sock. He stood with the piece hidden between his forefinger and middle finger. The buyer pulled out a crumpled five and some ones, and, with one smooth motion, Gunner grabbed the money and dropped the crack into the baser's hand. The buyer held it up for a glimpse at the prize, and a small smile broke across his lips.

"A'ight." The buyer was gone with no further ceremony.

"I'll be here all night, dawg," Gunner said, stepping out in the front yard.

The buyer didn't look back, scampering off to go get high.

A moment later, the same dark-colored sedan turned down Preston and headed toward Gunner. He froze, wondering if he'd been made. The cops were known to watch from the woods, but he hadn't seen any. The sedan didn't seem to slow, which meant he would keep rolling through, and they didn't see anything. Or he was just being paranoid. A noise crunched somewhere behind the house, and Gunner flinched, waiting to see what it was. He saw nothing, but suddenly, the sedan sped up. It pulled up to the edge of the yard and two narcs jumped out. "POLICE" was stitched boldly on their vests.

"Stop, police! Get on the ground."

Gunner broke his stance and ran the opposite way. He grabbed the handle of the thirty-eight through his oversized shirt, securing it while he ran. A few strides later, two uniformed cops materialized from the side of the house. They ran straight at him and Gunner was trapped. He stopped and held his hands up in the air. Without being prompted, he slowly went to his knees. One of the uniformed cops shoved him all the way to the ground and wrenched on a set of handcuffs.

"You're under arrest," he said, breathing hard through his nose.

The cops from the sedan came over and searched Gunner. Quickly, they found the thirty-eight stuffed in his waistband and the container of crack in his sock. They went straight for the contraband as if they knew it was there.

They must have been watching.

The narcs moved Gunner to the back of a nearby neighborhood center instead of straight to the jail.

"Let's see, George Sherman," the narc said, reading his name off an ID card. "You have a little bit of a history it seems."

"Huh?"

"You got popped last year for possession with intent to sell and the year before that, sale of controlled substance. Didn't get much time, I see."

"So?"

"So, you just got caught with a gun and some more dope, dipshit. You're a convicted felon. That's serious time. Feds could pick up your case, and that means you'd be doin' day for day. None of that, 'good behavior gain time' crap."

"Whatever, man. That gun ain't mine."

"Okay, whose is it then?"

Gunner sucked his teeth and looked away.

"That's what I thought. It was in your shorts, dumbshit. Doesn't have to be yours to possess it. Plus, it's got your disgusting DNA all over it, and when they show that to the jury, it's bye-bye little Georgie-boy."

"Man, whatever."

"Okay, don't say I didn't give you a chance. Have a nice life." The narc started to shut the door and end the fruitless interview, but before it closed, Gunner spoke up.

"Hold on." The narc hid his smile as he reopened the door. The kid had taken the bait. The excitement of investigative progress grew.

"I'm listening."

"Whatchu want to know?"

"Depends on how bad you want these charges gone? You can give me more dope, like more than this Chapstick container or give me a name of anyone doing these robberies or shootings?"

"A'ight. What if I know a little something about all the murders and shit? What'll that get me?"

Stunned, the narc had to process the information. He had expected the kid to flip on some next level up dealers, not inform on a murderer.

"Um, well. That'd probably clean your slate if you had some real intel."

"Okay, let's do that then. You in charge of the murder case?"

"No, but I can take you to who is?"

"And I don't get no gun charge, right?"

"Good chance, but like I said, it depends."

"A'ight. Deal, let's go. Take me to the guy in charge of the murder case."

Ten minutes later, Sherman stepped out of an unmarked police car, handcuffed in the front and shackled around the ankles. He was escorted from the back parking lot of the police station up to the Criminal Investigation Division. He looked around the parking lot cautiously, looking at each vehicle they passed while walking up to the building.

"There ain't nobody going to see you back here, relax."

***

Detective Chance Parker made a bee-line to the monitor room. The word of a street informant ready to give up information on the home invasions and murders had reached him out in the field. He hurried back to get on the front line of the information.

Parker's sergeant, Melvin Polk, and Detective Mike Durgenhoff were inside the monitor room. Chance acknowledged them with eye contact, but immediately turned to the big screen television mounted on the wall. It showed a live feed into the interview room where the potential informant sat. He wanted to see who was giving them an inside look at the underworld. Snitches, when truthful and transparent, validated what the police already knew but couldn't necessarily prove. That's what kept them relevant.

"Who's in there with him?"

"Sinclair from Vice." Chance nodded. Henry Sinclair had a good reputation for being thorough. Chance trusted him to talk with Sherman.

"They popped him down on Preston Street. After a quick squeeze, he offered up info on the murders."

"He bring it up yet?"

"No, he wanted to wait on you."

"Okay, good."

Chance didn't hesitate. He walked over to the interview room and entered unannounced. Sherman perked up and looked at Chance as he entered. Sinclair nodded as if he was expecting Parker. Sinclair took care of introductions and told Sherman that he was the detective over the murder case. Sherman sat up and scooted to the edge of his seat.

"So, just tell me what you know."

"Well, I was walking down the street when them dudes hit that house. When I heard the shots, I got the fuck out. Know what I mean?"

"You were there? You saw them go into the house?"

Sherman hesitated, but answered. "Yeah. I saw 'em. There was four of 'em."

"What'd they look like?" Chance hid his excitement and steadied his poker face. Sherman's mention of four suspects corroborated what the live victim said before clamming up.

"Dudes had on masks, but you could tell they were black guys. One guy didn't have a mask, though. It was the main guy, I think."

Chance nodded. This statement was consistent too, which meant Sherman was legitimate. "Did you get a look at him?"

Sherman looked away, as if suddenly he was reminded of the dangers of identifying someone for the police. Chance didn't want to scare him away so he glanced at Sinclair for help. He had already established the rapport. Sinclair read the cue.

"Hey, man, just remember what's at stake here, your freedom. It's not like you pulled the trigger. It's them who did this and put you in this position. Do the right thing, George."

"A'ight. Fuck it. I saw him. Scary lookin' nigga. Older, brown skin, low hair, decent build."

Chance formed an image as Sherman gave the description and immediately Antonio Toombs appeared. Seeing him at his brother's trial seemed coincidental at the time, but now Chance thought otherwise.

"You think you can ID him if I showed you a line-up?"

"Will I have to testify to that?"

Sinclair stepped up ready to field that question.

"First things first. Let's look at the line-up. Then we'll worry about testifying."

"Okay, man." Sherman looked over at Chance. "I'll look at one."

The case was building steam, and he reflected on what a positive identification meant. With it, he could start on forensic comparisons and search warrants. Chance was confident that would lead to an arrest.

Twenty minutes later, Chance walked back in with a line-up that included Antonio's picture. He placed the six-pack line-up on the table in front of Sherman and sat down, awaiting the outcome. He studied Sherman's eyes, gauging his reaction as the witness studied each image.

Sherman took a long time. Disappointment came strong for Chance Parker. The longer the witness took, the less likely an identification. He glanced over at the narc. Sinclair looked apologetic.

"Anyone look familiar?" Chance tried to hide the desperation in his voice.

"I mean, naw…, this guy is about the closest." Sherman pointed to an image that was not Antonio. It was an image of a filler who was currently in prison. Chance knew this because he had arrested the guy.

"So you don't recognize anyone?" Parker leaned closer to gauge his reaction.

"Naw."

Chance snatched up the line-up and exited the room. "Charge him."

"Hold on, hold on." Parker paused at the doorway. "Just cause I didn't ID anyone? Fuck it, if he's on there, just let me know, and I'll ID him for you."

"Shut up. You know it doesn't work like that."

Sherman looked up at the camera and then settled back down in his seat.

"So you gonna still charge me. That's fucked up, man."

"You gave me shit. You literally gave me a vague description of one of four suspects."

Sherman bowed his head as if he was debating something. He was holding something back, and Chance saw it.

"Hey, if you got something, now is the time to speak up. Don't hold back or else you're off to prison with that gun charge. It's your life, not mine."

"Fuck it. I seen that guy around before. Goes by 'T' or 'Tony' or something like that. I can find out where he and his crew be at."

Chance wanted to scream. He had just looked at the picture of "Tony Toombs" and failed to point him out.

Parker left and stepped into the monitor room. He wanted to discuss the possibility of letting Sherman go on the off chance that he could provide the location of the murder suspect. Polk and Durgenhoff wore tired, disappointed looks on their faces.

"What do you think? Do we kick him and let him come back with the location?"

"I think, based on what we have, we take the chance. No one else is talking and forensics isn't panning out yet."

Chance countered. "I think if we let him walk, we never see him again. If we charge him, at least we have that over his head. Make him bond out and then get the information."

"But, if you charge him, they'll be suspicious when he comes around asking questions. Especially when he ain't toting all that drug money."

"This sucks."

"Yes it does. But we have nothing to lose. Kick 'em," Polk said in a final decision.

Parker pulled Sinclair out of the room and told him that they were letting Sherman go. Sinclair didn't argue, willing to do what was best for the case. Sinclair and Parker explained the deal to Sherman and expected that he would report back by the end of the week or he would have warrants for his arrest.

Parker watched Sherman as he walked down the front steps of the police department. The feeling that he wouldn't see the informant again ate at him, but knowing he was out of options, he tried his best to ignore the feeling and hoped for the best.

***

Word of Gunner's arrest spread through the hood and reached Antonio. He was at his family home with Xavier.

When the knock came, Xavier got the door and led Gunner D through the living room and into the kitchen. The young man looked nervous.

"Sit down," Antonio said quietly. Xavier excused himself, leaving Antonio and Gunner alone.

Gunner stared blankly across the small table while Antonio thought of what to say. The silence grew and started to reach a dull hiss. The sound was broken up by Antonio reaching in his waistband and retrieving his nine millimeter. He set it down on the table with a heavy thunk and sat back in his chair, eyeing Gunner.

"You 'member what I said 'bout loyalty?"

"Yes, sir."

"I heard they picked you up?"

"Yes, sir, just like you said."

"And?"

"And you were right. I told them I'd snitch on a murder, and they took me right to the station."

"You saw all their undercover cars?"

"Yep, I got them all memorized. The ones I saw anyways."

"Good, well done. Who'd you talk to about the murders?"

"Detective named Parker."

Antonio nodded with recognition. He had asked around about Chance Parker after seeing him at Xavier's trial. He had a reputation of being a persistent pain in the ass and good police, therefore he was avoided.

"Do they suspect me?"

"Yeah, they had your picture in a line-up. I looked at it, but didn't point you out. Promise."

Antonio believed Gunner. He was too scared to lie, and that's the way he preferred it.

"So they brought me up first?"

"Well, kinda. I gave 'em the description like you said, and they came back with the line-up. Like they had you in mind, ya know?"

"Hmm." Antonio let this information marinate as he thought about what to do next. Gunner waited patiently, quietly at the table. Antonio noticed the young man seemed to be waiting for something.

"You did good, Gunner."

Gunner smiled. Earning his nickname back made the risky move of espionage worth it.

"Thanks, Tony Tombs. I told you, I gotchu, man." He balled his fist and patted his chest twice.

"Go write down all the undercover cars you can and make sure all the trap houses get copies. Make them memorize all the cars on your list and tell them not to sell to any of them."

"You got it, boss."

Gunner left the house, eager to follow directions. Antonio was pleased that his reconnaissance mission worked flawlessly. He was able to see the other player's hand before showing his. He couldn't help but let out a satisfying laugh at his genius.

"X, y'all get in here," Antonio called out.

A moment later, Xavier, Dookie, and Chris stood in the kitchen.

"Sup, Tony?"

"I need you to find someone tonight."

"Okay, who?"

"A loose end."

Chapter 16

Gary Levine sat in his recliner, watching Beau connect wires to the back of his television. All of the technology confused him. Input this, output that, he would say, but the game simulator was as genuine as flying a real helicopter. It was the only way Gary, in his condition, could ever get back in the cockpit, virtual or otherwise.

"So what are you going to do when the baby comes?"

Beau had confided in Gary about his situation involving Dylan, Wendy, and her unborn child.

"I don't know. Something tells me the baby is mine, which would be great in one sense and a fucking disaster in another."

"Hmmm." Gary thought on the subject. "I need a beer, want one?"

Beau looked over at Gary with a look that begged him to stop drinking. His skin was yellowing more and more as the cirrhosis worsened, but it was understood that Beau would not stop him from drinking. It allowed Gary to keep some degree of control in his life.

Beau erased the disappointed look on his face and answered, "Sure."

"You going to tell him or is she? I take it he doesn't know?"

"It should be me who tells him. And no, he doesn't know."

"Love makes us do dumb shit, don't it?"

"Yes, it does." Beau nodded his head and then let it hang.

"You'll figure out a way to make it right. It's who you are."

Beau wasn't so sure. The old man always gave him encouragement, but Beau didn't share the same confidence. He hoped it was true, but in his heart, he felt it was going to end badly.

Beau finished arranging the cables, and the television came to life. He set out a joystick and mock control panel to replicate the intricate functions of a helicopter dashboard. Beau found a sense of freedom he had never known at the helm of a chopper simulator, and the joy of seeing Gary get so excited was equally fulfilling.

"Okay, hot shot. When choosing an LZ, what's one of the things you have to take into consideration before landing and takeoff?"

Beau thought for a moment. "Make sure the area is big enough, clear of trees and guidewires, stuff like that."

"Yeah, yeah, that's true, too, but that's stuff you can easily see. It's the little things you can't that'll ground you."

"What do you mean?"

"Rocks and debris. Stuff like that can be disastrous. We caught this Viet Cong kid trying to sneak on base one day. Had a hand full of nuts and bolts in his pockets. We thought he was stealin' at first, but from where he was coming from, that didn't make sense. Then one of us noticed he was headed to the heli-pad."

Beau didn't follow. "He took them from the chopper?"

"No! He was going to throw them on the ground under the bird where we wouldn't notice."

"Okay?" Beau still didn't get it.

"If he had succeeded, and we started up the rotor, when it got good and hot, it woulda sucked all those tiny little things up in the intake and blown the motor. They woulda bounced around like BBs in a blender. They'd probably tear up the entire engine. Boom, now we're out of the fight."

"Huh. Copy that. Check the area for sinister Vietnamese kids." Beau joked.

"Ahhh." Gary scoffed at Beau's humor. "Smartass."

The muggy afternoon was spent with Beau running drills on the simulator. Gary barked instructions and tested him with complications, reliving his Army days. Beau had never seen the old vet get so animated as when he watched Beau fly. It was a glimpse into his past life. He hoped to pull some strings at the airport one day and get Gary one last flight under his belt.

Chapter 17

"You gotta be fucking kidding me?"

"No, sorry. Wish I was."

Chance Parker exhaled and tried to control his breathing. He put the phone back to his ear and told Sergeant Polk that he would be en route to the scene. He had just gotten home and needed a minute to change back into work clothes.

"You sure it's him?"

"Yeah, they made sure of that."

"They made sure of that?"

"You'll see when you get here."

"All right."

Chance ended the call and drove to the crime scene. Not only was there another murder, but Polk relayed it was the surviving witness from the home invasion robbery and murder that had started this mess.

Someone finished the job.

This was a knockout blow. Chance and his squad had noticed the quell in the violence, and hoped it was because of their hard work on the case. But, now this killed any momentum they had going. Chance was maddened that all of his best efforts seemed insignificant and meaningless.

Was it all just an illusion?

As he rolled up to the scene, yellow police tape fluttered in a stiff breeze. The setting sun shone through the treetops, and a crowd of expectant onlookers and news media were staged up the road. Detective Chance Parker sat in his car quietly, needing a moment to collect his thoughts. He bowed his head in defeat. Tonight was going to be another long night in a string of long nights, but this was the life.

Parker walked up to the scene ready to get to work. Mike Durgenhoff was standing next to Sergeant Polk; both stood with folded arms, studying the scene. Nearing the body, Chance took in the scene from the street and saw what Polk had meant by, "They made sure of that."

It looked different in the daylight. Chance hardly recognized that he was standing in front of the same house from two weeks prior. It wasn't a light distinction, but an overall feeling that changed between night and day. It reminded him there were two sides to every face, one good, and one evil.

The victim was face down and leaned slightly on his side with his knees bent. His arms and hands were tucked just behind his back, and his head lay in a pool of blood. He had seen the position before. It was something he would never forget. The man had been executed. Chance couldn't help but imagine what level of terror and agony the guy had faced just before he left this world.

Chance silently cursed to himself then stepped next to his sergeant and colleague.

"Any witnesses?"

"That we know of, no. Are there some out there? I would bet a month's paycheck on it. The problem is no one is saying shit. This crew has these people scared shitless."

Durgenhoff turned around to face across the street. "We've hit all the houses up and down the street and got nothing."

"Someone had to have seen something," Polk complained. "We got the call as shots fired in this area with someone lying on the ground bleeding. So, it had just happened, which means someone killed his ass in broad, friggin' daylight, and you know there are people walking around this neighborhood. That's just ballsy!"

"Jesus." Chance remembered foretelling of things getting worse the last time he was here. "So, they saw what happened. They just aren't going to tell us."

"Pretty much."

"This sucks." Chance walked off to get a better look at the body. He knelt down next to it, getting a closer look. As he keyed in on the victim's face, there it was staring back at him in glaring fashion. It was a message.

Sergeant Polk stepped up behind him, looking over his shoulder. "What the fuck is that?"

"Christ." Chance lowered his head. "A message."

Black string had been sewn tight around the victim's mouth, forcing his mouth closed. The crude piercing had caused the stitch points to bleed, but it was now dried.

"Looks like they did this before they shot him. Probably did it elsewhere, tortured him, and brought him here for emphasis." Chance stood up, disheartened. "Then shot him in the back of the head."

"Why would they do that? Why not just kill him?" Polk asked.

"You know the saying, Sarge."

"What saying?" Polk looked over at Chance and realized the correlation. "Cause snitches, get stitches—"

"Yep. And wind up in ditches."

"Christ."

"This guy didn't even say anything."

"Doesn't matter. He knew, just didn't tell us."

Chapter 18

The press conference was inevitable. The pressure for Chief Shaw to readdress the public was too much to ignore given the continued violence. He nervously waited for the Public Information Officer to call the conference to order, but he was busy trying to lay the foundation, ensuring generous questioning among reporters or they would stop the conference.

Shaw had reason to be upset. His city was falling apart with the heightened violence in just one of its neighborhoods. The perception was that the cops had lost all control of the area, and unfortunately, the reality met the perception. The taxpayers wanted peace and for the police to "Do something." Civil rights activists were targeting the department, specifically claiming racial disparity in policing the black neighborhoods versus the white ones, citing that the Chief allowed the violence to continue in those communities while actively policing others.

Meanwhile, behind the scenes, Shaw received reports that the Vice ops didn't net any arrests in the last two weeks while the violence was still going on. When he questioned Captain Carter about the problem, she relayed that it seemed like the dealers knew they were cops, and they couldn't get any traction. The investigators and undercovers had never seen anything like it before. The dealers were present, out in the open, but when approached for a buy, they blatantly passed as if they knew they were cops before contact was even made.

The updates from the home invasion and murders were just as discouraging. Sergeant Polk and his people were running into dead end after dead end. The home invasion murders had the most physical evidence with several different blood spatter patterns. One pattern had been isolated and was believed to have come from one of the shooters based on positioning, but a DNA profile had yet to be pulled from the sample provided to FDLE. The lag time was bothersome, but it wasn't a bust.

The rest of the cases were either opportunistic events on neutral turf or like the execution-style murder where there was an invisible wall of silence keeping them from any viable leads. The homicide unit had re-canvassed the neighborhoods, using disguises like postal carriers and meter readers, but camouflaging the fact they were cops didn't work for getting answers.

Frustration got to Shaw with the lack of arrests, and he was nearly out of options.

He stepped up to the lectern, ready to face the media and take his lumps with what dignity he had left.

***

Investigator Henry Sinclair was following up on a hunch before calling it a day. The street op was a bust and everyone went off duty, but he wanted to check on something that had bothered him for the last two weeks.

After arresting George Sherman, he had searched his person, wallet, clothes, and even under the soles of his shoes. Drugs were found in the weirdest places, and being thorough and willing to check the odd locations was the only way to keep evidence from slipping through the cracks. During the search of Sherman, he found a sliver of paper. On it was a handwritten phone number. It was the only thing written on the paper and seemingly unimportant. However, it was where he found it that made it odd and bothersome. The slip of paper was inside the liner of Sherman's hat. Sherman had a phone and a wallet containing other random life notes and females' phone numbers, but the number on the slip of paper didn't match anything else found. Research of the number came up empty, until he ran it through the City Utilities database.

The number came back to an address off Escambia Drive, belonging to a forty-one-year-old woman. There was little history for that address and no connection to Sherman that Sinclair could find. He wanted to run by the place and watch it for a while to see if anything happened, to see if there was something to the mysterious number, or to put it to bed as a nothing lead.

Sinclair found a dark spot on the side of the road where he could watch the address with some degree of concealment. It was an apartment in a row of townhomes in the shape of a U. The target address was tucked away in the corner, which forced the narc to park literally across the street. He killed the engine and sat reclined, giving the unmarked car the appearance of being unoccupied.

Inactivity and boredom led him to check his phone for any news updates. Movement from the apartment caught his eye, and he quickly stifled the light from his phone. A dark figure, silhouetted by the interior light, stepped out for a cigarette. He was young, about mid-twenties, slim build from what Sinclair could tell. Keeping his eye on the subject, he reached over and felt on the passenger seat for his binoculars. The enhanced view was just a closer look of the same shadowy figure.

The man finished the cigarette, stamped it out, and went back inside.

I'll give it another ten or so minutes, he thought. Probably nothing here.

***

"Yo, there's a car parked out by the street. I saw a light moving inside, like from a phone or something. Could be police?" Dookie announced as he shut the door to the apartment.

Antonio perked up and immediately looked at Gunner D with accusing eyes.

Immediately defensive, Gunner D said, "Hey, man, I didn't tell them cracka's nothin'. Only what I told you, Tony. I swear."

Antonio thought for a moment and eased up. He believed his young soldier. "Slip out back, take a look. See if it's one of the cars you recognize."

"Got it."

Five minutes later, Gunner stepped back in the apartment, after having crept along the back wall of the building where he spied on the suspicious car across the street. Although it was too dark to be sure, it looked like the same unmarked car he took the ride in to go to the police station.

"Yo, that's the same narc who took me to the station. Sinbad, Sin-something."

That was confirmation enough for Antonio. He stood up and eyed Dookie, Chris, and Gunner D. He removed his nine-millimeter from his waistband and handed to it over to Gunner.

"Take care of the problem, son. We can't have them knowing about this place."

Gunner revered the handgun as some sort of ancient relic with mystical powers. He took it, carefully shoved it in his waistband, and devised a plan of attack on the Vice cop. He told Dookie to go back outside and smoke another cigarette but walk away to draw the cop's attention from the backside of the apartment. They were going to flank the cop by sneaking out the back door and use the back side of the townhomes as a launching point.

"Sinclair," Gunner said.

"Huh?"

"That's the dude's name, Sinclair."

***

The digital readout on the dashboard said it was 9:09 p.m. One more minute, he agreed. He eyed the clock and watched it change to 9:10.

"Oh well. Dead end after all."

Sinclair sat up and put the keys in the ignition. At the same time, light flooded the front porch of the target address again. The smoker returned, but this time he shut the door behind him. The flame of the lighter lit up his face and, through the binoculars, Sinclair recognized the subject, although his name escaped him. Shithead, was all that came to mind. He watched for a moment, tracking the red embers of the cigarette across the darkened parking lot.

He released his hold on the keys and out of curiosity, watched a little longer. Even without a name, Sinclair felt that this guy was, in some fashion, in the game.

Suddenly, a loud crack and flash of light came from behind the townhome. Before Sinclair could react, his windshield cracked as a bullet hole appeared only feet from his head. Another loud bang, followed by another plunk of metal and glass breaking. Someone was approaching from the corner, head on. He swore it looked like George Sherman holding the gun.

His instincts told him to flee but he needed backup. He dove down in the seat and reached for his radio. As he did, his arm went numb, and a piercing hot pain radiated from just below his shoulder. Another loud bang was followed by a series of mutiple gunshots. He felt a hefty punch to his left leg and right knee that were both followed by more searing hot pain. Sinclair realized he had been shot and needed to move, or he would die. He cranked the car, hit the gear shifter to reverse, and punched the accelerator with everything he had left.

More shots came in from the driver's side as someone flanked him from his left. The barrage of bullets didn't stop as feeling quickly drained from Sinclair's limbs. Panicked that he wasn't going to make it out of there, he looked up in the mirror, trying to gauge where he was going. Another shot came in, and he saw the bullet hole appear just below his line of sight. He was afraid to find where it had landed.

There were bright lights behind him, and he aimed the car toward them. With lights, came people. With people, came help. Or so he hoped.

Sinclair backed the bullet-riddled car over the curb, then the sidewalk, and glanced off a utility pole before striking a parked car. He landed at a convenience store that sat at the corner of Escambia and Tennessee Street. He looked through the fractured windshield and didn't see his assailants advancing. It was time to get out of the car. He realized he was pressing the accelerator to the floor, revving the engine and pushing against the parked car that was wedged between his vehicle and the store's side wall. At that point, Sinclair could no longer breathe. He clutched his chest where it hurt, and it felt wet and warm. He wondered how oil had somehow sprayed him through the chaos because the thick substance felt slick like lubricant. He checked his hand and saw red. *Red oil*, he thought.

He pulled the door lever and spilled out of the car, crawling backwards up against the hard concrete wall of the store. His right arm was numb and defiant, so he reached with his left and retrieved the Glock twenty-seven from his ankle holster.

The clerk and a concerned customer peeked around the corner and saw the bloody cop lying on the ground. Another shot rang out in the darkness and plunked the bumper of his unmarked car.

"Get back!" Sinclair yelled. The distinctive metallic taste of blood overwhelmed his mouth. He spit to his side, a thick mixture of saliva and bright red blood. The clerk and customer quickly retreated.

He aimed his gun at the corner where the suspects would be advancing. The crashed cars and store wall gave him cover to the immediate left. He lay there, bleeding, waiting to kill whoever was trying to kill him—if he lasted.

Someone appeared at the edge of the parking lot. It was Sherman; Sinclair was sure of it now that he stood under the light. Sherman aimed a gun at him, but Sinclair sent a volley of bullets in his direction first, praying they landed somewhere vital. Sherman ducked out of the way and sought cover in the shadows. Sinclair waited. His left leg was numb, his right knee hurt like hell, and every time he took a breath, the pain was unbearable. A monstrous headache was taking form as well, adding to his misery. He took a deep breath, summoning courage from within to never give up, but it only caused him to have a coughing fit he couldn't contain.

Another attempt to gain ground was made by Sherman's accomplice, and Sinclair emptied the magazine in his direction. He reached in his waistband for another mag, but set the gun on the ground first. He pulled out the mag, clenched it between his thighs, picked up the gun, and slid it on top of the magazine all with his weak side hand. He cleared the slide lock, sending the gun back into battery and aimed it outward.

His chest was about to explode, and he felt unconsciousness start its stranglehold. His vision was closing in. He didn't want it to end like this; he wasn't done. Surprisingly, he wasn't scared. He was disappointed that he wouldn't be able to finish the fight.

His left arm sagged under the weight of the outstretched gun until it rested on his thigh. His eyelids drooped until they were completely shut. Before the rest of the world faded to black, a siren wailed in the distance, and a smile lined his face.

Chapter 20

Chief Shaw pushed his way through the crowd outside of the emergency room. He had to see his officer, despite his condition.

"Goddammit, move!" Shaw barked uncharacteristically. The officers made way, and he entered the trauma bay where Henry Sinclair had been taken.

Only Sinclair wasn't there. Used bandages stained red with blood, discarded plastic wrappers, and what he guessed was an amassed gallon of blood remained on the floor of the trauma bay. The gurney was gone, and a nurse sat before a computer, typing in data.

Fearing the worst, Shaw asked, "Where is he?"

The nurse hadn't noticed him enter and quickly realized he was asking about the wounded officer.

"He's in the O.R., but he's alive, for now."

He didn't like the caveat she gave, for now. That meant it was still a possibility that he could die. That was unacceptable.

"What happened?"

"Well, he's lucky to be here, really. He was unconscious and with a weak pulse when they got him to us. He was shot in the chest here." The nurse pointed to a spot on an X-ray above the computer station. "And in the arm here." She turned and looked Shaw in the eye and continued. "He had a through-and-through on the left thigh which we think landed in his right knee, but…" She trailed off letting Shaw brace for the pending bad news.

"What is it?"

"He also took a round to the head." Shaw's stomach sank. He felt lightheaded like he might fall. "It pierced the skull, but it doesn't look like it penetrated deep enough. Unfortunately, it caused swelling on the brain, which is a huge concern. They are going to drill on the other side of his skull to relieve the pressure and most likely induce a coma, put him on a breathing tube and wait."

"Wait? Wait for what?"

She held a skeptical look on her face. "For him either to recover or not."

***

Sergeant Melvin Polk was a veteran. He had been around the department for a while and had been a part of the homicide unit for the majority of his career. He had fielded countless calls requesting his assistance on shootings, suicides, homicides, and officer involved shootings. He was in the property unit as an investigator when a fellow cop was shot and killed in the line of duty. Every time his phone rang, he prayed it wasn't followed by news of another cop dying.

The one he received about Sinclair was close enough. The normally stoic sergeant was seething with anger when he got to Escambia Drive. He led the charge to secure the area and knocked on every door possible along that street, trying to find a lead. Unlike the other neighborhood, this area was mostly college students and young grads, not yet poisoned by the culture of silence. They had witnesses who spelled out how the two shooters appeared from behind the townhomes and attacked the parked car for no reason. The car backed down the street in a rush, taking rounds as it fled. Then after what sounded like a crash, more gunshots from the area of the store were heard. A few people had seen the shooters retreat toward the townhomes, but they were unable to pinpoint which unit.

The evidence found suggested the moving gun battle started in the middle of the block, out front of a U-shaped formation of townhomes. Detectives were talking with the residents, trying to determine where the suspects fled. The road was lined with different caliber shell casings, along with shattered glass from Sinclair's car and liquids from the engine compartment.

The store clerk had heard the shots and checked the side of his store. As he broke the corner, he saw the car driving furiously backwards and crashing into a customer's parked car. He called 911 from his cell phone as the cop fell out of his car and onto the sidewalk. The clerk recalled seeing the cop bleeding from the head, arm, chest, and leg areas while still managing to fire multiple shots, keeping the suspects from advancing.

When the first patrol officer got there, he and the clerk scooped up the wounded cop, putting him in the back of the patrol car, then headed to the hospital as the rest of the officers arrived.

***

Three hours later, Henry Sinclair was out of surgery and was medically induced into a coma. He was being monitored around the clock and fed through a tube. His wife was escorted to the hospital and sat by his side, grief-stricken and terrified her husband might not wake up.

Legions of cops showed up at the hospital for support. They lined the waiting rooms, parking lot, and anywhere they could congregate, exchanging hugs and even a few tears. The thought of losing a brother was too hard to fathom. Each one was dejected, knowing it could have just as easily been them in the Vice cop's stead. A somber mood filled the emergency room, and Chief Shaw stood at the epicenter. He had to leave. He needed to go home and hug his wife. As he walked out of the ER to the parking lot, he caught the stares of his officers, their eyes begging for answers. The problem was that he didn't have any. He was as lost as they were and desperate for help.

Chief Shaw had to find the resolve to fix this and wouldn't give up until he did. An idea that had formed weeks prior seemed to be the only option left. Tomorrow would be a new day, and with that, he would unleash hell.

Chapter 21

The executive suite of the Tallahassee Police Department sat atop the crystal palace on the third floor. Tucked in the corner, occupying a five-hundred-square-foot space, was the Chief's office, complete with an ornate cherry wood desk, leather couch, and a private bathroom. It was the penthouse of the station.

Beau Rivers fidgeted uncomfortably in the waiting area. He looked around, trying to figure out why he had been summoned to the Chief's office. The secretary didn't let on, and the only thing he got from Sergeant Mathis was to report to the Chief's office.

"You get hold of him yet?" Beau heard Chief Shaw ask from inside his office. The secretary answered that she had, and that he was on his way.

Who were they talking about? he wondered.

Beau tried to read the secretary for a clue, but she was glued to her monitor.

"Hey?" Beau tried to get her attention. "What's going on? Why was I called up here?"

"No, sorry." She gave him an apologetic frown.

Beau sat back in his seat and let out a frustrated sigh. The door to the suite opened and in stepped Dylan Akers. He walked straight to the secretary's desk, unaware Beau was behind him. "Hey, I'm here. What's going on?"

"Have a seat and I'll tell the Chief that you're both here."

"Both?" The secretary gave Dylan a head nod in Beau's direction. Dylan turned around. Beau met him with an expectant look.

They exchanged confused looks but didn't speak. Dylan sat down and stared ahead, lost in thought. Beau kept quiet, waiting.

The secretary alerted the Chief that both men had arrived.

While she was out of earshot, Dylan asked Beau, "You know what's going on?"

"No, not a clue."

"You think they found proof of anything?"

"I don't know. I don't know what else it could be."

"Yeah, this is weird."

"Hey, I think it's just us up here. Seems weird." Dylan nodded. Something occurred to Beau. "You think he's firing us?"

"Maybe."

"You think it's a trap? Some kind of trick by the Chief and Pritchard?"

"Dunno, but if it is, we've already fallen for it."

With a facetious tone, Beau said, "We can always shoot our way out."

Dylan grinned. It was as if the six-month absence had never occurred.

"The Chief will see you now," the secretary announced.

"See you on the other side, brother," Beau said as he stood up and led the way.

Shaw greeted both men at the door. The look on his face was plain and held no indication of the reason for the meeting.

"Candace, go ahead and call it a day. Head home early and see your kids."

The Chief's personal assistant looked surprised, but quickly accepted the free pass. She closed out her computer, gathered her things, and headed for the elevator. Shaw checked the rest of the executive suite, making sure it was empty.

"Thanks for coming, Beau. Dylan."

Dylan nodded, but Beau did not.

"Please, have a seat." As they settled into their chairs, the Chief continued, "There's no other way to put this, so I'll just come out and say it. As you know, our city has been facing an unprecedented spike in violence, most likely at the hands of a single criminal organization that seems to be getting bigger and more violent. All initial attempts at thwarting the violence have been unsuccessful. Any of the leads, however sparing, have wound up being dead ends. The communities are scared, scared of the violence in their communities, but at the same time, scared to come to us to speak out in opposition of the criminals."

Beau shot a glance at Dylan who looked flushed with guilt.

"What occurred six months ago was…." The chief paused, looking sternly at both men. Shaw continued, "Well, it was remarkable."

In unison, both men furrowed their brows in bewilderment. Remarkable was not what they were expecting. They shared an incredulous reaction.

"Yes, remarkable," he confirmed. "The cunning, the execution, and the planning that went into those killings was no doubt, impressive. I can appreciate the length you went to in the name of your daughter, Lieutenant Akers, and I am also very impressed with the loyalty you showed as well, Officer Rivers. Truly impressed."

Neither Beau nor Dylan responded, careful and knowing anything they said would be an admission. Beau figured this was just the latest attempt to get more evidence on the pair in an otherwise fruitless case.

"So, here I am. Stuck with one helluva dilemma. On one hand, I have a vicious criminal syndicate that has paralyzed my city with unprecedented violence. I've tried everything I can within my power and within my means. Still, it continues. On another hand, in my own department are vigilante cops who have done the exact same thing, but with masterful execution. The difference is the cops had an identifiable purpose, a mission if you will. The syndicate—who knows what their end game is?"

The Chief stopped talking and looked down at his desk, thinking about what to say next. "So, what am I to do?" he asked.

Beau shrugged his shoulders, remaining non-committal.

Shaw continued, "Well, a thought occurred to me, and you can thank Major Pritchard for planting the seed."

Beau scoffed, hating anything that Reginald Pritchard had a hand in.

"Hold on a minute, Officer Rivers. Here me out, please?" Beau gave him a reluctant nod to continue. "So, what am I to do? That is the question. He suggested that I fire you both, start a media campaign telling the public we got rid of the dirty cops, and ask for forgiveness. Hopefully that would be enough to rebuild the trust you two destroyed with those killings."

The Chief made his intentions clear. He had considered this, but the tone in his voice told Beau the Chief had gone in another direction. That gave him concern. He twisted in his seat. The job was the only thing that gave him purpose. Without it, he knew he'd be swallowed by the abyss.

Beau countered, "But you have no proof we did anything, Chief. We were cleared of any charges and have done our punishment following that bullshit IA investigation."

"Beau's right. You have no basis for firing us. We'll be able to get our jobs back and possibly even sue you for wrongful termination."

The Chief nodded in agreement, but redirected. "Yes, but do you think a jury, based on this set of circumstances, wouldn't think you had something to do with the deaths of Earnest McFadden and George Shelley?"

"Sounds like you're going to do it anyway?" Dylan asked.

"Depends."

"On what?"

"What you two think of what I have to say next."

They shot another glance at each other, thoroughly confused.

"Firing you is a viable option and Pritchard makes a compelling argument. But, like I said, I got to thinking more and more about the actual problem. I realized I was trying everything I could within my power. So, it's time I try something outside my means. I need you two. I need that pair of motivated men who are capable of taking out a threat while surrounded on all sides by the very cops they worked with. I need the pair who did all that and walked away unscathed."

"You want us to do what?"

"I can't make it any clearer, Dylan. I want you two to use your unique skills and target this group responsible for the violence. I want them eradicated and wiped from existence by whatever means necessary. I won't sit by and let these animals shoot more cops, not on my watch."

"You want us to kill these people?" Beau asked.

The Chief returned a sardonic look.

"Hey, you want to be clear, that's pretty damn clear," Beau snapped.

"What I want is them to be gone. Killed, arrested, disappeared, whatever."

Dylan leaned forward. "Chief, you have the wrong men. I know what you believe about us, but like Beau said, there's no proof we did any of that. You can't ask us to do this."

Shaw leaned back in his chair, swiveling side to side as he internally debated something. He placed his hands together in a prayer gesture. He looked down at his desk and focused on a file folder. He reached over and touched the spine.

"You sure about that?"

The confidence in Shaw's voice was unsettling. Beau grew nervous. Shaw slid the file folder across his desk in front of the pair. Dylan took it, opened it, and scanned the contents. Beau leaned over, trying to read what was inside.

It was easy to recognize the Earnest McFadden and George Shelley case file.

"Check the FDLE results page dated yesterday," the chief said, matter-of-factly.

Dylan found the page and read it. Reading his face, Beau could tell the implication of the lab results was catastrophic. Dylan lowered his head and closed his eyes. He handed the sheet over and Beau quickly read it. The blood drained from his face after he finished reading it.

"Like I said, gentlemen. I need you two."

"But how?" Beau couldn't fully process the results page.

"How? Really? That's what you can't figure out?" It was as if Shaw was toying with them.

"You were careful, very careful. I give you that. But give me some credit. I wasn't always an administrator. I was a cop first. A damn good cop."

Beau remembered Shaw was in homicide when he was a rookie. He had a reputation for being thorough which served him well in his climb up the department ladder.

"I went through the reports and evidence with a very, very fine-toothed comb. And that's when I found it." He glared at Beau. "That moment when you were pinned up against the transport van and Deputy Register had a shotgun pointed at you? You left a sweat mark on the side of the van from the back of your neck, the only part of you that wasn't covered. Left a healthy chunk of DNA."

"But..." Beau was stunned. Images from when the deputy pointed her shotgun at his chest flashed through his head. He remembered feeling the hard metal of the van on his back as he slid to the ground.

"How'd it go unnoticed until now?"

"Yeah?" Dylan chimed in.

"There were literally a thousand swabs taken from that one scene. It somehow fell through a crack and got overlooked, but what's important is that it's here now."

"Wait, how do we know you didn't make this shit up?" Beau asked. "Just to trick us."

"All three of us know it's legit, Beau. Don't reduce me to the level of someone who has to resort to parlor tricks."

Beau was about to rebut the point, but stopped. The Chief was right.

Silence fell in the Chief's office. Beau felt the weight of it all bear down. Although he had been limited, he was able to remain a cop for the last six months. That was about to come to an end.

"And the DNA match seals Beau's fate. But, I managed to grab some evidence against you as well, Lieutenant." The Chief had Dylan's full attention. "And I'll admit, this was clever. Ingenious, but it left a trail."

"I don't follow."

"The guns you used were from evidence storage. You used seized guns that were scheduled for destruction. And yes I know, those guns are now gone, but they matched the shell casings from those cases to the casings from your scenes."

"But you can't tie the guns to me?"

The Chief smiled, arrogantly. "Yes, I can. Circumstantially, but still tied to you. You used your proximity card to enter the vault before and after the murders. The timing was suspect, but being the section commander of violent crimes, you had access to the gun vault for inventory and inspections. The print out is in the file."

Dylan found it and read it carefully. Beau leaned over and saw that, on the dates of the kidnappings and murders, Dylan had entered the gun vault. It was circumstantial, but in conjunction with the other evidence against them, it painted an obvious picture.

To drive the point further, Shaw added, "Even with it being circumstance, coupled with his DNA and everything else we've got on you two, I'd say we've got you both by the balls."

The silence returned. The air left the room. Beau looked around. The feeling that the tactical team was staged behind the door returned, stronger than ever.

Shaw kept quiet, watching the pair from his chair. After brooding for what seemed like ten minutes in the quiet room, Dylan looked up. Beau had no idea what to say. He had been completely caught off guard.

Dylan seemed to perk up. He looked behind him suspiciously, like he could see through the walls into the rest of the executive suite.

"Who else knows about this?" he asked.

Shaw smiled. "Just me. The lab technician who ran the comparison wasn't given a name, only a sample. I pulled the vault logs myself."

"So, we could just kill you and go about our day?" Beau said coldly.

The Chief laughed. "That's why I need you two!" His smile erased instantly and he slammed his hands on the desk. "You were seen with me already. Don't you think they'd put that together rather quickly? Plus, I've already hidden copies of that case file in places you'll never find. That's twice you've insulted me, Rivers. Don't let there be a third."

Beau retreated.

Dylan said, "You're blackmailing us. Do your dirty work and avoid going to prison, is that the deal?"

"Essentially. I want to fight fire with fire."

"What if we say no?"

"I'd be lying if I said I wouldn't be disappointed. But it would be your choice, and I'd feed you to the wolves. I'll turn over the evidence to the State Attorney's Office and make examples out of you, discredit you, and make you both poster boys for corrupt cops."

"If we did say yes, how do we know you'd keep up your end and not turn us in anyway?"

"You don't. Make no mistake, men. There will be no record of this conversation, and you have no bargaining chips. You decided to take the law into your own hands, and this is your penitence. If you ask me, you have no alternative."

"Can we think about it, at least?"

"You have one hour. But you stay here, in my office. I'll be right outside."

Dylan and Beau exchanged another look. "Fine."

After the Chief left, Beau stood up and paced the room. "Fuck, fuck, fuck. Fuck!"

"I'm sorry, Beau. This is all my fault."

"Not your fault. It's mine."

"We both bear responsibility." Dylan was flustered, obviously caught off guard like Beau. "What do you think about his proposal?"

"I think he's got us by the balls, brother."

"No shit."

"When you think about it, that's a cold bastard out there." Beau pointed toward the door. "Shit, I underestimated him big time."

"What do you mean?"

"Think about it, he's got us on the hook for McFadden and Shelley. The community thinks we did it. Media thinks we did it. Hell, most of the department thinks we did it. So we go after these bad guys like he wants, and if we succeed, he's a hero for stopping the violence. If we fail or get caught, he's the hero for ridding the department of dirty cops. He'll deny any knowledge of our actions. It's like some CIA, black ops shit."

"And he thinks we're the smart ones. That's pretty diabolical."

"Seriously, we could just cap him in his office and make a run for it."

"Don't be ridiculous, Beau. The secretary knows we were here. Plus, he set this up. If I know Robert Shaw, he's got a fail-safe around here somewhere."

"Is there any way we could beat that evidence?"

"No, he's not bluffing. We both gave DNA samples so it seems legit. We'd be spinning our wheels, fighting that evidence."

"Fuck."

"And taking it to trial is such a gamble."

Beau stood, arms crossed and plagued by the situation. Dylan remained in his seat, immersed in thought.

"I think we should do it." Dylan said.

"What?" Beau retorted. "Are you fucking high? There is NO way he doesn't hang us out to dry. We can't trust that he'll keep his end of the bargain."

"Do you trust me?"

There was calmness in the way Dylan asked Beau for his trust. Oddly, that seemed to ease his skepticism. However, he left the question hanging unanswered. He was leery and did not want to be a part of some death squad.

"Do you trust me?" Dylan repeated.

"Last time you asked me that is when we got into this mess in the first place."

Dylan smiled.

"Well?"

"Yes, I trust you. It's the Chief I don't trust."

"I understand; but, like before, we're in this together. If he wants this problem of violence to go away so bad he's willing to make a deal with two devils to get it, I think we hold more leverage than he thinks."

"I doubt that. It seems like he's holding all the aces."

"I have a way to even the playing field."

"Okay, fine. If it keeps me out of prison for any length of time, let's do it." Beau had to trust Dylan. In a way, it had worked before.

Dylan called Shaw back in and told him that they accepted the deal, but he had conditions.

"Like what? I'm not so sure you have the leverage for any negotiations."

"We can't do what you want effectively with just the two of us. If I know the type of guys we're going up against, we'll need more, at least two more."

"I don't think so. Nothing about this will be sanctioned. I don't want to involve any more people than I have to."

"What if we got them to buy in, under your terms that if anything goes wrong, there is no liability on the department?"

Intrigued, the Chief asked who Dylan had in mind.

"Chance Parker."

"Parker, huh?"

"Yeah, he's worked for me before, and he knows the cases. He can keep us focused on the right people, and not waste time. That's good for both of us. So I want him and I'll take one other. You can choose the player."

The Chief smiled. He had just the right person in mind. "If you can convince Parker to help you out, done. Anything else?"

"Yes, you gonna keep Major Prick off our backs?" Beau asked. "Doing something like this is bound to catch his attention."

"That I can do."

Beau was being forced into this situation, but this was not a battle he was ready to fight. They were mercenaries, but without the paycheck. Fighting for their freedom on borrowed time.

As they got up to leave, the Chief gave some parting words. "Thank you. You'll see you made the right decision."
"Fuck you," Beau said, walking out of the executive suite.

Chapter 22

A hurried knock pulled Gary Levine out of his recliner and to the door. He cracked the door and saw Beau pacing back and forth on his front porch.

"Hey. What's up?"

"I'm fucked. Can I come in?"

"Yeah, sure." Gary sensed fear in his tone and knew his young friend was in a tough spot. He cautiously scanned outside and shut the door.

"How bad is it?"

"It's real bad."

Gary Levine was aware of the execution-style murders that Dylan and Beau had committed six months prior. A random call for service at Gary's house had brought Beau to his front door. It was a few weeks after Caitlin's death had made all the headlines. During the visit, Gary spoke his opinion about Caitlin's death and how he'd kill the son of a bitch responsible. Beau borrowed the machine gun with no questions asked. Gary put two and two together after the murders, but told Beau his secret was safe with him. After that, Beau had slowly opened up to the old man, especially since Dylan had become absent.

"Do they have proof of the murders?" Gary's tired old eyes widened with excitement.

Beau nodded. "They managed to get a fucking DNA hit from the transport van and found where Dylan used his security clearance to sneak out the guns we used from property and evidence."

Gary let the information soak in.

"But, that's not how we're fucked. That's just the beginning."

"How's so?"

"That fucking guy." A derisive smile came across his face, giving pause to his rant. "He's blackmailing us into doing his dirty work. He wants us to go after these dirt bags that are leaving a helluva body trail."

"Can he do that?"

"Oh, he's doing it whether it's legal or not. He's got us by the balls."

"Okay, okay. Relax. I'll get you a beer. Have a seat, and we'll figure this out."

Levine returned with a beer and sat down, finishing another while Beau filled in the details. He explained how the Chief gave him and Dylan the option to take out the criminal organization or face murder charges.

"Is he going to flush that evidence if you get rid of these guys?"

"He says yes, but I can't trust that."

"Hell, no you can't. That's taking out two birds with one stone, right there. Here's how I see it. He gets you guys to take out the trash and then sells you down the river. That's what it sounds like."

"Shit, you're right."

"Had a colonel try that same shit in Nam. Had some boys by the balls for getting drunk and rowdy in a bar. They fought with some Navy squids, and one of them wound up dead. He had some real pull over there and managed to get it covered up, so he tells them while they're out on a mission to take out some villagers known to hide VC."

Seeing the similarities, Beau asked, "What'd they do?"

"They agreed to take out the villagers to avoid a court martial, but turns out the villagers were friendlies, and the soldiers were killing innocents. Word got back of the massacre when another company came through, threw all of them in the brig with the colonel calling for their heads. Can you believe that? The same fucking guy who sent them on the mission sold them down the river."

"Dammit."

Beau leaned back on the couch, weighing out which was the worse fate. He sipped his beer and chuckled to himself.

"What?" Gary asked.

"It's funny, when you think about it."

"What's that?"

"When the culmination of bad decisions leads you to a point where you are forced to make another bad one."

Gary nodded in agreement as Beau thought deeply.

Looks like trouble found me after all.

***

Wendy sat at the kitchen table, nervously rubbing her extended belly after hearing about the Chief's ultimatum. "What did you tell him?"

"I told him yes."

"Dylan!"

"What? Maybe it's a chance to make things right after we did so much damage. I know you don't feel the same, but would you rather me go to prison?"

"Ugh, no. But, what are you going to do about these…criminals? Are you going to kill them?"

Dylan didn't answer. He didn't want to answer. Involving Wendy before was too risky, and he didn't want to repeat that mistake, not while she was pregnant.

"We dodged a bullet with them not knowing anything about your involvement. I'm going to do everything I can to keep it that way." Dylan glanced down to her stomach.

She understood his concern and knew he was right. She needed to stay off the radar. She walked over to Dylan, hugged him, and ran her fingers through his hair. He reached around her pregnant waist and held her tight.

Guilt cascaded over her body, knowing that the life he was trying to protect, the life growing inside her, might not even be his. She spent the afternoon, trying to summon enough courage to tell him the truth about what happened between her and Beau, but now with this latest obstacle, she couldn't make a bad situation even worse.

"Seems like it's your only option." She looked down at him with care. "To do what he asks for a chance at freedom."

"Yeah."

"I love you."

"Love you too." He squeezed her and buried his head in her arms.

"You're a smart man, Dylan. And a damn good cop. If anyone can figure a way out of this, it's you. I believe that."

Chapter 23

Shaw managed to make the personnel orders go unnoticed, buried in bureaucratic process. Rivers and Parker were moved under Akers's supervision in the Property and Evidence unit. It was a peculiar move, but with everything going on around the department, it was sure to go unnoticed. He had sent them a fourth person, as requested.

Desmond Holcomb was nearing the end of a questionable career. He had been recently demoted from sergeant down to officer after another excessive force complaint. Unlike the many that preceded, this incident was captured on a cell phone video. It showed Holcomb manhandling a teenager with no resistance and then drawing his weapon and pointing it at the kid. After going viral, he was quickly stripped of his rank and put on administrative leave. He was still at home awaiting the final decision.

Akers asked the Chief to grant them access to an off-site location to act as their headquarters. Shaw denied them official access, but suggested they quietly use the unoccupied offices at the Lincoln Neighborhood Center off Macomb Street. Originally Lincoln High School, a school for "colored" students during the pre-integration era, its central location was ideal for a health clinic and community center to take root. Those services used half of the space inside the old building, leaving plenty of room for his new squad to work unnoticed.

Beau and Dylan were first to arrive at the makeshift office. Rusted filing cabinets were shoved against the wall. Equally antiquated metal desks were stacked against another wall. The stale air smelled of abandonment.

"Good God, this place is a dump," Beau noted as he looked around. "It's perfect."

"I don't think anyone has cared about this place in a while. Hopefully, they won't notice now."

"Hey, Dylan?"

"Yeah?"

"We really doing this?"

"I don't see that we have a choice. Do you?"

"I don't know."

"Well, I do know that I want to see my son born, and if this is what it takes, so be it."

Beau swallowed his guilt, knowing that the son he spoke of could be his. Hearing Dylan talk about his unborn son made Beau think of the son he did have. The physical distance between them was far enough, but the emotional distance was profound. If going along with Dylan allowed him to see Scotty again, then he was on board.

The door squeaked open and echoed off the walls. Dylan and Beau turned to see Chance Parker walk in. Wearing jeans and a T-shirt, he dropped a duffle bag and some file folders onto a desk. The disapproving look on his face told them he was not happy to be there.

"Thanks for coming, Chance," Dylan said.

"I was told to be here. Not sure why. Did you ask for me?"

"Yes, I did."

"Why?"

"Because we could use your help."

"Help doing what? Whatever. Doesn't matter. I don't trust either one of you, so the sooner we can get this over with, the better."

"Agreed," Beau added.

"Don't kiss my ass, Rivers. I don't know why I'm here, but I'm pretty sure I don't have to like you."

"How about you stop being a dick, Chauncey?" Beau put a demeaning tone to Parker's given name, intending it to be an insult.

"Fuck you."

"Guys, really?" Dylan intervened. "We've been here less than five minutes. Can we take it easy, please?"

"Fine." Chance reigned in his attitude. "How about you tell me why I'm here?"

The door squealed again, announcing a new arrival. A tall, dark-skinned man with well-cropped hair, dressed in a designer polo and matching pants, stepped in. Desmond Holcomb normally looked the part of a high-roller rather than a local cop.

"I see I missed the start of the party. What's up, fellas?"

"Hey, Dez," Dylan greeted.

"Great, the who's who of fuck-ups," Parker said.

"You callin' me a fuck up?" Desmond squared up to the homicide detective.

"I didn't fuckin' stutter." He stepped up to Holcomb, getting in his face. "All three of you shouldn't be here. You're a goddamn embarrassment to the badge. I feel dirty just for being in the same roo—"

Beau Rivers had had enough. He grabbed Parker from behind and yanked him backwards, slamming him hard against a metal desk. Chance flailed, trying to break away, but Beau had him pinned.

"I've heard enough of your mouth."

Dylan stepped over and pulled Beau off. "Stop it, both of you. Especially you, Beau."

"Yeah, Rivers. Chill out," Parker said, rubbing his neck.

"As for you, get off your high horse. You're no goddamn saint, so stop giving us this shitty attitude and just listen to me for a minute. If you don't like what you hear, leave."

"Fine. Get on with it."

Dylan shot a look over at Holcomb who nodded back, and then lastly, he gave a glare back to Beau.

"I'm good," he answered.

Dylan lied to Parker and Holcomb, telling him that they were a part of a new test squad. He explained that the objective was to eradicate the central players in the criminal syndicate responsible for the upturn of violence.

Parker scoffed, not believing any of that.

"It's true. And this part doesn't leave this room. The Chief has given us carte blanche in how we take down this group."

"What do you mean carte blanche?" Holcomb asked skeptically.

"It means we can tip-toe over the line if necessary."

Holcomb nodded, but still in disbelief over the legitimacy of their mission. "So, we can just go bust some heads, shit like that? Old school style and he's okay with that? I mean, I'm not really on good terms in that regard, if you know what I mean."

"Have you seen the news? It's gotten bad out there. Shaw wants them to disappear. He doesn't care how, just so long as it gets done," Beau added.

"So, why you two?" Parker asked with cynicism. "He could have pulled from the entire department and, for some reason, he picks the two guys who are thought to have committed murder?"

"You don't pull any punches do you?"

Parker sat up in his chair. "No, Lieutenant. Not when I had to sit in court and have a jury question all of my sincere, honest hard work because you two assholes took the law into your own hands. To them, we're all the same. They don't see the difference. I see the look in the eyes of the victim's family when justice fails them, and all they do is blame me for what you guys did. I get why you did it, everybody gets it, but you crossed the line. There are some things a cop just can't do, and for that we all suffer. Just because we wear the same goddamn badge."

Dylan had no rebuttal. He lowered his gaze with a look of second-guessing on his face.

"That aside, Parker, we have a chance to make a difference without all the red tape, to go after these outlaws with damn near impunity. Isn't it at least worth a try?" Beau countered, coming to Dylan's aide.

Parker looked at Beau, still unsure.

"Come on, it's a chance for the good guys to even the score. Who cares if we have to cheat a little? Hell, the bad guys never play by the rules. It's time we evened the playing field. I know that has to sound appealing on some level."

"I don't know, Beau."

"Holcomb, what about you? You in?"

"You mean, I get to crack some skulls without getting in trouble, count me in."

"Parker, you willing to give it a try?"

"I don't think so, Beau. Seriously, you have the wrong guy."

"What can I say to change your mind?"

"Nothing. Sorry." Parker grabbed his belongings and walked out the door.

Dylan had a dejected look on his face. Beau stood up, grabbing the attention of Dylan and Holcomb.

"We can still do it with three."

"Good. I did not want to go back to answering phones in dispatch," Desmond stated.

"Okay, fine. You two go find us some cars to use." Dylan was out of the door and stepped back to add, "Get rentals, so nothing comes back to us or the department."

"All right, what are you going to do?"

"Go get our fourth man back. We need him."

Beau gave Dylan a suspicious look as he left the room. Dylan returned with a look Beau had seen before. It was the look he gave after they finalized the plan to kill George Shelley.

Chapter 24

The far corner of the car dealership parking lot offered a dark shroud of secrecy. It was fitting for the mission they were about to start. Three blocks away from the attempted murder of Detective Sinclair, Beau and Desmond waited for Dylan. Using an obscure radio channel to avoid any unwanted ears, Beau called for Dylan.

"Pulling up now."

An unfamiliar car pulled off the highway and found its way to the back corner of the lot.

Chance Parker stepped out of the passenger side. Surprised at his presence, Beau gave a questioning look to Dylan who shook him off. Parker's attitude had visibly changed, and for some reason, he was now joining them.

"Decided to join our little band of fuck-ups?" Beau asked.

"Yeah, something like that."

Business-like, Dylan said, "Hey guys, let's get started. Chance is going to brief us on Sinclair's ambush."

Chance briefed the team on the details of the shooting and what the investigation yielded at this point. He spread a map over the trunk of the rental and pointed to relevant points from the incident.

"Here's where he was parked based on glass fragments found on the ground, and here is where we believe the shooters came from, advancing on his position."

"So they used the townhome as cover or do you think they were in one of the units?" Dylan inquired.

"We couldn't tell. None of the witnesses could say for sure, but—"

"But, what?

"Could be nothing, but I found a fresh cigarette over here in the parking lot." Chance pointed to a spot on the map. "And when I did the canvass, I found the same cigarettes in an ashtray by the G unit, over in the corner."

"Okay, could be a witness that bugged out."

"Right, could be, but if you…" Chance reached in the rental and pulled photos out of a file folder and placed them on top of the map. "If you trace these sets of shell casings back from Sinclair's car, they lead directly to the spot where I found the cigarette."

Dylan weighed the evidence. "So he drew Sinclair's attention away while the other guy came at him head on?"

"Right."

"Who lives at the apartment?"

"That's the thing. It's a woman by the name of Flores. She's got no ties to any criminal types that I could find. None that are currently out of prison, anyway."

"Anita Flores?" Beau piped up. The name suddenly stood out.

Impressed, Chance answered, "Yes. How'd you know that?"

"I've been to her apartment before, long time ago. Her name came up in some phone records when I was working the Figueroa case."

"Okay, so?"

"Used to be Anita Baker, and she had a son by one of Figs's lieutenants, the kid should be in his early twenties by now."

Chance was astonished by Beau Rivers's recall. Coming up with empty searches was frustrating, especially with all the technologically advanced databases that are available. That technology, however, can never measure up to first-hand intelligence.

"Got a name?"

"Duquan Baker, but he goes by the street name 'Dookie'."

"Sounds like a start to me."

"Where can we find him?" Dylan asked.

"If he's a Northside boy, he'll be at the hill store at some point tonight. We can just wait there for him," Holcomb contributed.

The hill store lazily earned the moniker because it was simply a convenience store on top of the hill in a centralized location on Alabama Street and within walking distance of several neighborhoods. It was an attractive hangout for dealers, addicts, and hustlers.

Set up inconspicuously, Beau and Holcomb paired up while Dylan teamed with Parker. They watched the store while the activity increased as the sun went down. A few hours went by without a sign of Baker. They witnessed a few drug deals in the parking lot but ignored them, waiting for their target.

A tan-colored sedan caught Beau's attention. It quickly parked in front of the store, drawing looks from a few suspicious characters loitering around. The passenger door opened and out popped Duquan "Dookie" Baker. With a suspicious glare, he scanned the area.

"There's our boy," Holcomb said. Beau nodded.

Baker spoke to a few of the corner boys posted up in the parking lot and went inside the store. A small kid's backpack was slung over his shoulder, which immediately stuck out as odd.

"There he is. Now what?" Holcomb asked.

"Betcha there's dope in that backpack. Probably a decent amount, too. See how he gripped the strap tighter around those corner boys."

"So none of them get a wild hair and snatch it from him."

"Right."

Beau relayed over the radio that their target had arrived. "What do you want to do, Dylan?"

"I guess we get our hands dirty."

Beau looked over at Holcomb. "What the hell does that mean?"

"Dunno, but let's go find out."

Holcomb pulled around to the side of the store and both men eased out. Dressed in ballistic vests with the word "Police" stitched on the front, they had badges clipped on their belts. Dylan and Parker parked on the opposite side, but remained in the car.

As Dookie exited the store, he noticed the cops standing outside and slipped off the backpack, tossing it behind a trashcan. Beau saw him pat his waistband and assessed that was where Baker kept his gun. He made a mental note to watch his hands even closer.

Standing near the tan sedan, Baker called out, "Hey, what the fuck y'all want? Y'all po-leece?"

"This your car?" Beau asked.

"Nah."

"So you didn't just get out of this car and go into the store?"

"Nope, not me."

"No? Are you sure. Pretty sure we just saw you get out of this car."

Baker folded his arms and held a look of indifference. His silence was his answer.

Beau ignored the contempt and walked over to the trashcan, passing Baker. "Hmmm, what's this?"

Still no answer. Baker shifted his weight nervously.

"What could possibly be in here?"

Baker's contempt changed into worry.

"Still nothing to say?"

"Ain't mine so nothing to say."

Beau held out the backpack, weighing its contents. He looked around the parking lot. The crowd's eyes were watching, Dylan and Parker were out of their car and stood close to it. Without further consideration, Beau unzipped the small backpack, revealing a tightly wrapped brick of cocaine and several strapped bundles of cash. He let out a low whistle, impressed at the amount of contraband.

"Hey, man," Baker finally spoke. "You can't do that!"

Beau returned the indifference and ignored Baker. He zipped up the bag and looked back at Dylan. He nodded with an affirmation that there were drugs in the backpack.

Baker took a step toward Beau. Holcomb intercepted and stood next to Dookie.

"Whatchu lookin' at, nigga?" Dookie asked.

"Nothin'," Desmond answered with a contemptuous stare.

"Whatever, man. Y'all can't just take that shit man."

"Says who? You?" Beau asked.

"That shit ain't legal, man."

Beau ignored Baker.

Getting irritated, Baker spoke with a stern attitude. "Hey man, I'm talking to you."

"I'm done asking questions. I already did and you had your chance. Now I'm taking your shit, whether you want to admit it's yours or not. It's mine now."

"Fuckin' crooked motha-fucka."

Beau gave him a devilish grin that further served to aggravate the drug dealer.

Several of the corner boys scattered and immediately made phone calls. They anticipated something happening and had to be ready.

Beau stepped over to Parker and tossed him the backpack. Baker followed its whereabouts as if he were going to retake it.

"That's going to hurt, huh? Telling your bossman that half a key went missing with what looked like ten Gs. Hope you like walking with a limp, cuz I imagine he'll put a bullet in your ass."

Beau noticed a few of the corner boys had returned and doubled in numbers.

A loud, thumping stereo grew louder until a flashy car with shiny rims and tinted windows rolled up to the hill store. Two guys stepped out of the car, and Baker gave them a head nod. A message was hidden in the gesture, and they walked toward the cops.

"Who's this, backup?" Beau asked.

The two new players didn't say anything. The cacophonous stereo continued, drowning out the rest of the parking lot.

Dylan turned and Holcomb stepped away from Baker and next to Beau.

Dylan leaned over and whispered in Chance's ear who then turned and secured the backpack in their rental car.

"What are you boys here to do? You here to scare us?" Beau antagonized.

"Heard you dirty cops were harassin' my boy." The first player said, dressed in an over-sized black t-shirt and red and black pants with matching sneakers. He gave an intimidating grin, flashing his gold teeth, toward Beau.

"Who Dookie? Dookie's a grown man, aren't you Dookie? I mean, your name is synonymous with shit, so I'd say you have bigger life problems, but still grown."

"Fuck you, man." Baker shot back.

Beau held the two men's attention and walked over to their car. Steadily thumping and vibrating from the bass drops, he reached in and ripped out the stereo plate and held it up above his head.

The music went silent and was replaced by the protests of the crowd. "You can't do that, pussy-ass cracka."

"I just did. Question is, what are you going to do about it?"

The driver of the shiny car stepped up to Beau, clenching his fists and breathing heavily. Beau saw the motivation to fight in his eyes. Before he could react, Beau let loose a lightning quick punch to the driver's left eye, followed by a stinging left hook that crashed into his right cheek. Holcomb pounced on the passenger as soon as he stepped near Beau and threw him to the ground. He dropped his knee, carrying all of his weight on the passenger's neck, pinning him to the ground. Dylan stepped over, ready to address any of the corner boys if they wanted to join.

The scuffle lasted all of ten seconds while Beau wrangled his guy to the ground and Holcomb held his guy in submission.

"You had enough?" Beau asked under heavy breath.

"Yeah," the man answered, strained with defeat.

Dylan told Beau and Holcomb to release the two men. Parker was ready in the car. Baker stood watch, following the loot they had stolen.

The officers retreated slowly and left the area before they lost control of the situation. Rolling past the storefront, a car in the opposite lane slowed down, and Beau caught a glimpse of the front passenger. A ghost from his past, at least ten years, glared back. He would always remember the cold, icy stare of Tony Toombs.

***

They waited on Chance and Dylan to get back to Lincoln Center, but in the interim, Beau was bouncing off the walls with excitement. His head was throbbing from the adrenaline coursing through his veins, even rhapsodic from the altercation.

"Holy shit, that was fun." Beau smiled.

"And no arrests means no paperwork."

"Nope."

"When you hit that boy, he wasn't ready for that shit."

"Yeah, he didn't think that was going to happen, did he?"

Holcomb laughed and they relived the incident until Dylan and Parker arrived. They were less enthused than their cohorts, but nonetheless they looked pleased.

"We sent a clear message, that's for sure." Dylan summed up the interaction. "Do we know who's in charge of this gang?"

Parker answered, "We have an idea, but nothing solid. He's an old buddy of Beau's, from the Figueroa case, Antonio Toombs."

"Well, shit. I saw ole' Tony Tombs as we drove away. You think he's taking over?"

"I think as soon as he got out of prison, he began taking over by killing anyone in his way."

"He was the one I thought would be the hardest to catch. He was always so cold and calculating. Only reason he got convicted was because his own boss sold him out to save his ass. Not sure if he knows that or not. But now that I think about it, if he was rolling by after we roused those guys, it was probably his dope we took."

Parker replied, "Good. If he is in charge, hopefully it makes him mad enough to make a mistake."

***

Tony Toombs sat in the darkened room, brooding in silence. After ambushing the narc, they relocated their central hub to a house in a quiet neighborhood in northwest Tallahassee. It was unassuming, and he only allowed his top men to know its location. He had to preserve the sanctity of the kingdom, but that was secondary to what just happened.

Dookie relayed in detail what transpired at the hill. He believed the men were cops. They wore badges on their belts but acted different than police.

"What all was in the backpack?" Antonio asked.

"The Preston Street delivery along with ten Gs."

"Anything else?"

"Nah, I don't think so. Just that. I'm sure."

Antonio absorbed the information.

"They did all that but didn't take nobody to jail?"

"Nah, Tony. Not even the nigga that stepped up to the main guy. Shit don't make sense."

Antonio had locked eyes with that one guy Dookie spoke of. It was a face he would never forget, the lead investigator who had managed to penetrate the Figueroa fortress and send him to prison for the last ten years. He was willing to let it go, but if he was going to interfere a second time, he would make him pay and put a bullet in his head.

"It's the same guy from those murders last year, the ones on the news."

Antonio looked puzzled. "Huh?"

Dookie explained that Beau Rivers and Dylan Akers were believed to have executed the two men responsible for the murder of Akers's daughter. Antonio was still in prison at the time and somehow missed the news story.

"Really?"

"Yep. Dirty-ass cops, those two."

Antonio dismissed Dookie and told him to regroup later.

I need time to think.

Chapter 25

The lack of attention from the night before was surprising. No news reports or probing phone calls from the brass ever surfaced. With the current climate, the team figured someone would have complained, and the operation would be shut down immediately, but with no complaints came a new day.

Furthering the mission, Parker suggested targeting the dope houses up and down Preston Street near the double murder. Putting their own brand of pressure might prove to be more successful than the traditional ways that netted next to nothing.

The narrow residential roads of the small neighborhood offered an ideal terrain for the drug dealers. It made covert surveillance difficult and stealth hard to achieve with everything in earshot.

Changing up the rental car, Beau and Chance picked out a white pickup truck. Lawn equipment in the bed and dirt on the sidewalls completed the look of lawn maintenance workers. Spying on the Preston Street dealers, they had to wave off several streetwalkers who advertised oral sex at a discounted rate.

Turning down the offer, Beau asked one prostitute with confidence, "Hey, we're looking for twenty hard, honey. Can you hook that up?"

"Sure, baby. Blue house around the corner. Ask for Gigi. She got the gator, today. I could hook it up if ya'll want to party."

"Just lookin' to get high and finish out the day. Maybe later. We'll come back."

"Both of you?"

"If you can handle it."

"No, sugar. If you two can handle this." The woman strutted away, letting the possibility of a trick hang in the air. She flaunted her sex appeal, but the dirty clothes, overdone makeup, and the tone of desperation in her voice, showed just how much she was damaged. From top to bottom, she was broken and forced to sell her body to feed her addiction.

"Gross." Parker cringed. "What's the gator? That's new to me."

"It means the good stuff. Strong and not stepped on like weak crack. Alligators are known for their ferocious bite. So is the crack, so they call it the gator."

"Ahh. I guess that makes sense."

"So, Gigi's the player over there. That ring a bell in any of your cases?"

"No, not really. Haven't heard about any females being involved."

As the afternoon turned into evening and the night began to fall, Beau and Chance managed to get closer to the target on Preston Street. Gigi was quickly identified as the light-skinned female with pineapple dreadlocks. They watched as she barked orders at the basers who hung around like dogs waiting for scraps.

"She could pass for a man," Chance said after deliberation. "I mean, she dresses like a dude and hides her breasts in those oversized T-shirts. I could see it."

"Yeah, I agree."

Beau had managed to lure one of the addicts from the safety net of the drug house over to their truck. He finagled a deal for twenty dollars' worth of crack cocaine from the man, hoping to get additional information.

"Don't get me no white-boy crack, either!"

Chance mouthed "white-boy crack?" clearly new to this term as well.

"They'll purposely give the garbage crack to the white boys passing through, knowing they won't make much of a fuss at the quality. It's not like they'll report the dealers to the Better Business Bureau. They're the minority down here, and frankly, the dealers don't care."

"No, I guess they wouldn't."

The go-between returned with a small piece of crack, clearly already claiming his fee from the score. He handed Beau the dope and scurried off, ready to smoke what he'd managed to scrounge. Beau looked closely, examining it. He dropped it in a baggie and went back to watching the house, waiting for Gigi to make a mistake.

As night took hold, the wait was over.

Chance sat up in the truck. "Look!"

Beau focused his attention on the house. An able-bodied young man carried out a medium-sized duffle bag and got in a car with Gigi. The bag was elongated and carried something substantial based on the care and caution he used holding it.

"What do you think's in the bag?" Parker asked.

"Dunno." Beau sat up in the passenger seat. He smiled as Chance glanced over at him. "Only one way to find out."

Gigi, with her associate driving, pulled out of the driveway and left in a black sedan.

"We need to stop that car," Chance stated.

"Okay, but we're in a rental. No lights, remember? Same for Dylan and Dez."

"Shit, we need it stopped."

"We call patrol. Strike that, you call patrol. They'll think nothing of a homicide guy calling in a traffic stop. Just keep it casual so the Calvary doesn't show up."

"You're right. Let's follow them out of the area first."

"Good idea. I'll tell Dylan."

Beau relayed the plan to stop the sedan to Dylan over the radio. Chance stayed five car-lengths back from Gigi as they went north on Old Bainbridge Road toward Tharpe Street. The car turned east on Tharpe but failed to come to a complete stop with the sharp eye of Chance Parker watching.

"Got 'em. Didn't come to a complete stop." Chance fiddled with his radio, getting it back on the primary channel and requesting a marked patrol car to affect a traffic stop.

Five minutes later, while traveling north on Monroe Street, the black sedan was pulled over on a small side street. The uniformed officer who responded made initial contact and explained that they were observed committing a moving violation near Tharpe and Old Bainbridge. The officer looked back and saw Chance sitting in a white pick-up truck in a nearby parking lot.

After switching clothes from doing surveillance, Chance got out and approached the officer. Beau watched from the passenger seat as the uniform handed Chance a driver's license.

He could hear Chance ask the patrol officer about any obvious signs of contraband. The officer shook his head and Chance looked down at the license.

"Christopher Toombs, huh?"

"Yep, that's your driver."

Chance slowly twisted around and shot a glance through the windshield at Beau. A sparkle of excitement flashed in his eyes.

"You get the passenger's info?" Chance asked of the officer.

"No, says her name is Gaile Gaines, though." The name didn't stand out, but the initials supported the nickname of G-G, or Gigi.

"Thanks, I'll take it from here."

"Okay. You want me to stick around?"

"No, we're good."

The officer paused at Chance's use of "we." He glanced back at the white pick-up and saw Beau in the passenger seat. Beau kept his face hidden, and the officer didn't probe further.

The marked unit pulled away, and Beau exited the vehicle to join Chance at the driver's side door of the sedan.

"Go ahead and step out, please?" Beau ordered.

"What for?"

"Because I told you to."

"Whatever."

Chris Toombs stepped out of the car and spun around, putting his hands outstretched on the car, knowing the drill of a pat down. Beau reached around his waist and inner thighs for concealed weapons. He ran his hands down his pant leg and checked around his ankle. Nothing was there.

"You done feeling me up?"

"Don't flatter yourself. Where y'all coming from?"

"Nowhere. Ain't gotta tell you that."

Beau smiled and leaned down to address the female passenger. "Where y'all coming from?"

"Like he said, nowhere."

"Popular place, this nowhere." Beau looked over at Chance for direction. He shrugged. The normal course would have been to tip-toe around the fact they had done surveillance and casually inquire about what was in the bag. But the normal course took too long, and with the Chief's new edict, it was worth a shot to try something different.

"What about that gun case in the back? A-K or something else?" Chris's eyes bulged, giving Beau confidence in his guess. "Ahh, I see. It is a gun, not dope. Hmmm. Pretty sure you're not allowed to have an A-K."

"I don't know what you're talking about. Ain't no guns in there."

Chance remained at the back of the sedan, working the radio, running the plates and the occupants. He learned it was a rental car and relayed that to Beau. Again, he smiled at the young kid.

"Rental car, huh? I know you ain't over twenty-five, so I know you didn't rent the car." Chris averted his eyes. Beau leaned down again, "You rent this?"

"No," Gigi said.

"No? Well, hell. Who did? It's not stolen is it?"

Beau looked back and forth between the pair, neither one answered.

"Fine. Play it that way." Beau looked over at Chance and pointed to the passenger side. He understood the cue and asked Gigi to step out of the car.

"What's in the case?" Chance asked.

She shook her head.

Chance reached in the glove box and found the rental agreement. After looking it over, he turned to Beau and shook his head.

"Neither one's on here."

"Last chance, or whatever's in here may catch you a charge," Beau said.

She remained still, lips sealed.

"Fine."

Beau walked Chris to the back of the sedan and stood him next to Gigi. They avoided looking at each other. Their actions seemed rehearsed to Beau, like they were adhering to a code where anything other than silence was not tolerated. This was training instilled at a young age. Police interaction was not a matter of "if" to players like these, it was a matter of "when."

"What now?" Beau whispered to Chance.

"Watch them." Chance walked off, pulling out his phone and made a call. Beau stood guard.

Chris Toombs looked angry. He rocked slightly in his stance and stared directly at Beau. He returned the stare, identifying that the young man was working himself into a confrontation.

"Why are you eyeing me like that?" Beau asked.

"Cuz, you ain't shit."

Surprised by his boldness, Beau was taken aback. "Oh?"

"Yeah, you ain't shit, pussy-ass cracka."

"Man, that's twice I've been called that this week. I'm starting to get a little self-conscious."

"Whatever, you ain't shit without that little badge."

"This one?" Beau lifted his shirt exposing his entire badge.

"Yeah. Without it you just another bitch."

"A bitch? Really?" Beau played into the arrogant piffle.

"Take off that badge and see what happens, or are you a bitch?"

Cupping his genitals, Beau said "Nope, still a man."

He dropped the condescending tone and stepped up into Chris Toombs's face nearly nose to nose. He let the fire in his eyes burn outwardly into the outlaw's face, daring him to act.

I will unleash hell on you!

Chris's arrogance ignored the threat, "I knew it. You're too scared. Like I said, without that badge, you ain't shit!"

The tension filled the air until Beau took a step back.

"That's what I thought, pussy-ass cracka."

Beau slowly reached under his T-shirt and unclipped his badge. He reached past Chris and put it on the trunk. He stepped back, awaiting a response.

Beau held his arms out to the side invitingly, baiting the hoodlum.

Chris took a step from the car and widened his step. He balled up his fists and took a boxer's stance. It looked loose and amateurish, but his eyes held determination that Beau respected. With quickness, Chris threw a jab at Beau's face that he dodged. Chris reset and Beau moved to his right. Another jab missed. They circled around each other, remaining inside an imaginary ring.

"Get 'em, Chris!" Gigi shouted.

Chris leaned back and delivered a haymaker with his right. Beau blocked it with his forearm and buried his fist into the left jawline of his opponent. Stunned, Chris backed away and regrouped. Refocused, he ran at Beau, lowering his shoulder and picking him up with a full body tackle. Beau dropped a few elbows on his upper back before landing hard on the ground.

The kid moved with emotion while Beau remained calm, letting the heavy blows land on the back of the arms and shoulders as Beau shielded his head. These were favorable places where it would cause little damage. Beau could tell Chris was tiring out fast. He reached up and grabbed hold of his chest, letting the kid think he was winning. Chris pushed off, and before Beau could react, he caught a punch across the left cheek that sent stars popping in his peripheral vision like a camera flash. Beau threw his hands up to block the follow-up and intercepted his arm. Chris's weight on the follow-up blow moved to Beau's right. He used the momentum to shift into an arm bar and shoved the kid to the ground. Maintaining control of his arm, he continued morphing the hold into a pin. Moving with lightning speed, Beau was suddenly on top of his adversary who was now face down on the ground. Beau pulled back on his right arm, holding it perpendicular behind his body with his shoulder pinned to the ground. Beau then straddled Chris's arm and sat his left knee on the side of his head. Chris's body was trapped underneath Beau as he rested in a squatting position.

Using the lull, Beau caught his breath. Chris futilely squirmed. But the slightest lean by Beau would torque his neck and right shoulder, sending a tremendous shooting pain throughout his body. Chris let out a painful groan and stopped moving. This went back and forth until the hoodlum realized he had been bested.

"You done?"

"Yeah, man. Get off. This shit hurts."

"You damn right it does. They make us do it over and over again in training. I had this done to me several times. Believe me, I know it sucks." Beau wrenched his arm toward his head, sending another shooting pain into his shoulder. "Especially, when I do that."

Chris protested in a series of whines and moans, while Beau sat effortlessly in the hold. He glanced over his shoulder at Gigi, wondering if she was going to come to her partner's aid. She remained against the sedan, embarrassed for her partner.

Beau leaned over and spoke softly to Chris. "Guess I didn't need that badge, huh?"

Chris sucked his teeth in defiance, playing his role to the end.

"Not bad for a…, how'd you put it? Pussy-ass cracker?" Beau enunciated the derogatory name, mocking the insult.

"Fuck you, man."

"No…." With a violent jerk, Beau twisted his thighs one way and pulled Chris's wrist the other. "Fuck you."

An audible snap echoed and coincided with a pop that resonated through his grip. He stood up, releasing the hold, and Chris rolled to his side clutching his right elbow.

Chance walked over to Beau and saw Chris writhing around on the ground. His elbow was awkwardly bent, not as God had intended.

"What did you do?" he asked as he hung up the phone.

"What? He swung on me first. Plus, he called me a bad name."

Chapter 26

There was an extra hitch in his step. He bypassed the secretary and showed himself into Major Pritchard's office. Russell Trek had something.

With no preamble, Trek announced, "Rivers has missed the last two days of work and apparently Mathis has no idea where he is."

In his failure to obtain proof against Beau Rivers and Dylan Akers for the deaths of Earnest McFadden and George Shelley, Reginald Pritchard set up an alert through dispatch looking for any discrepancy in either man's work schedule. It was one of many administrative traps he had set for the duo. He was not going to allow them to sneeze louder than policy dictated without making a formal complaint. He aimed to annoy them into quitting or confessing. The plan hadn't netted any results until this morning when Trek walked through his door.

"Go ahead."

"I got the notice last night about the second day in a row. I verified this morning by calling Mathis. He heard that Rivers was transferred but knew nothing about it. He figured it was some kind of personnel realignment from the Chief's thing."

"Chief's thing?"

"The 'Kitchen Sink' operation."

"Oh, right. His knee-jerk reaction to the violence. Why would Shaw use Rivers for anything? That doesn't make sense."

"That's what I thought, too. So I dug a little deeper and found this down in Employee Resources, filed away." Trek placed a piece of paper in front of Pritchard. He picked it up and began to read.

The sheet rose suspicion at best, but it wasn't as damaging as he had hoped.

"They moved Rivers from the airport and put him under Akers in Property and Evidence? That really makes no sense." Trek summarized the information on the page.

"This was dated last week and signed by Shaw."

"Look at the other names."

Pritchard saw Parker and Holcomb on the list. "What the hell is going on?"

"I dunno, but something's up, boss."

Reginald Pritchard was no longer over Internal Affairs, but in his position as Major, he kept up to date on any and all developments in the one case he truly cared about. He wouldn't give up until Beau Rivers and Dylan Akers were in prison where they belonged.

***

Pritchard knocked first, but didn't wait for a response before entering the Chief's office. It sat on the other end of the executive suite from Pritchard's office.

Chief Shaw was on speaker phone with the City Manager. He saw Pritchard and waved him in while still talking. He wrapped up the call and leaned back in his chair, addressing his major.

"What can I help you with, Reggie?"

"You can explain what the hell you were thinking with this?" Pritchard held up the sheet of paper Trek had delivered.

Shaw feigned complete ignorance of the transfer order, waiting for Pritchard to show his hand. Reginald Pritchard would allow his emotions to get the best of him. "Well, what is it? I can't read that from here."

"It's a goddamn transfer order moving Beau Rivers down to P & E under Akers's supervision. Have you lost your damn mind?"

"What?" Shaw gave the best shocked face he could muster. "Let me see that." He reached across his desk and took the paper from Pritchard.

After reading it and holding a confused look, he replied, "This has got to be a fake, Reggie. I don't remember signing this at all. I mean, think about it. What the hell would they be doing down in Property? That doesn't make any sense."

"Okay, well then..." The unexpected reaction stalled Pritchard. "Then, you need to know I think Rivers is up to something, and he's missed the last two days of work."

"I'll get Inspector Shearer to look at it. She's thorough and will get answers."

"That's okay. Trek is on it already. I'll have him stick with it."

"No, I have Russell on something else right now. I'll get Shearer to handle it." Shaw's tone made the discussion final. Pritchard acquiesced.

"So be it." Pritchard stood up from the chair and Shaw remained seated. "You better not have anything to do with whatever they're up to, or believe me, I'll string you up next to them if you do."

Shaw replied with a crooked smile because, coming from Pritchard, the threat was meaningless. However, he had learned of the backdoor transfer. That gave the Chief concern, not only because it had his name on it, but because his faith of not being discovered depended on the abilities of Beau Rivers and Dylan Akers.

***

Russell Trek had already settled back at his desk in Internal Affairs when Major Pritchard strode through. The chime sounded as the door opened, and Trek's head turned to see who it was. Their eyes locked, and with a quick head nod, Trek bounced up and followed Pritchard out the door.

Huddled with Pritchard in the hallway, Trek knew something was up. It had to be additional information concerning the sheet of paper he delivered earlier that morning.

"You were right, Russell. There's definitely something going on," Pritchard assessed.

"I knew it."

"And I think Shaw is in on it."

"Really? The Chief?"

"He's dismissed it as some kind of mistake, but he's hiding something. I just don't know what."

"Okay. What do you want me to do?"

"Not sure. Keep your eye on Rivers and Akers. Who were the other two on that transfer order?"

"Holcomb and Chance Parker."

"Right, Parker." Pritchard nodded as a thought registered. "I want you to keep tabs on them as well. But don't get too close. If they are going to hang themselves, we'll let them. Then we'll be right there afterward to cut them down."

Chapter 27

The table rested on its side, overturned and next to a lamp that had been smashed against the wall, reduced to a dozen pieces. Drywall dust collected in a pile below the hole where Antonio had punched it repeatedly out of anger. The brooding turned into a violent outburst after learning that his cousin had had his elbow fractured and dislocated by Officer Beau Rivers. The attack was personal, not to just Chris, but to Tony Toombs, himself.

How dare he disrespect me!

His anger was directed at the furniture in the new headquarters. His wrath rearranged the entire room, implementing a post-destruction motif. The crew knew well enough to stay out of his way.

"If they think we playin', they gotta 'notha thing comin'. Fuckin' pigs. I'll kill 'em all. I'll kill their goddamn families, too," Antonio yelled as he paced the living room like a caged tiger waiting for his prey to come within reach. Xavier, Dookie, Gigi, Chris, and Gunner waited on the back porch. Antonio saw them huddled outside like scared idiots.

"Get in here!"

They all scrambled inside and encircled Antonio, waiting for instructions. Chris sported a thick cast over his arm that served as a reminder for the anger.

Xavier stepped up, "What we gonna do, Tony? We can't let this shit go unchecked, cops or not."

"Fuck, yeah. This is some bullshit!" Chris added by lifting up his casted arm.

"Hey, man, bringing that much heat on us ain't exactly what I signed up for. It's fucked up, what happened to Chris and all, but these aren't regular cops. Something about them has me a little scared." Gigi spoke with genuine concern.

"The way they jacked up that nigga at the hilltop store, shit. They ain't playin' by the same rules as the others, Tony," Dookie added.

"I see." He met each person's eyes, all with concern. "Do you think we should back down?"

Collectively, the group shook their heads. Some answered out loud, "No."

"Nah, Tony. But what can we do?" Dookie asked.

After a minute of thought, Antonio said, "Let's lay low for a minute." His decision was met with disappointment. "We have to be careful. We can't react with emotion out there in the street. That's when we get sloppy, and then we end up catching a charge. Ya'll feel me?"

"We feel ya." Gigi responded for the crew.

"We should go light up the motha fuckin' police station. That's what we should do," Gunner added with some animation.

"Nah, we need to send a message back to these particular cops," Antonio countered. Inspiration came and with an evil inflection, he said, "I think I know how we can change the arrangement."

Chapter 28

The rest of the week was surprisingly quiet. Chance and Beau made the rounds, checking on all of the operations tied to Tony Toombs. All were empty save for a few addicts loitering around, hoping shop would open for a quick score.

Chance parked their rental in a secluded spot behind a row of businesses off West Tennessee Street. Lulls in violence were always welcomed, but they were just that, lulls. Inevitably, the violence would spark again. Chance took the opportunity to call his daughter before bedtime. Beau gave him the car and stood outside, soaking in the cool night air.

Leaning against the hood, Beau studied the goings-on at a convenience store across the street. College students pumped gas as other customers came and went inside the store. Unaware of his over-watch, a patrol car pulled into the parking lot. The officer got out and went into the store. Beau pegged the visit as a welcomed bathroom break, having used the same bathroom many times while on patrol.

Beau looked back through the windshield and heard Chance talking on the phone, engaged in a deep conversation about first-grade drama. He turned back to the convenience store and saw an older, blue sedan with gleaming chrome rims pull up to the front of the store. The sound system thumped loudly and it reminded him of the skirmish at the hilltop store where he removed the faceplate from the would-be muscle. The memory invoked a prideful grin.

The bathroom break was over, and the officer exited the store. The music volume lowered as the cop paid attention to the flashy ride. Beau watched the exchange, waiting for a confrontation. The driver stepped away from his car, without any urgency, to listen to the cop. Beau was well out of earshot but read the body language loud and clear. The driver nodded and the music was turned off. Beau saw the officer point to the front of the car and noticed the car was in a handicapped spot. The cop was telling him to move.

The officer got in his car and slowly pulled away. As his back was turned, the driver stepped back out of his car without moving it as directed, and flicked his middle finger in the cop's direction. Adding to the disobedience, he sat back down in the car and cranked the music back to its annoying decibel level.

"Oh, no you didn't!" Beau stood up from the hood. "What an asshole." He looked back at Chance, still engrossed in the phone call, then started off on foot toward the convenience store.

Beau addressed the driver of the flashy car. "Hey, buddy. I need you to go ahead and move your car. Like the officer just told you to." Beau lifted his shirt, revealing his badge and gun.

The man glanced down at it and slowly turned the volume dial down, but he remained inside the car, indifferent to the demand.

"You gonna move it or not?" Beau asked, testily.

The driver looked around and past Beau. There wasn't any backup, no marked patrol car or anything official besides his badge. The driver replied, "Nah. I'm going inside to get something to eat. I'll move it in a minute." He locked his car, stuffed his keys in his pocket and turned to go inside the store. "You want it moved so bad, do it yourself."

As the violator entered the store, an elderly man stood down the sidewalk. A long expectant look was on his face. He walked with a cane and winced as he held his balance, making his way into the store. Parked behind him, Beau saw a car with a handicap placard in the rearview mirror.

Beau began to fume, but fought the urge to respond. A better idea came to mind.

"Do it myself, huh?"

Beau walked up to the driver's side door and pulled the handle. It was locked, true enough. He spun around, turning his back to the door, withdrew his Glock, gripped the barrel, and used the butt of the handle as a hammer to break the window. With a mighty whack, the glass shattered into tiny shards, littering the ground and the driver's seat.

He reached in, unlocked the door and pulled it open. He set the gear shifter in neutral then walked around to the hood. A small collection of people stopped pumping gas and watched, mouths gaped open in awe.

With a firm heave, Beau pushed the shiny blue car away from the front curb, using the concrete stop bar as leverage. The momentum grabbed the car, helping to move it backwards toward the pumps. Beyond the pumps was the perpetually busy three-lane portion of Tennessee Street. Coincidentally, the car was perfectly aligned with the entrance/exit of the gas station.

A final thrust with his legs and a push of the hood, the car gained enough speed to continue out into the road. The driver's door was still wide open and caught a yellow concrete pillar that guarded a pump station. The pillar held steadfast against the door and folded it backwards until it hit flush against the front fender. A loud metal crunch caught the attention of the rest of the gas station crowd.

"What the fuck?" The driver was exiting the store when he noticed that the commotion involved his car. The indifference of the driver quickly transformed into full-on concern as he watched his prized possession rolling backwards toward certain doom.

With the same level of empathy shown by the violator, Beau returned, "What? You told me to move it."

The man sprinted after the blue sedan, but it was too late. The pillar only slowed it down briefly. A small downward hill at the entrance sped up the car's momentum and flung it wildly into oncoming traffic. Cars honked and swerved, missing it initially, but an armored Brink's truck with a full head of steam failed to maneuver around the unmanned car.

The sound was horrific, but satisfying at the same time. People in the crowd applauded and others held an equally horrified look on their faces. It was the lack of common decency and just overall courtesy that bothered Beau the most.

Scanning the crowd, Beau was met with an appreciative look from the elderly man who nodded with thanks.

At that point, Beau Rivers understood what Gary Levine meant when he called him a sheepdog. It wasn't the traditional aggressiveness that Levine had talked about, but it was meanness all the same. He stood a bit taller, prouder in that moment. It wasn't about enforcing the law; it was about protecting the innocent herd. *I am a sheepdog.*

"Really?" Chance Parker's sarcastic tone came from behind Beau. He turned and was met with an irritated look, like that of a parent having to deal with an insolent child.

"What?"

"Do I have to ask?" Chance extended his arm, palm up toward the crash now at rest in the middle of Tennessee Street.

"He should've just moved the damn car."

"I don't know what that's supposed to mean, but whatever. Let's get out of here."

Chapter 29

The Golden Ale was a new addition to the midtown area. The bar specialized in having a variety of craft beers, open mic night, and weekly trivia contests. Garage-style doors that split the bar in two halves were rolled up, allowing the warm summer air to mix with the cooler indoor air conditioning. Beau and Chance sat at a high-top on the deck that overlooked Gadsden Street. The baseball game of the week played on the television.

Chance said his daughter was with her mother, so he agreed to join Beau for a beer, having no other suitable options.

"I wouldn't have thought of that," Chance said between sips. "Smashing his window and then pushing it out into traffic." He drifted off into thought. Beau didn't respond.

"I mean, all that for not moving his car from the handicap spot." Chance shook his head.

Beau felt an ounce of guilt, thinking maybe he went too far.

Chance swallowed more beer, set down the glass, and looked like he had something else to say. The last thing Beau wanted was a lecture. He was on borrowed time and didn't want to spend what he had left getting told about his shortcomings. He was already painfully aware.

Suddenly, Chance Parker broke out in a raucous laugh that caught the attention of other patrons on the deck. Beau watched vacantly.

"You said, 'He should've moved the car.'" Chance continued the boisterous cackle.

Easing up, Beau smiled and joined the laughter.

After a few choice comments that extended the laughter, silence fell on the pair who refocused on their beers. They weren't friends. They were thrown together because of Dylan and Beau's past transgressions, forced to get along under unusual circumstances, but in this moment, they were enjoying each other's company.

"So you wouldn't have done that?"

"No, I wouldn't have thought to do that."

"Hmm," Beau said as he finished his beer.

"What?" Chance asked. "You think I'm defective or something?"

"No."

"Then what?"

"Nothing."

"Spit it out. Apparently, we hold nothing back in this little band of fuck-ups. No reason to do it now."

"You're not the defective one at this table." Beau waved to the bartender for another beer.

"You say that like it's a badge of honor."

"No, it's not."

"Then what am I missing?"

Beau studied the younger detective for moment.

He is right, no reason to hold back.

"You're one of the good ones, Chance Parker, and there aren't many out there. You do the job the right way. There's a reason why you don't think like that. You have an inherent goodness inside of you that makes you special. It doesn't allow you to swim down in the depths of the abyss with the bottom dwellers."

"Is that where you are? With the bottom dwellers?"

"Me? Pretty much. Hell, I'm about as broken as you get. I've fucked up more times than I can count. Along the way, I lost something inside of myself. Unfortunately, I don't think I can ever get it back."

"And that gives you better insight over someone like me?"

"Insight, no. Instinct, yes."

"Instinct?"

"Yes, something as stupid as what happened back there at the convenience store. Guys like that don't respond to stern words from a badge, because he doesn't respect us. However, he does understand a personal attack, and there was nothing more personal to him than his car. So, instinct told me how to strike back. And that he'll respect."

"So, killing a guy trapped in a jail cell for raping and murdering your friend's kid—that gives you instinct?"

A deadpan look came across Beau's face. The bluntness of Chance's inference bothered him and felt like he crossed a line. Chance's face instantly turned apologetic.

"Sorry. Don't answer that."

"All I'm saying is that I'm wired different. We're both..." They locked eyes. "...Sheepdogs. We're just different breeds."

"Sheepdogs, huh?" Chance smiled at the comparison. He'd heard that somewhere before and liked the title.

"Don't ever believe anything different, and don't let anything change it. You are the real deal. Never lose sight of that."

Chance nearly blushed at the compliment.

"You know, there was a point when I very much looked up to you. I thought you were the sharpest detective there was. I believe there are people in this world born to be a cop, and you fit that mold until..."

Beau lowered his head, "Yeah, like I said, I've fucked up a few too many times, but you still have a chance to make a difference."

"Thanks. I won't have much of a career to worry about hanging around you and Akers."

"That's probably true." Beau grinned widely.

"Bet your ass." Chance raised his glass for a cheer.

A lottery commercial played on the television during the break between innings of the baseball game. Beau noticed it prompted Chance.

"Hey, can I ask you about the money thing, back in the day?"

With a what-the-hell look, Beau said, "Sure." It had unofficially gone down as being misplaced, but everyone in the department knew the real story; Beau had tried to steal it.

"Why'd you take it?"

"Moment of weakness, I guess. My life was shaping up to be shit at that time, and I thought I could take money that was from evil and use it for something good."

"Still stealing though."

"Yep. You're right about that." Beau downed a healthy pull of beer. "You gonna lecture me now?"

"No." Chance looked embarrassed for a moment. Beau saw that he was holding back.

"What?"

"Well—"

"We don't hold back, remember? Band of fuck-ups as you put it."

"Ever find out who ratted on you?"

A despondent look crossed Beau's face. He had tried to bury the past, but often it reared back from the dead and haunted him.

"No." He perked up with a thought jumping in his head, making him curious. "Why do you ask?"

It was the way Chance danced around the question, like he was fishing for information.

Sheepishly, Chance answered. "You may not remember, but I was on COPPS squad when the Figueroa raid went down."

Beau searched his memory bank until a vague recollection came. "You guys were on outside perimeter, right?"

"Yeah. After your people secured the house, we came in and helped search. Hell, it was my first dope search warrant. I remember being in awe of you back then."

Beau killed the accolade by ripping loose a throat-shaking belch. "Sorry."

"Anyways, I think I know who may have ratted you out?"

"Really? Who?"

"Well, um—"

"Just tell me, it's been so long ago. Like it'll change anything."

"You say that now."

"Dude! Just tell me."

Chance needed more liquid encouragement to divulge what he knew, which left Beau more annoyed. He waited impatiently.

"What's up, boys?" Dylan Akers appeared from behind Beau, putting his arm around his shoulder and interrupting the two. Desmond Holcomb followed and sat next to Chance, stealing a sip from Beau's beer.

"Hey, Dylan," Chance answered and quickly drank more beer, hiding from Beau.

Beau sighed out of frustration and jumped up from his seat to head toward the bathroom.

"What's his problem?" Holcomb asked.

"Nothing."

Five minutes later, when Beau returned from the bathroom, the group was talking about their next move to combat the violence.

"We need to cut the head off the snake. Without Antonio, those guys will crumble," Dylan said quietly, protecting the intelligence from unwanted ears.

As Beau sat down, he shot a menacing glare at Chance. Their conversation was sure to be continued. Conversely, talking about the Figueroa raid gave him an idea on how to go at Tony Toombs.

"Hey, Dylan, remember my informant from the Figueroa case? That guy you fileted on the buy-bust?"

"Yeah, why?"

"We saw him floating around the other day. He looked like he was still in the game. It may be worth a shot to see what he knows."

"Okay, that sounds like a good idea."

After finishing their beers, Chance Parker and Desmond Holcomb excused themselves and left the bar. Beau and Dylan remained.

"It seems to be going okay, right?" Dylan asked, thick with apprehension.

"I guess, man. Seems too surreal, like it's a bad dream."

"I need this to work out. I can't go to prison, Beau. I need to see my son born."

"I know, but I don't trust Shaw to keep his word."

Dylan nodded in agreement.

"Hell, you and Wendy should think about making a run for it. You know, try to disappear."

Dylan didn't respond and let the thought settle. He took a sip of beer and chuckled softly to himself.

Beau looked over. "What?"

"All hell broke loose the last time we sat on a deck like this drinking beer, contemplating doing something stupid for the right reason."

"Didn't quite work out the way we wanted, did it?"

"No, it didn't."

Chapter 30

Excitement and worry swirled together in the stomach of Inspector Russell Trek. It was a good thing he reread his emails before clearing out his inbox. The email from Chance Parker was shuffled somewhere in the mix and almost discarded. Parker claimed to have seen Beau Rivers exiting a house near the attempted abduction sight on his way to a late-night call out. After checking the Computer Aided Dispatch for any such corresponding service calls, he didn't find any. This time Parker was careful to check the surrounding houses as well. He believed that the visit was personal and generated a potential lead.

The issue was that this information had sat unchecked for nearly a month. As Trek walked down the hallway to Major Pritchard's office, he decided he was going to leave that part out.

"So I got something on the Rivers and Akers case I need to check out today. A new lead came in. Could be something."

Pritchard stopped reading his monitor and peered at the IA inspector over a set of readers perched on the end of his nose.

"Oh? What do you got?"

"Rivers was seen leaving a house over near the Shelley ambush a mo—a few nights ago. I did some digging and found out the guy who lives there is a Vietnam vet, worked in construction after that. Not sure how that fits, but it's worth a conversation."

"Hmm. Not sure how that fits either, but it does strike me as peculiar. Let me know."

Pritchard returned to the computer screen. Trek backed out, pleased that he didn't catch the near screw up. Plus, if the lead actually panned out, his ineptitude would easily get overlooked.

***

Trek pulled his unmarked car to the curb and stepped out. It was mid-morning and already sweltering. He studied the old wooden house and oversized porch as he slowly walked up the sidewalk and to the door.

After a knock, he heard slow-moving footsteps eventually make it to the other side of the door. It opened slowly, revealing an elderly and fragile-looking man with a ghastly yellow tint.

"Can I help you?"

"Are you Gary Levine?"

"Yes, sir. And you are?"

"Inspector Russell Trek, Tallahassee Police Department. I'd like to ask you a few questions, if that's all right. May I come in?"

Levine studied Trek carefully with suspicion, but welcomed him inside and out of the heat.

"Hot enough for ya?" Gary asked.

"Yes, it is."

"So, what kind of questions you got? Haven't had any issues with the neighbor for some time now. You guys came out and did a pretty good job puttin' the fear of God in 'em. Worked like a charm. Finally gave me peace."

"No, I'm not here for that. I'm with Internal Affairs."

Levine's hospitable demeanor changed as soon as he heard what unit the man worked under.

"I just wanted to talk about a friend that we have in common, Beau Rivers."

Levine didn't answer. His body stiffened.

"I know he was over here a little bit ago so don't bother denying that. What was the nature of his visit, if you don't mind me asking?"

The old man stood frozen. His silence emphasized his guilt. He reached for the recliner and eased himself down into the chair.

"Look, I'm not here to get you in trouble, but if you force my hand, don't think I won't haul your ass off to jail."

"He was here fixin' my AC. Damn thing crapped out on me and he came over to fix it."

Trek found his answer convenient.

"If you're protecting him, believe me, you'll be in the same jail cell as he is."

"I'm not protecting him. He doesn't need it. He's just a friend who fixed my AC."

Trek wasn't going to break through the old man's allegiance yet, but he wasn't ready to leave. He stepped away from the front door and moved into the living room. He glanced at the arrangement of pictures displayed on the mantle and around the room. He saw the picture of Levine in front of a helicopter in a jungle setting. He noticed a video gaming system under the television and thought it odd. Levine didn't strike him to be the gaming type.

After a moment of awkward silence, Gary asked, "So what's with all the questions about Beau?"

Trek turned to face the old man. With a wicked smile he said, "You damn well know why."

"Well, he ain't done nothin' wrong, so any other questions? If not, I think you should leave."

Trek didn't react and let out a disappointing sigh. Something in the corner of the room caught his eye, and then it clicked.

"What's that?"

Nervously, Gary replied, "What's what? It's nothing."

"That." Trek pointed to the odd-shaped item in the corner of the room with a blanket draped over the top. The outline of the sheet suggested it was a large gun or cannon.

"I told you, nothing."

"Bullshit." Trek crossed the room, ignoring Levine's protests and ripped away the blanket, revealing the M1919 Browning machine gun that Gary smuggled back from the war. To the side of the artillery was an ammunition belt that looked like the one Forensics found on the scene of the Shelley ambush. An explosion of excitement erupted inside of Trek's stomach.

"I think you ought to leave now, sir." Gary's voice was abounding with fear.

"Don't worry, I am. But go ahead and stand up. You're coming with me."

Chapter 31

After no answer on Gary's phone, Beau decided to drive by the Akers's house and park in his usual spot. He cut the engine and sat in silence, staring at the house. Coming back was like an addiction. It wasn't smart. It was unhealthy, but he couldn't stop. Wendy had a vise grip on his heart, and he lacked the ability to fight it off.

He tried calling Gary again, but there was still no answer.

Where could he be?

The light knock on his passenger window sent a shockwave of fright radiating through his body. For an instant, he felt weightless.

Calm replaced the fear as Wendy Akers's beautiful face peered inside his car. His heart thumped. It continued thumping because it was her.

"I'm sorry. I didn't mean to scare you."

"That's okay." Beau got out of the car and walked around to see her up close. He wanted to hold her, but stopped short, trying to hide his excitement.

"How are you?" she asked.

"Good."

"Good? Really?" Her right eyebrow furrowed. Her skepticism was obvious. "I highly doubt that."

"Yeah, I don't know why I said that," Beau said sheepishly. "My life is a complete mess right now. The Chief is totally setting us up, Pritchard still has a hard-on for me, and we're playing a very dangerous game with some very dangerous bad guys. And there's always…" Beau tailed off leaving the situation between himself and Wendy unspoken. "It's really quite awful."

"Okay, that I believe." She smiled.

Beau glanced down at her large belly.

"You shouldn't be out here," he said protectively. "You should be taking it easy. Does Dylan know you're out here?"

"Relax." She crossed her arms. "This isn't my first pregnancy and it is you that shouldn't be here." Her admonishment caused him to back down.

"I know. You're right." Beau hung his head. "I'm sorry. I'll leave."

As Beau turned, she called out, "Wait."

"I just wanted to see you."

Wendy uncrossed her arms and did a pseudo curtsy. "Here I am."

Beau let out a strained laugh.

"I've missed you," he said. It was more of a confession than a statement. He was glad to get it off his chest.

Wendy didn't respond. Beau could see she didn't feel the same or at least wasn't going to admit it if she did. He had complicated her life to the point that he couldn't understand why she didn't hate him. Her silence was answer enough, and he didn't want to impose further. She should be inside with her husband. Again, he turned to leave.

"I've missed you, too."

Her face was soft and angelic, even in the orange glow of the street lamp. He stepped closer and with no protest from her, held her tight, encasing her pregnant form in his strong arms. A spark reignited. She wrapped her arms around him and squeezed. He took a deep breath, taking in her scent, reliving memories of that pleasurable night. In that instant, the stress of the world faded, and Beau was transported somewhere between happiness and contentment, if only for a moment. Secretly, he wished they could run away to a private island, far away from criminals, cops, and the need for secrets or revenge. The vision of sitting on a private deck overlooking a serene ocean came to mind, Wendy nestled next to him.

Drawn closer by an unexplained magnetism, Beau moved in and kissed Wendy passionately, completely giving in to the moment. He caressed her face, making sure she felt his strength. She kissed back, but then pushed away, careful not to give in to further temptation.

Beau apologized again.

"That's okay. Don't apologize."

"No, it's not right. What happened should've never happened." Beau took a step back, letting go.

He bowed his head in shame. "He deserves to know."

"Yes. You're right."

"It should be me who tells him."

"No, it should come from me. I just don't know how he's going to react."

"It'll be okay. He loves you very much."

She smiled.

Beau glanced down at her stomach. "So, how are you feeling? Everything good?"

Wendy ignored the obvious topic change. "Yes, everything is good. The baby is healthy and on track."

He nodded. "Glad to hear." For Beau, the child growing inside Wendy was another chance at life. Another chance to be a good father and to have something worth living for.

"So, how are you doing?"

She bit her lip as she understood the question but didn't want to answer. A worried expression creased her face, which made Beau uneasy.

"I'm terrified," she said. A tear broke loose and rolled down her cheek.

"Why? You were a great mother. You will be a great mother again."

She shook her head. "It's not that."

"Then what?"

Her pause caused a sick feeling in the pit of Beau's stomach. Another tear came. "I'm scared to death the baby is yours."

His knees nearly buckled. He was stunned in disbelief. If they shared this child, they would forever have a bond. If the child was not Beau's, then there would be no reason for them to be connected. Her implication was obvious.

"That hurts," he eeked out.

"I know, I'm sorry. I don't mean to hurt you, but this is the way it has to be."

Beau fought back tears of his own.

"If it is mine, I want you to know that I'll do whatever it takes to be there."

"I know you would." Wendy looked away, unable to look Beau in the eyes. She blinked as more tears cascaded down. Summoning strength from the sky, she faced him with determination. There was more. "I've also decided that when the baby comes, no matter what, Dylan is going to be the father."

Her words pierced Beau's heart like a searing hot knife. It was hard enough imagining his life without Wendy, but bringing a child into the world that he could not hold or talk to was unbearable—and for a child not to know his father. Beau was shattered.

The hurt in his eyes was apparent, and she reached out to him. He stepped back.

"It has to be this way, Beau. Can't you see that?"

Her eyes were pleading with him to understand.

"If you care for me at all, you will let this happen," she said.

Reluctantly, Beau nodded, swallowing back the tears that desperately wanted to break loose.

"What about that night? What about just now? Doesn't any of that mean anything?"

"Of course it does, Beau. I will never forget that night and what we shared, but like you said, it should've never happened. But we can't change the past, no matter how much we want to. And right now, I need Dylan in my life, not you. I just pray to God that he forgives me for what I've done."

Beau's head swirled in a maelstrom of emotion. He needed a moment to grasp everything. Suddenly, he felt alone, but it was because of his own doing. He didn't know what he'd set out to accomplish by coming here. He longed for Wendy and to hold her again, but now that she was standing in front of him, he wanted to be anywhere but here. The illusion had been soiled and would never be the same, no matter how he felt about her. After what seemed like ten minutes of an awkward silence, Beau spoke.

"He's a good man. He'd be foolish not to forgive you."

She smiled with hope.

"You are a special woman, Wendy Akers. Don't forget that."

"I won't."

Beau glanced around. Instead of revealing his true feelings, he decided to say good-bye.

"You better get inside. He's probably starting to wonder where you are. I know I'd never let you out of my sight."

With a gentle touch, Wendy reached up and caressed the side of his face. "Good-bye, Beau." She reached up and kissed him on the cheek before walking away.

He watched her leave. She walked out of his life. She made her way to the house and disappeared inside. Outside in the quiet night, Beau contemplated everything that had just happened. Before climbing into the car and leaving, he paused. He looked back at the front door and said, "I love you."

Chapter 32

I'm terrified. I'm scared to death the baby is yours.

As soon as he awoke, Wendy's voice echoed in his head. The words stung just as deeply as they had the night before.

It was early, and Beau didn't sleep well. He was tired, but didn't want to go back to bed. He checked his phone and saw no missed calls. His thoughts moved to Gary Levine, and he wondered why he hadn't returned any of his calls.

Beau showered, dressed, and met Dylan at the Lincoln Neighborhood Center. Holcomb was already there, but Chance hadn't made it in.

"You all right?" Dylan asked, his face genuine with concern.

Beau lived on the edge, wondering whether Wendy finally told Dylan about their indiscretion. He looked for a hint, but the worry told him otherwise.

"Yeah, fine."

"Still want to find your old CI, see if he knows anything?"

"Yes. He probably won't be out until noon. Probably shouldn't go knocking on his door with everything going on, so I'll wait till then. First, I need to check on something."

"Want me to go with?" Holcomb asked.

"Nah. I got it." Beau wanted to check on Gary and make sure everything was all right. He had to go alone because he didn't want anyone else to know about him. "I'll text you when I'm done, and we'll go hunt my guy."

"All right, sounds good."

***

Gary was slow to answer the door. His jaundiced eyes were wearier than usual, and he looked completely defeated. His shoulders slumped and his head hung low.

"What's going on, Gary? I've been trying to call. Is everything okay?"

"Come in, Beau. Shut the door."

The tone in Gary's voice was serious. Beau shut the door and sat down in the living room next to Gary's recliner. There was an empty bottle of liquor on a side table and an ashtray full of cigarette butts.

"What happened?"

Gary shook his head, unsure how to start. He fiddled with another cigarette and lit it before answering. Beau searched the living room for clues of what possibly could have happened to render him in such a state. At first glance, he didn't notice, but when he slowed down he saw that the M1919 Browning was missing. He grew confused. This didn't seem like a run of the mill burglary. Something more was going on.

"Gary, tell me what happened?"

"IA came to the house last night, Beau. Some pencil dick named Trek started asking about you and then ended up finding the ammo belt next to the Browning. They said if I didn't cooperate, they were going to charge me with accessory to murder."

This was the second time in the last twelve hours Beau had been gut-punched. It didn't lessen the blow. Blood drained from his face, and he felt paralyzed. He took a deep breath.

"This isn't your fault, Gary. Tell me exactly what you told them."

"Beau, I swear, I didn't tell them shit. I didn't say anything about, you know…."

"Right. It's okay, Gary."

"They obviously got the ammo belt, though. That's bad, right?"

"No, it ain't good," he assessed. "I'm sorry my problems got you jammed up. Tell me what you did say."

"They seemed to know that you've been coming here for a while, like they were watching you or something. Some other asshole named Pritchard came in threatening me with prison and what-not. What a pussy, that guy."

Beau got up and checked the windows, peering down the street for surveillance. He didn't notice any on the way in, but he wasn't looking for it either. Satisfied no one was out there, he returned to Gary.

"Did they put anything in the house? Is anything missing or moved in anyway?"

"Did they bug my house? No. I spent most of the night checking. I didn't find anything."

"Okay, good."

Unable to sit, Beau paced the small room.

"So, you didn't tell them anything."

"Not a damn thing." A proud grin broke through his haggard face. "I told them bastards to leave you and Dylan be. I told them that if they were going to charge me, then do it or let me leave."

"Was anyone else there? Or was it just those two, Trek and Pritchard?" Suddenly, Parker's absence from the Lincoln Center seemed suspicious.

Gary thought for a moment, "No, it was just the two."

"Think of where they took you. Was it the second floor or the third floor?"

"Third floor, I think. It was a big office that had a large window overlooking an apartment building."

Confounded by Gary's description, he was lost as to where they took him within the department. Gary read the confused look on Beau's face.

"Pretty sure it was that Pritchard guy's office."

"His office?"

"Yeah."

"Why would he take you there?"

"Dunno. Does that break protocol?"

"Yes, it does. With what you're saying, you should have been identified as a co-conspirator in a criminal case. They should've brought in one of the homicide detectives. And if not that, because they're IA, they should've done the interview in the unit. Not Prick's office. For some reason, your contact was kept a secret."

"Don't know what to tell you."

"Okay, anything else I need to know, Gary?"

"No, that was it."

"All right, I gotta get going."

"Before you go, Beau."

"Yes."

"You need to start thinking of an exit plan, brother. This guy Pritchard is coming for you bad. I don't think he'll stop until you're behind bars or in the ground. I hope I don't live to see either happen."

Beau nodded in agreement.

"And if I can help you in any way, you know I will. Just ask." A smile broke through his tired face. "Us sheepdogs have to stick together."

"Thanks."

Chapter 33

Dylan used the back stairwell to go unnoticed up to the third floor. After getting a frantic call from Beau about Pritchard and Trek bothering the old man, he had to speak to Shaw. Beau's friend with the Huey machine gun was uninvolved, but he possessed inside knowledge that could be damaging. Dylan had to get Pritchard to back off. To do so, he needed the Chief.

The Chief's secretary, Candace, was busy on the phone when Dylan walked in. He managed to slip into Shaw's office without her noticing. Shaw didn't observe him until the office door clicked shut.

"What the..., Akers, you scared the shit out of me."

"Don't care," he said rudely and took a seat in front of his desk.

A scowl came over the Chief's face at the intrusion. "What is it?"

"Pritchard."

The scowl turned to concern with a hint of worry. He turned from his computer, giving Dylan his full attention.

"What now?"

"He's snooping around and has found a decent piece of evidence against us."

"Okay. Is it the same stuff I found or different?"

"Different."

"Is it enough to arrest you?"

"I don't think so. Something tells me if Reginald Pritchard has enough evidence, he'll jump at the chance to make the arrest."

"He hasn't come to me with it, I promise."

"Why would he keep it from you?"

"I don't know. He's a bastard, but a diligent one for sure. If he's found a piece of evidence, rest assured he'll use it."

"You have to run interference. We need him off of our ass."

"I don't think you have any bargaining power, Lieutenant. Why should I help you, further? I've held my promise thus far. What happens beyond my door is out of my control."

Dylan shook his head, fighting the urge to come across Shaw's oversized desk and throw him out the window. Dylan took a deep breath before responding. "You're right. I don't have many bargaining chips, but you have to see the progress that we're doing on this little project of yours. The violence is down, but it's not over. There's still a lot to do."

Shaw nodded. "I'm listening."

"We've landed a few vital blows, but no knockout punch. And, we have a plan."

"A plan? Is it something I should hear, or not?" Shaw was careful to phrase his question.

"We think we've identified the man in charge. The plan is to take him down. He falls and the rest of the crew falls with him, like the head of the snake. With this crew out of the way, it should allow for a more legitimate response to be implemented by the department and keep the violence down."

Shaw made an odd face while he thought about Dylan's request. "How much time do you need?"

"A week or two at least. It should go fast with a little luck."

"I can do a week. Anything more will be a stretch."

"It'll have to do." Dylan got up to leave.

"For what it's worth, I thank you for the work you're doing. I have noticed."

Dylan acknowledged him with an indifferent look and then exited his office as quietly as he had entered.

***

After Dylan left his office and spoke of needing help with Pritchard, Shaw came up with an idea. He reflected on their conversation. He admired Dylan for what he was balancing in his life. With everything going on, he still thought like a cop, even when his fate was sealed. Legitimate follow-up to this side mission was an idea Shaw hadn't thought about. He liked it.

Shaw summoned his major over operations just before eleven o'clock. He showed up and sat down in his office five minutes early.

"What can I help you with, Robert?"

"We'll get to that in a minute. Any updates from your bureau you need to share?"

Pritchard's eyes narrowed. Shaw felt transparent but kept up the façade.

"No, everything is pretty much the same since the staff meeting yesterday."

Pritchard was careful and held his cards close, so Shaw quickly moved on.

"Okay, good. Something has come to my attention, and it requires the utmost sensitivity. I need you to look into it."

"What is it?"

"It's about the Rivers and Akers case from last year."

Pritchard leaned forward in his chair, immediately interested. "Go ahead."

"I believe my predecessor, Chief Harrison, had inside knowledge of their plan and was instrumental in providing intelligence to execute it."

"Where did you get that information?"

"Not important right now. But I think you should begin a surveillance detail on him at once. Use one of your guys from IA, but limit it as much as you can."

"Why a limit, Robert?"

"Because, this is unconfirmed information, Reggie. We need to tread lightly as David Harrison is a former chief and should be afforded discretion until we have proof, don't you agree?"

"Not if he's dirty."

"Right, but until we have proof of that, Reggie, I'm ordering you to lay low. You uncover something and then we'll do the full court press."

Pritchard leaned back in his chair, mulling over the information, and then skepticism took root. "I worked pretty close with Chief Harrison on that case. Are you sure this information you have is good?"

"It's worth me mentioning it to you. Plus, think about it. All the access to Shelley's whereabouts?"

"I don't know, Robert. That's a helluva leap involving him."

"I told you it was sensitive. I need you on it ASAP, though."

"Okay, fine. I'll bring Osgood in for this. She needs the experience."

"No, not her." The Chief was quick to nix his choice. "I need her on the use-of-force case. That officer needs to be cleared and back on the street. Use someone else."

"Fine, how about Ruiz?"

"He's on the McNair shooting. What's Trek working on?"

"He's already got something on his plate."

"What case is he working on?"

Pritchard didn't answer. Shaw had called his bluff. His options were to give in or reveal the latest lead from the Vietnam vet.

"Fine, I'll get Trek on it."

"Good. I'll approve any overtime he needs."

"Anything else?"

"No, you're excused."

"I'll let you know what he finds out."

"Thank you, Reggie."

Reginald Pritchard stood up to leave. Shaw watched him go and instantly felt relieved when the door shut. Pritchard had taken the bait.

He picked up the phone and dialed a number from memory.

"Hello?"

"Chief Harrison, it's Robert Shaw."

"Robert, call me David. How are you? Helluva mess you're weathering right now."

"No kidding. Listen, you remember our little talk before I took the chief's job?"

"Yes."

"Well, I need that favor you offered, no questions asked."

"What do you need me to do?"

Chapter 34

Ten minutes after noon, and Beau's old CI was nowhere to be found. All men, no matter their status, were creatures of habit, keeping to what they know and what is within their comfort level. Hoping the CI conformed to normal behavior, all that was left was to wait.

Beau and Desmond found a spot on the edge of the historic Frenchtown neighborhood about a block away from the Save-N-Go convenience store. Beau watched as a young man limped awkwardly toward the store. Fixated on him and his plight, Beau stared as he ambled down the sidewalk in pain. The area was wrought with poverty, drug use, and oppression, which made life difficult enough, but to add a physical disability would make life even harder. Health care in these neighborhoods was economically driven and not the best for a patient who couldn't afford the top level of care.

"I remember him," Desmond said, breaking the silence.

"Huh?"

He removed the straw he was chewing and used it to point toward the store. "That kid you're staring at."

"What's his story?"

"Shot when he was fifteen. He's about twenty-four now. Got shot in a robbery he and his buddies tried to pull off at a convenience store. The clerk whipped out a shotgun from under the counter and filled that kid's ass full of buckshot. It shattered his hip and knee and caused that busted-ass limp."

Beau shook his head. He almost felt sorry for the kid before Desmond explained what happened. He compared the kid's mistake to his own and how one decision can impact you for life.

"We all live with the scars of our past, some are just more apparent."

Desmond looked over at Beau, with an impressed look on his face.
"You just come up with that?"
"Yeah, I guess so."

Beau adjusted himself uncomfortably in the passenger seat. The words weren't meant for Desmond but said for his own sake. He didn't want to continue this conversation.

"That him?"

Relieved by the interruption, Beau peered in the direction Holcomb was looking. "Yes, that's him."

"Okay, how do we handle it?"

Beau studied the layout of the area, trying to figure out what would work best.

"We could snatch him up and say he's got a warrant."

"Yeah, except for when we kick him loose, everybody will know he didn't go to jail. Needs to be something else."

"Right." Desmond settled back in his seat, steadily chewing on his empty straw.

"Let's wait until he leaves the store and just roll past him. He'll see me and then meet up down the road."

"Okay."

Ten minutes later, the subtle roll-by worked, and the CI jumped in the back seat of the rental car and laid down out of sight.

"Damn, Rivers. You tryin' to get a nigga killed 'round here, man."

"What do you mean?"

"Shiiiiit. You know 'xactly what I mean. Ery'one in the hood been talkin' 'bout you."

He grinned at the renewed notoriety. Like he told Chance, it was about earning respect. Something extremely hard to do when you play by the rules.

"Whippin' that one boy's ass at the hilltop, takin' they dope, breaking Chris's arm the other day. And did you really drive some dude's ride into oncoming traffic? Seriously, that's some straight-up goon shit, right there."

Beau didn't react or bother to correct the story. If that's what the street wanted to believe, there was no reason to set the record straight.

Desmond laughed at the CI's breakdown.

"You must be the 'black-up' to these crackas, huh?"

Desmond peered in the backseat, then shot a friendly glance at Beau. "Yeah, I guess that would be me."

"What else they saying?" Beau asked of the CI.

"A whole lot, brotha. A whole lot. But we need to get out of the hood. Can you take me somewhere?"

"Don't worry. We got you covered."

Beau told Desmond to head over to the Lincoln Neighborhood Center where they could debrief the CI out of the reach of the "hood."

***

The Lincoln Neighborhood Center had served its purpose for Dylan and his team. The dusty building was growing on him. It was essentially a relic holding onto its significance in the community. Dylan had said that he could relate, while Beau found it repulsive. The back end of the main hallway was where Dylan had set up the makeshift office for any day-to-day needs.

The CI, Clarence Biggins, sat comfortably in the dusty room used for storage. Leaning back in a swivel chair with his arms behind his head, strangely, he seemed to be at home. For Beau, it was a reminder that he was being forced to do the Chief's dirty work in lieu of prison. Being there made him long for the monotonous routine of the airport.

Dylan entered the room, joining Beau, Desmond, and Biggins. Beau saw the CI strain his eyes, trying to place Dylan in his memory. Before it clicked for him, Dylan spoke up.

"You start?"

"No. Waiting on you. Where's Chance?" Beau asked. Beau was still worried after talking with Gary Levine.

"Not sure."

Beau let it pass since there were more pressing matters. Dylan nodded for Beau to get started.

"So, you up for helping us out again?"

"Depends on what you wanna know and the payment plan."

"We'll take care of you, but it needs to help us out. None of the corner boy, small-time shit, either."

"What are you wantin' to know?"

"Tony Toombs," Dylan said, getting to the point.

The carefree attitude Biggins came in with suddenly changed. His jovial smile erased as a serious glower washed over his face.

"I don't think I can help ya'll."

"Oh, come on. I think you can do just that."

"You are wantin' me dead, ain'tcha?"

"Come on. It ain't like that Biggs." Beau used the informant's street name to make him more at ease.

Biggins started to rub his face, tap his heels, and swivel back and forth in the chair.

"Have I ever burned you, Biggs? You gave me the biggest case ever, which even included Tony, and it never came back on you, did it?"

"Come on, man—"

"Did it? Did it come back on you or not?"

"No."

"That's right. So, come on. Help me out again."

Desmond and Dylan leaned forward with anticipation, seeing that Beau's magic was working.

"I don't know, Rivers. That's a tall order."

"All this hemming and hawing lets me know that you got something, so let's hear it."

After a minute of internal debate, Biggins gave in. "Okay, so I might know of something that's going down tonight, something big."

Excitement came to Dylan. The idea of something going down meant that he was that much closer to fulfilling his servitude to the Chief.

"Tonight? You sure?" Dylan asked.

"Yeah." Biggins eyes bulged for emphasis. "Something is going down."

"When tonight?"

"Should be around eight or so. Depends on when the runners get back."

"Is Toombs going to be there?"

"Should be. He normally oversees stuff like this."

"Where'd the runners go?"

"Miami."

"Beau?" Dylan wanted to speak to him privately. They stepped out into the hallway.

"What are you thinking?"

"Let's move on this, now."

"I'm for it. We can set up and wait for these runners to get back, pounce on them, and catch Toombs dirty."

"Right. I like it."

"Could get hairy. They obviously know we're not fucking around. They're going to be armed, which means we have to go in heavy."

"That shouldn't be a problem."

Beau grinned at Dylan's confidence.

A noise clambered behind them, pulling their attention down the hallway. Chance Parker turned the corner and walked toward them.

"Hey, we got something. You ready to roll in a bit?" Dylan asked.

"Sure. What is it?"

Dylan explained the recent update provided by Beau's CI. He delegated Beau to get all the details from Biggins that he could about the deal. After he was done talking with Chance, he came back into the room alone.

"Where'd Chance go?"

Dylan glared at Beau, trying to wave off the question. When it didn't work, he replied, "I needed him to do something for me." Dylan moved his glare to Biggins and back to Beau, trying to communicate that he didn't want to discuss anything in front of the snitch.

Beau read the look and backed off.

"Hey, hey, you better write this stuff down, Rivers," Biggins interrupted. "I'ma give you this case on a platter, just like befo'."

"Yeah, right. I'm listening."

Chapter 35

Reginald Pritchard grew more irritated as the minutes passed. He couldn't place it, but something annoyed him and he felt like he was teetering on the edge of obsession. He had sent Trek after the former police chief based on a lead provided by the current police chief. It was getting late and he wanted an update.

Trek answered on the first ring. "Hello?"

"Got anything?"

"No. He made a stop at the store, got food, and then on to the house. Hasn't left since. Walked the dog, didn't pick up its shit."

"I get it, Russell."

"Seriously, he just left it there. Who does that?"

"Russell!" Pritchard snapped.

"Sorry. It's just..." Trek paused, trying to convey respect to his superior. "This seems like a waste of time."

Something clicked for Pritchard. "Yes, it does."

"I mean he's the Chief, so you would expect him to be careful, but this just doesn't feel right. I'm watching a retiree who has no life."

"Like its busy work." Pritchard said it more as a statement.

"Yes, just like that."

Pritchard ended the call and left out of his office. He walked the length of the executive suite with determination. He felt like he was being toyed with and didn't like it. The suite was empty, but the light was on in Chief Shaw's office. He barged in unannounced, hoping to catch him in the act of doing something wrong.

"Chief, I just need to ask you..."

The office was empty. Pritchard checked the private bathroom.

"Robert?" He called out to ensure he was alone. He stepped out and checked the executive suite again.

Reginald Pritchard suspected Robert Shaw of providing him with a red herring. For what reason, he could not figure out, but it only served to make him more suspicious. Presented with the opportunity, he scanned the paper-laden desk, hoping the answer lay somewhere in the mix.

I'm in charge of this investigation, no matter who's involved.

Pritchard moved behind the desk and sifted through the various piles of papers, files, memos, and documents. He shoved away the piles he recognized as budget proposals, new hire selections, and department memos. He sorted through what was left and didn't find what he was looking for. He sat down and moved the mouse in a circle, bringing the monitor to life.

Surprisingly, it wasn't locked. He guessed the mystique of the Chief's office was enough to keep would-be snoopers away. Pritchard saw things differently. He opened Shaw's email account but found nothing exciting. There were multitude of files stored on his desktop for multiple reasons, each with a label that had no meaning. There wasn't enough time to sort through each one, so he made a note to have the hard drive cloned and to put Trek on the task.

"Dammit!" Pritchard exhaled and leaned back in the large leather chair. He was hoping to find something incriminating, but resigned to the possibility his instincts were wrong.

He pulled the drawers of the oversized desk open, searching them before leaving. The center drawer was a collection, however extremely orderly, of necessary office needs such as pens, paperclips, and the like. The left-hand drawers contained file folders on his executive staff. Shaw was responsible for yearly performance evaluations for each member. The right-hand drawer contained necessary paperwork and blank memos. The bottom right was locked.

"What's in there, Robert?"

Pritchard searched for a key. He didn't find one in the center drawer that fit the tiny lock. He scoured the top of the desk again and then looked behind picture frames and the other knick-knacks displayed around the office. Nothing.

Irritated, he fell back into the seat. A thought occurred to him and he pulled the center drawer out. He reached up underneath the desktop checking to see if there was a key hidden there. Nothing.

"God dammit!"

As he sat back in the chair, defeated, his gaze turned unfocused. He contemplated getting a screwdriver and ripping the drawer open. The issue was that if the answer wasn't in that drawer, the damage would alert the Chief that someone had been snooping.

I could pick the lock.

But knowledge of lock picking was necessary, he submitted.

Pritchard's gaze took focus. It held on an ornate pen/pencil holder. A rabbit's foot was draped over the side.

"I could use some luck." Pritchard grabbed the lucky charm, adhering to the superstition, but what he found dangling on the other end was a small gold key. He didn't waste any time and went straight for the bottom drawer. It unlocked and the drawer slid open. A large case file with some other paperwork was on top. He grabbed the paperwork first.

It was the transfer sheet he had questioned Shaw about a few days prior. This was the original copy.

Liar.

He was on to something. The next few sheets were some type of after-action report. He scanned over the documents and read about a fight at a convenience store on Alabama Street where a large amount of drugs was seized. The next section mentioned a subject getting his arm broken. There were no case numbers associated, and Pritchard, an avid follower of the patrol summaries, didn't remember anything like this happening. The reports were sent by Dylan Akers to the attention of Robert Shaw.

Pritchard's eyes lit up with excitement. He quickly placed the paperwork on the desk and pulled out his phone to photograph them. He would take time later to read them word for word, but now he just needed a copy for evidence.

Was Shaw using Akers and Rivers to carry out some type of street justice?

He burst with excitement and fought the urge to scream, but held it in for the moment. He would wait for the resignation of Robert Shaw to celebrate, while on his way into the chief's office.

He finished photographing the after-action reports and reached for the case file. If it was being kept in the same drawer as these gold nuggets, it had to be a significant case.

A faint chime of the elevator came from the hallway. It drew Pritchard away from the secret drawer. Figuring it was Shaw returning, he had to get out of the office before he was caught. He needed to know more before he confronted the Chief. The idea of calling out Robert Shaw in front of his command staff and even the media made him smile. Trying him in the court of public opinion would be ideal.

Pritchard placed the paperwork back in the drawer and shut it, replaced the rabbit's foot and exited the office. He was sneaking out the back stairwell when Chief Shaw walked into the executive suite accompanied by his wife and a bag of take-out food.

Chapter 36

"See anything yet?" Dylan's voice crackled over the radio channel. He was paired with Desmond as Beau sat alone.

"No, not yet."

Positioned to watch the south side of the warehouse, Beau sat uncomfortably in another rental that smelled heavily of cigarettes. At the corner of Brevard and Dewey, the warehouse was situated at the southern edge of the infamous "Frenchtown" neighborhood. It had had many owners over the years and was still in operation because of its prime location. Beau had passed by the metal-sided eyesore a hundred times without suspicion. The only history he was aware of was the rare noise complaints that came when a local garage band used the space to practice. Currently, it was a mechanic shop with a plethora of auto parts and mechanic's tools lying around.

Trepidation settled as Beau grew wary of what was about to go down. The absence of Chance Parker caused his paranoia to grow, wondering if Dylan's trust in him was justified.

Cutting Desmond out of the conversation, Beau sent a text message to Dylan, asking where Parker was.

Don't worry about it. He'll be here in a minute, Dylan replied.

"Yeah, right," Beau said to the empty car.

Movement at the warehouse caught his attention. Two men walked up, one was carrying a large duffle bag. Beau noticed through the binoculars that the bag matched the one Chris and Gigi used to hide the AK-47. One of the subjects looked like the street thug they called "Gunner D." He didn't recognize the other.

"Got something. Two just went in from the south. One was carrying a large duffle bag like the one Chris and Gigi had."

Dylan acknowledged.

"When Parker gets here, you two go in. Me and Dez will cover the north and east sides."

"Copy that."

A few minutes later, a car pulled up and parked behind Beau's rental. He quickly made the driver as Chance Parker who got out and jumped in the front passenger seat with Beau before anyone noticed.

"Hey."

"Hey, got two inside already. You ready for this?"

"I guess so."

"Where you been?"

"Why? You miss me?"

"Yeah. Bunches. Seriously, where you been?"

"Taking care of something. Don't worry about it."

"Whatever. Let's go."

***

"Do you know why the warehouse is such an ideal spot for business?" Tony Toombs asked.

"It's right there in the hood," offered Chris.

"That's one reason." Antonio smiled as he watched the two cops walk up to the warehouse from the south. "The other is it's perfect for counter-surveillance."

Antonio checked his watch. It read eight-twenty p.m. He pulled out his cell phone and hit a pre-set number. While it rang, he marveled at the strategy he had designed and the fact his hunters were about to become his prey.

From the church across the street, they watched. The expanded fellowship hall had a second floor that conveniently overlooked the intersection. Antonio had the advantage of a field general surveying his battlefield. Watching his plan unfold, he felt like a god.

"Yeah?" Duquan Baker answered the phone.

"Dookie, y'all ready? They took the bait and are about to follow Gunner and the other boy inside."

"We're ready, Tony." Antonio heard an audible metal exchange on the other end of the line. Dookie racked his slide, loading his weapon.

"You see the other two? The one they call Akers and the black one?"

"Nah, not yet."

"Find them. These guys came from the south, so look for them on the north side of the warehouse."

"You got it, Tony."

Antonio hung up and hit another pre-set number.

"Hello?"

"X? You see the other two? Akers and the black cop?"

"I got 'em in a red truck parked over on Dunn Street by that little church."

"Okay, good. They just sitting there?"

"Yeah, talking on the walkie-talkie."

"Okay, good. Tell Dookie you got 'em over there."

"A'ight." Xavier answered then added, "I could hear one of them say they were 'moving in'."

A lascivious smile came across Antonio's face. He was nearly salivating over his prey. He made a few more phone calls, making sure all the pieces to his plan were in place. He gave out the last preparations as he watched Beau Rivers and Chance Parker disappear inside the warehouse.

***

Staged outside the bay door, Beau looked back at Chance. Beau mouthed, "Are you ready?" Chance nodded. Dressed in raid gear, both had their guns drawn and ready. Beau peeked around the corner and saw the two bad guys in the middle of the first large bay area. One was standing. The other was sitting. He didn't see any weapons, but knew they'd be packing. Beau held up his hand and gave Chance two fingers, moved them to his eyes, and pointed inside the warehouse. Again, Chance nodded in acknowledgement. Two men are inside.

Beau took a deep breath. The stench of stale motor oil filled his nostrils. It was time to move. He nodded for Chance to follow. He lunged forward and barged through the bay door with his gun aimed outward, leading the way.

"Police, get on the ground! Get on the ground."

Beau Rivers and Chance Parker were a two-man team, but flooded the large room with speed and surprise that overwhelmed the two subjects. They froze in place like deer caught in headlights. The cops moved at an angle, quickly flanking their targets and ordering them to the ground.

Gunner D let out a few choice words but was physically compliant, as was his sidekick. Both went to their knees and interlaced their fingers behind their heads as a sign of submission. Beau held his gun on the suspects while Chance took the opportunity to go look in the duffle bag for the spoils.

"What do you got?" Beau asked.

"Stand by."

Chance stood so he could open the bag and watch the suspects at the same time. He unzipped the bag and reached inside. Beau noticed an odd look on Parker's face as he tried to register what kind of contraband they had found.

"What is it?"

Parker didn't answer. An uneasy feeling rumbled in the pit of Beau's stomach. Parker shouldn't be confused looking at seized drugs or weapons. He looked back at the two men on their knees and studied their faces. Something wasn't right. They had gone down too easily.

"What's in the bag?"

A smirk creased Gunner D's face. Beau saw it, and the uneasy feeling grew.

"Nothing but fucking paper." Parker pulled out a fist full of the paper from the duffle bag and held them up for Beau to see. "This is wrong, Beau. This is all wrong."

Beau instantly recognized them as Crime Watch flyers handed out by the Community Relations Unit to help neighborhood awareness.

Confused, Beau was slow to process what those flyers meant. Parker flung the duffle bag to the ground and stood next to Beau, equally baffled. Headlights flooded the room through the open door as someone pulled up to the front. Additional engines were heard pulling up on the back side of the warehouse, followed by several car doors slamming and footfalls moving fast.

"This is a set-up." Beau kept the gun trained on the two men with one hand while he reached for his walkie-talkie. As he reached it, he could feel the vibrations from it transmitting something out, but it was too excited and garbled.

"We gotta get out of here, Beau. Something bad is about to happen." Parker's face was panicked.

"You got that right, pig. You fucked with the wrong niggas. See you in hell, Rivers!"

Beau and Parker looked at Gunner D who, along with his sidekick, fell to the floor. Automatic gunfire erupted from everywhere. Beau and Chance dove under a large workbench for cover. Beau flipped the table on its side for more protection.

Thunderous and deafening, the shots burst through the metal siding, creating pinpoints on the wall. A combination of the headlights and streetlights filtered into the warehouse with each round. Bits and pieces of shrapnel flew wildly from each bullet that ripped through, finding a piece of a car, a tool, or some other random object that stood in its path.

Beau and Chance hunkered down behind the workbench, trying to weather the volley of bullets. Debris rained down and pelted the cops. Gunner D and his buddy crawled like snakes out a side door. Beau was about to suggest they follow, but the hail of lead projectiles striking the cement floor between their positions convinced him otherwise. To follow would guarantee multiple gunshot wounds.

"We need a way out!" Beau screamed above the chaos.

Chance nodded and frantically scanned the rest of the warehouse, looking for an escape. Suddenly, the gunfire stopped. A ringing sensation assaulted Beau's eardrums. He popped up from behind the workbench to see that the entire wall of the warehouse looked like a piece of metal Swiss cheese. Movement near the door caught his eye, and he quickly fired a few shots. Someone had tried to enter and ducked back outside.

"Cover the back, Chance!"

"They're still alive. Go again," someone yelled from outside. The voice was familiar.

"Get down!" Beau fell on top of Chance as a second volley of automatic gunfire blasted, nearly taking them out. The workbench took the steady onslaught of bullets. Leaned against it from the safe side, Beau could feel each bullet hit resonating through to his side. It would only hold so many bullets, Beau thought, and it was fast reaching its limit.

With his attention averted to the front, Beau was sure he and Chance were being flanked. He checked the side exit and kept it in his peripheral vision while he scanned the back of the warehouse. He held his gun aimed at the back door, waiting for an attack. He was pinned down and hated every second of it.

"We need to move, now!" he yelled.

Chance patted his shoulder and pointed to a door opposite where Gunner had made his escape.

"There!"

The corner was darkly lit, and it was difficult to see the door. It was deeper into the warehouse, but away from the gunfire, so he agreed it was their best option.

"Go! I'll cover you."

Beau kneeled around the workbench and laid down covering fire while Chance scurried to the hidden side door. It was locked, but a quick shoulder jolted it open. The room was dark, but it was still more inviting than staying put.

"Come on, Beau."

His gun ran dry and he performed a quick reload before moving. After negotiating a maze of automotive junk, Beau dove through the door leading into the adjacent bay.

The automatic gunfire was slowing down to an intermittent staccato. From inside the warehouse, additional gunfire from a slight distance was heard, followed by yelling and running. The automatic gunfire stopped. Beau listened, trying to figure out what was happening.

"Over here!" Chance yelled out. Beau scanned the dark room but couldn't see him. "Here, Beau." Finally, Chance was standing by a dirty window in the back of the warehouse near another door that presumably led outside.

"Where does it go?"

"Look. There's a car right there, two shooters positioned on both sides, waiting for us to come out of that other back door. They were trying to flush us out."

"Mother fuckers!" Beau stepped up and looked outside the grimy window. He looked in the opposite direction to make sure no one else was set up outside of this door.

"If they're heavy out front and the back, they probably aren't covering the side like they should."

"Maybe, fuck! That's a big gamble."

"Got any better ideas? We can't stay in here."

More gunshots were heard out front, but the expected hits in the other bay didn't register. The bullets didn't follow them to the second bay, which told Beau their movement went undetected. They looked curiously at each other.

"Dylan and Dez?"

"Got to be."

"We should go now, then. If they're drawing fire away from us, we have to move."

"Fuck it, you're right."

"Is it unlocked?" Beau asked.

"Yeah. I'll pull. You lead the way. We haul ass out to the right and don't stop until we're out of range."

"Sounds good." Beau bowed his head and sucked in a deep breath. "This sucks!" He nodded to Chance.

Chance pulled the door. Beau took one step through the threshold and aimed in the direction where he saw the shooters waiting. Caught off guard by their emergence, Beau managed to catch one of them in his sights and hit him with a few rounds before he sought cover behind the car.

"Go, Chance, go!" Beau steadily laid down fire on the car, plunking the hood, fender, tires, and shattering the windshield as he backed away from the warehouse. Chance moved alongside Beau, watching his back. As they cleared a small collection of woods, the front of the warehouse came into view. Chance stiffened as he saw the shooters behind cover, shooting across the street away from the warehouse. Beau glanced back to see Chance take aim and fire his gun, sending rounds down range.

As they continued to move, Beau could see the entire front of the warehouse from a block away. Looking at where Chance was shooting, he was unsure if his hits landed, but he saw a man dart behind cover in the front yard of the warehouse.

Checking across the street, they saw Dylan Akers in a shooting stance from his knees, shooting around the front fender of a red truck.

"Dylan! Dylan!" Beau yelled. Dylan looked and smiled in relief. He turned his head and yelled something to his left. He assumed he was talking to Dez. Soon, they too, were retreating. Akers pointed off to the east, the direction they were running. Beau nodded, understanding what he meant: keep in that direction and he would soon find them.

With their backs to the warehouse, Beau and Chance were in a full out run. Sirens wailed in the distance, undoubtedly responding to reports of a gun battle. Adrenaline streamed through their veins, and Beau wasn't sure he had exhaled yet. He felt a throb in his lower back and reached under his vest, but didn't feel a hole or blood, only sweat and dirt. Relief set in and he focused on running forward.

"You okay?" Beau asked Chance.

"I think so." Chance patted his chest, stomach, legs, and butt. "Yeah, I'm good."

"Fuck me!"

"That was way too close."

The adrenaline continued as anger seethed throughout his body. They had just tried to murder him and Chance, set them up like rats in a cage just to shoot them dead.

Cowards.

Finding an empty parking lot several blocks away, Beau and Chance stopped to catch their breath and wait for Dylan and Dez. Thoughts of revenge swirled in Beau's head.

"That goddamn snitch, Biggins. He set us up, that fence playing piece of shit."

"Of course," Chance agreed.

"And that little shit, Gunner—"

"Pretty obvious who's pulling the puppet strings."

"Yes, it is. Toombs. They're all going to pay. I swear to God, they're going to pay."

Chapter 37

"Are you guys all right?" There was honest concern in Robert Shaw's voice. Dylan Akers had called him as soon as the team rallied back at the Lincoln Center. Thankfully, there were no significant injuries suffered, but there were enough near-death experiences to go around.

"Yeah, thank God."

"Any of them get hit?"

"Dunno, but there were bullets pretty much flying everywhere, so who knows."

Shaw let out a disappointed sigh.

"Sorry to disappoint," Dylan said sarcastically.

"I'm just glad y'all are all right."

"We're fine." Dylan's tone caught the attention of the other three.

"Listen, keep me updated on what you do next. Sounds like you have them hot and bothered. I got the deputy chief beeping in, probably to inform me about this shooting. I still have you covered on my end, but you might want to think about laying low for now."

"I'll think about it."

Shaw hung up on his end. The conversation had a bad aftertaste that lingered, and Dylan felt ill. Shaw was telling him to lay low, but that burned time he didn't have. The longer this project lasted, the more the likelihood of exposure. This gunfight would cause all sorts of ripples that would complicate everything. It would affect life in that neighborhood, life inside the department, and the lives of his team.

"What did he say?" Beau asked Dylan.

"Nothing important."

"You sure everyone is okay?"

The team gave a collective "Yeah."

"What's our exposure on the red truck rental?" Dylan realized in their haste, they had had to abandon the truck. No doubt it was part of the crime scene now.

Holcomb answered, "I used my alias. It shouldn't lead to us. Plus, I did it online and picked it up after hours."

"Okay, good."

Beau stirred in his seat. He looked uncomfortable. Dylan ordered everyone to make the necessary calls to their loved ones and let them know they were okay, something he'd learned was essential after being involved in a shooting. Beau remained in his chair, fidgeting. Dylan realized he had no one to call.

"Goddammit." Beau sprung out of his seat, ripped off his raid vest and set it on a nearby table. "What the hell? My back hurts like hell now, feels like I got kicked by a horse."

"What?" Chance ended his personal call and helped Beau check his back. "Lift up your shirt."

Chance saw a large bruise forming on Beau's lower back. He stepped over to the raid vest and flipped it over.

"Dude, you got shot!"

"What?"

Dylan and Desmond turned to see. Chance held up the raid vest, displaying a smushed nine-millimeter slug in the lower portion of Beau's vest.

Silence took over the room. The need to mention what could have been if Beau had not worn the vest was pointless. All of them knew the vest made the difference between life and death. The bullet was near his spine and could have dropped him where he stood.

"Fuck me," Beau said, quietly.

"Must've happened in the shop room after the gunfire started," Chance stated. "Waited until our backs were turned by that table? Opportunistic asshole!"

Silence came again.

"Hey, we're still here, right? They tried their best to take us out, and we walked right out of there," Dylan hailed. "Hell, they had to trick us to do even that."

"So what do we do now?" Desmond asked.

Dylan shrugged his shoulders. "I don't know."

Asking the team to move on was a high price. The stakes were far more serious than they had originally anticipated. He knew Beau was on board because of their circumstances, but Parker and Holcomb were innocent.

"Those assholes tried to kill us. Just like they tried to kill Sinclair." Chance spoke with emotion and stood up to emphasize his statement. "Fuck that. I say we hit 'em back, and put 'em in the goddamm ground."

"So we stay on this crew until they all go down. You're all still on board with that?" Dylan asked.

Collective nods went around.

Dylan eyed Beau and could read a distant hate behind his eyes. It was the same look he had that rainy night he told Dylan he would help kill George Shelley and Earnest McFadden. Now the hate was for Antonio Toombs.

"Good." Dylan was pleased. With the streets crawling with cops and detectives, it was too late to do anything tonight, and he suggested they head home.

Curious, Dylan asked before everyone left, "Y'all hit anyone? You think we killed any of them."

"Hell, I don't know," Holcomb answered. "Probably, but can't say for sure. I mean, I didn't see anyone go down."

"Pretty sure I hit one coming out of that back door with Chance. He's probably dead," Beau offered, playing back the scene in his head.

Chance snickered. His whimsical laugh seemed inappropriate during this conversation and everyone turned to Chance.

"What's so funny?"

"He's not dead." He looked at Beau. "That guy you shot."

"Oh yeah? How do you know that?"

"Easy. Two reasons." Chance held up his hand and counted along. "He wasn't confined to a jail cell and he was armed."

The air was instantly sucked out of the small makeshift office. Incredulous looks were shared among all except for Chance who sported a proud smirk. It was widely speculated throughout the department that Rivers shot a caged George Shelley in the basement of the courthouse, just not proven. Dylan appreciated the wit, but thought the burn crossed the line. He didn't need any dissention amongst the group.

Beau exploded in a boisterous laughing fit that quickly spread to Desmond and then on to Dylan. Chance reveled in his comment as everyone laughed. It alleviated some of the stress of the night, giving them a much-needed release.

Chapter 38

Melvin Polk stood on the familiar side of the police tape. Disorder and confusion spread out before him at the crime scene, and it all felt overwhelming. Too many questions surfaced, and there were not enough answers. Never a good start.

"You mean to tell me no one was killed? Nothing at the hospital yet?"

"Nope." Senior Detective Mike Durgenhoff stood next to his sergeant. "It started out here in the yard. You can see tire tracks in the dirt right there. Clearly, they left in a hurry, spinning out in the wet grass and mud."

Polk nodded.

Durgenhoff pointed to the east and across the street from where they stood.

"I got a shit ton more shell casings over there on the sidewalk, like whoever was shooting over there used those bullet-riddled cars for cover."

The light from the street lamp glinted off the shell casings that littered the street like tiny pinholes in the asphalt. The number was staggering and probably neared the century mark. Forensic Specialist Brennan Headley was busily working the scene in a white Tyvek suit. Her blonde ponytail bounced furiously as she moved from one point to the other.

"That two-twenty-three casings in the front yard?"

"Yep. Witnesses heard an automatic start first. Probably an AK or SKS rifle."

"What's that over there?"

"Forty caliber."

Polk nodded again.

Another detective, Daniella "Dani" Del Rio, called out to Durgenhoff from the side of the building.

"Hey, Mike? Got something over here."

Polk and Durgenhoff ducked under the tape and met Del Rio by the corner of the building. She shined her flashlight on the exterior and explained her find.

"Look there. The angle of those rounds coming in puts the shooter over there." She spun and pointed further to the east, through a clearing and away from where Durgenhoff found the forty-caliber casings. "Gives us another shooter."

"Or one of the shooters started here and moved over there, or vice versa."

Del Rio had not thought of that, which gave her slight embarrassment. The fluidity of a shootout had escaped her train of thought.

"Anything else?"

"Yes, look here." Excitement was added to her voice as she moved the beam of light to another spot on the wall.

"That," she said with satisfaction. Polk and Durgenhoff leaned and studied the small, red mark. "That is blood, boys. Fresh too. Whoever was shooting from over there hit someone standing in this area."

"Sweet. Make sure Brennan swabs that. Double check and make sure the crime scene tape goes around this entire property. This could have expanded to this whole damn street."

"Will do." Durgenhoff winked at the younger detective, pleased with her help. She smiled in return.

They continued to work the scene, trying to glean what happened from the evidence left behind. The number of bullet holes, shell casings, and various swabs taken throughout the mechanic shop was staggering and exhausting. Polk cursed the Chief for taking Chance Parker away from the unit and settled on making a formal complaint with the Chief's office in the morning. He needed manpower and that included one of his best detectives.

Special project, my ass.

After sifting through the scene in the front of the warehouse and across the street, they searched the inside of the shop. Surprisingly, there were no dead bodies. They were puzzled at how anyone could have survived had they been inside during this assault.

Not much evidence was found inside. More forty-caliber shell casings were on the shop room floor. There were some scuff marks on the ground like someone was crawling toward the side door. A large workbench was overturned, and the thick, top layer had absorbed a multitude of projectiles. Forensics carefully examined the first bay of the mechanic shop as it was the focus of the barrage, based on all the holes in the wall, but they didn't find any blood. Oddly enough, they found an inexplicable duffle bag filled with Crime Prevention flyers from the Tallahassee Police Department.

"Filled with what?" Durgenhoff asked.

"Flyers from the police department, strange right?"

"That makes no damn sense. You think it's some kind of message for us?"

"Who knows?"

As the focus of the crime scene processing moved to the back of the warehouse, Del Rio called to Durgenhoff again.

"I should just make you lead on this mess, Dani."

"Afraid I'll solve it faster than you?"

He chuckled back. "Yeah, probably would. What do you got?"

"Another shooter."

"Geez, another one. How many are we up to?"

"Shit, at least six or seven. Maybe eight."

"So what did you find?"

"By the car, more holes coming from over there by that door. I checked with patrol. They found it like that."

Durgenhoff looked at the side of the building and focused on the door. It was still open.

"Hmm."

"Found about four casings by the door and then a trail leading back toward the east. He was steady shooting and moving that way. I think whoever the shooter was right here, moved to the other location I found. Probably came from inside the warehouse. Maybe made a run for it that way."

"Makes sense. We just got to figure out who the hell these people are."

"No shit, right. But that tells you there was at least one guy in there when they started shooting."

"And no blood?"

"Not yet."

"Lucky guy. Do me a favor and double-check all the hospitals. I want you to call, not dispatch. They'll fuck it up by not asking the right questions."

"You got it. Hey, found more blood over here too. On the ground right here. Some more tire tracks in the mud, backing out over to Dunn Street."

"Great. Make sure we get it all. Good job."

Chapter 39

"Holy shit!" Gary Levine said, eyes wide with amazement after hearing Beau's story. "You know, I heard that shit all the way up here."

"You did?" Gary's neighborhood was about fifteen city blocks to the north of the warehouse, positioned on top of one of the city's seven hills. It was no surprise the gunfight could be heard at that distance.

"Hell, yeah. I was takin' the trash out and heard ratta-tat-tat-tat, ratta-tat, ratta-tat. Hell, thought I was back in Nam. Glad you're okay, brother. Seriously." Gary put his hand on Beau's shoulder as he worked a cold beer.

"Thanks."

Beau's mood grew somber and quiet. Gary could see the experience left his young friend shaken. He had seen the look before. It was expected back in the jungle.

"You know, soldiers who were in the country for the first time and survived their first assault went through the same thing. Many times they were battling survivor's guilt over their fallen buddies, but it's all the same bad shit."

"Bad shit is right." Beau pulled up his shirt, showing Gary the bruise, now a deep purplish color.

"Oh, damn, son." Gary got up from his recliner and retrieved a pack of frozen peas from the icebox. "Here, lie back on that. Should help. Brought you another beer, too. That will help."

"Thanks." Beau winced as he leaned back on the peas.

After more silence, Gary spoke. "You know, the bad shit I was referring to isn't the physical hurt. It's in your head."

"Yeah, I know."

"Talk to me, son."

"I'm fine, Gary. Really. It's not the shooting. It's not the near dying. It's something else."

"Oh. I see. It's not the shooting and it's not dying…."

Gary Levine had simplified his life in his later years. He'd led a life worth living and shared his wisdom with Beau during their short friendship. There wasn't much in all his years that he hadn't seen. He just wanted to help.

"Must be a woman," Gary said. He lowered his voice. "It's about Wendy, isn't it?"

Beau stirred. Gary was close.

"Talk, boy. I may die soon and God knows I can't have you hurting this bad without at least me trying to help!"

Beau smiled and looked at the old man. A few minutes of silence passed before he started talking.

"You know, losing my wife, my son, and even my self-respect, and then making things worse by killing a man in cold blood and falling in love with a woman I can't have…" Beau paused before moving on.

"It's okay. Keep going."

"After all that shit, I found myself holding on to a job where they don't give a shit about whether I'm dead or alive. The only friend I had in the world, I betrayed in the worst way. He'll find out soon and hate me, or shoot me…."

Another pause. Gary waited patiently, listening.

"All that shit just piled on top of more shit. The pile is so big that now I face a life sentence in prison or take a chance at being gunned down by criminals."

"I give you that, Beau. You've been through more than most, buddy."

"No kidding. But going through all that shit, all that stuff, I figured death was just waiting around the corner. I didn't care if I died, didn't care if I left behind my loved ones because I wasn't worth having around. I just stopped caring." Beau continued, "So, inside that mechanic shop when those bullets went flying…"

Another pause, but Gary finished the thought. "You realized something?"

"Yes."

"You realized you didn't want to die."

Beau nodded. "Yep."

Gary smiled with relief.

"Beau, that's a good thing."

"I could have just as easily walked into the gunfire, ensuring Chance could escape, or stayed in the warehouse and let them come get me. It would be worth the sacrifice."

"But you didn't. You fought back. You survived. You wanted to live."

"But what's there to live for, Gary? Prison? A best friend who is destined to hate me? A woman who wants nothing to do with me and a job that is trying to get rid of me?"

"You have a point, son." Gary thought for a minute. "But I never said being a sheepdog was easy, did I?"

Beau chuckled, welcoming the levity. Gary was wearing his tank top again, exposing his tattoo.

"What are you going to do?"

"Not sure, Gary. Not sure. But I need to do something."

"You'll figure it out. But remember the world needs more sheepdogs, Beau. There are far too many wolves out there."

***

Gary Levine had long since fallen asleep in his recliner. Beau didn't want to be alone so he stayed the night. He had practiced on the helicopter simulator game for hours until Gary had finally nodded off. The freedom of flying, albeit virtual, was addicting. He imagined how exhilarating it would be in real life. He checked his watch; it was nearly three in the morning.

Beau stifled a yawn and looked over at his old friend, nestled comfortably in his chair. He got up and adjusted a blanket up to his shoulders. As he did, Beau got a closer look at the sheepdog tattoo on his right arm. The ink was faded, but the image of the protector stood proud and gave Beau a warm feeling inside.

Beau sat on the couch and restarted the game. He chose a single engine EC120 model helicopter. Typically used for news choppers, he thought they looked like a dragonfly with a bulbous head and thin tail. It was the model in which he was most proficient. He let the rotor warm up and pulled back the cyclic for lift off. He worked the levers at his feet and built up enough speed to do an imaginary serpentine in the air. Weaving through the air, bobbing left and right, he realized that, along with the freedom, flying gave him a sense of control. He was in charge of his path, no one else.

Gary had taught him to scan the ground periodically and not to rely solely on the instruments for guidance. Beau saw the value in this for police tracking purposes, but he also figured it was a holdover from Gary's Vietnam days. He imagined the old salty pilot keeping a watchful eye on the rice patties for snipers.

As he continued the simulator, he saw a digital outline of trees and water from a lake. He pulled left and went over the blue expanse of the virtual water. He grew tired and wanted to end the flight. He let up on the left foot pedal and intentionally caused the chopper to spin out of control. He fought it for a minute, but then abandoned all control, allowing the helicopter to spin until it crashed into the imaginary lake.

A red light blinked. Words scrolled across the screen: *You are dead.*

He shut off the game and sat in silence. Gary slept peacefully in the recliner. A tremendous burden had settled on Beau's shoulders, and he was feeling crushed by the weight of it all. Gary had confidence that he would make it, but Beau was not as optimistic. His destiny, as was his practice, was to mess things up. He had no reason to believe this situation would turn out any differently. He was lost in a swirling vortex of bad shit.

Chapter 40

Detective Mike Durgenhoff looked up from filling out a property receipt to see Major Reginald Pritchard walking up to his scene. The hectic scene had drawn attention from command staff, but an actual in-person visit was unwarranted. Nonetheless, since Durgenhoff chastised Pritchard following the interrogation of Beau Rivers, he chose to stay clear from Major "Prick." Pritchard had seen fit to interfere with Durgenhoff's interview of the cop suspected of murder. Making demands that went beyond his expertise had soured the one chance they had at getting a confession. The Major's ego and incompetence had allowed Rivers to walk.

Pritchard walked straight up to Durgenhoff. "Detective, can you tell me what you've got here?"

"Hello to you too, Major."

"Yes, hello. What happened?"

"Excuse me, sir, but Sergeant Polk made all the notifications before taking off. Do you have some special interest in this case?"

"Detective," Pritchard repeated the rank as if it were an insult. "Do I need to hold some special interest to be briefed on a case?"

Durgenhoff relented. "No."

"I am merely concerned, as you are, with all the violence going on. I figured I would try and lend a hand."

It'd be a cold day in hell before I ever let you help me on another case!

"That's interesting, sir. I haven't seen you out on any of the other calls?"

Pritchard quit with the pretense and scowled at the homicide detective. "Just tell me what the hell happened."

Durgenhoff told him how the call of gunfire came in on 911 and that the officers didn't find any victims or suspects upon arrival. He told Pritchard of the numerous different shell casings, but that it was too early to determine who was involved.

"Looks and feels like a gang shootout over turf or maybe even some kind of drug deal gone wrong."

Durgenhoff withheld the presence of blood and did not mention the police flyers. He didn't know how they factored in just yet and didn't want Pritchard to muck things up.

"Gangbangers, huh?"

"Yes, sir."

Pritchard moved past the detective to survey the scene with his own eyes. Durgenhoff went back to cataloging the evidence. Pritchard stepped across the street to get an angled look behind the warehouse. He scanned the street where little, yellow, numbered markers stood in place of the myriad shell casings.

"That's a lot of shell casings," Pritchard said.

Durgenhoff looked up from his receipt, but didn't respond after he realized the Major hadn't actually posed a question.

"Any of these forty caliber?"

Annoyed, Durgenhoff stopped again and answered.

"Yes."

"What kind?"

"What kind?" Durgenhoff did not hide his irritation.

"Yes, Detective. I'm asking what kind of forty-caliber shell casings did you find?"

Durgenhoff looked over an arsenal of brown bags at his feet. Brennan Headley exited the warehouse door, carrying another identical brown bag and set it down with the others. It was full, like the rest, of collected evidence. She grabbed an empty bag and turned to head back inside. She didn't even notice Pritchard.

"Hey, Bren. Do you know which bag has the forties in it?"

"Are you fucking kidding me right now, Mike?"

"Easy, Bren." She spun around to scold the detective directly to his face, but abruptly stopped when she noticed the Major looking expectantly at her.

She bit her tongue and started sifting through the bags in search of the forty-caliber shell casings. She suddenly stopped going through them and looked up at Pritchard.

"Sorry, sir, but I put them in a white envelope and they've all been sealed already. And there are close to a hundred of them to sift through. I have my notes, but we won't examine them until later when I'll have some help."

Pritchard exhaled with disappointment.

"I could show you the pictures on my camera, if you like?"

"That'll work."

Moments later, after retrieving her camera from her truck, Brennan showed Major Prick the up-close photographs she had taken of the shell casings.

He thanked the Forensic Specialist and Durgenhoff and walked away from the scene.

"What's he looking for?" Headley asked.

"I don't know. He comes across as wily, but I think he's an idiot."

"But specifically shell casings? That's odd."

Durgenhoff was exhausted, but gave thought to the exchange with Pritchard.

"You're right. That is odd. And to asked specifically about the forty caliber. We have, what, like five other kinds of casings?"

Brennan counted in her head, then nodded. "Yes."

"Whatever. I don't know what he's thinking and, right now, I don't care. But what I do know is that this shit ain't going to collect itself."

"Ugh, it would be great if it did, though."

***

Due to the late hour, Reginald Pritchard opted for the elevator instead of climbing the three flights to his office. He bypassed the executive suite and pushed open the door to Internal Affairs. A groggy Russell Trek stood up from his cubicle.

"What did you find out?" Trek asked.

"Not a lot. Durgenhoff thinks it's a gang shootout, but…"

Trek cringed, "I don't think so."

"No, but we don't know it was Akers and Rivers just yet."

"I know, sir, but with those after-action reports you found." Trek stopped to formulate the rest of his thought. "The guys they referenced in the reports work that area, and it mentions that guy Antonio Toombs. When I ran utilities at that warehouse, it came back to an old lady with the last name of Toombs."

"I know."

"It's not a friggin' coincidence. Were there forty-caliber casings on scene?"

He nodded passively and added, "They were Winchesters."

Trek's face lit up, knowing that was the same as the department-issued ammunition. "That's going to be them. It's got to be."

Pritchard was not quite ready to buy. He had learned from his mistakes in the first bout with Dylan Akers and Beau Rivers not to act too hastily.

"I agree. But we need emphatic evidence first. Hard proof. We're not going to be able to match their Glocks, but it does add to the total circumstance."

"That has to be enough."

"No, not yet. I refuse to be humiliated again. But if we're right, and Akers and Rivers are involved in this, we will also have proof that Shaw knows about it and has overlooked or even sanctioned their actions."

"That's huge."

"Very."

"What do you want me to do about Harrison?"

"Huh?"

"The order from Shaw to follow Harrison. Could he be in on it, too?"

"No, dummy. That was a red herring. He wanted to throw us off his scent by serving up Harrison as a distraction and making himself look like he was helping and innocent. I'm willing to bet Harrison has nothing to do with any of this."

"Ah. Gotcha."

"Go home. Get some sleep. We're back on Akers and Rivers tomorrow and we won't stop until they both go down."

Chapter 41

Dawn broke, and the morning sun peeked through the thin slats of the blinds. Wendy Akers lay awake after a night of restless sleep. The discomfort of the pregnancy was bothersome enough, but after Dylan told her of the warehouse shootout, she nearly fainted. Only managing a few hours of sleep, her anxiety found her again thinking about their conversation.

***

After he had told her the night before, Wendy had flung her arms around his neck. "I'm so glad you're okay."

"It's going to take more than that to keep me from you and the baby."

She cried while he held her in his arms.

"It's not worth continuing this thing you're doing for the Chief."

Dylan didn't respond. She ran her fingers through his hair as he thought. He had told her it always seemed to soothe him no matter the level of stress.

Eventually, he'd spoken. "I underestimated him."

"Who?"

"This guy we're going after. We were lucky tonight, for sure, but I don't think we can stop. Not now."

"Why not? It's past dangerous. I can't lose you, Dylan. I've—we've lost too much already."

"It's for us, why we can't stop. I have to believe Shaw will hold up his end of the bargain if we take this guy down. I hate having it held over my head, but I can't really see any other option. He holds too many of the cards with the evidence he found."

Wendy nodded as a tear escaped. Dylan had wiped it away with a gentle swipe of his thumb.

"Don't cry," he'd said with a gentle smile. "We have to face the consequences of what we did for Caitlin."

The sound of her daughter's name caused her to let out a sob. Dylan had pulled her close and held her until she stopped. He had carried her to bed and they'd eventually fallen asleep.

***

She rolled over, the fear still present. Dylan was still asleep.

Wendy had been a cop's wife for over fifteen years and had dealt with the rollercoaster of emotions that came with the title. She never feared for him more than when she watched him sleep that morning. She was afraid that he was fighting so hard to be there for a son that might not be his. The thought of Dylan failing and the child belonging to another man paralyzed her to the core. Guilt washed over her, and she suddenly feared the future.

I have to tell him, today.

Wendy slowly rolled back over and struggled to sit up. She got out of bed and waddled her way to the kitchen. She started the coffee machine and poured herself a glass of orange juice. The life inside of her had a fondness for the drink. After a glass, he would do somersaults inside the womb. Sometimes he would jab her in the ribs, causing her to wince, but the reassurance that he was real and not just a mirage gave her joy.

She finished the juice and waited for it to filter down to the baby. As she scanned the refrigerator for breakfast ideas, she felt the first flitter of the day. She smiled.

"Good morning, my love." She rubbed her hand over her stomach.

"Let's see, what should we make for breakfast?" She looked blankly, not finding anything.

The baby kicked and rolled over.

"Oh yeah? Is that right?"

Wendy chuckled.

Suddenly, an excruciating pain shot through her bowels and caused her body to constrict. She leaned against the counter and gritted her teeth, bearing through the discomfort. Holding her stomach, she waited for the pain to subside. It lessened for a moment and Wendy stood up and exhaled, blowing out the pain. "Wow, that hurt. What are you doing to me?"

She took a step back to shake off the episode, hoping it was not the start of labor. She was only eight months pregnant and wanted to avoid complications before getting to full term.

Wendy looked back at the refrigerator and debated whether to open it or not in case it was the cause of those pains. She pulled it open. As the cold air blew against her face, her insides seized up and it felt like the baby was tearing his way out from the inside. She let out an audible groan, but stifled it, trying not to alert Dylan. She reached underneath her stomach trying to ease the pain, but her knees buckled, and she fell to the ground.

Panic set in.

No, it's not time. I haven't told him yet. I need more time.

Chapter 42

Strangely enough, it was the silence that woke Beau Rivers. The eerie calm in the small house was foreign. His body was stiff from the brief night's sleep on Gary's cramped couch. He glanced up and noticed it was mid-morning based on the sunlight coming in the window. He wiped his face awake and checked his watch: nine-thirteen a.m.

Beau stretched out his legs and arms, and let out a groan. He propped his head up to look around the living room, wondering about Gary. He kicked off his blanket and sat up, yawning and rubbing his face again, trying to wake up.

Out of the corner of his eye, he saw Gary still in the recliner. He startled Beau.

"Jesus, Gary. You scared the shit out of me, buddy."

Beau was met with silence.

He looked over at his old friend and saw he was still sound asleep in his favorite chair. But something was off. He was too still. Beau studied Gary's face. There was a strained look of pain. Beau realized Gary was awkwardly slumped over.

"Hey, buddy? You all right?"

More silence.

"Gary?" Beau shouted.

"Shit. Gary!" Beau leapt from the couch and reached for Gary. He checked his pulse and thankfully found one, although weak. Beau shook him, trying to rouse him awake. His body felt disconcertingly cold. Gary's body sat limply in the chair and didn't react to Beau's efforts.

"Come on, Gary. Don't do this to me, buddy. Come on."

Beau rubbed his knuckles roughly against Gary's sternum, but there was no reaction. Beau reached for his cell phone and dialed 911. He yelled out Gary's address and the need for an ambulance then tossed the phone aside. He pulled Gary from his recliner and carefully laid him on the floor.

"Gary? Gary? Come on, buddy. I need you to wake up, okay?"

The sunlight fell directly on the floor where Beau placed him. Illuminated by the natural light, Gary's color was a sickly yellow, more disturbing than usual. Beau checked for a pulse again. It had weakened from the moment before. Gary's chest rose and fell, but it was slight. Beau bent over and put his ear close to Gary's mouth. Air was moving in and out, but a laborious wheeze was present.

Without warning, Gary's body went totally still. Beau searched for a pulse and didn't find one. He listened for breathing but it had stopped. "Shit, no, Gary. C'mon!"

Beau leaned over Gary's torso, placed both of his hands in the center of his chest and began chest compressions. He counted each thrust aloud. It had happened so fast, the moment slipped into the surreal as he realized he was trying to keep his friend from dying. Only seconds ago, he had been asleep.

The silence was alarming. The only sound was Beau counting. His arms started to grow tired, and the muscles in his shoulders ached. Stopping wasn't an option. He needed Gary in his life and wasn't ready to go on without him. He was the calm in the middle of a chaotic storm and feared what would happen if he lost that part of his life.

After several rounds of compressions, he checked again for a pulse. He felt a faint bump, but there was not a second.

"Fuck!"

Beau let out a guttural cry and continued the CPR. He ignored the fiery burn that stung his shoulders and arms. But with each thrust, the pain grew. He feared his arms would seize, forcing him to stop and helplessly watch his friend die. Exhausted, he abandoned the counting.

The siren's wail of the ambulance broke the silence as it neared the house. Beau slowed the compressions when he heard the vehicle pull to the curb.

"In here!" Beau jumped up and opened up the door. "Bring a defibrillator. I just lost the pulse."

The EMTs heard the order and quickly reacted. One grabbed a small hand-held machine from just inside the ambulance and ran toward the front door. The machine looked like a boom box stereo with a small LCD screen in the middle and paddles on the side. They followed Beau to the living room.

"I found him in his chair over there. He had a pulse at first, but after I got him on the floor, I lost it. I've been doing compressions for several minutes now."

"Okay, does he have a pacemaker?"

"No."

The EMTs knelt next to Gary, cut his shirt off his chest, and applied two adhesive pads, one to his chest, and the other on his side just below his ribcage. The machine ran a diagnostic test based on its reading.

"Come on, come on." Beau watched nervously.

The machine spoke in a robotic voice. "Stand Clear." A buzz sounded and Beau saw Gary's body convulse and arch upward. The same robotic voice said, "Check for a pulse and reassess the patient."

"I got a pulse. Get the stretcher."

Beau ran out with the second EMT and helped him bring back the stretcher. Together they got it up the porch steps and into the house in record time.

Moments later, Gary was loaded in the back of the ambulance with Beau holding his hand. One of the EMTs steadily worked on Gary while the other drove. She asked Beau a barrage of health questions about Gary. He answered what he knew but it wasn't much. He felt ashamed he didn't know more.

She ran a line on Gary's right arm and began administering a saline drip. She reached across Gary and into a cabinet in the back. She pulled out a small box, ripped it open, and removed a syringe. She looked at Beau who was wide-eyed and worried.

"Epinephrine. It'll give him a nice jolt," she said.

As soon as the drug made its way into his veins, Gary's eyes fluttered. Beau squeezed his hand, willing his friend to revive.

"Hey, Gary. Can you hear me?"

His eyes still fluttered, but he didn't answer. Beau looked over at the EMT who gave him a sympathetic smile.

"Just keep talking to him. Seems to be working." She was just patronizing him, he knew, but it proved comforting. He smiled and nodded back.

"You're going to be okay, Gary."

She went back to the cabinet and got another small, brown vial, punched the seal with another needle, sucked it up the tube, and pushed it in the line leading into his vein.

"Gary, stay with me, buddy."

As the ambulance drove up the long ramp to the emergency room, Gary's tired eyes flipped open. He searched his surroundings. Beau squeezed his hand again and leaned in.

"Hey, Gary. You're in an ambulance on the way to the hospital. You passed out on me, man."

Gary responded to his voice and looked at Beau. Locking eyes with him, Gary suddenly relaxed. An odd reaction given the circumstances, Beau thought. It was like he'd been searching for Beau, and now he was found. It must be the drugs. Gary turned his head to look at Beau. He gave an endearing and thankful look.

Beau read it and understood. "You're welcome, brother."

The ambulance parked, and the rear doors opened.

"They're going to take good care of you, buddy."

Gary gave a weak nod. Beau released his grip, but Gary held on. Gary had something to say. Beau leaned in but nothing came out. Frustrated that he couldn't speak, Gary lifted his left hand and touched his right bicep, just under his sheepdog tattoo, and then lifted his finger at Beau and pointed toward his chest.

The message was clear. Beau smiled, then let go, allowing the EMTs to take him into the ER.

You are a sheepdog.

Relieved that he and the EMTs were successful, he took a minute to relax and sat down on the back of the ambulance. He wondered what could have happened if had he chosen to go home last night instead of bunking on Gary's antiquated couch. He envisioned finding Gary slumped over in his chair, lifeless.

Beau shook off the thought and gathered himself. He got up and walked into the ER to stay with Gary for a little bit longer.

"Hey, I'm with the guy they just brought in by ambulance," Beau told the nurse at the check-in desk. "Which room did they take him to?"

She scanned a monitor in front of her, "Ummm, no." She looked again to verify her answer. "He's in trauma bay One."

"Okay. Trauma bay?"

"Yes, sir. It's down that hallway," she said pointing behind him.

Concern turned into fear. The trauma bay was for patients who need immediate medical intervention. He tried to tell himself that was just where they took all patients who had near-death experiences. On the other hand, Gary had been stabilized and should have gone to an observation room instead.

Approaching the open double doors to the trauma bay, he saw a swarm of nurses scurrying around a patient and a masked doctor calling the shots. A machine above the gurney was holding a steady tone as the doctor yelled more orders. Beau felt the onset of shock as he looked in the middle of the chaos to see Gary Levine's fragile body lying still. After a minute, the doctor took a step back and, with his hands out to the side, called the time of death.

Chapter 43

Betting the late night kept Mike Durgenhoff away, Chance Parker snuck into the Criminal Investigations Division early the next morning. Unable to sleep after the warehouse shootout, he needed to know what was found at the scene. The Person's side of the division was quiet. Polk hadn't made it into the office, only Dani Del Rio was at her desk.

Chance walked quietly past her cubicle and over to Durgenhoff's. He peered over the partitions, looking for anyone else. When no one noticed, he ducked into Durgenhoff's cube and sat in his chair. A pile of paperwork sat on the corner of his desk. The papers were dated the day before and were stacked in no particular order. As was the senior detective's method, it would be sorted later. Property receipts, statement forms, and some supplemental reports made up the stack. He flipped through what he could, putting together bits and pieces. Scanning quickly, he didn't see any mention of his name. Beau's, Dylan's, and Desmond's weren't found anywhere either. Chance felt a sense of relief, but it was trailed by guilt. He hated keeping his fellow homicide detectives in the dark and hoped that wouldn't be the case for much longer.

After looking through the paperwork, Chance slipped out of Durgenhoff's cube and went to his own desk. His own pile of paperwork waited for him. He leaned back in his chair then reflected on the shooting. He had never been that close to the fire, but living through it gave him a confidence he wasn't sure he deserved.

He stared at a picture of his daughter, Victoria. After the divorce, she was his entire world and the shooting nearly ended everything. At that moment, Chance realized he needed to end this game they were playing with Antonio Toombs.

"Hey, Chance."

Startled, he turned to see Dani Del Rio standing in the opening of his cube. He greeted her with a friendly smile.

"Hey."

"Where the hell have you been?"

"Oh, nowhere and everywhere."

"Oh, shut up. Seriously?"

"Secret squirrel stuff, Dani. I'd have to kill you if I told you."

"You suck."

She scowled at him and pursed her lips, pouting. He smiled back.

"You hear about the shooting last night?"

A nervous twinge poked Chance, but he kept a straight face. "Yeah, I heard something. Heard no one got hit. Is that right?"

"Yes. So weird. I think there was, like, a hundred rounds found on scene. That's crazy."

"That is crazy."

"Them fools need target practice or something."

"Any idea who's involved?" Chance probed casually.

"Not really. I found some blood on scene, so hopefully, we get a DNA hit. Oh, hey. That reminds me, did Polk tell you about the CODIS hit on your double?"

Chance sat up straight with interest. "No."

Administered by the Florida Department of Law Enforcement, the Combined DNA Index System was used to compare evidence samples to known DNA samples. This was a treasure trove of investigative leads and almost always led to an arrest. Chance welcomed the news.

"Yeah, came in late yesterday, and we were going to jump on it, but then that shooting came out, so we scrambled to handle that."

"Where is it?"

"Somewhere in this mess you call a desk. Seriously, clean this shit up, Parker."

"Ha! Thanks, Dani."

Chance immediately sifted through the pile of paperwork looking for the FDLE letterhead. It was near the top. He pulled it from the stack and scanned the results sheet. The name that matched the DNA stood out in bold letters accompanied by identifying numbers. Excitement burst inside as Chance reread the name, making sure it was real and his eyes weren't playing tricks. It was a name he was very familiar with.

A minute later, he pulled out of the parking lot and dialed Dylan Akers's number.

***

The odd noise woke Dylan. He rolled over and reached for Wendy, but he was met by cold sheets. He looked around the room for her, but she wasn't there. The strange noise continued until he realized his cell phone was ringing. He grabbed it off the nightstand and read the caller ID. Chance Parker's name was on the display.

"Hey, Chance."

"We got him!"

Confused, Dylan drew a blank on what Chance was talking about. "Huh? Got who?"

"Xaxier Toombs. We got him."

"Okay, Chance, I just woke up. What the hell are you talking about?"

Dylan's first thoughts were that Xavier was one of the people shot last night in the shootout and had been found dead.

"Remember the double on Preston Street?"

"Um." Dylan thought. "Yeah, two dope dealers shot in the living room. A third jumped out of the window."

"Right. Well, one of the shooters took a hit in the doorway, left some blood on the wall."

"You got a DNA hit?" Dylan sat up, invested in the conversation.

"Yep, came back to Xavier Toombs."

"Oh, hell yeah."

"How do you want to handle it? I mean, it's not Antonio, but you know he's wrapped up in this."

"Let me get up and get dressed. Call Beau and Dez in. Let's meet in an hour."

"Okay."

Dylan hung up the phone and got out of bed. He showered and dressed while he thought about a plan for how to use the information Chance had just relayed. Given the difficult position Chief Shaw had placed him in, he had to ensure whatever move he made was maximized.

Contemplating what to do, Dylan suddenly realized he hadn't heard or seen Wendy since waking. He stepped out of the bedroom into the hallway.

"Wendy?" he called. Dylan looked around the living room and peeked outside to make sure her car was still in the driveway.

"Wendy? Babe, you here?"

Dylan made the corner and heard a light whimper from the kitchen. Behind the kitchen island, he saw her legs lying on the tile floor in a position that immediately caused distress. He rushed to her side. She was writhing in pain, holding her stomach.

"What's wrong?" he asked, his tone stricken with fear and panic. There was too much riding on the birth of this child.

"It hurts, Dylan. Something's wrong. It's different than before."

"Okay, I'm calling an ambulance."

Dylan grabbed the house phone and dialed 911. He told the operator to send an ambulance and spat out the address.

Back by her side, he held her in his arms. "It's okay, babe. The ambulance is on the way."

"Okay. I'm sorry, Dylan."

"Sorry? For what? We're going to get that baby delivered safe and make sure you're taken care of. You're strong, Wendy Akers. You can do this."

Wendy winced as she endured another wave of body-wrenching constrictions in her stomach and bowels. Dylan held on helplessly as she weathered the pain.

"It's okay," he repeated as he stroked her hair.

Wendy exhaled through pursed lips. The wave passed, but it left her exhausted.

After a few more minutes of waiting, Dylan heard the sirens of the approaching ambulance.

"I'm sorry, Dylan."

He chuckled at her. "It's okay. You have nothing to be sorry for. Hold on a second." He stood up. "I'm going to go let the EMTs in. I'll be right, back."

"No, Dylan. Wait?"

Confused, he asked, "Wait? Wait for what?"

Wendy hesitated.

"Let me go let them in. You need to get to the hospital."
"No, Dylan. I need to tell you something."

Chapter 44

Beau left the hospital and drove aimlessly. The bad shit had piled so high it would take a lifetime to shovel. Numb and distant, he was on autopilot, just wandering.

As he stopped at a traffic light, his subconscious broke him out of his trance. He looked around with an apathetic appeal. A red neon sign that read "Tattoos" hung above a small corner business and grabbed his attention. It glowed, even in the mid-afternoon sun, beckoning him. Instantly, Beau decided something and pulled in.

The tattoo parlor had just opened for the day. The man behind the counter who greeted Beau had both arms fully sleeved, hooped earlobes, dark-rimmed glasses, and a short hipster haircut. His skinny frame suggested he ate anything listed as organic. His eyes were slow, still blood shot from whatever he had ingested, injected, or consumed the night before. Beau didn't care.

"Can I help you?"

"Um, yes." Beau looked around the walls of the shop, studying the many options on display. There were homages to just about everything in pop culture, retro cliché's, sports, music, fantasy, animals, and an entire panel of skulls with various adornments.

"See anything you like?"

"Not really. You got more stuff?"

"Yeah, I got, like, literally several thousand images. Why don't you tell me what you're thinking about? If we don't have it, I could probably draw it."

Beau thought for a minute. "How about a sheepdog?"

"Like a German shepherd?"

"No. A sheepdog."

"Hmm." The tattooed hipster stepped in a back room and returned with a three-ring binder of plastic sleeves. It looked like a perp book.

He opened it to reveal hundreds of additional images. It was a perp book of tattoos. The hipster flipped to a specific few pages that had numerous breeds of dogs. He searched earnestly until Beau noticed an image that was nearly identical to that of Gary's right arm.

"That one. I want that one."

"Okay, great. I have some paperwork for you to fill out real quick and then we can get started."

Beau was directed to a back room with a chair that looked like it belonged in a dentist office from the 1950s. He sat down and thought about Gary while he waited. He missed him already.

After ten minutes of signatures and initials, the hipster donned gloves and the machine hummed to life. Beau sat there, still numb to everything. As soon as the needle pierced the skin of his right bicep, he felt the sharp bite of pain. He gritted his teeth as it felt like a knife digging into his flesh. Counteracting the numbness, he welcomed the pain. It reminded him he was still human. The hipster tried to carry on a conversation while he worked, but curt answers kept it one-sided until there was just the whir of the iron.

The sting of the needle lessoned as the artist continued. He finished the outline of the sheepdog and was now working on the intricate details of the fur and face. Beau sat still so the majesty of the animal could be captured. He wanted it to be perfect. He glanced down at the progress and saw the makings of a beautiful image. He sat back, thinking of his friend and shed a tear. He ignored it and let it roll down his cheek.

Chapter 45

"That it?" Antonio Toombs stood next to Clarence Biggins as he peered down a hill and through a thin patch of trees. He glanced over at the baser whose life he held in his hands.

"Yeah." Biggins was nervous and visibly shaking.

Those ten years in prison had left Antonio ample time to figure out that Biggins was the person who'd sold him and Figueroa out to the police. After coming up with the plan to lure Beau Rivers and his partners into a trap, he knew Biggins was the perfect bait. Convincing the snitch to go along was easy. A nine millimeter shoved halfway down his throat might have been the deciding factor.

"You sure?" The inflection in Antonio's voice was accusatory.

"Yeah, Tony Tombs, I swear."

Antonio raised a pair of binoculars to study the scene further.

"We went around back." Biggins pointed off in the distance. "Over there."

Toombs watched as his mind worked feverishly, contemplating his next move. He had to strike back, and after the failure at the warehouse, he was going to take matters into his own hands. The realization came that, although loyal, his crew lacked a certain finesse in their abilities. They were too sloppy and rough around the edges. Ten years of prison had managed to smooth out his own edges. He had used all that time to rethink his life and how he would, once out in the world, regain control and be the notorious leader he dreamed of being.

"So, no one else is there at night?"

"Nah, the clinic closes at seven. The other offices, I think, close at five," Biggins answered. "It should just be them."

Antonio nodded, pleased with his reconnaissance. He lowered the binos and took in the entire campus of the Lincoln Neighborhood Center. The neighboring cemetery offered public access and a thin tree line to watch and observe. An evil grin creased his face.

"Can I go now?" Biggins asked.

The grin erased from Antonio's face. He looked at the informer, allowing his soulless black eyes to bore into the pitiful man, making him cower.

"Do you see where we're standing, Biggs?"

Biggins looked around. "Yeah."

Before Biggins turned back to him, Antonio pulled out his nine millimeter and held it inches away from his head. Instinctually, Biggins fell to his knees and started to beg.

"Please, Tony. Please. Don't, man. I'm sorry. I did what you asked. Just let me go."

"You crossed me one time before, and that's one time too many."

"No, c'mon, Tony Tombs. Please?"

The man was a pathetic sight. Putting a bullet in his head would just end his miserable existence. Antonio leaned in, placing the barrel on the man's forehead, now beaded with sweat. Biggins closed his eyes. Tears pushed out from under his eyelids and streaked down his face. He sniveled and mumbled something that sounded like a plea to God.

"God can't help you now."

Antonio prolonged the man's agony as he slowly moved his finger into the guard and on the trigger. This was the best part. His life hung on a simple finger pull. Adrenaline coursed through Antonio's body, making it buzz with power. He reveled in the moment.

The sound of a car engine approaching interrupted him. Antonio pulled the gun away from the informant's head and shielded it behind his back. A car crested the hill and drove toward them. As it neared, Antonio knelt and put his arm on Biggins's shoulder.

"Don't move or say anything."

Biggins nodded, too afraid to do anything else.

As the car passed, Antonio buried his face as if in prayer. The car pulled down the hill and stopped in front of a gravesite. Two elderly women wearing big hats and matching dresses slowly climbed out. One carried flowers. They paid no mind to the two men up the hill.

Antonio stood up. He wanted to kill the weasel who sold him out all those years ago. But if he did, the women down the hill would hear and, in a matter of minutes, the entire area would be crawling with cops. That would ruin everything.

"Leave town. If I see you or hear of you, I will kill you, your family, and anyone who knows you and then bury you in this cemetery."

A glimmer of hope flashed in Clarence Biggins's eyes. "Yes, sir. I will Tony Tombs. I swear. I'm gone today."

"Get out of my sight."

Biggins stood up and tried to shake hands.

"Nigga, get out of here. I don't want to shake yo' hand."

"Okay, sorry."

"Run, snitch!"

Biggins took off on a trot, over the hill and disappeared. Antonio turned back toward the Lincoln Center and thought more on his plan.

Chapter 46

Chief Shaw called the afternoon meeting to order. He addressed the necessary budget and other internal issues as per the agenda, but it seemed rushed to Major Pritchard. The Chief was distracted like something was weighing on his mind. Pritchard bet the reason was the black op squad he had sanctioned with Dylan Akers and Beau Rivers. The shootout was less than eighteen hours ago, but he assumed it was fresh in Shaw's mind.

As the agenda was met, the Chief asked if anyone had anything.

"If there is nothing more to discuss, let's adjourn."

"Chief, I'd like to discuss something." Pritchard watched as the Chief hid his annoyance.

"Yes, Reggie."

"I noticed there was a quell in the recent violence, no doubt due to good police work, but with the shooting at the Dewey Street warehouse last night, I have concern that our response isn't working like we thought."

He noticed, albeit slight, the Chief winced at the mention of the warehouse shooting. Pritchard grinned and waited for his rebuttal.

"I haven't been updated by Sergeant Polk, but the way I understand, it's being worked as rival gangs shooting up the place."

"So the violence is still prevalent?"

"Now, Reggie, I never said we would completely fix the problem within the first several weeks. Things like this take time."

"But we've thrown so much manpower at this, you would think we'd have arrests by now."

"I have confidence in our guys to make the best case they can."

"Which guys are you referring to, Chief?" Pritchard couldn't hold back any longer. His verbal jab was met with suspicious eyes across the conference table. An uncomfortable tension filled the room.

After a moment of silence, Shaw broke the tension. "We're done with this meeting, today. Reggie, if you don't have anything helpful to contribute to the problem, keep it to yourself."

Pritchard rolled his eyes, noticing that Shaw avoided his question. It gave him confidence that he was right.

***

As Shaw rinsed his hands in the executive bathroom, his mind raced. He couldn't shake the thoughts of the shootout after hearing from Dylan Akers. He and Beau agreed to go after the criminals, but Shaw couldn't help but feel responsible if something terrible happened.

On top of the guilt, Shaw replayed the interaction with Pritchard. Pritchard had a confidence that concerned Shaw. He needed to know what he knew and mitigate any exposure. It could prove too costly if Pritchard interfered to further his personal agenda.

Shaw walked out of the bathroom and decided he needed to talk to Dylan Akers. He needed to get a handle on what they were planning next. As he finished drying his hands, he was met by Reggie Pritchard standing in his office. Candace stood behind him at the door with an annoyed look on her face.

"I'm sorry, he just walked in."

"It's okay, Candace. Please excuse us."

Pritchard had an impish grin on his face. He sat down and waited for the Chief to sit.

"You look like the cat that ate the canary, Reggie. What the hell?"

"You know, Robert. Don't give me this phony act anymore."

"What exactly am I being phony about?"

Pritchard came out swinging. "Let's start with those after-action reports in that bottom right-hand drawer."

"What!" Shaw sat straight up in his chair and his eyes went wide at the mention of the reports.

"Thought so. You did sanction Rivers and them to do all that stuff didn't you?"

"Hold on, Reggie. Hold on. You broke into my office and then into my desk? What authority do you have to even do that?"

"Don't change the subject, Robert. It doesn't matter how I got it, and we both know that. What matters is that you put together some sort of 'hat squad' to go take out these drug dealers."

Shaw deflated, knowing Pritchard was right. All the property within the walls of the department was not legally protected like in a house. It could be searched with little reason, if any was needed, under the authority of administrative regulations.

Pritchard continued, "First, I have that transfer order you initially lied about, which is also in the drawer. Then I have the reports in your desk that back it up. I'm sure if I keep digging, I'll find more."

Shaw remained silent, buying time to think his way out of Pritchard's crosshairs.

"I think I could get used to the title of Chief." Pritchard rested briefly in his seat. "Chief Pritchard. Nice ring to it, don't you think?"

"You're such an asshole, Reggie."

Pritchard smiled, relishing the moment.

"Can't you think of someone other than yourself?" Shaw sat forward and looked hard at Pritchard. "Can't you see that there has been a real difference made out there? Hell, we've seen almost a whole month of no violence because of what those guys are doing. In a neighborhood wrought with poverty, drug use, and historical indifference, those guys are actually turning the tables on these thugs."

Pritchard kept silent but with a smug look on his face.

Shaw continued, "I don't recall seeing you at the hospital that day Henry Sinclair was ambushed and nearly died. You didn't look in the eyes of those officers waiting to see what the hell I was going to do about it. Well, I'd had enough and I made something happen. If you can't see the honor in that, Reggie, then you can kiss my ass. You wanna be Chief so bad, you have to make tough decisions and not just sit in judgment of others."

Pritchard slowly nodded. He stuck his bottom lip out like he was in agreement. "I don't know what part of honor allows cops to brutally beat people."

Shaw had no answer for that.

"I don't know what part of honor says that it is okay to overstep the laws we swore to uphold just because you lost control of your city."

"But—"

"No buts, Robert. You allowed cops to abuse their authority. Dirty is dirty. That's something I think your predecessor failed to realize with that fiasco with Rivers and Akers. I thought you were going to be different and learn from his mistakes, but you're just as dirty. Actually, worse! You have them doing your dirty work."

"I know it is fighting fire with fire, but something drastic had to be done."

"Stay with the desperation angle, Robert. It might keep you from getting indicted."

"You're such an asshole."

Pritchard made a move to stand up and leave.

"What now?"

"What now? I'm not sure. I think maybe I bring you and the rest of those miscreants up on corruption charges, excessive force, abuse of power, and a whole lot of other shit I'll find."

Shaw sunk in his chair. Pritchard held his fate in his hands, which gave him a sickening feeling in the pit of his stomach.

The Major hesitated before leaving then turned back to Shaw. "I have one more concern, Robert?"

"What?"

"What else do you have locked up in that drawer?"

Shaw's heart stopped. He was sitting on a powder keg with a short fuse. If Pritchard learned of the evidence linking Dylan Akers and Beau Rivers to the murders of George Shelley and Earnest McFadden, everything would explode into a fiery ball of chaos. It would start a chain reaction he was confident he could not stop, not even with the best public relations specialist.

The hesitation was noticeable, but Shaw kept from reacting further.

"Robert," Pritchard said, sternly. "What else is in that drawer?"

In front of Shaw, was a line. Remaining on one side meant he was aiding and abetting murderers. If he stepped over, he admitted knowledge of a murder and failed to act, violating his vow of duty.

"Haven't you sucked enough blood from me already?"

Pritchard smiled arrogantly. "Never. Not until all dirty cops are removed from my agency. Even if that includes you."

Shaw's head lowered. He couldn't bring himself to just hand over the evidence. Pritchard stepped around to Shaw's side of the desk and opened the bottom right-hand drawer. Shaw had to fight every urge to wrestle him away and break his jaw for being such an insolent jerk.

Pritchard removed the case file, stepped back, and flipped it open, wanting to know what else had been kept secret. Shaw looked away, unable to watch. Pritchard devoured the contents of the folder and gasped as he found the proverbial smoking gun.

"Oh, Robert. I am thoroughly disappointed in you but, at the same time, impressed."

"Oh, fuck off, Reggie."

Pritchard laughed out loud as he left the Chief's office with the case file in hand. "Whatever makes you feel better. I'll be in touch, Robert!"

Chapter 47

After leaving the tattoo shop, Beau tried to check in with Dylan. There was no answer on his phone, so he called Chance. Chance rushed the conversation, but told him to come to the Lincoln Center and that something big was going down. Given the morbid start to his day, it was hard for Beau to get excited about "something going down," no matter how "big" it was. He parked around back and started up the outside stairs. His right arm ached from the tattoo.

"Hey, Beau. Where you been?" Chance was heading out of the back door and down the stairs.

Beau hesitated, so Chance kept talking. "Doesn't matter. We got something big. I got a DNA hit on Xavier from that double murder last month. We're going to jump on it tonight. I have a plan I think will work."

"That is big."

"Right. And hopefully we catch a break, and we're able to take out the whole crew."

"What about his brother, Antonio?"

"We'll need some luck to add him to our list because we don't have much on him. If my plan works, we should get some good evidence and go from there."

"Sounds good."

Chance started down the stairs, but stopped for a second and noticed the bright ink under Beau's right sleeve.

"What's that?"

Beau noticed Chance staring at his new tattoo. "Just something I felt like getting." Beau tried to cover it up.

"Come on, let me see it."

"Fine." Beau pulled back his sleeve, revealing his tattoo. The vibrant green was enhanced by an Aquaphor sheen. Chance leaned in and studied the details of the image.

"A sheepdog?"

Beau nodded.

"Nice. I like it."

"Thanks." Beau looked around and back to the parking lot. "Where's Dylan? I've been trying to call him."

"Oh, you didn't hear?"

"No, what?"

"Wendy had to be rushed to the hospital. He's there with her. They're going to deliver the baby today."

Panic gripped Beau's throat in a viselike squeeze. He tried his best not to overreact to the news, but his thoughts were consumed by Wendy and the fact he hadn't told Dylan what had happened between them.

"Shit, it's early. When are we moving on Xavier?"

"I got a few things to check out first, but at dark we need to move."

Beau checked his watch and noted the time. "All right, I'll meet you back here."

They parted ways, and Beau drove straight to the hospital. On the way, he rehearsed what he was going to say to Dylan; but no matter what he said, the scenario didn't play out in his favor.

But he deserves to know.

***

His patience had paid off.

The snitch was right.

Antonio Toombs removed the binoculars after watching the two cops talking on the back stairs of the Lincoln Center. He recognized Beau Rivers and Chance Parker, even from up the hill in the cemetery. He watched both leave in separate cars and wished he knew what they had said.

He played back the interaction in his head, trying to glean any additional information he missed at first glance. Parker had been in a hurry and Beau had ambled up with no sense of urgency, but as they spoke, Rivers tensed up and left in a hurry. It told Antonio whatever Parker had told him, caused Rivers anxiety. It felt personal to Antonio. Something that caused a reaction like that is a weakness and ripe to exploit.

The ladies with the fancy hats had left the cemetery. No one else was around. Antonio removed the nine-millimeter Beretta from his back waistband and double-checked the magazine. It was loaded to maximum capacity. He slammed the magazine back into the well and gripped the pistol tight in his right hand. He loved the sense of power the gun bestowed. He ignored the compulsion to fire off a few rounds just to exude that power, stuffed it back in his pants, and set off down the hill.

He pulled out his cell phone and dialed Xavier's number.

"Hello?"

"X, it's Tony. Y'all hangin' out at the new crib?"

"Yeah, where you at?"

"Don't matter. Y'all stay put, but be ready to scramble if I hit you back, a'ight?"

"Yeah, a'ight."

"But, remember I'm there at the house, ya here?"

"I gotchu, Tony Toombs. I gotchu."

Antonio hung up the phone. He was on the other side of the fence that ran the length of the cemetery and bordered the back side of the Lincoln Center. He checked the surrounding area and quickly scaled the fence. Now on the property, he crept up to the back door and let himself in.

It was time to take matters into his own hands.

Chapter 48

Parked underneath the Women's Delivery Center, Beau sat in quiet. He gathered his thoughts while watching the dash clock, knowing he was procrastinating. The fact that he may now have a son seemed surreal, but it also meant facing Dylan. He took a deep breath and forced himself to get out of the car.

He walked to the building and rode the elevator up one floor to the reception area. He had a drone-like awareness, as if he was watching himself.

"Can I help you?" The nurse at the reception desk addressed Beau.

"Um, I'm here to see Wendy Akers, I was told she came in earlier. Has she had the baby yet? Is she okay?"

The nurse typed on the keyboard and read the monitor that faced away from Beau. He tried to read her face while she typed, but she didn't give any hints.

"I can't go into detail, but yes." A genuine smile put Beau at ease. "A healthy baby boy arrived at three-fourteen p.m. and Mom is doing good."

A tremendous sense of relief came over Beau, and he shared a smile with the nurse. He had had the same feeling when Scotty was born. Visions of holding a newborn came to him. The robotic feeling faded as he felt his heart beat again.

"Would you like for me to let them know you're here?"

"Um, well, it's not too soon is it? I'm sure they want to be alone right now."

"I can call back there and ask."

If the baby was his, Beau desperately wanted to see him and hold him. But, hearing the good news of a healthy delivery and that Wendy was doing all right, he was surprisingly satisfied. He could turn around and go, leaving his sordid past behind. Ruining the moment was the last thing he wanted.

"You know what, on second thought, I'll just come back later," Beau told the nurse.

She was in the act of dialing the room when she stopped and hung up the receiver. "Oh, okay. I'll let them know you stopped by. What was your name again?"

"Beau," he said, as he turned for the elevator.

He pushed the down button willing the doors to open. He escaped any dramatic confrontation, and suddenly, he wanted to disappear. He remembered what Wendy had told him a few nights before. No matter whose child it was, Dylan was going to be the father and raise the boy. Beau's feelings did not factor into her equation of family. She wanted to cut him completely out of her life. He was the mistake she needed to erase. Beau's heart ripped in half, knowing even if he was the father, he would never be a part of his child's life.

He furiously stabbed at the elevator button as if it were directly related to its response.

"C'mon, goddammit!"

A chime dinged and the doors opened. Beau stepped inside and punched the ground floor button. He watched the doors close and instantly felt better about leaving. He exhaled. Just as the doors closed, a hand reached in and the doors retracted. As they peeled back, Dylan Akers stood on the other side. He stepped in and joined Beau for the ride down.

Oh, shit!

"Hey, Dylan. How's Wendy?" Beau didn't know what else to say.

Dylan turned and faced Beau without a response. His eyes told Beau that he knew everything. There was no denying. It was all out in the open. Immediately, Beau's shoulders sank, his eyes lowered. He was standing at the base of a mountain as an avalanche of bad shit came rumbling down: he was about to get buried.

The elevator stopped at the ground floor, and the doors opened. Newly made grandparents of another newborn stood with flowers, gifts, and smiles, waiting for a ride up. Beau scooted past them as did Dylan, and they exited out of the small ground floor entrance and into the parking lot.

As soon as Beau got about ten yards from the door, he turned to address Dylan. He wanted to apologize. He was met with a right hook across the jaw. The blow knocked him to the ground, and stars flashed in his peripheral vision. Dylan advanced and as Beau tried to get up, he was met with another crushing blow, this time to his left cheek.

Beau stayed on the ground, bleeding from the corner of his mouth. Dylan hovered over him with clenched fists and flared nostrils, seething with hate.

"Get up!"

"No."

"Get up and fight me!"

"No."

"Get up, Beau!"

"I'm not going to fight you. I'm done fighting. I'm done with everything."

Dylan pushed Beau between two parked cars that shielded them from prying eyes. Dylan pulled out his gun. He pointed it at the head of his longtime friend.

"Go ahead, Dylan. I don't blame you. I deserve it. Do it."

"Are you in love with her? Is that why you park down my street and watch, because you love her?"

"Yes."

"Goddammit, Beau! How could you?"

"I'm sorry."

"Sorry isn't good enough."

Dylan pushed the barrel against Beau's head. He could feel the cold steel flushed against his temple. Only the pull of a trigger would end everything. He imagined the hot lead tearing through his brain and the insurmountable pain that would follow before blinking into death. It wasn't a question of if—Dylan was capable of pulling the trigger. It was when. He closed his eyes and waited for it to be over.

"Ahhhhh. Fuck you, Beau." Dylan removed his gun and stepped back. "Fuck you!"

Beau shrunk even lower, realizing he wasn't even worth killing. "She loves you, Dylan."

"What?"

"She loves you. Always has, always will. What happened between us was nothing more than a mistake. And although I hate being apart from her, I can't imagine life without you as my friend. You're the only one I have."

Dylan didn't respond. He let the gun hang loose by his side. Leaning up against a car, he caught his breath.

"I've realized that I will always be a fuck-up, Dylan. Somehow, bad shit seems to follow me everywhere I go. Why you've been my friend for this long, I'll never understand, but I am grateful. I've done something unforgiveable, so I won't even ask."

"Shut up, Beau." It was slight, but there was a friendly tone to Dylan's voice. "I know I wasn't the best husband after Caitlin died. I can see where I pushed her away and shut her out. I can see where she would've been drawn in by another man who gave her attention, but you as my friend, what we were going through at the time. You shouldn't have done it. That's crossing the line."

"I know. You're right."

"I'm still not there, but it's taken a lot to even want a family again. Losing everything like that made it hard to want to love anything again. I couldn't bear the thought of losing someone again. I knew I wouldn't survive. But the day Wendy told me she was pregnant, something came alive in me again. I found life was worth living, and with time, I too could heal."

"You deserve to be happy. Both of you do."

"I was, until I heard about you and her."

Beau sank back down to the ground.

"Although, I am angry with you, I feel somewhat responsible."

"Don't. I take all the blame. I should've sent her back home to you that night. Instead, I gave in."

"I don't want to hear any more."

"Sorry."

Dylan holstered his gun and stared blankly off into the distance. He stayed leaning against the car like he wasn't ready to leave. Beau got up, dusted himself off and checked his bloody lip. It was beginning to swell.

Beau stood next to Dylan as he always had. He was relieved that Dylan finally knew. The awkwardness that he felt around Dylan evaporated and gave him the ability to move on. Forgiveness wasn't an option, and Beau knew the friendship was over. But he found solace knowing that Dylan could move on and live his life with Wendy.

"He's mine, you know."

Beau looked over at Dylan with a puzzled look.

Dylan read the look on Beau's face. "The baby, he's mine." His tone was final. "He looks just like Caitlin did when she was born with the same smushed face and pouty lips. I don't need a DNA test to tell me that baby is mine. I know the timing of everything, but I got to thinking after Wendy told me there was a chance the baby was yours. The night Caitlin went missing, we actually had a date night and were intimate. It got overshadowed and forgotten because of what else happened that night, but that must've been when we conceived."

Dylan was convincing enough that Beau didn't question his conclusions. He grew saddened and disappointed. He had imagined, if the child had been his, it would be a bright shining light in the eternal darkness of his life. But it was not meant to be, and he was thankful at the same time because it was for the better.

***

Dylan looked down at his right hand and tightened his fist. His knuckles ached and the pain was excruciating. However, he felt better beating on Beau after an afternoon spent riding a hellacious roller coaster of emotions. In the last few hours alone, he had learned of his wife's infidelity, held his newborn son, and punched out his best friend. Staring blankly into the distance, he hadn't the slightest clue where this ride was going next.

"Good, I'm happy for you." Beau spoke after Dylan explained the baby was an Akers. "You're the best father I know."

Beau meant well, but the praise felt a little empty given the circumstances. Dylan let it hang in the air.

He checked his watch and noticed he'd been gone long enough. He needed to get back to Wendy and baby Phoenix.

"I need to get back up there."

"Okay." Beau sounded rejected, but Dylan wasn't ready to care.

Without saying good-bye, Dylan walked off toward the Women's Center, leaving Beau behind. As he reached the door, his cell phone buzzed in his pocket. Expecting a well-wisher, he pulled it out and answered. It was Chief Shaw.

"Hey, Chief."

"Whatever you're going to do with regards to our side project, it needs to happen now."

Dylan froze.

"Okay, why? What happened?"

"Pritchard found the evidence against you and Beau. He's coming after you. I'm sorry. I can't protect you any further."

"Goddammit!"

What else could go wrong?

Shaw spelled out how Pritchard became aware of the evidence linking them to the murders of Earnest McFadden and George Shelley.

"How the hell did he do that?"

"That's not what you should focus on right now, Dylan."

"Easy for you to say. You're not on the other end of this thing. What aren't you telling me?"

"I'm not getting into that right now. Just push forward. I'll be in touch."

"Wait—" The line went dead. "Shit!"

Dylan spun around to see Beau standing just a few feet away, listening to his end of the conversation.

"What?" Beau asked.

"Fuckin' Shaw. He said Pritchard knows about the evidence against us. Says he's coming after us. He didn't say how long we have."

"Fucking Shaw! I knew he'd double-cross us."

Both fell silent, letting their minds soak in the news. After a few minutes, Dylan spoke first.

"He wants us to keep going after Toombs."

"Fuck that! Why should we do anything for that man? He sold us out and I bet you he did it to save his own ass."

"I don't know."

Dylan let his thoughts move and digest the information. He considered several different angles and settled on a course of action. He was angry, but he wasn't surprised.

"I can't. I need to be here, but I need you to go with Chance and Dez tonight. Finish the job."

"Dylan, I'll do anything for you, but this is stupid. We're going to get arrested. Why do something more stupid? Or were you thinking about going out in a blaze of glory?"

"No, I'm hoping not to go anywhere."

"I don't know, Dylan."

"Listen, if you want to start making it up to me, go! Take care of business and finish the job." Dylan had a pleading look in his eyes that managed to change Beau's tune. "Please, just trust me."

"Fine, I'll do it for you."

Chapter 49

Lying in wait, Antonio Toombs patiently sat in the adjoining room of the cop's headquarters. He had crept up closer to the Lincoln Center after Beau Rivers and the other cop, Parker, had left. He watched as the last clinic worker departed for the day and slipped through the back door. He snooped around and found some paperwork and other things left behind by the dirty cops, making it obvious this was their base of operations. He scavenged through some of the old desks pulled from a larger pile in the corner, looking for anything describing their next moves against his crew, but he found nothing. He checked his nine millimeter in his waistband. He removed the magazine and rubbed his thumb over the bullet in the top of the stack. He shoved it back in the well, pulled back the slide and let it rip.

I love that sound.

Making his way around the room, Antonio opened a door to what he thought was a closet, but it actually led into another identical room. He stepped inside and pulled the door shut. He stood with his nose to the frame and, through a tiny crack, could spy into the first room. Taking inventory of what was in the neighboring room, he saw more desks and piled up junk. Thoughts of trapping the corrupt cops inside and using the old desks to burn the place down came to mind. He would stand on the top of the hill in the cemetery and watch them burn to death.

However, they had proved themselves more than resourceful, escaping from the warehouse, and a fire wouldn't be as quick as a carefully aimed bullet. He was going to do it up close and personal. He stared at the chrome slide of the Beretta gleaming in the waning daylight. Its awesome power reverberated through his body, giving him a sense of supremacy.

He waited in the darkened room for his prey to return. He was the spider and the Lincoln Center was his web. It was now a matter of patience and discipline; two things he had mastered during his ten-year prison stint. *All I have to do is wait.*

***

On the way to the Lincoln Center from the hospital, Beau came up with his own plan. He was tired of all the bad shit following him around and needed to make things right. It was time for action; he just needed to figure out how. He thought about how his inaction had led to Caitlin's death, acting on his lust for another man's woman, and taking the life of a man in cold blood. It was a resume fit for the damned, not for him. He thought back on his academy days with Dylan and how he had sought to change the world. He grew angry at how he allowed the disgust of the world to stain his soul and turn it black. He had once believed he was strong enough to fight back.

Gary Levine had believed Beau was a sheepdog, a protector. Beau didn't feel the label was justified. He did not feel worthy to be called a sheepdog and felt more like a selfish wolf. Rubbing his face, he felt the welt forming on his cheek where Dylan had punched him. It was already tender to the touch.

Beau pulled up to the Lincoln Center and parked. Chance and Desmond weren't there. He texted Chance, asking where he was and if he was set to go after Toombs. He was ready to get it over with. There was no telling when Pritchard would drop the hammer if he had found the evidence to arrest him for murder.

Beau checked his phone, but Chance had not replied. Beau sat in his car and looked around the empty parking lot. All the county workers and clinic employees had gone home. The stillness of the quiet car was calming, and Beau actually felt relaxed. A gust of wind kicked up and blew past his car. There was dampness in the air. He looked up at the treetops whipping around and the dark clouds swirling above. A storm was coming.

How appropriate.

As the wind howled and the gray clouds swirled, Beau walked up the back stairs and into the Lincoln Center. The rear entrance was left unlocked, and he walked in, strolled down the hall and into the small makeshift office. The occasional whistle of air from the approaching storm broke the silence; otherwise, it was still.

Beau walked in and sat down at a desk. He thought about Dylan and all the pain he had caused him. He rubbed his cheek again. The welt had already set, making his face feel tight.

How can I make it up to him?

As soon as Beau considered this, the answer came in a sudden revelation. It was so simple and yet so easy, he was ashamed he hadn't thought about it sooner. He turned to tell someone and hear it said out loud, but then realized he was alone. He turned back to the desk and immediately felt compelled to write it down, to let Dylan know how he was going to make things better. He searched the desk for paper but it was bare. He walked out into the hallway and down the corridor to the county offices. The door was locked. He checked the clinic and the offices were also locked. He figured as much. He checked the reception area and saw a copy machine off to the side. He pulled out one of the paper trays and snagged a few blank sheets and made his way back to the office.

Motivated by his newfound idea, he took to writing his plan for Dylan's eyes only. He let the pen work its magic. It was like the words already existed on the paper, he was just making them visible.

A shuffle noise broke his concentration. He perked up and twisted in his seat to look at the back of the room. He glanced out of the windows, seeing the beginnings of the storm. He moved back, pegging the noise from just beyond a door in the back of the room. He fought off an eerie sensation that someone was watching him as the paper and pen begged him to finish the letter to Dylan. A gust of wind whisked through the outside screen, and Beau figured it was the source of the noise and went back to writing.

As he finished the letter, he signed his name and added his badge number. A muffled clank came from down the hallway. Someone had walked in the back door. Footsteps followed and Beau folded up the letter he had written. The makeshift office door opened, and Desmond Holcomb appeared in the doorway.

"Hey, there you are. Chance has been tryin' to call you. You ready to roll?"

"Yep, I'm ready."

"Good, let's go. He's waiting on us over by the new target."

"Okay, gimme a second. I'll follow you over there."

"All right. But Chance wants to roll now, says it's important we don't let this window close."

"Okay, I'm right behind you."

Desmond let the door close on the office, and Beau heard his footfalls lead to the back door. He picked up his letter to Dylan, but the shuffle noise from the back of the room returned, this time it was louder. He put the paper and pen down and gave his attention to the noise. He moved stealthily to the back of the room. He took careful deliberate steps, minimizing the sound, and slowly removed his gun from the holster. He pulled it up to his waist as he neared the door.

The noise stopped but he was invested to the point he couldn't back away. If it was Pritchard or his do-monkey, Trek, spying on him, he was going to make things difficult. He stopped within arm's reach of the door and listened. There was no sound, no heavy breathing, or the scratching of a scavenging rodent. Beau slowly reached for the doorknob with his left hand, gripping his Glock tight in his right. He turned the knob ever so slightly until the lock was free from the frame. In a quick violent pull, the door flung open and he lunged into the closet ready for a confrontation. Only it wasn't a closet. It was a small anteroom that opened up to another room, the same size as the makeshift office. Beau stepped clear of the connector room, searching the larger, darkened room with his eyes. Only a sliver of daylight peered in the room. From what he could tell, it was identical to the headquarters, and it too was used to stockpile old student desks, bookshelves, and other antiquated stuff, but nothing was there.

Beau stood at the threshold, staring into the darkness. There were infinite places to hide and suddenly he felt vulnerable. As many times as Beau had stared into the abyss, it never got easy knowing that one day it would not let him go.

"Hey, Beau? You comin'?" Desmond barked. He startled Beau, and it broke him from his ghost chase.

"Thought I heard something."

"Come on, Chance is waiting. Says we have to do it now or never."

"All right."

Beau holstered his gun and followed Desmond out. It was time to end this game they were playing with Antonio Toombs. He didn't understand why Dylan wanted to stick with their plan despite the Chief giving up the evidence to Pritchard, but he made a promise to his friend that he intended to keep.

***

Through the tiny crack in the door, Antonio Toombs watched Beau Rivers sit at a desk with his back turned. He waited and watched. The room was too large for him to sneak across and shoot him. He knew from his earlier reconnaissance, the door he stood behind creaked when it opened. The noise would be a dead giveaway, and he needed to win the ambush, not give the dirty cop a fighting chance.

I need to lure him to me.

Antonio gripped his Beretta tight in his hand and pushed a chair across the dusty terrazzo floor. It scooted just enough to catch Rivers's attention. Antonio kept spying through the crack. Beau turned and looked his way, but it wasn't enough for him to investigate. The wind kicked up outside, and Antonio figured Beau would blame the noise on the weather and think nothing of it.

Suddenly, another noise arose beyond the room, giving Antonio pause. Rivers didn't seem concerned about it as he remained sitting. The door opened and just beyond his sight line, he heard another man's voice speak. He listened carefully and quickly realized it was one of the other dirty cops. Antonio panicked, thinking that his plan didn't account for two cops. This had to be done methodically and with no traces left behind.

The second cop left and Antonio watched as Rivers began packing things up. Antonio heard the outer door shut and knew he and Rivers were the only ones in the building. Even with the second guy outside, he could kill Rivers and escape before he came back.

This was his opportunity. He kicked the same chair, sending it sliding several feet and making a loud shuffle sound. Rivers turned and keyed in on the door. He slowly walked toward the door and out of Antonio's sight. Toombs backed up and quickly took a position in the rear of the room, hidden in the shadows. He aimed his Beretta at the connector room, which he was counting on Beau Rivers to come through any second.

The door flung open and Rivers stepped in, straining his eyes to see into the black. Spending the last hour in the room, Antonio's eyes were well adjusted. He slowly rose his gun and took aim at the head of Beau Rivers. Looking through the sights, there was a faint glimmer on the chrome barrel. His heart thumped as the power surge flowed through his body and into his trigger finger. Beau stood there as if he was waiting for death to appear. Antonio was going to oblige him. He closed his eye, steadying his aim. He slid his finger down and around the trigger.

This is it.

"Hey, Beau? You comin'?" The other cop suddenly returned, his voice boomed inside the room. Antonio quickly ducked behind the pile of desks, sitting quietly. *Dammit.*

Ambushing one cop was one thing, but taking on two at the same time would increase the odds of failure. Antonio needed that certainty. His empire demanded it. He wanted to be king, not a martyr.

Antonio remained ducked in the dark corner and listened carefully as he heard the men finally leave. He heard two different cars speed away and then gave it an extra minute before he stood up from behind the pile of desks.

"Dammit!" he yelled, his voice echoed in the dusty room.

He walked through the connector room and back into their headquarters. Rivers had been at the desk, doing something intently for quite a while. He had looked to be writing something. Antonio checked out the large, paned windows and unlocked one from the inside. He wasn't ready to abandon his idea of attacking them on their home turf. He wanted another avenue to use in his favor.

While unsatisfied with the failure of his plan, he was pleased that, at least, the venue wasn't tainted, and it left the chance for another opportunity. Walking past where Rivers sat, Antonio saw a folded up piece of paper left behind. On the perpetual hunt for intelligence on his opponents, he picked it up and read it. As he absorbed the contents, his eyes widened in disbelief. This was no mere nugget; this was a treasure trove of intelligence. He reread it again from start to finish, making sure he fully digested its contents. It was nearly too good to be true.

"Now, I got you both."

Chapter 50

The new place felt foreign. Far removed from the ghetto and in a west Tallahassee neighborhood, it was hard for Xavier to feel at home. Antonio promised it was the smart play, but he was uneasy about all the moves his older brother was making without considering his own input. It was quiet and "off the radar" of the police, Tony said.

Xavier checked his phone, hoping to hear from Antonio who had been secretive about what he was doing. When he had left earlier, Xavier had asked him what he was up to.

"Don't worry about it, little brother."

"C'mon, man. I can help. Hell, I used to lead this crew."

"Not anymore," Antonio said with a sharp glare. "Listen, I'ma go take care of some business and less you know the better. You hold it down here. And just cover me, okay?"

Xavier sucked his teeth. "Whatever, bro."

"Hey? I got you. I need you to get me, okay?"

"A'ight, Tony, I got you."

Shouts and laughter came from the recreational room in the back of the house. All the guys, and Gigi, were hanging out, playing video games and listening to music. Xavier checked the large bay window and saw the wind whipping the trees around outside. He grew worried about the storm moving in and eyed his prized possession, the '86 Monte Carlo, sitting in the driveway. He stared at the car, reveling in the new coat of wax he had just added that afternoon.

"Yo, X. You comin' bro?" Chris was inviting his cousin back to the party.

"Just checkin' on my ride."

"What? You think some jit gonna break into it out here?" Chris flashed the handle of the pistol stuffed in his waistband. "I don't think so!"

Xavier laughed.

"That's what I thought, dawg. Come get some Call of Duty, and let's get fucked up!"

"Ah'ight, sounds good."

Xavier followed Chris into the rec room. Once an outside porch, it had been converted into a family room by the previous owners. Now it served as the hangout for the crew of Tony Toombs. The rest of the house was the new base of operations, moved to this location just before the warehouse shootout.

The pungent odor of burnt cannabis filled the room. Dookie had a blunt hanging from the corner of his mouth while he fidgeted in his seat, working the game controller. His efforts were displayed on a large screen television mounted on the wall. Gunner D was next to him, working the second controller and screaming at Dookie in makeshift military terms he picked up from playing the simulated war game.

Just as Xavier reached for a cup of liquor, the lights dimmed, pausing the flow of the party, followed by a sharp crack of thunder that boomed and shook the house.

"Holy fuck."

Other choice words followed then laughter resumed the party.

"You jumped like a little bitch, X." Dookie teased.

He cackled before taking another hit from the joint. "Fuck you, Dook!"

***

"Now is as good of time as any." Desmond's voice came over the radio. A bright flash of lightning lit up the night sky and a deafening clap of thunder chased as the approaching storm announced its arrival.

Chance looked outside as the raindrops started plunking the roof of his car and blurring the windshield.

"What do you think?" he asked Beau who sat in the passenger seat.

"You're call, bro. Storm's going to get nasty and will probably cover any noise we make going up."

Nervously, Chance nodded, taking in the suggestion.

"You think this'll work?"

Beau grinned, sensing his partner's anxiety. "Only one way to find out,"

Chance relayed over the radio to Desmond that they were ready.

"Copy that. They're all smoking weed and playing video games in the back room."

"Okay, we're moving up now. Stand by for the distraction."

Beau and Chance slipped out of the rental car and gently pressed the doors shut. The rain was light, but steady, giving the ground a thin layer of moisture.

"Distraction. Good word for it," Beau mused.

"Let's just hope it works."

"Have faith."

Beau and Chance used the shadows to sneak to the front of house undetected. The Monte Carlo in the driveway let them know they had the right place. The house was quaint and didn't fit the personalities of the hooligans housed inside. Chance stopped for a moment, appreciating the new headquarters. Tony Toombs was hiding his empire in plain sight.

Positioned behind a large tree, Chance stood by while Beau took a position next to the door. Once set, Beau nodded across the lawn back at Chance. Nervousness laid siege to his stomach, and Chance felt the onset of dry heaving.

Get it together.

He kept a loose grip on the baseball bat as he stepped up to the driver side door of the Monte Carlo. He hoisted it back over his shoulder, prepped for an over the fence swing and glanced at Beau. He nodded that he was ready. With purpose, he swung the bat down as hard as he could, smashing the windshield. Glass shattered and shook the car, setting off an audible alarm that echoed down the quiet street. Broken glass in an outline of the barrel remained and let rainwater seep into the interior. Chance backed away from the car and behind the tree.

"What the fuck?" Xavier Toombs stormed out onto the porch, staring at his car. His eyes searched out in the night for who was responsible. Chance stuck a portion of his body out from behind the tree, catching Xavier's attention.

"Who's there? I'm gonna fuck you up for messin' wit' my car." Xavier leapt off the porch and raced across the lawn. Chance moved from behind the tree, giving Xavier pause. He read the recognition in his eyes.

Xavier said, "You fucked up, comin' alone, Detective Parker."

Chance smiled.

The hard end of Beau's gun barrel poked Xavier in the back of the head. "Who said he's alone?"

Xavier tensed, and after weighing his position, he relaxed and let his shoulders sag in defeat. He lifted his arms slowly out to the side. Chance took the opportunity and searched his waistline for weapons. Tucked in the back was a gun, which he quickly removed and secured.

"Where's Tony Toombs?" Chance asked.

"Don't know who that is." Xavier began his stance with defiance.

"Liar." Beau kicked Xavier in the back of his leg, causing him to fall to his knees.

"Oww, fuck, man. You ain't gotta kick me."

"Stop lying."

"I'm not lying."

Beau responded with another kick to the back, shoving Xavier down to the wet ground. Desmond appeared from behind the house.

"Let's take this inside," Chance said. He looked at Beau, then Desmond. "You ready?"

Beau answered and Desmond nodded.

Beau grabbed Xavier by the collar of his shirt, keeping his gun trained on the back of his head.

With Xavier leading the way, they all walked through the front door and into the house. Chance followed as Beau pushed Xavier toward the back where they knew the rest of the crew was. As soon as they stepped into the light of the rec room, Desmond and Chance split off toward the corners to get a better angle on the group. Outnumbered by the thugs, they used surprise to gain the advantage.

"Oh shit, what the—"

"Don't fucking move," Chance barked. He waved his Glock with authority, gaining compliance by displaying the business end at the group.

Duquan and Chris froze, wide-eyed on the couch. Gunner stood up, but Desmond quickly addressed him with a shotgun pointed at his midsection. Gigi slipped off a barstool and raised her hands in submission.

"All right, let's just calm down and no one gets hurt," Chance ordered. "Where's Tony Toombs?"

His question was met with silence.

"I said, where's Tony?"

More silence. Xavier snickered at the way their allegiance irritated the cops. He was met with another swift kick to the legs by Beau. This time, he fell all the way to the ground.

"Fine. You got this?" Chance asked Beau.

"Yeah." His focus stayed on the suspects. "Go check it out."

Chance backed out slowly and began searching the rest of the house. He moved carefully and quietly in case Antonio Toombs was hiding somewhere in the house. He checked several bedrooms, the bathroom, and the garage. There was random evidence of drug use scattered about the house, some ammunition here and there, but no sign of Tony Toombs.

Making his way back to the rec room, Chance saw that Beau was nose to nose with Gunner D. The tension in the room was palpable. Xavier, Duquan, Chris, and Gigi were all lined up and on their knees with their hands interlaced on the top of their heads. Desmond stood guard with the shotgun.

"You the one that shot me in the back?"

Gunner didn't answer. He stood up straight, all five feet six inches, to Beau's six-foot-two frame and stared him in the eyes.

"What did I miss?" Chance interrupted.

"Nothing. I was just asking young George here if he was the little pussy that shot me in the back."

"I told you, man. My name is Gunner."

"You still haven't answered me, George."

"Fuck you, cracka."

With a lightning fast jab, Beau's fist connected with Gunner's nose, catching him off guard. Gunner fell back, and as he caught his balance, he reached under his shirt in his front waistband.

Fear gripped Chance as he read the threat. Gunner was reaching for a gun. It was a move ingrained since the academy that all cops were taught to watch for. But Beau reacted, like he had anticipated it. As Gunner reached the grip of a pistol, Beau's left hand was clamped on the outside of his, keeping it stuffed in his waistband. Gunner was unable to muscle against the leverage Beau had on him. Before Gunner could do anything else, Beau withdrew and placed his handgun between Gunner's eyes and pushed down.

"Don't even think about it, George." Gunner stiffened and stopped fighting. Beau peeled his hand back and removed the gun from the young man's beltline. With a quick glance, he noticed it was the same caliber as the round found embedded in his Kevlar vest.

"Was this the gun you used, you little fuck?"

Gunner didn't answer, but his eyes gave it away as they bulged from the guilt.

"It was you. I knew it." Beau grew angry and shoved the smaller suspect backwards. He tossed the gun to Desmond and turned to face Gunner.

"Beau?" Chance called out. His tone held a degree of worry.

"What?" he snapped.

"Chill out. Remember why we came here?"

"No, Chance. This little shit shot me in the back, and that doesn't really sit well with me. I think I'm going to question the suspect a little more."

"Beau, c'mon. Keep it together."

"Fuck you, Chance. I'm tired of this shit. We always have to play by the rules while these assholes do whatever the hell they want. How 'bout I'm going to do what I want now. And that's find out why he shot me in the back."

Beau snatched Gunner up off the floor and dragged him into a smaller room off the recreational area. Chance figured it was some type of storage closet.

With the four other threats still in the room, Chance was anchored and couldn't stop Beau without leaving Desmond alone with four dangerous suspects. He stutter-stepped toward the smaller room, but reconsidered.

"Yo man, that guy's gone crazy. You need to do something, call back-up or something," Xavier spoke up.

"Shut up." Chance felt panicked and hoped it wasn't showing.

Yelling came from beyond the door and silenced the room as they all listened. Beau demanded Gunner tell him that he was the person who shot him. The shouting was bookended by the sounds of punches and groans as Gunner failed to answer.

"Check your boy, detective."

Chance ignored Xavier and nodded for Desmond to check on Beau. He acknowledged and stepped over to the door. It was locked.

Desmond knocked. "Beau, open up man."

"No, go away Dez. Everything is fine in here."

The shouting grew angrier and angrier as it neared a crescendo. The rage radiated through the door. Fear registered on the faces of Gunner's partners.

"C'mon, Beau. Chill out, man. This has gone too far."

"Does anyone care that he tried to fucking kill me?" Beau screamed from the other side of the door.

"Of course, man, but let's be cool."

Silence followed.

"Beau?" Desmond called. "Beau?"

The sharp crack of the pistol deafened the room. Desmond's eyes lit up and beat on the door. Chance immediately stepped over the remaining four suspects, trying to keep them calm but still at a position of disadvantage. He had to maintain control as best he could.

Duquan and Chris attempted to get up.

"Sit the fuck back down, now!"

"That ain't cool, man. You gunna let his crazy ass just kill us? You hav'ta get us out of here."

"No, shut up."

"Damn, man. This is fucked up."

Chance regained control of the remaining four and stood closer to the door where Beau had taken Gunner.

"Beau, come out of there."

The small interior door flung open and Beau appeared through the threshold. He was not himself, but the image of a demon thirsty for revenge.

"That's one down. Who's next?"

"Beau, no!" Desmond reached out to hold him back, but Beau pushed him off with a violent shove. He stepped over to Duquan Baker and grabbed him forcefully.

"You're the other asshole from the warehouse. You're coming with me." Duquan struggled to get away, but Beau twisted his arm to the brink of breaking it and led him into the small room.

Before the door could shut, Desmond stepped inside and began arguing with Beau, leaving Chance alone with the other three.

"Parker, man. You can't let him do this, get me outta here." Xavier was desperate.

Lost in worried thought, Chance didn't answer.

"Parker!"

"Fine." Chance helped Xavier up, grabbed him by the arm and rushed him outside, leaving Gigi and Chris to fend for themselves. He stuffed Xavier in his car and got behind the wheel.

"Your boy's off the chain, man."

"I know. I've never seen him like that. I never wanted to believe he actually killed those men before, but now, I see that he's capable." Chance let out a deep breath. "It was not supposed to go this way."

"No shit."

Chance cranked the car and sped off before anything else happened. The rain was beating down steadily, drenching the earth and flooding the roads.

Chance continued, "I don't know if he'll stop until all of you are dead. And the problem is I don't know who to trust right now."

"You gotta take me to a safe house or something, man."

"Why the hell should I do that?"

"Cuz, that crazy ass cop just killed Gunner and prolly Dookie, too. Hell, sounds like he was intending on killing us all. Prolly you and the other cop, too. You said yourself, he's probably capable of anything."

Chance thought to himself as he drove. After a few minutes, he turned to Xavier, the man he had despised since he arrested him for murder only to be acquitted by corrupting the system in his favor.

"I have an idea, but you need to trust me."

"Whatever, man. Just keep me away from that asshole."

Chapter 51

"Here? Are you fucking joking?" Xavier looked through the blurry windshield as sheets of rain fell from the sky.

"No, I'm not," Parker said.

"Nah, man. I don't think so."

"Okay, fine. Get out."

Xavier weighed his options, looked out the window again, contemplating the alternative.

"It's the best option and we both know it."

"Yeah, but the jail?"

"Sure, think about it. He can't reach you in here. Hell, he tried to kill one of the deputies during that whole fiasco seven months ago. You think they'll let him just walk in this place?"

Xavier conceded the point, but was still unsure.

"I'll even book you under a fake name, ask the deputies to put you in a separate holding cell until I can come get you."

The internal debate waged inside of Xavier's mind. The facial expressions that resulted let Chance know he seriously considered taking his chances with Beau Rivers.

"I can't help you if you walk away. This is a one-time final offer."

"Fine, shit." Xavier looked as if he betrayed some higher code of conduct.

"Good, first things first."

"Whatchu mean?"

"I mean, I help you, you help me."

"How?"

"The double murder on Preston last month?"

Xavier Toombs's face turned to stone. "Don't know nothin', Parker. I wasn't there."

"Aww, c'mon, Xavier. Yes, you were."

A cocky smile creased his face, "You gotta witness or something?" Xavier sounded cocky, rubbing it in that he and his crew had executed the only witness in that case. The only problem was Chance couldn't prove it.

"Nope," he replied with confidence.

This threw Xavier. Chance saw the curiosity in his eyes.

"So, what then?"

"I know you were there, standing in the doorway." As Chance let loose of that investigative nugget, he could see the memory recall flash in Xavier's eyes. The DNA test had proven its worth. He just had to get Xavier to come around.

"You stood there and killed the first guy, but you didn't see the second guy come from the hallway until he fired on you. I would think that your back-up, probably Duquan, eliminated that guy for you, but you still got hit. And you left a little blood on scene, didn't you?"

Rain pelted the top of the car as there was silence between Chance and Xavier.

"You can't dispute DNA, Xavier. Do yourself a favor, talk to me. Let it all hang out, and I can protect you."

He didn't answer. That was the detective's best card to play, but it hadn't delivered the knockout blow. Chance needed a different angle.

"I know your brother calls the shots. He pretty much booted you from the throne since he got out of jail, didn't he?"

"We were soft. He has vision and he's a good leader."

"Oh, really?"

"Yeah."

"Okay, if you say so." Chance let his speculative tone hang between them, hoping Xavier took the bait.

After a minute of silence, Xavier asked, "What do you mean, if you say so?"

"Where was Tony tonight, seriously? Don't bullshit me?"

"Honestly, Parker, I don't know."

"What if I told you, I did?"

"Huh?" Xavier keyed in on the detective.

"Ask yourself this, Xavier. How do you think we knew where your new house was, and that it just so happened that Tony was nowhere to be found when we came knocking?"

"Whatchu tryin' to say, Parker? You sayin' Tony snitched us out?"

Chance responded with only a shoulder shrug and a facial expression that said, "You do the math."

Xavier waged an internal debate, and Chance waited a moment.

"With you and the crew out of the way, he could take all that money and do whatever the hell he wants with it. Oh, shit, I forgot about this. Ask yourself another question. Where was he during the warehouse shooting? Was he down in the trenches with Gunner and everybody, or was he hiding somewhere safe?"

Xavier's brow furrowed into an angry "V" shape. He was fuming on the inside.

"Fuck, yeah. That nigga just sat in the church during the whole thing while we were on the front line. Shit! I ain't gonna take a bullet for his ass. Blood or not."

"Exactly."

"That motha fucker just gets out of prison and takes the fuck over. What about me, dawg? What about me? I had it runnin' just fine till then."

"Hell, you beat a murder. I should know."

"Yeah, I should be king, not him."

"So, like I said, Xavier. Help me out, so I can help you out."

"A'ight Parker, I talk to you, but you better get me a deal."

Chance Parker walked Xavier Toombs up to the sliding security door in the sally port and into the jail's booking room. It was just them and the receiving deputy. The rest of the intake unit was quiet. Chance was able to convince the deputy to hold him in a separate holding cell for the night and once finished with the search protocol, he accommodated the request. Xavier was led to the cell, and after the deputy departed, Chance stepped in and sat down.

"Let's go over this nice and slow. I got all the time in the world."

Two hours later, Chance left the jail with a signed confession from Xavier, spelling out his role in the Preston Street double murder and how his older brother, Antonio Toombs, had given the orders.

Chapter 52

The tiny curl of his lip and the tiny squeak he made while he slept was breathtaking. Despite everything that surrounded the birth of his son, Dylan Akers found solace by just being with him. Everything else seemed insignificant.

Phoenix Akers's soft gray-blue eyes blinked open and stared back at Dylan. Instantly, a broad smile crossed Dylan's face.

"Hi," he said. "I'm your daddy, and I'm never going to let anything happen to you." Thoughts of Caitlin came to him, and a tear escaped and rolled down his cheek. "I'll tell you about your sister one day, okay?"

Baby Phoenix became uninterested and yawned. Dylan could feel him try to stretch within the swaddled blanket. His perfect little eyes closed, and he fell back to sleep.

"That's okay, buddy. Go to sleep."

Dylan rocked back and forth while cradling the baby in his arms. He had forgotten about the emotional scene that played out earlier in the afternoon with Beau. He glanced out the hospital window to see the rain pouring down. He wondered if Beau, Chance, and Desmond were able to get to Antonio Toombs with success. There was a good chance it was the last opportunity they would have to get close to him, knowing that Pritchard had gotten hold of the evidence in the McFadden and Shelley murders.

He didn't want to think about that right now. Today his son was born, and there was nothing more important.

Wendy stirred in the hospital bed. She had dozed off after dinner. Dylan looked over at her, curled up and comfortable in her warm bed. He hated what had occurred between her and Beau, but she proclaimed it was a one-time mistake, and she had done it only in the interest of convincing

Beau to help them murder George Shelley. In retrospect, he wasn't sure that was a good enough trade, but he had to remove any bad thoughts because what was done, was done. What happened can't be undone; the death of his daughter taught him that. No matter what he, Beau, or Wendy did, she was still gone. Surprisingly, Dylan didn't harbor any ill feelings toward his wife for what she'd done. She made it clear who she wanted to be with all along, and because of that, he had already forgiven her.

Wendy awoke. She stretched and let out a gentle moan and a yawn. It was cute, but not as much as the baby yawn.

"Hey," she said softly with a smile.

"Hey."

"How long have I been asleep?"

"A few hours."

"How is he?"

Dylan looked down at the sleeping baby. "He's perfect."

Wendy smiled. "Good." She sat up in her bed and fixed her hair in a ponytail. "How are you?"

Dylan knew it wasn't his general well-being she was asking about. Before dinner and her falling asleep, he told her about the confrontation with Beau and the phone call from Chief Shaw. Her question about how he was ran much deeper.

"I'm fine." Dylan continued rocking the baby. "I'm better than fine. I'm happy, and I love you."

Pleasantly caught off guard, Wendy replied, "I love you, too."

A knock rapped the hospital door. It was heavier than the nurse. Plus, they weren't due for at least another hour to check on the baby. They weren't expecting any visitors this late either.

Another knock came, just as heavy as the first but with a sense of urgency.

"Who is it?" Wendy asked.

"Major Reginald Pritchard, ma'am, with TPD. May I come in?"

Panic-stricken at the announcement, she looked to Dylan with a desperate look of indecision. She mouthed, "What do I do?"

Calmly, hiding his anger from Wendy and the baby, Dylan eased up from the chair and handed the sleeping child to his mother.

"It's okay. This was going to happen one way or the other. Remember, I told you that I'm happy and that I love you."

"But what can I do?"

"Try not to worry. You are doing the most important thing in the world right now."

The knock came again.

"Dylan?" Wendy cried.

"I'm coming," Dylan called out. He leaned down and held Wendy's face in his hands. She had begun to cry. "Don't cry baby. I love you." He kissed her on the lips. Tears fell from her eyes, making his good-bye kiss a little salty.

"I love you, too, Dylan."

Dylan released his hold and stepped out of the hospital room. Major Pritchard was joined by Russell Trek and two other Internal Affairs inspectors.

"Major," he addressed Pritchard as he shut the door behind him. "Couldn't wait until I brought the baby home?"

Pritchard shook his head adamantly. "Lieutenant Akers, you are under arrest for the murders of Earnest McFadden and George Shelley." Trek grabbed hold of his wrists and ratcheted on a pair of handcuffs as Pritchard spoke. "You have the right to remain silent. Anything you say, can and will be used against you in a court of law."

Dylan listened as his rights were read to him as he was led down the hallway to the elevators. He caught stares from the nurses, doctors, orderlies, and everyone they encountered all the way out to the parking lot.

"Seriously, Pritchard, you couldn't wait one more day until I got the baby home? I'm not going anywhere."

Trek helped Dylan sit down in the back seat of his unmarked sedan.

"No, I've waited long enough to nail you for this. Rivers is next."

Chapter 53

The deluge that soaked the city lasted until midnight. Beau Rivers was exhausted, but pleased with how the operation unfolded. Antonio was unaccounted for, which was a loose end, but they made the best of what they had. Bad guys were going to jail, and that's all that mattered. At the moment, home didn't sound appealing. Pritchard and his lap dog, Trek, would most likely be waiting for him to return. If not now, then first thing in the morning.

He pushed all thoughts related to the operation aside and focused on the plan he had penned earlier for Dylan. He searched his pockets for the letter, but it wasn't there.

Shit, I left it at the Lincoln Center.

Welcoming any excuse to avoid home, he changed course and headed for the makeshift headquarters in the dusty old building. The outcasts and downtrodden were left to wander the rain-soaked streets. Beau weaved his way through the damned and pulled into the empty parking lot. He got out and went into the office. He flipped on the lights and looked around the desk he had been sitting at earlier, but there was no letter.

Where the hell is it?

Beau checked everywhere. He stopped and played back in his head what he could remember after writing it. He was done writing and then came the odd noise. Beau looked at the back of the room. The noise had pulled him into the other room, but he remembered leaving the letter on the desk. That he was sure of. He checked the desk again and looked between it and the wall. Still no letter.

Maybe I did grab it and it's lost in the car somewhere.

He flipped the lights off and walked down the corridor to the back stairwell. He glanced off in the distance and through the tree line over the cemetery grounds. Everything was still and quiet. Peaceful. It was moments like these that made him envy all the normal people sleeping soundly in their beds, clueless to the battles waged in their defense.

A sheepdog never sleeps.

Walking down the steps, an engine revving louder and louder through the parking lot broke the silence. Beau studied the approaching car and reached for his hip. The headlights washed over him and soon two more cars broke off from behind the lead. Moving to opposite sides, they surrounded Beau. Reading the situation, he quickly realized they were department cars. Their blue lights flipped on and blinded Beau with their strobe effect. He moved his hand away from his hip and straightened up, a sign of submission.

"Beau Rivers," a voice boomed from an open door behind the bright headlights. "You are under arrest. Please place your hands on top of your head and walk back to my voice."

In a moment of defiance, Beau remained still. His eyes narrowed, a deadpan look on his face. Through the light stream, he stared at the dark image with contempt.

"Do it now! We know you are armed. We will shoot you if you do not comply."

Through his peripheral vision, occupants of the backup cars stepped out and aimed their weapons at Beau. He was outnumbered at least four to one.

"Oh, please, do something stupid. By all means, make this easy on us," a new voice said. This one, however, was unmistakable. Beau strained to see the unflattering form of Major Prick as he stepped away from the wall of light to lock eyes with Beau.

I'll never give him what he wants, ever.

Beau stood erect and slowly moved his empty hands to the top of his head. He kneeled to the ground and turned his back to the officers. Seconds later, his gun was removed from the holster, and he was shoved to the ground. A heavy knee dropped in the middle of his back, and he was placed in handcuffs. Beau didn't fight. That would only aggravate things.

"Beau Rivers, you are under arrest for the murders of Earnest McFadden and George Shelley." The elation in Major Prick's voice was obvious.

Beau's face was expressionless. One officer read his Miranda rights as he was stuffed into the back of an unmarked sedan and whisked off to the station. His thoughts quickly moved back to the letter. He was flooded with questions that volleyed back and forth in his head about where it could have gone. If they found the letter, then everything would be ruined.

***

The bigger the job, the more of the little stuff there seemed to be. It was nearly three a.m., and Chance Parker was finishing what had started outside of Antonio Toombs new headquarters some seven hours before. Back at the station with all the evidence, he cataloged, logged it in, and deposited everything in the safe where it would be collected the next morning.

Chance let loose a loud yawn and stretched out his arms and back.

"Damn. I'm tired," he said to the empty room.

In perfect timing, his cell phone trilled as if it was responding.

"Hello?"

"Chance? It's Mike." There was a hidden excitement in the senior detective's voice. "Are you up?"

Temporarily forgetting it was sleep time for the rest of the world, he realized he'd just answered the phone like any other time. Suspicious of the phone call, he wasn't sure how to play it. Did Durgenhoff know something about what went down at the Toombs's house?

"Uh, yeah. What's up?"

"Well, you ain't gonna believe this, but Pritchard just ten-fifteened both Akers and Rivers for the McFadden and Shelley murders. They're up in CID now."

"Really?" Although he wasn't sure why, Chance hid his disappointment.

"Yes, sir. Seems that Rivers only wants to talk to you. Can you come in?"

The air was knocked out of Chance Parker. Stunned at the news, he failed to answer Durgenhoff.

Why would he specifically want to talk to me?

"Chance, you there?"

"Uh, yeah. I mean, yes I can come in. He asked for me? Are you sure?"

"Yep. What's that about?"

"Not sure," Chance lied. He figured Beau had come to trust him, even under these circumstances.

"Okay, whatever. See you in a bit."

He wants to talk to me?

His exhaustion abated and was replaced by a spark of energy. He had been so enthralled with the case at the onset, even half a year later, a personal connection had developed. As he left the Property and Evidence night deposit room, he slowed his step. This was such an important case for the department to get right, however, working with them for nearly a month he had grown close to the two men involved. He felt his loyalties being divided.

Is Beau asking for me because he wants me to cover for him?

Showing up five minutes after being called would probably get noticed and draw unwanted attention to why Chance was at the station at such a late hour, so he walked over to the nearby convenience store for some caffeine. It would also give him time to put his thoughts together.

Chapter 54

Beau stared blankly at the same off-white colored walls. This time his left hand was handcuffed to the chair. The last time he had walked away, but that would not be his fate for the second. He found peace with his decision to give up and was ready to accept responsibility. However, with his letter undelivered, he needed to talk before they questioned Dylan. Stuck inside the room, he wondered how he was going to make that happen.

Activity stirred outside the interview room. Beau figured they had finally reached Chance Parker and called him in. He had probably just finished from the operation at the Toombs's house. Getting Chance to come do the interview was a key piece in his plan. He was glad they listened. Major Prick was going to try to claim all the glory, so when Beau listed his one demand, the look on Pritchard's face had been priceless. It was as if his favorite toy had been snatched right out of his hands and given to the new kid. The sight of Reginald Pritchard squirming and giving in to his demand was almost worth confessing to murder.

The interview room door opened, and Chance Parker entered. With the hidden camera to his back, he gave Beau a look that begged, "What are you doing? Have you lost your mind?" Chance knew the command staff, the State Attorneys, and anyone else privy to the case were all watching.

Beau responded with an easygoing smile and confidence.

As Chance shut the door, Russell Trek caught it and stepped in behind Parker.

"Nope. Sorry, Rusty. This confession is for Parker's ears only. It's him or nothing."

Trek stood there with a dumbfounded look on his face, also, equally satisfying as slighting Pritchard. Beau went silent waiting for compliance.

"Fuck you, Rivers. You're either going to talk or not. It doesn't matter who's in the room."

Beau slowly turned his head to address the Internal Affairs inspector. He looked at the man with disgust that was immediately recognizable.

"What?" Trek asked.

"Inspector Trek," Beau began. "You are investigating a double murder that involves a police officer as the suspect. You and Major Prick have already managed to screw up this investigation so badly, the only thing left to save it is a bona fide confession. Now, I make a simple request in exchange for the needed confession, and you want to screw that up too?"

Chance was leaning against the wall, watching with amusement. A small smile was stuck on his face.

"But…," Trek stammered. A second later, he checked an incoming text on his phone. His face turned a shade of red, and he looked up at Beau.

"Bye, Rusty."

"Whatever." Trek stormed out of the room, and Parker took a seat across the table from Beau.

"Thanks for coming," Beau said.

"I'm not sure you gave me a choice, buddy."

"You could've said no."

"You're right."

"So why didn't you?"

"Something you said before. About being in this job for the right reasons. It stayed with me. Doing it right is the only way."

Very pleased with his answer, Beau nodded. "That's why I asked for you."

"Okay, so it's pretty damned late. Can we get started?"

Beau chuckled. "Sure, I ain't got anywhere to be." He pulled up his shackled left arm to show Chance.

"Have they read you your rights yet?"

"Out in the field. Nothing on video."

"Okay, I'll read it again if you're cool with that. And you're sure you don't want a lawyer to come at least sit with you?"

"No, I'm good, Chance."

"Okay, I guess we'll get started."

"Go for it."

Beau studied Chance Parker's face. He'd placed him in an uncomfortable situation given their recent professional connection. The situation was surreal and he assumed it was the same for Chance.

After rereading Beau's Miranda warnings, Chance had him sign the form acknowledging that he understood his rights. It was the first and crucial hurdle to any interview.

"So how do you want to start?"

"From the beginning, I guess."

Beau Rivers began talking about how, after the death of Caitlin Akers, he learned of the traffic stop of George Shelley. The timeframe of the traffic stop was after she was kidnapped but before her murder. Beau explained that the idea of her still being alive during the traffic stop and his not intervening made him sick to his stomach.

"That was the motivation for the murders," he said.

Chance nodded in acceptance and then furrowed his brow in thought. Beau read the confusion.

"What?" Beau asked. "Didn't know about the traffic stop?"

Typically, Chance wouldn't dare acknowledge not knowing something in an interview. His normal reaction was to tip-toe around the issue and maintain that he was all knowing. This interview was different.

"Nope. We didn't think of that."

"It's okay."

"So, after learning about the traffic stop and the subsequent motion by the defense, you chose to go after McFadden and Shelley?"

"Yes," Beau answered. "I found McFadden's court schedule through the clerk's office website and devised my plan to capture him. I rented a van under a fake name and waited for the transport van to pass me on Pensacola Street. Once I crashed into the van, it rolled over. I laid down covering fire to keep the deputy pinned and then extracted McFadden from the cargo hold."

"Covering fire?" Chance probed, hoping to get Beau to expound.

"Despite what your team may have thought, I had no intentions of hurting the deputy or any cops for that matter. It was McFadden or nothing."

Chance nodded. "Durgenhoff thought that too. That you intentionally missed the deputy to keep him pinned down. You do the same with the machine gun set-up over off Bronough?"

"Yes. I aimed it to take out the engine of Shelley's van, or rather what I thought was Shelley's van, and to scatter the SWAT team, nothing more."

"Okay, so let's get back to McFadden and after the kidnapping."

"So, I stashed him at a nearby warehouse until the search went cold. Then I slipped him out of there and over to that billboard area off Thomasville Road."

"Was that to send a message?"

"Yes."

"Where'd the winch come from?"

"Nearby construction. It was one of the reason's that place was chosen."

"Did he say anything? You know, before you killed him?"

"He apologized. But it was too late."

"He apologized for what?"

"Killing Caitlin."

Silence fell in the room. Beau watched as Chance withdrew slightly, something clearly plagued his thoughts. Beau recognized it wasn't easy on Chance to do what he was asked to do, so he wanted to make it easier.

"You want to talk about the courthouse thing or the failed attempt on Shelley?" Beau pressed forward for Chance's sake. Another first in homicide interviews, the suspect driving the confession.

"Up to you."

"We'll stay in order."

Beau continued with the set-up for the ambush attack on the transport van that was ultimately found empty. He described how he built the remote-activated switch for the machine gun, set the Altima on the crash course, and the confrontation with the female deputy.

"So the DNA found on the side of the van was put there when you were confronted by Deputy Register?"

Chance was trying to corroborate the evidence. Beau respected the thoroughness.

"Yes."

"So after slipping away, you ran to the house on Fourth Avenue and changed clothes?"

"Yes."

"So, you did leave that receipt on the ground during this escape and not while on a routine patrol call the day before as you stated in an earlier interview?"

Beau replayed that earlier interview in his head. He was in a different place in his life. Now he was accepting responsibility. He stopped for a moment and noticed he was inexplicably calm.

"Well, I'm not sure. I didn't actually notice when it fell out, so it could have been during the escape or could have been during that call for service."

"Fair enough. Doesn't matter now."

"No, it doesn't."

"Pretty ingenious how you covered that up, by the way."

"I agree." Beau smiled. The credit belonged to Dylan, who had placed the fake call generating a call for service to explain his presence, but he would keep that to himself.

"So, now that we've covered everything else, let's move to the courthouse."

"Okay. Like you may have already figured out, I snuck a gun into the courthouse and was able to bypass the metal detector. When a commotion outside distracted the bailiffs, I was able to steal an access card from one of them, and I took the freight elevator down to the transfer center. I fired two shots into the ground to lure out the deputy in the center. Once he left, I let myself in with the access badge and shot George Shelley in the head."

The silence returned. Beau took a deep breath. A line he had sold to many felons in his position held true. It felt better getting it off your chest. It had been lip service until this point, but now he could relate. However, this information could not be rebottled. It was out there, forever.

Chance Parker spent the next hour going over the little details of the investigation that had left him and Durgenhoff questioning, such as the location of the warehouse, where Beau got the Altima from, and so forth. Beau volleyed back each question with an answer and refrained from any posturing or procrastination. Chance took advantage of having a cooperative suspect, even though Beau was a police officer who knew the process, to better his understanding of working a murder case. It was rare that detectives were ever met with this level of cooperation.

At the end of the interview, Chance sat back in his chair. Beau could tell he was taking a mental inventory and searching for any detail that was missed. Beau knew there was an importance piece Chance hadn't covered.

"Okay, so I think I'm about done here."

Beau didn't answer.

The vibration of Chance's cell phone was amplified as it sat on the table's surface. He ignored it, but another text came in right behind it. He picked up the phone and read the message. Beau saw a change in his face.

"What do they want you to ask me?" Beau asked.

Chance didn't respond. He looked uncomfortable.

"It's okay. Remember, do it the right way."

Not hiding the fact that Pritchard, Polk, Shaw, and many others were watching the interview in the monitor room, Chance answered, "Tell me how Dylan is involved?"

This was the missing piece Beau was waiting on. He was ready.

"He isn't."

"I'm sorry?"

"He isn't involved."

"Okay, Beau. I want to believe you, but we both know that's not true." Chance sat up straight. "There's no way you pulled off all this stuff by yourself. Plus, you can't deny your connection through the cell phone plants and all of the proximity card hits where he went to Property and Evidence to get the guns you used."

"I see your point, but he's not involved."

"Beau, you've sat there and confessed to two murders. Why would you lie about that?"

"Exactly. Why would I lie about that?"

"I'm not sure, but how do you explain that? I mean, at the courthouse, it was Dylan outside creating the distraction for you to make your way down to the transfer center."

"I never said it was a distraction, I told you that there was a commotion outside, and that I used the opportunity to gain access to the freight elevator. I never knew he was even outside in the hallway. I was inside the courtroom, remember?"

"That's pretty convenient though. I mean he just happens to be there, has a mental breakdown fighting Trek and several deputies while you slip down a freight elevator and kill the man responsible for murdering his daughter. I don't believe that was just a coincidence."

"You can choose to see it that way. I don't."

"Okay, answer where the guns came from then." Chance adopted an irritable tone to confront Beau. "It was Dylan's proximity card used to get and return the guns, the same make and caliber of guns used in the murders."

"That's easy. I stole his proximity card and used it to slip in Property and Evidence to get the guns. I returned it to his office when he wasn't there."

"So you took the guns?"

"Yes. Me, not Dylan."

Chance's phone vibrated again. And again. It continued to buzz until he turned it off and stuffed it in his pocket.

"So, you are telling me that Dylan Akers had no part in the murders of George Shelley and Earnest McFadden?"

"That's right. I take full responsibility for both murders. He had nothing to do with either one."

Chance sat back in disbelief. "I'm sorry Beau, I don't believe that Dylan had no knowledge of this whatsoever."

"I understand your frustrations, but that's the truth, and that's my statement. I did it for him. There is no denying that, but I acted alone."

Beau was taking a small leap of faith in that moment. Over the last month, Beau noticed that Dylan had held private meetings with Chance. He assumed it had something to do with the case against Antonio Toombs, but he wasn't absolute. If Dylan had confided in Chance about their plans to murder Shelley and McFadden, this play would soon die on the vine and expose him as a liar or make Chance an accessory.

"Okay." Chance seemed disappointed. "Anything else you want to get on the record?"

"No. That is everything."

Chance pushed away from the table, wiped his tired face, and stood up. Beau hated to lie to Chance, but it was saving Dylan from a life in prison. He was giving Dylan the chance to be the father he wanted to be. It was the right thing to do.

"Thanks for coming, Chance. You're a good cop."

Chance paused at the door. He turned to Beau and then extended his hand. Beau reached over with his free hand and in a moment of sincerity, shook Chance's hand.

"Good luck, brother."

"Thanks, but it's not luck I'm after."

"What then?"

"Redemption."

Chapter 55

Sitting in solitude, waiting for the pendulum to swing back, Dylan struggled to keep his eyes open. Starting the day a little under twenty-four hours before with the birth of his son, his body had started shutting down. He forced himself to stay awake and alert, careful not to succumb to the exhaustion. He checked his watch; he'd been sitting in the interview room for over two hours.

Russell Trek had stuck his face in the room earlier and Dylan took the opportunity to request a lawyer before any questioning. He assumed the long delay that followed was due to Trek trying to find a lawyer. At one point during the wait, he was certain he heard Chance Parker's voice outside the door. He wondered if Parker had been called in or if he had shown up on his own.

He didn't see Beau, but Dylan was sure he had been brought to the station, just like before. He wondered how his interview went and how he was holding up. The image of putting a gun to Beau's head flashed through his consciousness. He regretted how angry he had gotten, but given the circumstances, it was how he had felt in the moment. Now, he felt like he needed Beau more than ever.

We're in this together.

Prison was a realistic possibility. Jail would be just a glimpse, he thought. Prison would be the equivalent of hell on earth for a cop like Dylan, a notch just waiting to be made on some lifer's belt. He shuddered at the thought.

A muffled voice came from beyond the interview room door.

The lawyer must be here.

"I'm going to tell him. Deal with it."

Sergeant Melvin Polk entered the room. He was casually dressed in jeans, given the late-night call out. Dylan strained his neck to see past Polk while the door was still open. He caught a glimpse of Chance Parker's profile. He looked tired.

"Melvin," Dylan addressed the homicide sergeant.

"Hey, Dylan. I know you asked for a lawyer, so obviously you don't have to respond, but I felt you needed to know something."

Dylan looked up at Melvin Polk with anticipation but didn't speak.

"Beau has confessed to everything."

The blood drained from Dylan's body.

"He did what?"

Polk lifted his hand up to cut off Dylan. "He confessed to everything. As in, he did everything. Said you had no part in it at all. Copped to stealing your proximity card to get those guns out of Property and Evidence."

"But, why?"

"He didn't go into detail but said he did it for you. Something about a traffic stop he did. Apparently, he stopped Shelley in the minivan the day after your daughter went missing and let him go."

The blood hadn't quite returned. Dylan was still hung up on the idea of Beau confessing. When he asked why, he was referring to why did he confess, not why did he do the crime. He wasn't going to clarify his question. As his brain played catch up, he processed what Polk said about the traffic stop. Dylan had found out about Beau pulling over Shelley. He used the information to guilt Beau into helping him. Then he realized it was part of the investigation he wasn't supposed to know about.

He feigned anger. "Traffic stop? He let him go?"

"Yeah, says that was the motivation for why he killed both McFadden and Shelley. Pretty much to avenge Caitlin's death."

Dylan was lost, yet relieved, but also disappointed. A mixture of emotions swirled in a chaotic frenzy, leaving him stunned. The look on his face was that of a confused man, which happened to be appropriate for the situation.

"I know you're confused, but like I said, he confessed to everything."

"So what does that mean?"

"Well, we ran everything by the State Attorney's Office, and even though Major Prick out there is dead set on charging you, with Beau's confession that is corroborated through DNA and other evidence, it was decided you are going to be released."

Dylan listened and quickly ran down the long list of the evidence. Shaw had found the circumstantial proximity card readout that showed his card accessing the evidence vault to check in and out the guns used in the kidnappings and murders, which Beau now confessed to doing, even though it was part of the plan he was responsible for. There was the burner phone incident and his presence in the courthouse during the execution of Shelley, which in and of itself was not damaging, it was still circumstantial—mainly because he held the most motive to kill McFadden and Shelley. But Beau had provided a viable motive to kill the pair. Plus, it was Beau's DNA on the transport van, so it would make sense that they would latch on to his altered story. Dylan wanted to know more about what Beau had said in the interview, but that would be asking too much of Melvin Polk.

Beau had given him an out.

That bastard, he put it all on himself so I could walk.

This gift of a second chance was too generous. Dylan's emotions overwhelmed him, and his eyes welled up. A single tear ran down his cheek, and he quickly wiped it away. This meant he could go back to his wife and child.

Melvin Polk didn't understand the reaction.

"Dylan? You okay?"

"I've been through enough and even accused of murder, but now it's over. Now that the truth has come out." He lied.

"We're writing up the probable cause now, but I wanted to tell you that you're free to go."

"Thank you, Melvin." Dylan stood up and followed Polk out of the interview room. Trek, Pritchard, Shaw, and many others stood outside the interview room. They watched him walk out. Trek and Pritchard tracked him with leering eyes, sold on the fact that he had just gotten away with murder. Shaw's face was more apologetic. Dylan figured it was because Shaw had exploited him into the Toombs investigation based on evidence that was now pinned to Beau Rivers.

"This isn't right. He should go down with Rivers, too," Pritchard barked.

"Reggie, shut your mouth," Shaw chastised.

"Whatever." Pritchard motioned for Trek to follow him as he headed for the stairs.

Shaw turned to Dylan, "Go to your wife and child, Dylan. I'll call you later, and we'll figure this all out."

"Thank you, Chief."

Shaw gave him a knowing look to play it cool with regards to the Toombs investigation. Dylan caught the message and returned an acknowledgement.

He looked over at the closed door of the first interview room. He knew Beau was inside. He must feel so alone.

"I'll give you a ride back to the hospital," Polk said.

"Okay, umm..."

"What?"

Dylan glanced over at the interview room. "Can I talk to him? Just for a minute?"

An uneasy look came over Sergeant Polk. Shaw overheard the request and looked equally uncomfortable.

"I don't think so, Dylan. That's not a good idea."

"C'mon. At least just to say good-bye?"

Polk looked at Shaw for his approval. He nodded.

"Fine."

Polk opened the door to the interview room. As Dylan stepped in, Beau lifted his head. A smile donned his face as their eyes met. Fighting the urge to run over and hug him for his selflessness, Dylan stood silently, beaming with gratitude. Beau's eyes lit up in acceptance. They held each other's stare, wanting to share more than a look, but restrained themselves given the circumstances.

The message was clear though. Thank you.

Beau smiled, clearly keeping his own emotions at bay. He tilted his head slightly in a discreet nod.

"Good-bye, my friend," Dylan said.

"Good-bye, Ace."

Another tear escaped and Dylan quickly wiped it away. He turned and left the small room. With Polk at his back, he let more tears flow. They were for his friend who had just sacrificed everything so he could be with his family.

That thoughtful, sweet bastard.

Chapter 57

Wendy was trapped. Policy mandated the baby remain at the hospital under care for at least forty-eight hours. It was early morning and rolling into hour forty. The remaining eight seemed a lifetime away. The baby was agitated as he adjusted to life outside the womb, and Wendy was overwrought with thoughts that her husband would spend the rest of their lives in prison, leaving her alone to raise the child. She sat at the edge of the hospital bed, rocking the fussy child, trying to hold onto her last few shreds of sanity.

"Shhh, baby. It'll be okay. Let's pray Daddy comes home soon." Wendy tightened her hold on her newborn son, wanting to believe her words, but her doubt was crushing.

The baby squawked and fidgeted uncomfortably. He then let out a painful cry that made Wendy's heart sink, making her feel even more helpless. Mixed with her anxiety over Dylan and the exhaustion from childbirth, she was on the verge of collapse.

"Shhh, Phoenix, please. Shhhh, it's okay." She sped up the rocking to try and sooth him back to sleep. "Come on, I just fed you. It can't be that." She checked his diaper and the little color line on the outside indicated he was dry. "You're dry, little guy. What is it?"

Baby Phoenix let out another blood-curdling scream, like he was in agonizing pain. It was as if the baby knew something was wrong.

"Oh please, shhh. Mommy's right here."

I can't do this. Not alone.

Wendy could no longer be strong for the baby and began to sob. She was weak. She couldn't help feeling lost, and she was only on day two of the baby's life.

Through his rant, Xavier quickly realized he had been tricked. It was all for show. That Beau Rivers cop dragged Gunner D into the other room, pretended to be angry, and fired a round, making him think that Gunner took a bullet. That was the only explanation.

Xavier's anger boiled over into a violent outburst. He had confessed to everything because of that!

"Ahh, hell nah. Damn you, Parker!" Xavier began to swirl in a confused tailspin. "Oh, hell nah. This shit ain't right. I want my mothafuckin' lawyer, now!"

The deputy and two others flooded the small room and snatched up Xavier, pulling him out into the hallway. Still shackled by the belly chains, he managed to kick and resist like a deranged madman. After a bout of wrestling around on the floor, he was finally restrained under the weight of three jailors.

He yelled out, "You s'posed to be dead, Gunner. You was dead, boy! Goddammit, you was dead!"

The inmate cowered against the man on his other side as Xavier stood up. A deputy quickly intervened.

"We got a problem here?"

"No, sir. No, we don't." Xavier collected himself and sat back down. The respect level rose, mainly because of fear, amongst the lot.

"Good, scoot down more. We got a few late check-ins for first appearance."

Xavier stood up again and eye-balled the little man who squeezed into a smaller section of the bench to make room. Xavier sneered at him, continuing his show of dominance.

All the faces in the room watched the threshold to see who else was joining their party of miscreants. Xavier didn't care, but he looked out of amusement. When he turned, an apparition walked through the door that completely stunned him from head to toe.

It can't be!

Staring back at Xavier, also dressed in faded jailhouse blues and tan slides, were the tired eyes of Gunner D. Downcast and sporting a puffy left eye, he looked surprisingly whole and alive.

He's alive?

His face displayed a pathetic look as he hung his head low, avoiding eye contact with anyone else. He moved to the end of the bench and sat. Before Xavier could say anything, his cousin, Chris, and then Dookie followed Gunner D inside.

Incredulous, Xavier burst out of confusion. "What the fuck, nigga? You was dead. How the hell is you here right now?"

The three crew members avoided eye contact with Xavier and each squirmed in their seats, unable to answer for why they now sat in first appearance.

"Hey, shut your mouth. I'm not telling you again. Now sit down," ordered the deputy.

Xavier ignored the command. His confusion morphed into paranoia and called out each man as they ignored his pleas for explanation.

"But, I saw him take you in that room and shoot…"

Gunner finally lifted his head and looked Xavier in the eye then slowly shook his head.

"But, I heard the gunshot…."

Chapter 56

Ordered to be silent, the inmates moved as directed into the waiting room. The only sound was the clanging of chains and shuffling of feet. Xavier stepped in and reverence replaced the silence. No stranger to the first appearance protocol at the jail, a video chat with a judge where charges are formally read and bonds issued, he sat down, confident that his deal made with Chance Parker was making his stay only temporary.

Being a witness to a cold-blooded murder by a cop during a police raid gone bad guaranteed he could write his own ticket. It was only a matter of waiting at this point. He would make it back out and take his rightful spot at the top of the empire.

Selling out the crew, like that. You gettin' what you deserve, big bro!

The inmates going in alphabetical order, Xavier Toombs sat at the end of the bench that ran the length of the room. Looks of respect and head nods came from the other inmates, clearly aware of the recent exploits of him and his crew. Conquests made in the streets echoed inside the jails and prisons. To some players, prison was just an inconvenience, a mere physical reassignment and nothing to be feared.

"Yo dawg, what they got you for?" The inmate, a small nervous man seated next to Xavier, whispered.

"Don't matter. Ain't gonna stick anyhow."

"True."

Xavier tried to ignore the inmate, but he continued. "Hey man, when I get out, do you think Tony Tombs can hook me up?"

Angry, Xavier's face crumpled at the sound of his brother's name, and barked, "It's my crew, nigga. Not his. You want a job, you come to the king. That's me!"

The door was pushed open and Wendy inhaled quickly and wiped her face, hiding her sorrows. She didn't want the nurse to see her like that. She stood up with her back to the door and placed the baby in the rolling bed. It was probably time for a check-up or something.

"Hey." The warm voice of Dylan Akers startled her as she was expecting the intrusive nurse.

Wendy spun to see her husband. Speechless, she stood frozen, unable to comprehend how he came to be back.

"Hey," Dylan repeated.

Wendy snapped to and ran toward Dylan with her arms wide. He caught her in a loving embrace and squeezed her tight. He lifted up her small frame, and her bare feet were left dangling. She wrapped her arms around his neck and buried her face into his shoulder. She resumed her sobbing and just let it out, all while Dylan held her, never wanting to let go.

Lost in the emotion of the moment, Wendy's senses came back, and she noticed the baby stopped crying, as if he sensed the restoration of their family balance.

Wendy retracted from Dylan, and he eased her back down to the floor, "But, how? How are you here? I heard them say you were under arrest."

Dylan's eyes watered as he thought about his answer. Wendy grew worried, wondering if this visit was only temporary and if he was on his way to jail.

"What is it?" Her tone turned serious. "Tell me, Dylan."

"Beau," he mustered.

"Beau? I don't understand. Did something happen to Beau?"

He shook his head. "Beau is why I'm here and not on the way to jail."

"I still don't understand. What's going on?"

Dylan sucked in a cleansing breath, clearing his unsteadiness.

"I was up there at the station; they were going to charge us both with murder. I didn't talk, so they left me in the room for hours just waiting. Finally, Polk comes in, tells me that I'm not getting charged."

"What?" Wendy gasped. "But why did they change their mind like that?"

"Like I said, Beau." Dylan smiled. "He confessed to everything, but told them that I had nothing to do with it. He told them that he stole my access card to get the guns out of Property."

"He did what?" Wendy heard her husband's explanation, but her response was more disbelief than an inability to understand.

"Basically he covered for me. For us." His eyes lowered and watered again as Wendy processed the information. She watched tears fall down his face as he thought about his friend making such a huge sacrifice.

"So, you won't get charged? With anything?"

"Doesn't look that way. Polk said they consulted with the State Attorney, and they said no. Usually that holds up unless more evidence is found."

"Okay, but can they charge you later? What if Beau turns on you or something? I mean, with our history you never know what could happen."

"I don't think he'll do that, Wendy."

She nodded in agreement. She didn't think Beau would ever do something like that either.

"When I left, they let me say good-bye, and the look in his eyes..." Dylan choked up, but continued. "It was like this was his way of making everything okay. Everything from not stopping Shelley on the traffic stop that day, and being with you, and even ending our friendship all those years ago. It was like it was a debt repaid."

After a moment of reflection, Wendy spoke, "So he confessed to both murders, even McFadden's?"

"Yes."

Wendy now understood why Dylan was so emotional. She recalled the night Beau parked down the street for the last time. She had been harsh but for good reason. There were lingering feelings she felt would always be there, but they were an unwarranted distraction. Severing ties was the right thing to do. It was hard, but she ignored her heart's cry. The more she thought about what Beau did, the more overcome with a mix of joy and sadness she became. The joy was for the return of her husband and family. The sadness inside her heart was love for Beau. An unrequited love that could never be nurtured, but she would always hold a special place just for him.

Chapter 58

Busily working on her second basket of complimentary tortilla chips, Victoria Parker noticed her father staring back at her, and she offered a wide smile. Her freckles and dimples counteracted the missing teeth on the spectrum of cuteness.

"What?" she asked with embarrassment.

"Nothing, honey. I've missed you, that's all."

"It's okay, Dad. I know you've been busy putting bad guys in jail."

It put Chance at ease that she had some level of understanding about what he did when he was away. It lessened the guilt. Also, it was the same reason he let her choose where they ate lunch. Her affinity for chips and salsa made her favorite Mexican restaurant the obvious choice.

"I'd rather spend time with you," he said.

"I like hanging out with you too, Dad. Especially, when you get me out of school to come here." She ended her enthusiasm with an exaggerated bite of a chip.

"I'm glad."

Chance had awakened after only a few hours of sleep. The last thing he heard before going home was Beau Rivers confessing to two murders. Murders that had shocked the city and shifted the public trust to public suspicion. The storm from the night before had blown through. The city survived without any damage. Chance took a moment to notice the sky was clear, and the air was comfortably warm, carrying a sense of tranquility.

Longing to be around something pure and innocent, he arranged lunch with his eight-year-old daughter. There was no better embodiment of innocence than his daughter. Pulling her out of school for a lunch date required a few hoops, but it was worth it in his mind.

"So are you and Mom getting back together?"

So much for an easy lunch date.

"I don't know, sweetheart." Chance shifted uncomfortably in his seat. "But please know I love you so very much, and there isn't anything that will ever change that."

"Mom told me the same thing." She considered the chip in her hand and scooped a big helping of salsa and crunched down. After she finished, "So is that a no? She didn't answer me either."

"You're way too smart little girl." Chance saw her smile at the compliment and studied her further. His relationship with her mother had soured to the point of separation, and the last thing he wanted was for it to negatively impact Victoria. He watched her work on chip after chip and saw an inner strength, a resolve to deal with unfavorable situations with positivity and grace. It gave him hope that she was going to be okay.

The server came and set down a cheese quesadilla for Victoria and a chicken burrito for him. Chance changed the subject, and they discussed the ongoing playground gossip of the third grade at Shady Oaks Elementary. The fascination of the tales, at least in her eyes, rivaled that of the trendiest reality shows. Chance just smiled and enjoyed the sound of her voice.

As lunch ended, Chance checked the time on his phone. It was nearing twelve-thirty. He needed to get her back to school, but he was also waiting for an important text. Last night's operation culminated in more work that spilled over into today. He hoped today would be the last of it.

Thinking about the confidence game he ran on Xavier and the rest of the crew made Chance smile with amusement. He imagined all of them sitting at first appearance with confused looks plastered on their faces, wondering what the hell happened. But most of all, he wanted to see the look on Xavier Toombs's face when he realized he'd been had by the detective he entrusted to help him out of a murder charge.

A laugh escaped during the drive back out to Victoria's school.

"What, Daddy?" she asked.

"Nothing, honey. Just thinking about work stuff."

"Work stuff? Funny?"

Chance had broken some paradigm of police work in her mind. Apparently, it was all serious with no room for humor. "Don't worry about it, honey. I'll tell you when you get older."

"Aww."

"Here we are, Vic. Thanks for going to lunch with me. I hope we get to do this more often."

"Me too, Daddy. Especially when they're serving meatloaf in the cafeteria. Yuck!"

Chance laughed. "I'll make a note of that."

He kissed his daughter and sent her on her way back to her classroom, sure to be envied for her lunch locale over the humdrum school cafeteria.

In perfect timing, the text he was anticipating came through.

It's signed and ready.

That meant it was time to get back to work. Chance replied that he was on his way.

Twenty minutes later, he walked down the second floor of the courthouse to the county judge's chambers. Chance was then escorted through the thick, double doors and down a narrow hallway into an office. The judge's assistant waved Chance into a larger office and took a seat behind her desk. He rapped lightly on the doorframe to announce his presence.

"Come in, detective." Judge Roy Fowler stood up from behind his desk and extended a friendly hand out to Chance.

"Thank you, sir."

They shook hands. "Nice to see you again. Have a seat."

Chance sat while Fowler searched his desk for something. Finally finding it, he pulled out a sheaf of papers held together by a paperclip and waved it back at Chance. Peering over a set of bifocals resting on the end of his bony nose, he looked skeptical about its contents.

Last night before leaving the station, Chance had drafted a probable cause and a warrant for the judge to review. He had someone drop it off first thing while he slept, with instructions to call or text when it was done. The warrant was the first of many dominoes that needed to fall. Chance had corresponded with Sergeant Polk and told him he was getting a warrant for Antonio Toombs and that he needed some help making the arrest. Polk didn't question how, just complied with the request.

Worry fell over Chance, but he sat patiently, waiting for more than just a look to respond.

"This is quite a read, Detective. Let's talk about it."

"Yes, sir." Fowler was a former prosecutor. He always scrutinized what he was asked to sign and discussed the faults that may prove troublesome. He sat down and scanned the documents again.

"So he wasn't there? I take it all of the others were arrested, charged like you hoped?"

"No, he wasn't there like we planned. And yes, sir. It all worked out. That's what gave us the probable cause for that right there."

"I see. And you got Xavier Toombs to rat out his brother, just like that?"

"There was more substance to it, but essentially, yes. He confessed and dimed out his brother on tape. It'll be hard to refute that. And coupled with all the evidence we've been able to compile the last month on him and his crew, I feel like we'll be giving the State Attorney's Office a heck of a case to send these guys away for a long time."

Chance saw no point in mentioning the ruse that went along with the confession. Not yet anyway.

"Right, I remember you coming to me all those times." Fowler smiled and gave Chance a playful look through the bifocals. "Even the late night calls to the house."

"I apologize for that. And to your wife for bothering you all those times."

"Oh, no. It was no bother, Chance. When Dylan Akers called me and told me what you guys had planned, and how you were going to do it, I was happy to help out."

"Yes, sir. And we all thank you."

Fowler held a warrant for the arrest of Antonio Toombs. The charges were racketeering, drug trafficking, multiple counts of attempted murder, and murder. He looked over the paperwork one more time, set it down on his desk, and signed his name, making the warrant active.

He handed it over the desk. Chance stood up to accept it but Fowler held onto the documents to get his undivided attention. He had one more thing to say.

"I trust that this was all done above board, Detective. I don't need anything coming back to bite me in the ass."

"No, sir. We're good."

Fowler released his grip, and Chance took the documents. There were a few more steps to make and more work to be done. He thanked the judge again and found his way back through the double doors and down to the clerk's office.

He pulled his cell out of his pocket, found a contact, and hit send.

"Hello?" Polk answered.

"Sarge, it's Parker. The warrant is signed."

"Okay, I'll let the task force know. They should have him within the hour."

"Good."

Chance hung up and stood anxiously in the clerk's office, waiting for the girl behind the counter to file and enter the warrant into the system.

Chapter 59

"He's been in there for about twenty minutes," a voice, hushed for safety, said over the radio.

"You sure it was him that went in?"

"Positive. I repeat, positive it was the target."

"Okay, hold what you got. We can wait him out. What does the source say?"

Another voice chimed in, "Source puts him in the house."

"Okay, copy that."

Chance was listening to the U.S. Marshal's channel. They had been tasked with finding and apprehending Antonio Toombs. They had tracked him to a dead end on Richmond Street, deep in the Lincoln Heights neighborhood. It was the neighborhood that Tony Toombs had grown up in only to later return and terrorize as he built his so-called empire. That was all about to come to an end.

From a concealed spot on the next street over, Chance watched the face of the small green house through a pair of binoculars. Antonio Toombs stepped out of the front door and made sure it shut behind him. Calmly, he stood at the top of the wheelchair ramp and looked up at the late afternoon sky and smiled.

"Target's coming out."

"Okay, units move in."

Antonio remained on the porch as heavy engines roared up the short street. Footfalls from the path next to the house grew louder as heavily armed men ran up to the side of the house. Their vests read: US MARSHALS.

"Don't move, don't move. You are under arrest."

With an eerie anticipation, Antonio took in his surroundings, filled with swarming cops and machine guns, yelling and screaming. Chance focused on the man's eyes, not seeing any stress or anxiety, like he knew they were coming. That caused him to worry. A man with nothing to live for is the most dangerous.

As the arrest team approached, Antonio obeyed the verbal commands and allowed the Marshals to handcuff him with no resistance. Chance keyed in on his face through the binos, trying to get a feel for the kingpin. Toombs held a cocky grin that worried Chance.

Chance pulled his unmarked around to the dead end of Richmond Street. Antonio had been seated in the back of a Marshal's car. He sat up straight in the seat, not slouched like someone doomed. The worry grew. Chance opened up the door and leaned in to talk.

"Mr. Toombs, how are you today?"

Antonio turned to see who was addressing him, recognition flashed in his eyes. "Detective Parker. I'm fine even though I find myself in handcuffs."

"I could help you out if you feel like chit-chatting for a little bit. We can get out of this God-forsaken humidity and talk like men."

"A tempting offer, Detective." Chance could feel the rejection coming. "But no, I would like to seek counsel before making any statements."

Chance bit his tongue. He knew someone like Antonio Toombs would hide behind the shield of an attorney. He had played the game long enough to know not to talk. Chance knew he had to build a rock-solid case when going after a high-caliber target like Toombs. It would come down to good police work.

"Fine. Let's go ahead and call him now."

"I did, earlier. He'll be meeting us at the jail."

"You knew you were getting arrested?"

"I don't have to answer that, Detective, but yes. You can't throw my entire crew in jail and not think I wasn't going to hear about it."

"Fair enough."

Chance followed the Marshal who escorted Toombs out to the jail, and as promised, Toombs's lawyer stood outside the fence to the sally port.

"Counselor," Chance greeted.

"Detective, uh?"

"Parker."

"Yes, Parker. Thank you for bringing my client in unharmed." The attorney shot a glance over to Toombs with an I'll-take-it-from-here look.

"That's how we prefer it, counselor." Chance hated the insinuation that the more dangerous the criminal the more likely they are unjustly beaten.

The lawyer removed a folded piece of paper from a briefcase and presented it to Chance.

"This is a court order to have my client redirected and held at the Federal Corrections Institute until trial."

Confused, Chance took the paper to check its legitimacy. He looked it over and asked, "What for?"

"What for? Seriously, Detective. You can see the dangers posed to my client if he is housed here."

"He's been here before and with his street cred at an all-time high, I would think he's perfectly safe. What are you trying to pull here?"

"I'm not trying to pull anything, Detective."

"So why the court order?"

"It is my understanding that Beau Rivers is being housed here as of late last night."

Chance nodded in confirmation and added, "So?"

"So, he is charged with two counts of murder. Murders that he committed in cold blood with devious calculation. Matter of fact, one of his victims was in custody at the Leon County Jail at the time of his death and the other under the protection of the Bailiff's unit. He's proven resourceful and cunning."

"But there's a difference. Beau wasn't in jail at the time. Now he is."

"He killed those men under the nose of your entire department, Detective." The jab went straight to Chance's gut. "And am I understanding that Beau Rivers assisted you in this case against my client?"

Fuck!

"Yes, but his mere involvement shouldn't affect the merit of this case. If you weren't so concerned with smoke and mirrors in your defense, you'd see that."

"We'll let a jury decide that, Detective."

"Okay, whatever." Beyond irritated, he shoved the court order back at the lawyer. "You have to clear your little motion with the jail before he can be transferred."

The Marshal pulled Antonio out of his backseat and walked him past Chance and his attorney. The cocky grin remained.

Chance followed him with his eyes, refusing to be intimidated. The attorney told him he would follow him inside to talk more. Antonio acknowledged him and looked straight at Chance.

"Tell Beau that I received his letter."

"Huh?" Confused, Chance didn't understand the meaning. "What are you talking about?"

Antonio laughed like a jackal and ignored Chance as he was led into the mechanical doors of the jail.

Chance looked at the attorney. "What the hell did that mean? What letter?"

With a genuine absent look, he said, "I don't know. He mentioned something about a get-out-of-jail-free card. I'm not sure if that's what he's talking about. He never told me anything more than that."

"Sure he did."

***

Chance felt out of place, a foreigner in a strange land. Never having visited the jail in this capacity, he felt awkward as he waited on the other side of the glass partition. He brought arrestees to jail or talked to an inmate about a case in the unit where they were housed. Never did he visit one. But he needed an answer. What Antonio had said moments ago bothered Chance, and he wanted to ask Beau the meaning.

When he badged the deputy at the front desk and asked to speak to Beau, he received a glaring look and a foul mood. Chance wondered why the attitude until he remembered, it was Beau who had shot at one of their transport deputies and butt-stroked another with a shotgun. He was definitely not their favorite prisoner. Chance checked at his watch. Fifteen minutes had passed from when he requested to speak to Beau. The tardiness was probably a result of their distaste.

A moment later, Beau stepped into the room on the other side of the partition. Not knowing the etiquette, Chance smiled to greet Beau. He shot a smile back, sat down, and picked up the direct connect phone on the wall.

"What are you doing here?" The smile vanished and Beau's tone became harsh.

"Well, hello to you, too."

"Sorry. Thanks for stopping by, but you shouldn't be here. Is there something wrong with the case?"

"No. Actually, everything turned out as we hoped. I think it'll be a great case."

"Good. So why are you here?"

"Well, really, I'm here as a friend with a curious question, not as an investigator. Something just came up, and I wanted to ask you in person, if that's all right."

"Okay, what?"

"We got Antonio this afternoon and we just brought him in."

Beau considered the news and nodded with acceptance. "That's good. Is that what you wanted to tell me?"

"No, it was something he said just a bit ago when we got him here to the jail. He wanted me to give you a message."

Beau leaned forward, now more invested in the conversation. "A message? What is it?"

"He said to tell you that he got your letter. What does that mean? What letter is he talking about?"

Chance noticed Beau's face turned a few shades whiter. The message meant something, and it registered deep inside. It silenced Beau. Stunned, he didn't respond.

Chance knocked on the thick glass, trying to get Beau to snap out of whatever trance the message caused.

"Hey, Beau? What does that mean? The lawyer said it could be his get-out-of-jail-free card. What's he talking about?"

Beau shook his head and stared off somewhere behind Chance.

"Beau, talk to me. What is it? Let me help?"

"No, don't do anything. Everything is fine. He's just messin' with you."

"Bullshit. I can see it in your eyes. You know exactly what he's talking about. You know!"

"Good-bye, Chance."

"Beau! C'mon, man. I can help. What's he talking about?"

Beau stood up and turned his back, ignoring Chance's pleas. He banged on the metal door until the jailor opened it and let him out of the small room. Chance watched him leave and was left more confused than when he had walked in.

What letter were they talking about and what the hell did it say?

Chapter 60

The tragedy of losing a child to murder is that it's hard to focus on the good memories without the bad trespassing. Dylan constantly battled with this, trying to remember Caitlin as she was in life. Now, he remembered one of the most peaceful things in this world to do is watch a newborn baby sleep. They are so innocent and vulnerable. They beg for care even when they are content in dreamland. Dylan and Wendy had just made it home from the hospital and put baby Phoenix down in his new crib. Exhausted, physically, emotionally, and mentally from the last forty-eight hours, they stood in the threshold of the newly painted bedroom and watched him sleep. He was bundled tightly in a blanket cocoon with a perfect pout fixed on his lips.

Dylan inhaled and let out a sigh. He reached around his wife and held her close. She arched her neck down resting it on his shoulder, sharing the moment.

"I'm terrified it'll happen again." It was a fear that was too heinous to mention, but weighed heavily on them both.

Wendy's body tensed. "Me, too."

"I don't even want to think about it anymore."

"Then don't. He's here. He's home and we're here, too. Together. Let's not let fear cripple us."

"You're right."

Dylan leaned down to kiss Wendy. They held the kiss despite being near collapse.

"I need a nap," she declared.

"Well, we have about an hour or two, tops, since he just went down. Lead the way."

Wendy stepped back from the doorway, but only after one more look, one more assurance that her boy was safe, then she headed for the bedroom.

As Dylan followed, a buzzing in his pocket stopped him. He pulled out his cell phone. The caller ID read: Robert Shaw.

"The Chief is calling," he told Wendy.

"What for?"

"Dunno." Dylan hit the answer button. "Hello?"

"Dylan, it's me. I know you're probably home right now, but I need you to come in to the station."

"Why? I was just there last night. I thought everything was settled."

"I know. It was on that thing. This is about the other thing."

Dylan instantly knew Shaw was referring to the side project he had forced upon him and Beau.

"What do you mean?" Dylan knew. He was hoping to get more information out of the Chief.

"You know what I mean. I'm talking about the case against Antonio Toombs and his people. Apparently, Pritchard went to the State Attorney's Office after he found out about it and then contacted Toombs's lawyer. He's obviously on a rampage now, saying the arrests were all illegal and we should all be arrested. I got them to hold off on going to a judge just yet to give us a chance to explain ourselves."

Dylan nodded. Given what he knew about Pritchard, he was not surprised that he went over the Chief's head.

"What time?"

"Now, Dylan. They are headed up here and we need to get..." Shaw paused on the other end. He lowered his voice, "We need to minimize the damage here. There is too much at stake."

Dylan could hear the fear in Shaw's voice.

"Fine, let me get some things together and I'll head up there."

"Can we explain things, Dylan?"

"We'll see." He hung up before the Chief could respond.

The more he thought about it, he felt Shaw was scared because Pritchard had something on him as well as Dylan and the squad. Shaw thought only of himself, and that made Dylan angry. That was not the Robert Shaw he once knew.

"You have to go back?" Wendy stood, arms folded, in the bedroom when Dylan entered.

"Yes."

With a guarded look, she asked, "You coming back this time?"

Her eyes bore a pain that sat on the edge of surrender. His heart ached for her because she had endured the tumultuous roller coaster of the last few days.

He went to her and held her close. "Yes. Of course, I'm coming back."

She stifled a sob, and Dylan hoped what he said was not a lie.

***

The drab eight-by-eight jail cell was anything but inviting. However, it was quiet. The silence accentuated the isolation. The muffled sounds of metal doors buzzing and clanking shut down the hallway made for the only external sounds. Internally, Beau's mind was furiously working through the news Chance Parker had just delivered.

Somehow, Toombs had gotten hold of the letter. That's the only logical explanation for his message sent through Chance. The letter spelled out how he was going to take the fall for Dylan, allowing him to be free of any criminal charges. He was willing to sacrifice his own freedom so his friend could live in peace, free from the cloud of suspicion cast after they killed McFadden and Shelley.

That was now in jeopardy. If Toombs exposed the plan, it would be disastrous for Dylan and guaranteed to send him to prison along with Beau. It would also erase any validity Beau had, which wasn't much to begin with.

He rocked back and forth with nervous energy, letting his mind work, thinking of how to deal with this problem. He grew frustrated as he came up blank. He had to do something, but he was stuck inside of a bleak concrete box, locked behind a thick metal door, and guarded by men who despised him.

Anger boiled within. He needed to get to Toombs before he could use the information in the letter. If Toombs was smart, he would have hidden it somewhere, somewhere he knew it would be kept safe and be used on his terms, not his lawyer's. But getting to him or anyone was out of the question.

Beau needed help. He had phone privileges, but who the hell would he call. He couldn't further involve Dylan or risk bringing in Chance. He trusted no one else.

A sickness fell in the pit of his stomach.

Beau let out a low groan wrought with helplessness. The sick feeling was crippling, and he curled up on the thin mattress, grabbing his stomach.

I have to do something, but what?

An epiphany struck, and suddenly everything was clear.

Chapter 61

Lieutenant Dylan Akers walked through the front doors of the police department with his head held high. The stigma of wrongdoing seemed to hang in the air, but he wasn't going to give it further credence. He nodded to the duty officer who watched him suspiciously from behind the safety glass. Dylan proceeded through the double doors, down the hallway, and into the elevator. Hanging on the wall, amongst the Hall of Heroes, was a small plaque with his image encapsulated in the middle, along with a brief narrative. It was for the medal of bravery. He had earned it by shooting a man who was about to kill Beau Rivers following a harrowing shootout and car chase. It seemed a lifetime ago, but it served as a reminder that he was capable of good in this job.

As the elevator doors opened on the third floor, Chance Parker was pacing back and forth. Under his arms was a thick, three-ring binder full of paperwork.

"Good, you brought it."

"Yeah." Chance acknowledged the binder. "Let's hope it's enough."

"It will be. Let's go."

Dylan pulled open the doors of the Chief's conference room. Shaw stood in the back corner. Pritchard sat in the middle with a lascivious grin on his face. Trek and members of the command staff filled in the rest of the room.

"Lieutenant Akers, please have a seat. Detective Parker, we didn't call you here, just Dylan." Pritchard asserted himself early. "You may be excused."

"I called him here, Major. He's essential to the case and will help explain everything. That is why we're here, right?"

Pritchard's grin was replaced by a look of concern. Dylan exuded confidence, and he noticed the Major was picking up on it.

"Fine. Parker can stay."

Shaw found a seat, and Sergeant Polk entered the room. He apologized for being late and took a seat close to Dylan.

"Thanks for coming, Melvin." Pritchard stated.

Polk nodded as he adjusted in the chair.

"Lieutenant Akers, let me start by saying I believe you should be charged with the murders of Earnest McFadden and George Shelley, but that's another matter I consider unresolved. Right now, I am deeply disturbed at what you and your team have been doing. You and Beau Rivers have given this department a black eye that will last for decades and this...," he paused as he searched for a word for emphasis, "brutality you call police work, will not stand. I will not allow it, and I will see you burn."

Dylan remained calm and stoic. Chance stirred nervously in the seat next to him.

Pritchard continued, "And don't deny it this time. I have the proof, and Beau Rivers can't cover for you." Pritchard shot a glance over at Shaw who slinked down in his chair.

"Russell?" Pritchard addressed Trek, giving him the cue to step up.

"Yes, sir." Trek opened a file in front of him and removed several papers. "This is the transfer request signed by Chief Shaw, placing you in charge of a three-man squad consisting of Beau Rivers, Chance Parker, and Desmond Holcomb. You can see the original signature of the Chief, and a records search proved that it was never disseminated to the department as required by our policy."

Dylan glanced over at Shaw who looked uncomfortable. He felt no empathy toward the Chief; this was his doing, and he deserved to be called out.

Trek pulled out another sheet and held it up. "Here, we have after-action reports from you, Lieutenant Akers, to the Chief, detailing what you did on several occasions, the first of which, outlines taking a kilo of cocaine out of a backpack with what looks like no established probable cause."

Dylan waited. Trek searched for something else within the file. "And I see here that you did, in fact, charge Duquan Baker with cocaine trafficking based on this seizure. That's an improper search and an illegal arrest. You had no authority to stop or detain him. You had no authority to search the backpack and no authority to take the drugs."

Trek set down the paper and looked at Dylan for a response. Dylan didn't give one, remaining steadfast.

"Nothing to say, Lieutenant?" Pritchard asked.

"Not at this time, sir. I'm sure you have a lot more stuff in that file folder, so I'll let you just get it all out in the open."

"Suit yourself. It'll be your funeral—or trial, rather."

Trek continued. "Moving on, the next after-action details another illegal search and seizure on a traffic stop involving Christopher Toombs and Gaile Gaines. This led to the procurement of an assault rifle in which you later charged young Christopher. Also, of note." Trek looked up from the paperwork. "This encounter resulted in an excessive use of force by Officer Beau Rivers when he broke the arm of Mr. Toombs."

Dylan flinched as he heard the news of the excessive force. He looked at Chance who gave an embarrassed grin and shrugged his shoulders.

Trek added, "Again, you overstepped your authority in taking the gun which will be deemed as inadmissible in court."

"Still nothing to say, Dylan?" Pritchard addressed.

Dylan shook his head defiantly, but he was too busy processing something Trek said. The only way they knew about the excessive force was from one of two sources. The first being Christopher Toombs, which he knew never happened. That was the catalyst for the warehouse shootout, so why would Antonio have had the boy claim excessive force, only to turn around and try to kill them. That didn't make sense, it wasn't his style. The only other way that information made it up to Internal Affairs was from within.

"Anything else you want to embellish?" Dylan said.

"Embellish!" Pritchard yelled, nearly coming out of his seat. "This is not embellishment, Lieutenant. This is a simple fact laid out in your own writing. We've already compared samples of your reports to this and got a match, so don't deny that you wrote it. This is blatant disregard for the law. You and Rivers continued your vigilante ways, taking the law into your own hands, and I will not stand for it. It ends now!" Pritchard calmed himself. "So, please by all means sit there with that smug look on your face like you did nothing wrong, and I'll nail your ass to the wall. The only reason you are here is that we promised the State Attorney to hear you out before charging you with theft, false imprisonment, aggravated assault, and the list goes on. You may have slipped from the noose on the McFadden and Shelley thing, but by God, I've got you dead to rights on this."

Dylan withheld any reaction to Pritchard. All eyes in the room fell to him. "Didn't happen like you said."

"The hell it didn't. It's right here in black and white."

"I know what that says. I wrote it. But it didn't happen like that."

"Oh, so you admit to writing it?"

"Yes." Dylan said as if Pritchard were slow and not paying attention. "But again, it didn't happen like that."

"Well, I beg to differ, Lieutenant. That will be your word against the witness's, and, coupled with the after-action reports you just admitted to writing, I think it will be enough to convince the State Attorney to prosecute." Pritchard scoffed and looked around the room, stopping at the legal advisor and then looked over to Shaw. "Really, this was a complete waste of time. Why bother continue—"

"Witness?" Dylan interrupted and then looked over at Chance who shook his head in confusion.

Pritchard reengaged. "Yes, Dylan. You think I'm taking any chances in this investigation. We've done our homework, too."

"You going to make me guess at who it is, or what?" Dylan asked.

"As much as I enjoy watching you squirm, I will fill you in," Pritchard said. "Matter of fact, he's out in the hallway waiting. Trek?"

Russell Trek got up from his seat and stepped out into the hallway. A moment later, he re-entered with Desmond Holcomb following. Holcomb was dressed in a navy pinstripe suit, a white dress shirt with a pink collar, and a matching handkerchief in the pocket. Dylan noticed his bracelet, watch, and rings were all the color gold, not silver.

He is the source within. Makes sense.

Holcomb avoided eye contact with Dylan or Chance as he found a seat across the room. Dylan looked over at Shaw for an explanation, but he only offered a pathetic and submissive look that said, *My hands are tied.*

"Dez," Dylan welcomed.

His eyes heavy with embarrassment, Holcomb gave a head nod back to Dylan.

"So this is your witness?"

"Yes, Sergeant Holcomb is willing to testify and validate everything in the after-action reports and more."

"They promised to give your stripes back, huh, Dez?"

"Got to take care of me, Dylan. I'm sorry."

Chapter 62

Deputy Luke Brackens worked the night shift on the "Blue Ward," a name given to the wing where law enforcement affiliated inmates were housed. He'd gotten word that Beau Rivers had been officially charged with the murders of Earnest McFadden and George Shelley and couldn't wait to get to work to see for himself. He wanted to see the man who had shot at his uncle, Les.

At twenty-two years of age, Luke took seriously his oath to protect all under his control, but Beau's reckless behavior became personal. Although, Uncle Les had told him to hold no grudge, Luke fostered a hate toward the man who had crossed the line.

"Time for rounds, Luke. You're up," his sergeant reported.

"Copy that, Sarge."

Brackens left out of the unit and entered the long hallway. Aside from Rivers, two other inmates were on the floor. One was a former cop from Louisiana who had committed some fraudulent schemes and awaited trial. The other was a state trooper in New York before getting hooked on painkillers and moving to Florida. He had pulled a gun on a neighbor during a narcotic-induced tirade and then barricaded himself in his townhome. TPD's Tactical Apprehension and Control team was called out to deal with the situation. They had flushed him out with gas and taken him into custody.

Brackens hoped, during his stay, Beau Rivers would try something, anything. It would be the excuse to pulverize him and pay back what he did to his uncle.

Continuing his rounds, Brackens heard a faint groan down the hallway, a sickly groan that was normally the precursor to some made-up illness. Inmates constantly complained; a trip to the infirmary broke up the monotony of solitude. Brackens paused, pinpointing where the noise came from. It was down a few cells on the right, Rivers's cell.

If this was a trick, he was ready.

***

Holding his stomach and writhing in pain, Beau heard the key enter the lock and the cell door open. A baby-faced deputy stared at him with glaring eyes.

"What's wrong, Rivers?"

"I don't know, but my stomach hurts like hell. Like I got kicked by a Clydesdale."

"It's called remorse. It'll pass when you realize you did something wrong."

"No, I'm pretty sure somethings wrong, Deputy. Can I go to the infirmary, please?"

The deputy looked down the hallway for something and then back at Beau.

"I ought to just leave you in here and let you suffer, you son of a bitch."

Still lying on his side, Beau replied, "I'm not sure what I've done to you, Deputy, but whatever it is, I'm sorry. I need medical help, I swear."

Beau let out another groan, gritting his teeth and clenching his eyes.

"Infirmary's busy right now. You'll have to wait."

The deputy was just being malicious.

"Ahh, c'mon, Deputy. Please?"

Another episode came and he pleaded with the deputy.

"Fine." The deputy requested over the radio to escort Beau to the infirmary. A minute later, permission was granted.

"C'mon. Get your ass up."

"Can you help me?"

"You're a grown man. You can do it yourself."

"C'mon, please?"

The deputy hesitated. Beau saw his eyes narrow as he thought about something before he acted. Beau extended his hand as he lay helpless on the bed. The deputy chocked the door open and cautiously entered the small cell. The deputy's eyes never left Beau's.

The deputy reached down. Beau clasped onto this arm firmly and felt the deputy tense. There was an awkward moment in the tiny cell, holding each other's hand. Beau then pulled himself up to a seated position.

"Thanks."

"Let's stand up."

With more help, Beau stood up next to the deputy. They stood nearly eye to eye, Beau slightly taller. His eyes darted to the nametag on his chest: Brackens.

"Ahh. That makes sense." Beau bowed his head and stepped toward the hallway.

"What's that?"

"You must be related to Les Brackens. That's why you hate me."

The deputy was caught off guard. He stammered, "Well, um…, I don't hate you, but—"

"Les your dad or something?"

"Uncle."

"Ahh." Beau nodded, still keeping his eyes downcast. "It's okay to hate me, if you want. I understand. I would probably do the same in your shoes."

Beau continued down the hallway, out of the unit, through a locked door and out into the center of the jail. Brackens walked closely behind, just off Beau's right shoulder.

During the brief elevator ride down to the bottom floor, Brackens stood poised on the far side of the car, carefully watching.

"I'm sorry. I don't hate you. I guess I'm just mad."

"I get it. You must think I'm a monster. I've faced a few monsters in my career. I won't be the last for you either."

Brackens nodded in agreement.

"What's the L stand for?"

Brackens glanced down. "Oh, Luke."

"Luke. Nice to meet you. I'm sorry about your uncle. I don't really know him, and we… met… under unusual circumstances."

"I'll say. You were firing an automatic rifle at him."

"Please tell him I'm sorry and I never meant him any harm. I was just trying to get to the guy in the back."

"You should tell him yourself."

"Is he here? I'd be glad to tell him personally."

"No, but he very well could be the guy taking you to court and whatnot."

"Well that's a little ironic, isn't it?" Beau let out a chuckle, but instantly winced and hugged at his core.

The elevator came to a stop, the doors opened, and Brackens directed Beau down a long wall to another locked door.

"You know, Uncle Les actually told me that I shouldn't hold a grudge against you."

"Oh, really?"

"Yeah. He's an exceptional man. Very forgiving. I mean, if he's willing to let you off the hook, I don't know how much more forgiving someone can be."

"Well, tell him I'm grateful for his forgiveness."

Brackens opened the door to the infirmary and informed the nurse of Beau's symptoms. Directed to a table lined with thin paper, he sat down and the nurse took his temperature, blood pressure, and examined his eyes and ears. Beau was the only inmate in the triage area and Brackens the only deputy. Cautiously, he stood guard at the door.

Chapter 63

The inquisition continued with Pritchard leading the charge. "Let's hear your side, Lieutenant Akers. Or shall we inform the State Attorney's Office that they can go ahead and file charges."
"You'd like that wouldn't you?" Dylan said.
"That's why we're here."
"Well, I hate to disappoint you, but you've got it all wrong."
Pritchard waited attentively in disbelief.
"We can start with the first stop at the hilltop store," Dylan said. "We had all the authority we needed, Major."
"I'm listening."
"We were conducting follow-up from Detective Sinclair's shooting. We developed a suspect by the name of Duquan Baker based on where the incident originated. Prior intelligence suggested that he frequents the hilltop store, so that's where we went."
"Prior intelligence?" The concept seemed foreign to Reginald Pritchard.
"Yes, prior intelligence."
"What does that mean?"
"A real cop wouldn't ask that, but since it's you, Major, ask Desmond. It was his suggestion."
Pritchard turned to Holcomb with an irritated stare. Clearly, he had omitted some things in his debrief. Desmond blurted out, "I told him if Baker was a north-side guy, he'd be hanging out at the hilltop store."
"Go on."
"Eventually, Baker showed up and we conducted a citizen encounter. We all saw him exit the vehicle and go into the store. He had the backpack

on when he went in but slipped it off as he exited the store. When asked about its ownership, he denied knowledge of it."

Pritchard wasn't following the rationale. Dylan realized he needed to spell it out.

"It was abandoned property. He ditched it and gave up any and all rights to it. It was abandoned, so that allows us to search it."

"But you saw him with it earlier? It was his."

"And then he denied it. He did what any street player would do, separate themselves from it. That was his choice, not ours. He walked away and verbally denounced it several times, even in front of your witness."

Holcomb, hidden behind his hands, gave Pritchard a raised eyebrow look that said, "He's right."

"After seizing it, we got his prints off the bag of cocaine and DNA off the zipper of the backpack." Dylan worked his way around the room seeing the validation that this was, in fact, a good arrest settle on the faces. "I'm no prosecutor, but that sounds like a pretty damn good dope case if you ask me."

Several nods of agreement came from the room, most notably the legal advisor.

"Okay, fine, Dylan." Pritchard's irritation rose a level. "That's one case out of many you bungled. But you're not going to explain away the illegal seizure of that AK-47."

"Can I try? That's why I'm here, right?"

Pritchard leaned back in his chair with disgust imprinted on his face.

Taking the reaction as a go-ahead, Dylan continued. "Matter of fact, that case is just as clean as the first. Detective Parker and Beau saw Ms. Gaines commit a moving violation and called a patrol unit to affect the stop. Doesn't matter they were in a civilian car. The probable cause for the stop transfers between officers. Basic rookies know this. During the stop, they determined the car was a rental, the preferred choice of dopers, and upon finding the lease agreement, neither Ms. Gaines's nor Christopher Toombs's name was on it."

"That doesn't give you the right to search it and seize evidence," Trek spoke up, thrusting his knowledge outward.

"You're right, Rusty. Good job."

Trek's face turned upside down.

"That's why a good cop continues down any available avenue."

"Which was?" Pritchard asked.

A grin crossed Chance Parker's face. Dylan answered, "Call the rental car company. Many have a policy that if their car is stopped and the leasee is not present, they will ask the police to take control of the car until they can take custody. It voids the contract with the lease, and the leasee gives up any and all rights to the car. As the vehicle's lawful owner, the rental company can grant permission to search the car for any contraband. It just so happened that Chance and Beau located that AK-47, during their inventory search, before they returned the car to the rightful owner."

Major Pritchard's face became forlorn and tired in just a short matter of time. His golden case, he realized, was actually made of fool's gold.

"And let me add, Major, that Detective Parker sent off that rifle to be compared to the double murder on Preston Street and found it matched several slugs found in the victims and projectiles found at the crime scene. I'll let you take one guess whose DNA came back on the trigger guard?"

Pritchard looked uneasy, the disgust still emblazoned on his face. "Who?"

Dylan slapped his hand on the table in an overly dramatic way. "Mr. Christopher Toombs."

Pritchard had enough. "Okay, okay, I get it. You covered your tracks on those cases, but Desmond told us everything about the shootout at the warehouse. First of all, you had no authority to be in there, and second of all, you failed to alert any part of your chain of command that you were involved in a use of force, especially deadly force. You let the department respond and work that scene without the faintest bit of a heads up!"

"Let's not forget they were ambushed, Reggie," Chief Shaw chirped trying to mitigate what he could. "I mean, they barely escaped with their lives."

"Now you weigh in, Robert." Pritchard turned in his seat and gave the Chief a scowl. He turned back to Dylan. "I get it that you were ambushed, but one could argue it wouldn't have happened if you weren't trespassing. The way I see it, you have the property owner defending themselves against trespassers and you shooting back. I call that attempted murder."

"It's not trespassing."

"According to Desmond, who you were with the whole time, Parker and Rivers just walked into that warehouse hoping to interrupt a drug deal. Trespassing."

"Not trespassing. Not when you have a signed search warrant."

"Huh?" Pritchard, Trek, and Holcomb all shared the same incredulous look.

"Chance," Dylan addressed. Chance pulled open the large, three-ring binder and removed several stapled sheets of paper and slid them in front of Dylan. "Thanks." Dylan turned back to Pritchard. "Signed by Judge Fowler. The probable cause was established by the credibility of a verified informant and followed up by circumstances that validated his claims."

Trek interjected, "Is that the same informant that set you up to be ambushed?"

"The same. The thing is Russ, we didn't know we were going to get ambushed. We went in based on what we knew at the time. Not what came afterward. So, not trespassing."

"Where was the knock-and-announce? Why did you serve it with only four people? That's an officer safety concern."

"Yes, it was. But this was a calculated risk we were willing to take and Fowler agreed that we didn't need a knock-and-announce warrant, based on the circumstances."

"Like what?"

"We knew they would be heavily armed, which we were right about. We knew there was a high propensity for violence, which was also right. All our fears outlined in the request for the warrant were validated by what happened."

Pritchard was now drowning in a pool of misconceptions. He tried to salvage any aspect of his case. "Never mind the authority level and the criminality of the shooting, how do you explain the shootout? Failing to report a use of deadly force is a serious violation."

"I did report it."

"Liar!" Pritchard boomed. "That is a flat out lie, Lieutenant. You did no such thing. If you did, then where is the use-of-force report?"

"I was not asked to do one, as is the protocol for an officer involved in a shooting."

"But you failed to report it, bottom line."

"That's false. I did report it."

"To who?"

"My chain of command."

Pritchard searched the room for the captain who supervised Dylan. Finding him, he asked, "Did he tell you about this shootout?"

"No, sir. He did not."

"There you have it, Lieutenant. You are a proven liar."

"The only thing proven here is that you cannot listen. I did report it. Isn't that right, Chief?"

Shaw tried to dissolve into the chair and deflect attention, but once Dylan called him out, he begrudgingly sat up.

"Take out that little transfer order, Russ. Read it off again?"

Trek ignored the request until Pritchard nodded to proceed. Trek read out loud and informed the room that Rivers, Holcomb, and Parker were under the command of Dylan. But Dylan was directly under Chief Shaw.

"So, after the shootout, I called Chief Shaw and informed him of the shooting. He told me that he would take care of the department notifications."

Silence fell on the room, waiting for Shaw to say something.

"He did call and that's what I told him." There was a degree of humility in the Chief's tone. "I saw no point for him to stop and secure the scene, because they had just been ambushed. I was just glad they were alive. I was going to give Sergeant Polk and his team time to figure things out and inform them, but things moved a little too fast."

"So, it's you who was negligent?" Pritchard concluded.

Shaw clenched his jaw and sent a bitter glare at his major. "Looks that way."

The focus moved back to Dylan. "And I suppose each member of your squad informed you of the shoot out?"

"Since I was there, yes. They did."

"Goddammit!" Pritchard launched out of his seat. It flung backwards and crashed against the glass wall. "Trek. Hallway."

Dylan allowed a small smile of victory to himself as he watched the Major storm out of the room.

"We're not done, Lieutenant. Get comfortable. Holcomb, you too. Hallway, now!"

***

Twenty minutes later, Pritchard came back to the conference room, refreshed. Trek and Holcomb looked like they had been through the spin cycle. Dylan inhaled as he readied for whatever Pritchard was going to bring this next go around.

"You must think you're clever, Lieutenant, but I know what you're doing. You are bending words and bending the law to cover up you and your loose cannons' wanton disregard for the law. Rivers is a lost cause, but Parker over there had a promising career. Now, you've tainted him by dragging him down to your level."

"I didn't drag anyone down, and he still has a very promising career ahead. He's a great cop. I specifically asked for Parker, but he initially turned me down, for reasons which I understood." Dylan turned to his right and smiled sincerely at Chance. "But, I convinced him to join me in this endeavor. Do you know how I did that, Major?"

"No, enlighten us."

"I told him that we would do everything the right way. We would never overstep our bounds. We would always have legal authority, and we would make the best case possible. That was the only way he would agree."

Chance nodded in agreement as Dylan continued. "Of course, we toed the line and responded with force, but only when necessary and justifiable. It's called police work, Major. Sometimes you have to get your hands dirty. It's something you haven't got the slightest clue about."

"Watch your tone, Lieutenant."

"It's true. You had nothing but hard-nosed police work in front of you this whole time, but you still chose to see what you wanted, bad cops. You brought us here, wasting our time with this foolish witch hunt, when we need to be working together. You're so blind and ignorant, it's dangerous."

"Hard-nosed police work? What about one of your own? This was how he perceived things as they happened. He was there. Right, Sergeant Holcomb?"

"Yeah, but I mean—"

"It's not his fault. He didn't know what was going on behind the scenes. He didn't know, and I purposefully kept him in the dark. Hell, Beau Rivers didn't know either."

"What? But why'd you do that?" Holcomb sounded hurt.

"Sorry, Dez, but I've never been able to trust you to do what's right for this department. You've always been out for yourself. I kind of anticipated you'd be in this room in this manner, and that's why I didn't tell you."

"That's fucked up."

"Don't care."

Holcomb threw his arms up and fell back into his chair, pissed off. "What about that shit Rivers pulled on that last thing, pretending to shoot that kid?"

"Yes, Lieutenant. Let's talk about that." Pritchard stepped in.

Dylan pushed away from the edge of the table and turned to Chance. "I'll let Detective Parker talk about that one."

"Again, we had Fowler sign a search warrant for the residence. We had all of the forensics come back from the cocaine, the AK, and from several other shootings. I was able to tie-in that house and show they were going back there after each incident. I had court orders to go up on their phones to ping their locations, but we needed more on Antonio Toombs. He was the main target, the head of the snake. He'd been elusive, but we knew he was dirty. We just needed proof."

"Which meant we needed at least one of them to talk," Dylan interjected.

"Right. So I came up with the ruse, which they bought. Rivers had the reputation of going off the reservation. The news about his impending arrest for the murders of McFadden and Shelley was known, so they saw him, as you put it, as a 'loose cannon.' So I just let human nature and their fears play into it."

Chance continued, "Rivers did his thing with the little guy, Sherman, and took him into another room. He put on a show and it caused Xavier to jump first. I took the opportunity and was able to exploit that into a full confession against his brother. I would have taken whoever the first one to jump would have been, but we hit pay dirt when it was Antonio's little brother. He gave him up on the Preston Street murder, the hit on the witness, the drug trafficking, you name it. It gave us plenty of ammunition to make the arrest."

"So you scared him into confession. That's coercion, you can't do that," Trek stated.

"Yeah, I saw Beau shoot at that kid," Holcomb added.

"No, you didn't," Chance said.

"Okay, I heard it. Plain as day."

"Did you, Desmond?"

Holcomb furrowed his brow in confusion, thinking earnestly about whether he heard the gunshot or not.

"Yes, I heard it. I know what a gunshot sounds like."

"Okay, but I was there too. It was also thundering and lightning something fierce outside. Who's to say that wasn't a thunder clap just outside the window? It was perfect timing if you ask me."

"Nah, I heard a gunshot."

"Did you see him shoot at the kid or not?" Pritchard's impatience was palpable.

"No."

"Was it thundering at that moment when y'all were in the house?"

"Yes, sir."

"Did you ever see a shell casing or anything like that?" Chance jumped back in.

Holcomb thought, but then shook his head.

"No, I didn't."

The room stood silent. Dylan heard Parker exhale and relax. He watched Pritchard, turned to Trek, and then glanced at Shaw. The Chief looked relieved, like a burden had been lifted away by Dylan and his forethought.

"Wait a minute. Even if it was a ruse, and Xavier thought you shot his buddy, it's still a tainted confession," Trek announced.

"Technically, yes," Parker admitted.

Pritchard scooted back up to the table with new life. He asked, "So you obtained an illegal confession based off coercion?"

"No, sir."

"But you just said you got a confession after he was led to believe his friend was shot. You said, technically that it was tainted."

"Yes, only if I obtained the confession at that moment. I took measures to remove that fear from Xavier before I got the confession."

"How so?"

"If he thought Beau was going to kill him, which was reasonable, although it was part of the ruse, I had to remove him from the house.

Which was technically at his request. I drove him to one of the most secure facilities we have in this town, the jail, and then talked to him."

"He could argue he was still scared, and that's why he confessed."

"He could, but it would contradict what he said on audio tape." Chance held up a tape recorder to emphasize the fact.

Doubtful faces adorned the room. Chance clicked play on the tiny recorder. A voice, deep and slow, seeped out. "I make this statement without promise or coercion to Detective Parker. I swear all is the truth, the whole truth, and nothing but the truth. So help me God."

Chance's recorded voice followed, "Thanks Xavier, you did the right thing."

Chance clicked the stop button and set it down, letting Xavier Toombs's words erase any doubt in the room. He held up a sheet of paper for the room to see. "He read that from this sheet which he signed." Chance set it on the table and slid it over in front of Prichard who ignored the justification it proved.

"If he makes the claim, Major, that's fine. I think we'll let a judge and a jury decide who's right," Dylan chimed in.

Pritchard futilely attempted to rehash the battle once again. Members of command staff finally weighed in and admonished Pritchard for continuing his pursuit of false claims and that the lieutenant and detective had proven their case. Dylan remained steadfast and again defended each and every one of his actions.

A loud, short buzz vibrated on the table in front of Chance. He picked up the phone and moved it in front of Dylan, letting him read the text message: Positive ID, 100%.

Dylan nodded, beaming with more confidence.

"What's that, Dylan?" Shaw asked.

"That's confirmation of another attempted murder charge for George Sherman and Duquan Baker." He turned to Pritchard. "Since your head's been so far up this case's ass, you should know that Detective Sinclair came out of his coma a few hours ago. He's doing well and alert. The doctors let us show him a photo line-up and he ID'd both men as the shooters. Not to mention, we have Sherman's nine millimeter from his arrest which I'm confident will match the slugs they pulled out of Henry."

Pritchard glared at Dylan, but the rest of command staff smiled, pleased at the news of Sinclair's improved health as well as the establishment of the additional case.

"I don't care how you cleaned this mess up, Dylan. You will always be dirty in my book, and you'll always be a murderer."

"I pity you, Major. I really do. You just don't get it. You can't fight fire with fire in our line of work. The bad guys don't play by any set of rules. They are smarter and more dangerous than they have ever been. We have to fight back and the only way to do that is being smarter than we have ever been before. And we don't need assholes like you getting in the way."

Pritchard ignored the righteousness and scoffed at Dylan.

"If there's nothing else, Major, I'd like to get back home to my wife and newborn son."

The disgust on his face turned to a painful combination of fury and defeat. Pritchard shook his head and stormed out of the conference room. Trek remained, twisting childishly in his seat, looking lost and out of touch.

Shaw stood up, buttoned his jacket proudly, and stepped up to Dylan.

"Good work, Dylan. You saved your ass, and I think you saved my ass big time."

"All due respect, sir, go to hell. I didn't do this for you."

Shaw was taken aback. He wasn't expecting that from Dylan.

"I did it because it was the right thing to do. I just played into what you wanted to get my way, and it worked. Shame on you wanting us to fight dirty."

"That was a helluva gamble, then."

"With a stacked deck." He glanced at Chance Parker as he collected the binder and grinned. "I took a Chance."

Dylan walked out of the room and stepped into the elevator. Chance followed and stood next to him with a smile from ear to ear.

As soon as the door closed, Dylan said, "You can stop smiling now."

"That was fucking awesome. You're my hero!"

"Pick someone else, Chance." His stoicism remained. This was nothing to be celebrated.

"Aww, c'mon. That went as good as we could have expected."

"Yeah, but that's the problem. Should've never gotten to that point. This kind of police work should be going on all the time."

"I agree."

Quiet fell on the ride down. Dylan's mind was whirring in the aftermath of the meeting. Making a fool out of Pritchard stood out. But something came to him, like a shot out of the dark.

"Hey?"

"Yeah?"

"That true about the lightning? Beau didn't shoot at that kid?"

"Oh, no. He shot right next to his head, scared the kid shitless. But you had Holcomb turned upside down with everything else, I figured I could get that on the record, and it worked."

Dylan broke from his seriousness and laughed as the elevator doors opened. Chance joined him.

Chapter 64

The late hour in the infirmary cast a foreboding feeling throughout the room. The silent hum of machines was broken only by the movements of the nurse checking Beau's vitals and then conferring notes at a desk. Deputy Brackens stood unwavering by the door. He seemed on edge to Beau.

Lying on the crinkled paper liner, Beau watched the nurse bounce around the room, and he kept the deputy in his peripheral vision. The nurse had given him some low-level pain relievers and told him to lie still for a while after her initial assessment.

Coming back from her desk, she held a thermometer in her hand.

"Open up."

Beau obliged.

It beeped a minute later, and she studied the results.

"Am I going to live?"

She barely broke a grin. "Yeah, you'll live."

"Probably stress-induced. There's nothing I can find that warrants anything further. Let the pain relievers work for now and get some rest. If the cramps come back or get stronger, just ask to come back down, and we'll try something else."

"Okay, sounds like a plan."

The nurse scribbled something on a chart, ripped off a sheet, and told Beau it would be filed with his paperwork.

"He's ready to go back, deputy."

"All right. Let's go, Rivers."

Beau slipped off the table and stepped back into the large hallway with Deputy Brackens following close. It was after "lights off," and only the reserve lights were on, giving the jail a somber mood.

Beau paused at the elevator and waited for the deputy to push the button. He noticed Brackens was careful not to get too close and kept his strong side bladed away from Beau in case of a close quarter attack.

I didn't know I was such a threat.

The doors opened, and the deputy made Beau go first. Again, he took a post on the far side of the car. Beau stood still, hands held in front of him, head submissively bowed. He didn't want to be a threat.

"Did they really kidnap and… rape that lieutenant's little girl?"

Beau read sincerity in the deputy's eyes. He replied, "Yes."

Brackens shook his head, his disgust obvious by the glower on his face. "So, that was why you did what you did?"

"Am I on trial here, deputy?"

"No, no. I know you don't have to answer, but that's just for me. I'm asking. I was just thinking about what I would do if I was in your shoes, you know?"

"I see. Well, I hope you are never in my shoes, Luke. But, to answer your question, ask yourself this: would that be enough motivation for you?"

Brackens thought for a moment, then replied. "Hell yes, it would."

"There you go."

The elevator chimed, and the doors opened. Beau stepped out. Brackens followed through the door and then down the long hallway back to the unit.

"And what you're saying is that you meant to shoot around Uncle Les? You didn't want to hurt him?"

Beau stopped and faced the young deputy. "Would you believe me if I said, yes?"

"But why?"

Beau smiled, it was obvious to him but lost on the young man. "Because I didn't want your uncle to shoot me! I needed to keep him pinned down so I could escape with McFadden."

Brackens squinted, processing the answer. Finally, after a minute of silent deliberation in the cavernous hallway, Brackens said, "I can see that."

"Good."

"All right, let's get back to the unit."

Brackens escorted Beau back into the unit and down the smaller hallway of the Blue Ward. Adhering to protocol, Beau stood with his back to the wall while the deputy radioed that he had returned with the inmate.

"Okay, Rivers. Turn around. Arms out to the side."

He obeyed. Brackens then searched Beau. He started by grabbing around each ankle, to the calf and up each thigh. He swiped along the belt line, front and back, and then did the unpleasant duty of checking Beau's groin. The grope caused Beau to wince, more out of embarrassment, until the deputy removed his hand from his genitals. Brackens continued and grabbed up under his arms, chest, moved his arms down and checked his shoulders. After a quick run-through of his hair, the last place to check was in Beau's mouth. Nothing.

"Back on the wall." Beau stepped back and leaned against the wall. Brackens grabbed the ring of keys on his belt and unlocked his cell door. He pulled it open and told Beau to enter.

"Thank you, Luke."

"Sorry I came off a little strong, but you can understand that, right?"

"Absolutely." Beau stepped into the tiny room and offered Brackens a smile. "It was nice talking with you."

"Thanks. It definitely gave me some insight."

Beau held out his hand for the deputy. "Any time."

Brackens braced the door with a foot and grabbed Beau's hand to shake.

"I'm sorry, Luke."

"For—"

The lightning quick brachial stun to the right side of Deputy Bracken's neck caused him to fall instantly. As he crumpled to the floor, Beau caught him in a choke-hold and squeezed, slowing the blood flow to his head. He held tight until he went completely limp. The heavy metal door started to close shut and was sure to trap him inside with the unconscious deputy. Beau pulled an ink pen from the deputy's uniform shirt and leapt toward the door catching it just before it closed. He eased the door near the frame, and used the pen to keep it cracked. He had to move fast. There was much to do.

"I hope you'll understand why I did this, too."

Chapter 65

Loud thumps from the front door shook the whole house. Dylan jumped out of bed and reached for his gun. Dazed and half-asleep, he listened. More thumps followed by a muffled voice called out for Dylan.

"Who the hell is that?" Wendy's voice was groggy and irritated.

"I have no idea." The alarm clock read six-forty-nine a.m. It was still dark outside.

"Check it out. They're going to wake the baby."

As if on cue, Phoenix's faint cry came from his room.

"Dammit."

The loud thumps returned, again followed by a muffled voice asking for Dylan. He threw a pair of shorts on over his boxers and kept the pistol in hand.

He flipped on the porch light illuminating the early morning callers. He opened the door to see a tall blond man, strong, purposeful, and wearing a U.S. Marshals badge.

"What the hell?"

"You Dylan Akers?"

"Yes, and you?" Dylan looked past the large man. Several other officers, deputies, and U.S. Marshals stood in the front yard. Dylan recognized them as members of the Violent Fugitive Task Force. The tall man at the door, he didn't know.

"Deputy Marshal Cole Grayton."

The name did not register anywhere. Dylan set the gun down on the hallway table behind the door. "Okay, now that you've successfully woken a sleeping baby, how can I help you Deputy Marshal Cole Grayton?"

"We're looking for Beau Rivers. He's escaped."

Instantly, Dylan's knees felt weak, and the blood drained from his face. He couldn't believe what he had just heard.

Am I still dreaming?

"What?"

"You heard me. He escaped late last night from the county jail." Grayton paused after he delivered the news. Then he added, "Is he here?"

"Huh? No, of course not. I thought he was in jail."

"So he's not hiding in your house?"

"No! I just answered that." Dylan was getting angry at the Marshal.

"Good, then you won't mind us coming in and looking for ourselves."

The deputy took a step inside the doorframe, but Dylan stood in his way.

"Actually, I have a newborn in here that we're trying to let sleep, so yes, I kind of mind."

"We have reason to believe you may have assisted in his escape. I'll have a search warrant signed in thirty minutes."

"Wait, what? Assisted?" Dylan looked past the rigid Marshal, trying to get a hold on what exactly was happening. "What makes you think I helped him? I didn't even know he escaped until you just said something."

Grayton stalled in answering and looked back to his men for direction. He was met with affirmative nods to continue.

"Listen, I'm fairly new to the area, so I don't know you, and I don't know Rivers. But I do know he escaped last night around nine p.m., and around ten p.m. an alarm went off in the evidence vault at TPD. When they pulled up the activation report, it was your card that was used to gain access, but it was your boy Rivers on the video surveillance. Given your recent history, so I've been told, I'd be stupid not to check here first."

"My card was used?"

"Yes, sir."

Dylan stepped off the porch and walked over to an unmarked sedan parked by the garage. Grayton followed. Dylan walked around to the passenger side and stopped. The passenger side window was broken. Tiny shards of safety glass littered the ground.

"Well, shit!" Dylan said.

"What?" Grayton asked.

"It's gone. He must've come here and taken it. Smashed out the window to get it."

Grayton stepped over and looked at the evidence. "I still need to look inside."

Dylan looked at the front door. Wendy was standing in the threshold, holding the baby. The look on her face said, "Just give them what they want."

"Okay, fine. Don't mess anything up, please."

Grayton gave the cue for the rest of the men to go inside the house. Wendy stepped aside and joined Grayton and Dylan.

"So, Beau escaped? Is that what I heard you say?"

"Yes, ma'am."

"How?" Dylan asked.

"He managed to knock out a guard, switch into his uniform, and walk out. He managed to pass as a deputy all the way to the parking lot. It wasn't till about an hour later that the deputy came to and started yellin' for help."

"Is he all right?"

"Yeah, he'll be fine."

"That doesn't make any sense." Dylan was thinking out loud.

"No, it doesn't. I mean, why confess to double murder and then all of a sudden break out of jail and go on the run."

"Exactly."

Dylan stared off in the distance. The late summer morning was cool for the moment, but carried the promise of heat and humidity.

Something must have changed. Something worth breaking out of jail and risking everything for.

"You got something, Akers?" Grayton asked.

Dylan noticed the Marshal watching him. "Uh, no.... No, I... I was just trying to think of where he might go."

Grayton's men were coming out of the house, unfruitful. They shook their heads, letting Grayton know Beau was not inside.

"Nothing?" he asked.

A deputy answered, "No, sir. No sign he was ever inside. Probably grabbed the ID and left for the station."

"Okay, let's pack it up."

"Hey, you said the alarm went off in the evidence vault?" Dylan asked.

"Yeah, why?"

"Did he take anything?"

"Dunno. They were reviewing the video when I left. Wasn't much. I heard someone say he had a duffel bag. But we're assuming he took at least one gun, probably more."

Dylan struggled to find an explanation for why Beau would escape. The Marshal was on to something. Why would Beau cover for him on the murders just to escape a day later? Was this part of an end game that Beau kept to himself? Confusion soon turned to anger.

Grayton thanked Dylan for his cooperation and handed him a business card.

"You know the drill, Lieutenant. If you hear from him or know where he's at, please call me. Don't get yourself involved in this and just a friendly reminder," Grayton leaned closer to Dylan as his face turned serious. "Do not get in my way, or I will run you over."

Dylan remained unbothered.

"Have a nice day," the marshal added. Grayton turned to Wendy and the baby, "Ma'am, sorry to barge in, but just doing my job."

Wendy didn't answer either. Both waited until everyone was gone before speaking. "Dylan? What the hell is he thinking?"

"I don't know."

"They'll kill him this time, for sure."

"Maybe."

"And you don't know anything about this?" She studied his face as he answered.

"No, not a thing. But why didn't he come here for help? Or at least some money?" Suddenly, sadness weighed heavy, "Or to say good-bye?"

Wendy freed a hand from under the baby to console Dylan by rubbing his back.

"What are you going to do?"

"I don't know. I have to find him, but I don't want to leave you and the baby."

Wendy rocked back and forth from nervous energy rather than trying to sooth the baby. She seemed to weigh her comfort level of Dylan leaving again. "Go. We'll be fine."

"Are you sure?"

"Yes, you bring him in safe."

Chapter 66

They were taking no chances. It was like using a steamroller to crush an aluminum can. The Sheriff's Office SWAT team was prepping for the run, double-checking their gear, and going over the route. One operator stood and waved the Bearcat as it backed into the sally port. The armored transport vehicle barely fit through the rolling gates.

Antonio Toombs stood at the center of attention. A belly chain was wrapped tightly around his waist and tethered his hands in a pair of handcuffs; he was ready. His attorney stood behind him: ensuring his safety was a priority.

Next to the attorney was the Major who oversaw all jail operations, an older man, perfectly silver coiffured hair, a pressed green uniform, and an intense stare that came with thirty years of experience. He was beyond frustrated from the escaped prisoner; the stress compounded as he was subjected to this spectacle just to protect a known murderer.

"Has the route been pre-checked, Major?" The attorney asked.

"Yes, it has."

"Good. We don't want any fiascos happening again."

The Major ignored the dig.

"We're just about set, Major," the SWAT Team leader announced. He was decked out in his full kit, thick-plated vest, and a ballistic helmet. It had been one of the only times assault weapons had been allowed inside the jail. Normally a secure facility, they cleared the receiving unit of all inmates to accommodate Toombs's transfer to the federal prison.

"Thank you, Lieutenant." The Major turned to the attorney. "This is where you part ways, counselor. Only room for him in the back of that thing."

"Antonio, I'll be over to the prison tomorrow or the next day to check in. Do you need me to bring you anything?"

"Nah, I'm good. Just need these boys to get me there safe."

"Let's hope they will do their jobs."

"We're moving him in a by-God, armored truck with teams of men trailing him, carrying assault weapons. The helicopter is already up monitoring the route, and the Marshals are out hunting the man that caused all this. We don't do this much security for the Governor, so keep the passive aggressive crap to yourself or I'll find a cell just for you."

"I'm sorry, Major, it's just that Beau Rivers has proven himself resourceful and willing to do what it takes to get his way, even if that means putting an entire agency at risk. And right now, we can only assume he has my client in his crosshairs."

"I understand the precaution. I just don't like the insinuation."

"Fine, I apologize."

The Major nodded, accepting the apology. "Sooner you leave; the sooner we can get this show on the road."

"Yes, sir," he acknowledged. "Antonio, I'll see you soon."

"A'ight, man."

The diesel engine of the armored truck rumbled as it idled in the sally port. The hallway from the holding cell to the door was lined with heavily armed SWAT operators. Antonio shuffled his way through the line and into the back of the Bearcat. Once seated, he was joined by three of the men, all poised with machine guns.

The drive from the west-side jail to the northeast prison location went quickly. A motorcade fit for a president ran in advance of the Bearcat and blocked traffic, allowing smooth passes through otherwise busy and congested intersections. Scouts ran on the parallel streets looking for and stopping any panel vans or suspicious vehicles that could attempt an assault. The helicopter hovered at an obvious four hundred feet, calling the run over the radio and spying for potential threats.

***

Antonio couldn't help but grin. His anger over Xavier's betrayal had waned overnight. *That snitch will get what he has coming, plus, I'll be out soon, and I'll rebuild with another crew.* Xavier only served to hurt his own cause by squealing to Detective Parker. Once his get-out-of-jail-free card was cashed and he was out of the reach of Beau Rivers and Dylan

Akers, he would be back on top of the world. He figured that trading places with Lieutenant Akers would take less than a month. If his luck continued, they would soon catch and kill Rivers, ridding him of the problem all together. His escape was only an inconvenience.

Can't help but smile.

"What are you smiling at?" one of the cops in the back asked.

"Nothing, just can't believe all this is for little ol' me."

A deadpan look came over the cop's face. "I'd just as soon shoot you now. Say you were the one trying to escape."

Antonio's smile widened. He wasn't intimidated. Cops all acted brave when talking to someone in handcuffs. Most lacked the fortitude to follow through, bound by their precious laws.

"All this for some drug-dealing murdering piece of trash. Complete waste of time."

Antonio shook his head in quiet response.

"Got something to say?"

"All this…" He paused to look around and then nodded outside to the legion of cops assisting, "is because of a cop, not me."

Reeling from the verbal hit, the deputy looked away, ending the conversation. Antonio sat back and returned the grin.

***

Cole Grayton and his team tailed the motorcade which crossed the city at break-neck speeds. They hovered on the outer perimeter, hoping to catch Beau waiting in anticipation of striking out against Toombs. They opted for transporting him in the Bearcat rather than one of the unmarked vehicles. It wasn't necessarily Toombs's safety he was concerned with, but it was using Toombs as bait to catch Rivers. Nonetheless, his idea was ignored, and they went with plan B.

"Anything?" he asked over the radio. "Anyone got anything?"

"Nope."

"Nothing here."

"Negative Cole."

He shook his head, out of ideas. This was his only play.

"Only way he makes a dent in that steel beast is a dadgum fifty caliber. Only thing strong enough to pierce the armor. Or an RPG, for Christsake."

"He did break into TPD's evidence vault. You think they had one of those laying around?" someone asked over the radio.

"Who knows? I'm sure Mr. Toombs hopes not, but might make our job easier."

Grayton let the conversation wither as he thought about other avenues to take to catch his man. Lifting the mic to his mouth, he asked, "Where's our buddy, Lieutenant Akers?"

"Left the house about ten minutes after us and went straight to the police station." A pause followed. His team was pinging Akers's cell phone for an updated location. "He's still there. The only call he made was to a Chance Parker."

"Who's that?"

"Detective with the city, worked for Akers recently. Matter of fact, he's the one that worked the Toombs case."

"Oh, he came to Richmond Street when we got Toombs, right?" Grayton was still shaking off the newness of his reassignment.

"Yeah, that was him."

"What's he calling him about, ya figure?"

"Not sure. We can check him out if this doesn't pan out."

"Okay, sounds good."

***

With lights flashing, the Bearcat made the northbound turn from Orange Avenue onto Capital Circle. The federal prison was a straight shot ahead, just a few more miles to go. The armored truck raced by while the motorcycles held up traffic to let it pass. The civilians stuck in traffic watched with curiosity as it cleared the intersection.

"There's a white van heading south toward the Bearcat's location," someone announced over the radio.

The SWAT operators, in unison, scooted to the edge of their bench seat, getting a better view through the front windshield. The wide expanse of the six-lane road would give ample room for an ambush attack. If Rivers was going to make an assault, they wanted to see it coming.

Fear was evident in their eyes. One grabbed Toombs and shoved him down on the floor of the Bearcat, making him a harder target.

"It's still southbound, coming up to the parkway now," the same voice updated.

"Can you intercept it?" the SWAT Team leader asked.

"Trying to catch up now."

One of the operators in the Bearcat said, "Shit, we're almost to the parkway. Can you see it?"

"No, not yet," another answered.

The voice on the radio spoke, "It made the light, L-T. We're not going to catch up."

"Someone get to that van, now!" the SWAT Team Leader ordered.

"Can you make this thing go faster?" the operator asked the Bearcat driver.

"Not too much more, but hold on."

The Bearcat lurched forward steadily as its speed climbed to nearly seventy miles an hour. Its heavy frame lumbered up Capital Circle, but every bump and imperfection in the road resonated into the cab, jostling all the passengers.

"There it is." The operator spotted the white panel van from the back of the Bearcat. "It's in the inside lane."

"I want that van stopped now!" screamed the Team leader.

The operators inside the Bearcat watched as the van passed going south. Three unmarked cars, dashboard lights lit and flickering, gave chase to the van and closed in fast. Following the action, the operators looked through the rear windows. The van slowed to the side of the road, and their teammates approached with weapons drawn. A few seconds later, they were too far north and out of view.

Listening to the radios for updates, they stared at each other, waiting for a report.

"It's not Rivers. Everything is ten-four. He's just a plumber."

The SWAT cops exhaled as they felt the Bearcat slow significantly. Turning to see why, they saw the welcoming sign of the federal prison. The armored truck raced up the driveway and around back to a specially designed unloading zone and backed in.

The operator leaned over Toombs, still on the floor and wrapped in chains. "Looks like you made it in one piece."

Chapter 67

"You can't really tell what he takes out of the evidence vault. Some type of duffel bag for sure," the evidence technician said. "You can see the top of it there and the strap over his shoulder there."

She pointed to the screen and worked the controls of the video surveillance system. Dylan Akers, Chance Parker, and Sergeant Polk hovered, watching over her shoulder.

The image was grainy due to the minimal lighting of the late hour. Beau had already managed to change out of the deputy's uniform and into all dark clothing.

"What's the timestamp, again?" Dylan asked. He struggled with why Beau would make this move, coming back to the station after escaping jail. It was a huge risk that would provide a lead to what he had planned.

"It was ten-fifteen p.m."

"So, a little over an hour to walk out of the jail, find a car, and come to the station," Chance summarized.

"Apparently, he made a stop at my house before coming here," Dylan said, reminding Chance of the early-morning raid at his house by the U.S. Marshals.

"Right."

"So, have y'all determined what's missing?" Dylan addressed the evidence tech.

"No," she answered.

"No?" Polk asked with a hint of anger.

"Have you seen how much stuff is back there? It's like taking a pin from a haystack of pins. We can't just go in there and say, oh, that thing is missing right there!" The technician's sarcasm was obvious, but she did make a good point. Polk eased up.

"Okay, so how long will it take to find out? It could really help us figure out where he went and what he's up to." Dylan's concern matched his tone.

"I would say a few hours," she told him. "We'll have to scan everything and then compare it to the logs to see what's missing."

"Okay, thanks. Call me as soon as you have an answer."

"Yes, sir. Will do."

Dylan walked out of the Property and Evidence room. Chance and Polk followed. They stepped outside in a small, tucked-away corner of the police station. The isolation allowed them to talk in private.

"I got nothing." Dylan turned and looked at Chance and Polk. "You guys?"

"No." Polk shook his head.

"Not really." Chance said.

"Shit. What the hell is he thinking?"

"Whatever he's up to, it's got to be about Toombs. But what?" Polk asked.

"The letter," Chance offered.

"The letter? What letter?" This was the first Dylan had heard of any letter.

"When Toombs was brought to the jail, he told me, 'Tell Beau I received his letter'."

"What the hell does that mean?"

"Dunno, but I tried to ask Beau and he completely shut me off. He said to leave it alone. Whatever it meant, it clearly bothered him enough to break out of jail, because it was just a few hours later when he jumped the deputy."

Dylan tried to digest everything. "So, Toombs tells you about this letter from Beau, you tell Beau, and that night he escapes jail and breaks into the evidence vault to steal something."

The other two also let the information soak in, trying to make sense of it all.

"What was in that letter?" Dylan asked.

"Shit, that's the million-dollar question."

"Whatever it said, it was worth risking his life for."

"Where do we go from here?" Polk asked. "Sitting around theorizing ain't going to find him."

"I got an idea," Dylan said. "I'd like you to come along, Chance."

His sincerity seemed foreign given the circumstances, but Dylan knew he'd asked too much of Chance Parker already.

"Absolutely. Us sheepdogs have to stick together."

Relieved, Dylan smiled. "Come on, I'll drive."

"Call me with updates, Chance," Polk requested.

"Yes, sir."

Leaving the alcove toward the parking lot, Dylan turned to ask his younger counterpart, "Sheepdogs?"

"Yeah, Beau never told you about that?"

"No."

"Hell, he got a tattoo of one on his arm."

Chapter 68

Pulling up to the small house in the Levy Park neighborhood, Chance Parker took in his surroundings. "Hey, I know this place."

"You do?" Dylan asked.

"Yeah, I saw Rivers walking out of here early one morning. I was on the way to a shooting, so I relayed it to Trek in IA."

"You what?"

"Hey, I chased you clowns—or just him, apparently—for months after the McFadden and Shelley thing. I was invested in finding the truth. I knew it was still open, so I shot Trek an email, seeing if anything would shake out."

Dylan couldn't fault the young detective for doing his job, even though he had been on the other side of the investigation.

"That was before." From Chance, this sounded like an apology.

"Come on."

After five minutes of knocking and no answer, Dylan stepped off the porch and wandered around back. When he returned several minutes later, he announced, "No answer back there either."

"You sure it's this house?"

"Pretty sure. Mailbox says Levine on it. Beau told me his name was Gary Levine."

An elderly woman walking a small terrier stopped on the sidewalk to study the two men loitering.

"Y'all here looking for Gary?" she yelled out.

Dylan turned to address her. "Yes, ma'am. Have you seen him?"

"No, but his son came by late last night to check on things. Said Gary had passed."

"Gary passed? You mean he died?" Dylan asked, surprised.

"Yeah, said it was liver failure."

"Oh wow. We didn't know that." Dylan recalled the old man was a widower and didn't have any family. The mention of a son visiting late the night before told him he was on Beau's trail. "So, you said the son came by?"

"Yes, nice young man. I wish my kids visited me as often as that boy visits Gary."

Chance removed a printout from the evidence vault surveillance video and showed the old lady. "That him?"

"Why yes. Did he do something wrong?"

"No, ma'am. We just want to ask him some questions."

Dylan asked, "So he was here last night? Did you talk to him?"

"Just for a minute while I let Peetie out to go potty."

"What did he say?"

"He said he was taking care of a few things around the house while they get the arrangements settled."

"Was the son carrying anything or taking anything in or out of the house?"

"Oh, I don't know. I don't see too good anymore. I was across the street there with Peetie." She turned to point to her house. "Is there something going on I should know about?"

"No, ma'am. But if you see the son, would you call me immediately?" Dylan handed her a piece of paper with his number on it.

"You're a policemen?"

"Yes, ma'am."

"That sweet young man couldn't have done anything that bad."

Dylan smiled and envied the woman's ignorance. Chance waited until she was well out of earshot to speak. "So this guy died?"

"Didn't know that," Dylan said.

"Makes this place as good as any to hold up."

"Agreed. Let's go around back." Dylan sized up the old wooden door. The wood was cracked and the doorknob looked to be original with the house. Gaining entry would not be much of a challenge.

Chance pulled out his pistol and held it by his side, ready.

Dylan noticed Chance arming himself and stopped. "You really think you'll need that?"

Chance looked down and contemplated the question. "Might."

"This is Beau, not some random bad guy. He won't shoot us."

"You maybe, but me…, I haven't known him as long."

"Put it away, please."

"Fine."

With a swift kick, the well-worn door flung open. There was no reaction in the house. The two fanned out and searched the small house, looking for signs of Beau. The living room, kitchen, and bedrooms were all clear. Medical paraphernalia was strewn about the living room, which confirmed what the neighbor said about the ambulance being there a few days prior.

"Can't tell if he's been here or not," Chance called out.

Dylan had checked out the bathroom across from what looked like the old man's bedroom. The shower curtain was removed and what remained in the bathtub was a mystery.

"Chance, c'mere. Take a look at this."

Chance found him in the small bathroom and immediately keyed in on the tub. "That ice?"

"Yeah. A lot of it."

"Hmmm."

"Hasn't been there long. Only about a third has melted."

Standing there, the two men were perplexed at the find.

"What the hell was he keeping cold?" Dylan asked.

"Don't know. That's weird." Chance knelt down to get a closer look at the tub. He inhaled, trying to get a whiff of any detectable odors. "Got nothing," he reported.

"Could be nothing," Dylan stated.

"Or something big."

"C'mon. Let's get out of here."

Chapter 69

"You really think he came back here?" Chance asked, thick with skepticism.

"No. He's many things, but dumb isn't one of them," Dylan answered.

"So, why are we here?"

Sitting in the parking lot outside Beau's apartment, they stared at the face of the building as if they expected it to say something.

"He may have a left a clue or something. I don't know."

"A clue? Are you a Hardy boy now?"

Dylan chuckled. "No." He realized it did sound odd. "No, I guess it's more wishful thinking, hoping he left something behind. I hate to think he'd leave like that without saying good-bye."

"I'm sure he has his reasons."

"I'm sure he does. I just wish I knew what they were."

After a few more minutes of waiting, Chance spoke up. "We going in to look around?"

"Yeah, but we're not the only ones here."

"Huh?"

"Black Tahoe parked over by the entrance."

Chance twisted in his seat to look toward the entrance. He spied the truck and came to the same conclusion as Dylan.

"Marshals, probably."

"That makes sense." Dylan kept his focus on the apartment building. "C'mon. Let's get this over with."

As they neared the front door, Dylan noticed a distinct boot print next to the doorknob. The Marshals had already been inside. Covering their bases, they left someone behind in case he or someone else showed up.

Fuck it! I can't just let this go. I need to find something.

Dylan stepped through the broken door and took in the bleak apartment. It was empty and depressing. Realizing he had never set foot inside Beau's apartment before, its sad aura was infectious. There was minimal furniture and personal items, and what was there had been searched through or thrown on the floor. There was no obvious starting point so Dylan wandered around the small apartment while Chance searched through the wreckage.

"Lot of empty bottles," Chance said.

"Yeah."

"Like, a lot. You think that's his plan? Break out and just get plastered one last time?"

Dylan looked sideways at the young detective. "No."

"Well, there's nothing here. Literally, this guy lived like a hermit."

"He was lonely. Keep looking."

"Fine."

Dylan walked around, trying to get a feel for the apartment, but nothing was revealing itself. He was still lost as to the motivation of Beau's escape and not getting any traction was aggravating.

Frustrated, he lashed out. "What the hell are you up to?"

No answer came. The apartment kept silent.

"You say something?" Chance asked from another room.

"No."

"If there was anything here, safe bet the Marshals grabbed it."

"Okay, let's get out of here."

Chance led the way, but something caught Dylan's attention in the living room. There was nothing hanging on the walls, no pictures or art, no decorations of any kind, so a picture frame lying face down on top of the television stood out. If it was the only picture in the apartment, it held special meaning, and Dylan was curious as to what it could be.

As he lifted the small wooden frame, disappointment set in. It was empty and only his reflection stared back in the glass. He studied the small wood frame, hoping to glean some type of clue. It was old and bore the scars of several moves, but there was no indication of what it had held. The Marshals didn't take it as the backing had been replaced, something they would've tossed to the floor in their haste. Whatever picture it held had some importance in Beau's life.

"You coming?" Chance asked.
Wiping a tear away, he answered, "Yeah, I'm coming."
Dylan set the picture frame down and walked out.

***

"How long have they been in there?" Cole Grayton asked his deputy Marshal, tasked with watching Beau River's apartment.
"Bout ten minutes."
"You boys miss anything they might find?"
"Doubt it, Cole. We turned that place inside out. Besides empty liquor bottles, wasn't much of anything in there."
"Okay, I'll be there in a minute."
"Copy."
Five minutes later, Chance Parker and Dylan Akers stepped out of River's apartment and walked back to their car. Grayton pulled up behind their unmarked, blocking them in.
"Hey, boys. Whatcha doing?"
"I think it's pretty obvious, Grayton," Akers answered, not playing along with the pretense.
"Trying to find your boy before me?"
"I just want him brought in safe. I figured a quick look around wouldn't hurt. I might have found something you and your guys missed. You know, some personal insight."
Grayton scrutinized the two city cops, trying to figure out their reason for being there. He was new, but he wasn't going to let deep personal ties get in the way of catching his man.
"And?"
"And what?"
"You come up with anything? You know, you're 'personal insight' as you put it?"
"No, nothing."
"You're not holding back on me are you, Lieutenant?"
"No."
"Remember what I said right? About getting in my way?"
"I remember."
Grayton gave him a stern look of caution. "Good."

The blacked-out Tahoe pulled away, leaving Chance and Dylan alone. Dylan sat in deep thought while Chance stirred. Unable to hold his tongue, Chance had to ask, "Didn't want to mention the ice at Levine's place?"

"No."

"Okay—"

"I'm not ready to trust Grayton yet. Plus, we don't even know what that's about."

Chapter 70

Just after ten o'clock, the lights in the house blinked off. A quiet calm swept over the home, giving it a peaceful feel that Beau Rivers hated to disrupt. A quick glance up and down the street showed him it was clear to proceed. He slipped out of the borrowed car, and careful not to attract attention, casually strolled up to the side of the house where he found a large bush to hide behind.

Before he continued with his plan, this was the one stop he had to make. The short drive east to Jacksonville was worth the risk. This would be his only chance.

Settled behind the bush, Beau waited and listened for any movement within the house. Knocking on the door and asking to speak to his son wasn't an option. Calling his ex-wife from the burner phone earlier was equally pointless as she immediately yelled at him for his reckless behavior, endangering their son. She was too much of a hurdle, so he was going to side-step her and go around. If she caught him, she would call the police and ruin any chance to see his son. He wasn't going to put her in that position. He just hoped Scotty would want to see him.

Beau palmed a fistful of pebbles used in the landscaping and stepped away from the bush. He tossed one up to the second-story window, creating a soft tick on the outside. Another easy toss and the light flicked on.

Trepidation gripped Beau as he stood totally exposed in the side lawn of his ex-wife's house. When Scotty's face lit up with excitement instead of disgust, Beau felt a wave of relief wash over him, replacing the trepidation with joy.

Since learning that Wendy's baby was not his, he'd yearned for his son. It was too late to repair all the mistakes, but he was going to give it a try.

"Hey?" He called up in a hushed tone.

"Hey, Dad. What are you doing here?"

Beau shrugged. "Can I come up?"

"Uh, yeah."

Beau hopped up on the air conditioning unit, stepped on the top of the privacy fence, and then jumped for the ledge of Scotty's room. It wasn't graceful, but he managed to hold on and pull himself in with minimal noise.

Scotty tugged at his pants, helping him inside the bedroom window. Once inside, Beau grabbed his son and hugged him tight. Sitting on the floor in his room was the only place he wanted to be.

"Does Mom know you're here?"

"No, son. And I'd like to keep it that way, okay?"

The boy smiled, he was intrigued by the mystery visit and nodded his head in acceptance. It was an excuse to be defiant.

"So, how have you been?" Beau looked around the boy's room. It was a stark contrast to his room in Tallahassee, but he was just an infant then and had outgrown everything. The notion of Beau missing that portion of his life made him depressed. He liked the half space ship, half baseball theme.

"Good, I guess."

"How's school going? Sixth grade, right? That's middle school isn't?"

"It's fine and yeah, middle school. Big difference from last year. We have to go to different classrooms like every hour. I got lost on the first day. That school is super huge."

An authentic smile creased the face of Beau Rivers. The innocence of his son and how he spoke warmed his heart. He realized it gave him a temporary escape from all the bad shit that surrounded his life, and it worked so much better than booze. It was genuine.

"I bet. I got lost several times at school, too."

"You did?"

"Sure. How's baseball going? Still playing?"

"Yeah." The boy's mood suddenly changed.

"What's wrong, Scotty?"

"Mom said you did a bunch of bad things, like you killed people. And now you're going away for a real long time. Is that true?"

Revenge killing, murder, and justice are things a sixth grader shouldn't have to gauge, especially when it involved a parent. Beau's heart cried out for the boy. Bringing these complications into his life was his fault, and he needed to fix that.

But no sense in hiding the truth, he thought. "Yes, but there's a reason. And I'd like to tell you, if that's okay?"

Scotty reacted maturely, willing to give his absentee father a chance to explain.

"Those men did a really bad thing, Scotty. Really bad. And they hurt someone very close to me and my friend."

"Uncle Dylan?"

"That's right." Beau had never heard Scotty say that before, he liked it. Uncle Dylan.

"And the person they hurt was Caitlin?" he asked.

"That's right. So, I made sure they were punished for what they did."

"But isn't that what judges and lawyers do?"

He wasn't wrong. "Yes. Most times they do, but sometimes judges and lawyers get it wrong and don't really help the people that need it."

Scotty cocked his thin eyebrow as he considered this. "But, why would they get it wrong? Isn't that their job?"

"I don't know, son. I'm still trying to figure that one out."

"So, you killed those men because they hurt Caitlin?"

Beau wished he didn't have to answer, but he wanted Scotty to hear this from him and no one else. "Yes."

Scotty pulled his legs up and hugged his knees. He went into deep thought and subconsciously started to rock back and forth on the floor. Beau waited him out, worried that his candor would scar him too deeply.

"Would you have done the same if those men hurt me? Like they did Caitlin?"

"In a heartbeat, son."

He nodded. "Good."

"I'm sorry you would ever doubt that, but please know I love you more than anything in this world, and I'd do anything to protect you. I know I haven't always been around to show you or tell you, and that's my fault. Not yours. But I do love you!"

"I love you too, Dad."

Beau reached out and grabbed the boy, bringing him in for another hug. He needed to hear those words more than anything. They warmed the darkest part of his heart, giving him a sense of hope and purpose. Two things he'd lacked since that fateful night he stepped in the Akers's home and been asked to help kill two men. Beau enveloped his skinny body with his strong arms and fought back the emotions. He felt the pressure of a tiny squeeze around his waist, Scotty returning the love. Then he pushed Beau away.

"But Mom said you got caught and went to jail?"

"That's true."

"Then how are you here and not there?"

"Um, they—"

"Did you escape?"

"Well…, sorta…."

"Oh, man. That's so cool. Did you dig a tunnel or pretend to be dead so they'd carry you out?" Scotty's voice rose with his excitement.

"Shhhh. I don't need your mother coming in and finding me here."

"Sorry."

"But no, I didn't do any of those things. I kind of just snuck out when they weren't looking." Beau spared the details of assaulting Deputy Brackens and stealing his uniform.

"Okay, that's pretty cool, too."

"No, Scotty. It's wrong, but there is something I have to do before I go back."

"Like what? Can I help?"

"No, son. I have to do it myself."

"Will it make things better or worse for you?"

"Worse."

"Then why do it? Mom always tells me to not make things worse after I get into trouble."

"Smart woman. She's right. You should listen to her."

"So, why don't you stop now?"

"Because, it may be worse for me, but it will be better for someone else. Someone I care very much about."

"Who?"

"It doesn't matter. And I don't want you to worry about me, okay?"

"Are they going to kill you, Dad?"

Fear overshadowed his big brown eyes, and although death was a distinct possibility, he wasn't going to admit it to the child.

"No," he added a half-hearted smile.

"So, if you go away to prison, how will I see you? What if I need you?"

"I've already thought of that."

"You have?"

"Yes, turn on your computer."

"But, Mom says no computer after bedtime."

"Scotty, I think this one time will be okay. But…" Beau pulled the boy close. His eyes bore straight into Scotty's, emphasizing the importance of his message. "I need you to promise me something and you can't tell anyone, son. I mean it, no one. Not even your mother. Can you do that?"

The boy blinked. Bestowing such a secret was a monumental privilege, and he didn't answer.

"I need to know you can handle that, Scotty?"

"I can, Dad. I promise."

"Good." Beau smiled and tousled his already messy hair.

Beau spent the next hour going over step-by-step how to contact him at any time. He laid down explicit instructions and made him repeat them until it was engrained deep inside his mind. Once Beau was satisfied, the boy let out a lengthy yawn.

"Can you spend the night, Dad?"

"Uh, well. I'm not so sure that's a good idea."

"Please, Dad?"

"If you want me to, sure, I'll stay."

Scotty jumped into his small bed, and Beau eased down behind him, cradling him in his arms like when he was a baby. He was much bigger now, but he held tight as the boy nestled inside of the warm grip of his father. There was one last thing Beau needed to address.

"I need another promise, Scotty?"

"Sure, Dad. Anything."

"You're going to hear some bad things about me, more bad things, but I don't want you to believe any of it. Okay?"

"Okay, Dad. I promise."

Another yawn came from the boy. Beau could feel his body relaxing and drifting off to sleep. A tear of joy welled up and let loose down Beau's cheek, tickling as it descended. He wanted this moment to last forever. He reached down and kissed the top of his son's head. He closed his eyes and drifted off to sleep.

Chapter 71

"Confirmed, it's the white two-story house with the privacy fence in the back."

Grayton smiled. Rivers was as good as in custody. He had monitored the phones of all the people in Beau River's life, which weren't many. His ex-wife in Jacksonville was among them. When his tech guy relayed that a new number had called her out of the blue, he got suspicious. Tasking him with follow-up, he learned it came back to a burner that came active a few hours after the escape. As further confirmation, it hit towers in Tallahassee on the southwest side of town before moving on to Jacksonville.

They moved on the burner phone's location and tracked it straight to the ex-wife's house.

"Copy that. Everyone get in position. Let's hit it before he has a chance to wake up."

The pre-dawn light was beginning to stretch over the eastern sky, but the shroud of night still wore. Cole Grayton was pleased about how this worked out and was ready to finish the job.

"I want a team on the back, a team up front with me, and then four units for perimeter in case he manages to jump out of a window on us."

Grayton's orders were followed, and the team responded with their accepted duties. Ten minutes later, they were set and ready.

***

Booming thumps came from downstairs. Scotty's eyes slowly peeled open as the noise repeated. Something was wrong. He heard his mother's voice yell something, and then men yelling back and storming through the house.

Dad!

Scotty flipped over in the bed to wake his dad up and warn him, but the other side of the bed was empty. He was gone. He looked at the window and it was left cracked open, evidence of his stealthy departure.

A wave of sadness came over him, but as he thought about his dad coming to see him, telling him that he loved him, and spending most of the night, the sadness transformed into happiness.

Scotty's mother was steadily yelling out for him and before he could answer, his bedroom door flung open. Filling the entire doorway was a tall man wearing a thick, bullet-proof vest with a machine gun in his hands. His arms were huge and flexed as he gripped the rifle. He stepped in and quickly looked around the room.

"Is he in here? Tell me now!" the man said.

Unable to answer, Scotty froze.

"I told you he's not here. It's just my son in there, goddammit!" his mother said.

"Is he in here?"

Scotty saw the serious look on the man's face and then looked at his mother. Her face was crinkled with worry.

Scotty managed to get out, "No, he's gone."

The man searched the room and was followed by another, also wearing a bullet-proof vest. A patch across their chests and backs read: US MARSHALS.

The men left from the room and Scotty bowed his head. His mother had that look on her face again. It was the face before restrictions were given. But she did something that surprised Scotty. She came in the room and hugged him, tight.

He hugged her back.

"I'm sorry, Mom. I just wanted Dad to spend the night, that's all."

"It's okay."

"Don't be mad at him, please? He came to say good-bye."

"Good-bye? What do you mean?"

"He said, he's going away for a while, so he wanted to spend time with me."

His mother began to cry, but Scotty couldn't understand why she was sad. She just hugged him while they sat on the bed.

***

"Found it upstairs in the kid's bedroom." One of Grayton's deputies presented him with River's burner cell phone.

"Dammit." Having the phone was okay, but he wanted the man attached to it. "Anything on it? Other phone calls made, texts?"

"No, just the one call made to the ex-wife yesterday."

"Shit!"

This was a big swing and miss for Cole Grayton. What started as a promising lead, fizzled out fast.

"Talk to the ex. I'll talk to the boy."

The deputy stepped into the living room to address the woman while Cole took the boy back into his room.

"What's your name, buddy?"

"Scott."

"Scott, cool name. I'm looking for your dad. Do you know where he is?"

"No."

"Would you tell me if you did?"

Scotty didn't answer and looked away.

"What did y'all talk about last night when he came to visit?"

"Nothing. We just hung out."

Grayton nodded. The boy wasn't going to trust him. He had to appeal to the kid in another way.

"Do you want your dad to get hurt?"

Scotty's face creased in anger. "No!"

"Good. Me neither, but if he keeps running like this, he may get hurt. So, if you know where he might be, I think it'd be best if you told me."

The logic registered in the boy. He sat silently, thinking. But he needed a little more coaxing.

"Did your dad leave that phone for you? So you could reach him?"

Scotty's eyes lit up, but he didn't answer. Grayton took it as a yes.

"Why did he leave the phone for you? Is there a number he told you to call?"

"No." The answer came too quick. The kid was a bad liar.

"Scott, remember we don't want your dad to get hurt. Give me the number he gave you."

Scotty didn't answer. He fidgeted with his hands, full of nervous energy. Grayton keyed in on the boy's face. His eyes gave it away again. He kept glancing at the computer desk.

"Did he write the number down?"

No answer.

"He did, didn't he?" Grayton got up and snooped around the boy's computer desk. He probed around the monitor and an organizer, and then underneath the keyboard. There, he found a torn piece of paper with a handwritten phone number.

Grayton didn't bother looking back at the boy. He left the room immediately to follow the lead with a renewed purpose. He was back on the trail, and this time, Rivers wasn't going to slip away.

Chapter 72

After leaving the ex-wife's house, Grayton asked his team to meet down the street at a grocery store. As soon as his tech guy rolled up in his decked out conversion van, he fed him the number, eager to see where it led.

"Punch this number in and see what it comes back to." Grayton handed him the sliver of paper and the tech typed the number into the computer. This was a slow process and Grayton's impatience began to nag. "Anything?"

"Not yet, Cole. Hold on. It's thinking."

"We just missed him here, I know it. We're right on his heels and that's a world of difference from yesterday. I want to keep the pressure on. I wanna catch this guy!"

The computer provided a result.

"It's coming back to the Tallahassee Police Department. It's one of their extensions."

"What?" Grayton sounded surprised. He thought about the possibilities. "It's got to be Akers's."

"Makes sense," the technician said. "And it would've flown under the radar if anyone checked the phone records, assuming we didn't have the burner number, that is."

"I agree. It has to be Akers's." Grayton processed everything and considered his next move. Coming to a decision, he told the tech guy, "Get me Akers's location."

"You got it. What are you thinking?"

"I'm thinking I go ask him face to face."

***

Dylan wanted to be away from the station, so he asked Chance to meet him for breakfast. An homage to the tree-covered county roads of Tallahassee, the aptly named Canopy Roads restaurant was a few blocks from the station and served a great breakfast. Squeezed between two other businesses, the small restaurant was a popular choice, and on the weekends, a crowd normally waited outside. Dylan was amused that several sandwiches were named after the Indiana Jones movie franchise.

Late the night before, Dylan and Chance had followed every lead they could think of to find Beau. After leaving the apartment, they went to the jail to see if they could look in his cell, but like his apartment, it was barren. Word got back just before breakfast that the Marshals had hit his ex-wife's house in Jacksonville based on a phone track.

Chance slurped his coffee. "Where do you want to start today?"

"I was thinking we head out to the airport. Maybe he had a locker or something out there we can look at. Also, maybe there's someone there we don't know about who helped him out. I don't know."

"I guess. Not much else right now."

"I know. I feel like we're grasping at straws."

Dylan forked some scrambled eggs and took a frustrated bite. The waitress, a tattooed young blonde with a helpful smile, came over to refill their drinks. The conversation paused until she stepped away.

"I wonder if the Marshals got anything at his ex-wife's house?" Chance asked.

Dylan shrugged and offered, "I could probably call her in a little bit and ask."

"You think that guy, Grayton, would share if they did get something?"

Dylan smirked. "No."

"Yeah, didn't think so."

After breakfast, Dylan grabbed the check and they walked outside to the car. He hit the remote fob, unlocking the doors, but before they climbed in, a sleek, black Chevy Tahoe eased up behind them. The window rolled down, and Cole Grayton peered out from the driver's seat.

"You following me, Grayton?" Dylan asked.

"I think I ought to be."

"Why is that?"

Grayton looked out the windshield, not answering the question. Dylan grew impatient at the stall. He glanced past the Tahoe and suddenly realized that Grayton wasn't alone. He counted at least three other Marshal vehicles in the parking lot.

"I think you lied to me, Lou-ten-ant!"

"Lied to you? About what?"

"Helping your friend, Mr. Rivers. I think you are his pipeline through the department."

"Pipeline?" Dylan huffed. "Look, I don't know what the hell you are talking about. Tell me, arrest me, or leave me the fuck alone, understand?" Dylan stared at Grayton in a challenging manner.

Grayton eased out of the Tahoe and walked up to Dylan. He spoke in a low tone, implying a threat. "I found your number at the ex-wife's house. It's a way for the boy to keep in touch. Through you. I could have you arrested for aiding a fugitive."

"You found my number?" Dylan sounded confused.

"Yep."

"Okay, Grayton. I'll bite. What number of mine did you find?"

Grayton rattled it off, not needing to check first.

Dylan immediately smiled and shook his head. "That's not my number."

"That's what I would expect you to say."

"Go to hell, Grayton. Listen, I'm telling you that's not my number." He fished his cell phone out of his pocket. "I don't know whose number it is, but I can find out."

Something registered in the Marshal's face.

"You're telling me that's not your number?"

"No, Grayton. It's not. But if it's a lead to where Beau is or who may be helping him, I'll help you find out who. I want him brought in, safe and unharmed. Hopefully, that's what you want to."

"Fine. How would you find out?"

"I have the department directory on my phone right here." Chance offered, holding up his cell phone.

"Find that extension and see whose it is." Grayton said it more like an order than a request.

After a moment of searching, Chance found it. He stared at his phone and then laughed.

"What is it? Who does it come back to?" Dylan asked.

Between laughs, Chance answered, "Major Pritchard."

Dylan chuckled, also finding the humor in who the number belonged to. Grayton stood dumbfounded, irritated that he wasn't in on the joke.

"Can you explain why that's funny?"

"Sorry, you're new." Dylan quelled his laughter. "Pritchard hates Beau Rivers with a passion. Has for a very long time, and there is no way in hell Pritchard would be helping him. And equally, there is no way Beau would ever ask that man for help. Trust me."

"Could be part of his plan? Throw me off his scent."

"Grayton, you can ask anyone you want. Seriously, ask any officer at the department if they think Pritchard would help him."

"I don't understand. Why would his number be hidden in Scott Rivers's bedroom after we know Rivers was there?"

Dylan looked at Chance for an answer. He shrugged with no ideas.

"I think Beau's messing with you. I think he's telling you to leave his family alone," Dylan offered.

The Marshal's jaw tightened. His temples flexed, and his nostrils flared. "You may want to find him before me, Lieutenant. I'm not in the business of letting fugitives mess with me."

Chapter 73

Beau slipped out of the borrowed car and made his way through the woods. Fighting against a terrible sense of déjà vu, he studied the back of the Akers's house for any signs of counter-surveillance. He crossed the yard and quietly knocked on the back door.

Before opening the door, Wendy Akers stared incredulously through a crack at Beau with wide eyes of disbelief.

"Get in here!" she hissed, grabbing his arm and pulling him inside. "What the hell are you thinking? I have a newborn here. Everybody and their mother are out looking for you. Hell, Dylan left out early this morning to try and find you."

"I'm sorry. I don't mean to bring any danger to you or the baby. I won't be long."

Her anger dissipated. Her angry scowl turned into a sympathetic pout. She moved closer and threw her arms around his neck. Taken aback by her response, he was slow to accept the embrace.

"I'm glad you're okay, and thank you. Thank you for what you did for Dylan, for us."

She pulled him closer, emphasizing her appreciation.

"You're welcome. He belongs here, with you. Not in prison. It was a cost I was willing to pay."

"Was?" She pushed away. "You having second thoughts?"

"No, of course not."

"So, what do mean was?"

"That's not your concern."

"Okay, so why the hell did you escape?"

"It's better you don't know. But it'll be over soon."

"That scares me, Beau. I'm terrified for you."

"Don't be. Like you said, it's for the best."

She gave him a friendly smile.

A subtle baby's cry came from a few rooms away. She heard it and headed toward a back bedroom.

Beau had been going on autopilot since leaving Jacksonville, and now that he stood alone in Wendy's house, he suddenly felt impulsive and selfish. She had clearly stated how she felt about Beau and where he fit into her life. Nothing was going to change that. He was foolish to think otherwise.

Wendy returned with an awakened baby Phoenix. He glanced down at the child. It was their first meeting.

"Hi," he said gently. The baby's blue-gray eyes blinked and met Beau's. "He's beautiful, Wendy."

"Thanks."

Beau stared at the boy's tiny face, seeing a perfect image of an infantile Dylan Akers. He was right. The baby was his.

"I need to go," he said with urgency, changing the mood.

"Wait…, ugh!" Wendy looked hurt. "Why did you come here?"

"I don't know."

Wendy scrambled and set the baby down in a swing. She stood up with her hands on her hips.

"That's not good enough, Beau."

"I… wanted to tell you…" The words didn't seem to come. "I wanted to tell you…, good-bye."

"Good-bye? I don't understand?" She formulated a thought and responded. "You broke out of jail, hiding from everyone wearing a badge, just to come here and tell me good-bye?"

"Something like that."

"No, that's bullshit. Why can't you just say it?" Wendy was irritated.

"Say what?"

"That you love me!"

The air left the room. He had hidden that fact for the better part of a year, but he was more transparent than he thought. Beau felt exposed and had a pathetic look on his face. "That obvious?"

A comforting grin broke across her face. "Yes," she added, "All those nights you waited down the street were a pretty obvious clue."

"Yeah, I can see that."

She inched closer and placed her hand on his arm, trying to put him at ease. "It's okay."

He managed the courage to look her in the eye. The sparkle of the soft topaz-colored gems mesmerized Beau. Transfixed by her beauty, he held her stare, making the moment harder to end.

"I really do need to go. I've already put you in enough danger."

She didn't argue, nodding in agreement.

He reached up and lightly ran his fingers down the side of her face. "Good-bye, Wendy Akers."

A twinge of fear flashed in her eyes. "Wait? Why are you saying it like? I'll never see you again?"

Beau didn't answer. He didn't want to lie.

"Beau? Please," she pleaded. "Whatever you're planning on doing, it's not worth your life."

"I think it is."

Wendy was lost for words. She shook her head, mouth gaped open, speechless.

"I don't understand, Beau?"

"You will soon."

Tears welled up, blurring the sparkle in Wendy's eyes. Beau let his hand roll off her shoulder and down to her hand, holding it in his. As he stepped away, his hand slipped out of hers, letting if fall by her side.

He opened the back door, peeked left and right and turned back to Wendy. "You're right. I love you. Always have, always will. And everything I've done, I've done for you."

Before she could respond, Beau disappeared out the door and was gone.

Chapter 74

"What do you mean he was just there?" Dylan stopped walking and stood out front of the airport's main terminal. He held the phone to his ear and stared wide-eyed at Chance.

"He just showed up, but was only here for a minute," Wendy answered.

"Did you see which way he went?"

"No."

"Did you see what car he was driving?"

"No, he came up through the backyard."

"What!" Dylan spun and ran his hand through his hair. He was angry and frustrated. "Well, what did he say? Did he say where he was going? What he was doing?"

"No, Dylan, but that's why I'm scared. He came to say good-bye." Wendy paused. He could hear her stifle a sob on the other end. "It was like he was never coming back."

"Shit."

Dylan shared his wife's fear. All the moves Beau was making were made by a desperate man nearing the end. Going back and looking around his house for him was futile. Beau would be long gone by the time they got there, and they would be chasing a cold trail. Dylan had to get out in front.

The Tallahassee Airport rarely saw the hustle and bustle of the larger airports, but its steady and modest trickle of vacationers and business travelers kept it busy. Dylan and Chance strolled through the main terminal and walked past the ticket counters and baggage claim. Dylan had called ahead to Sergeant Mathis, and he had agreed to meet them out front of the TSA checkpoint. Mathis was waiting near a set of stairs that led to the airport administration wing.

"Thanks for meeting me, Leo."

"Sure."

"We're trying to find anything we can that may tell us where Beau might have gone. We were thinking he had some kind of locker or something?"

"Sure, we have a small locker room by our office. I'll show you."

Mathis led the way upstairs, through a secured door and down a hallway. He came to a door that displayed the department logo on it and opened it with a key.

"The Marshals came by yesterday evening, looking for the same thing, so if there was something, they probably found it."

"Figures."

"Still want to take a look?"

"Yeah, might as well."

"It's through that door on the right."

"Thanks, Leo."

Dylan and Chance stepped into the locker room. It wasn't much bigger than his old office in CID. Two of the walls were lined with numbered lockers, most had combination locks hanging from the latches. A small wood bench sat in the middle.

"We didn't ask which one was his," Dylan realized.

"This one." Chance stepped to number eight. "The lock's been cut."

"Ah, nice of Grayton to leave it there, unsecured."

Chance removed the broken lock and opened the locker. There was an empty gym bag, toiletries, and an extra uniform hanging from a hook.

"Nothing here, man."

"Check the pockets of the uniform."

Chance looked flatly at Dylan, knowing he was getting desperate, but did as he asked.

"Still nothing."

"Dammit!" Dylan felt useless. He sat down on the bench and buried his face in his hands.

"Like I said, he has his reasons."

"UGH! I know, but—"

"Hey, I got an idea. Let's just go ask Toombs what the hell this letter is about? Maybe we can figure out what Beau's up to from that angle?"

"He's already at the federal prison. We wouldn't be able to talk to him today. Too much red tape to get through, and then if we did, he'd have to actually agree to talk to us. And there's no way they'll let me in right now."

"Okay, what else you got?"

"Shit." He buried his face again and rubbed it furiously, trying to wipe away the helplessness. "I got nothing."

"I've never seen you like this. This…, emotional before."

"Well, deal with it. I'm trying to keep one of my only friends alive, and I'm failing miserably. He's not making it easy on me." It was the truth, but Beau covering for him was a huge part of the way he felt.

The locker room door opened, and an elderly black man with a friendly face and cleaning supplies entered.

"Hey, how ya'll doing?"

"Fine, sir. Thanks," Chance answered while Dylan collected himself.

"That's good, that's good."

The janitor made his way around the small room and checked the trash can. Leaving it alone, he scanned the cleanliness of the lockers.

"Uh oh. What happened to that lock?" he asked.

Dylan replied, "Someone had to cut it to get inside." He didn't want to say that they had done it because the officer who it belonged to was a wanted fugitive, and it may have contained evidence.

"Huh." The old man considered something and stared at Beau's locker. "I guess trouble managed to find him after all."

Dylan and Chance immediately turned to each other, making sure they had just heard the same thing. He pulled the door open and stepped out into the office area.

"Excuse me, sir? Do you know Beau Rivers? He's the one the locker belongs to."

"Yeah, I know Officer Rivers. He's good people," he said defensively.

Dylan looked down and read the name on his ID card. Malcolm.

"Yes he is, and you're right. Trouble did find him. Do you know where he is?"

"No, didn't ask."

Chance picked up on something and asked, "Didn't ask? So, you talked to him recently?"

The old janitor began to shy away from the two cops. He turned to walk away, letting the door shut, ignoring the question. Dylan and Chance followed. He pushed a cart of cleaning supplies toward the main entrance.

"Wait, Malcolm, please," Dylan pleaded.

"I told him I wouldn't say anything. Now I done said something too much. Like I said, he's good people. Leave him alone."

Dylan stepped in front of Malcolm, blocking him from leaving. Malcolm was frightened by the move.

"Look, Beau is my friend. Please hear me that I want to help him, but to do that, I need to know where he is. I've been looking all over this city for him and got nothing. If you know something, please tell me."

"You his friend?"

"Yes, I am."

"You Dylan?"

Surprised to hear his name from the mouth of a stranger, he answered, "Yes."

Malcolm's fear erased as he measured carefully what to say. Dylan could see that he knew something.

"He came here to the airport late yesterday." He cut himself off, unsure if he should continue.

"Okay, and what did he say? Did he tell you anything?"

"Um, well—"

Again, Chance picked up on something. Dylan was too focused on what the old man knew to see it. "Did you help him in some way, Malcolm?"

His eyes darted away.

"That's okay, if you did. Listen, we're not here to get you in trouble, I swear. If you helped him, that's fine. We're the guys you need to tell."

Chance's sincerity struck a chord with the janitor. "Yeah, I saw him in the parking lot, and he asked for help. Asked me to come here and get him some clothes out the gym bag and then asked to borrow my car."

"Your car? Did you let him?"

"Yeah."

"Does he still have it?"

"Think so."

"Is he going to meet you somewhere with it or leave it somewhere?"
Again, his eyes averted. His trust wasn't fully earned by the two cops.
"Malcolm, please?" Dylan pleaded.
"Okay. I'll tell you."

Chapter 75

Malcolm's car was back safe and sound as Beau had promised. Grabbing a backpack out of the backseat first, he locked up the car. He hid the keys under the back tire, as instructed, and walked slowly toward the sidewalk.

The interaction with Wendy was still heavy on his mind. Her beauty would never escape him, and his heart ached knowing he could never be with her. But as she said, it was for the best.

With a deep breath, Beau took in a lung full of air and blew it out, clearing his mind. He still had much to do before he was finished.

Walking toward short-term parking, he turned toward the terminal, giving the illusion that was where he was coming from. He kept his head down, avoiding the cameras. He just needed to make it to the employee gate that led to the back of the terminal and the tarmac. From there, it was a short distance to his destination.

As he neared the terminal, a woman stepped out of an SUV with a small, rolling suitcase. She wore an expensive pant suit and high heels. Beau needed to get past her but she paused and turned toward him.

"Excuse me, ma'am."

She stepped back, but caught a glimpse of his face. Recognition flashed in her eyes, giving Beau a sick feeling in the pit of his stomach. He kept walking, head down, hoping if she did recognize him, she would soon forget and let it go.

Then Beau heard her say to someone in the SUV, "Hey, that was that guy the cops are looking for, something Rivers."

Shit.

Beau stopped. The woman stepped back, and while keeping an eye on him, grabbed her cell phone. He calculated something quickly in his mind and knew he couldn't continue his current plan if she called the police. It would ruin everything. He could salvage it, though. He just needed a way.

"Yes, 911…, I see that wanted cop, Rivers, here at the airport."

It was time to move. Beau spun around and took off running toward the rental car return. They would have keys on hand, he thought. He crossed the driveway, ran down the stairs and into the parking lot, not looking back at the woman. He kept the pace as he neared the rental return. A man, dressed in a suit, tie removed, stepped out of a car. The timing was perfect, and it didn't matter the car. The man grabbed a matching jacket and his suitcase from the backseat. Beau spied the rental car attendant and saw he was busy on a computer. Beau stopped, took a deep breath and approached.

"I'll take those for you, sir."

Beau had appeared out of nowhere and startled the man. "Oh…, uh, Okay." He handed Beau the keys and stepped away from the car.

"Any issues with the car we need to know about?"

"No, it ran fine. Thank you."

"Okay, we'll take it from here."

Beau let the man walk away thinking the transaction was legit. He walked around the car and tossed his backpack on the passenger seat. Suddenly, the make and model of the car registered.

Just had to be a red Mustang, didn't it?

As he was about to step in the car, his name was called off in the distance. The voice sounded familiar.

***

Hurrying out of the main terminal, Dylan and Chance jogged down the sidewalk toward the employee parking lot. Malcolm told them Beau was going to leave the car for him around three p.m. Dylan's watch read three-fourteen p.m.

They had split up to cover more ground, and as they made it down the slope, Dylan called out, "You see him?"

Chance yelled back, "No."

Dylan made it to the edge of the parking lot and climbed up on a railing that bordered the lot. He craned his neck to scan over top of the cars, looking for Malcolm's car or Beau. A few employees had parked and were walking toward the terminal, watching Dylan.

"Dammit."

He climbed down and darted between the cars, visually scanning each one for Beau's familiar face. Chance took the opposite side, and after a few minutes of fruitless searching, they met in the middle.

"Here's Malcolm's car," Chance shouted. Dylan stood tall over a row of cars to see in Chance's direction. "It's clear."

"Dammit!" Dylan spat.

"He's already come and gone."

"Yeah, but where's he going from here?"

"I don't know."

They stood in the parking lot, lost. Dylan threw his hands up in frustration. Suddenly, the radio beeped breaking the silence. It was the emergency tone that preceded a "hot call."

"Any units in the area of the airport, please respond to a sighting of fugitive, Beau Rivers. I repeat, any unit, please respond to the airport for a sighting of Beau Rivers."

Instantly, Dylan and Chance perked up and looked back toward the main terminal, frantically searching for Beau. Dylan couldn't see anything from the distance. He pulled his radio from his belt and turned up the volume.

"Complainant is standing by the front and will flag down an officer. She stated she saw Rivers walking in the parking lot toward the rental car return area."

Officers chimed in and responded. Dylan and Chance took off running. The rental car return was on the other side of short-term parking, on the opposite side of the airport. He kept listening to the radio traffic and heard Grayton key up and advise that he and the Marshals were en route.

I have to get to him first. Dylan sprinted toward the terminal with Chance following. A woman stood near the front with a cell phone to her ear, pointing furiously further into the parking lot. Dylan turned to look where she was pointing and headed that way.

As he and Chance neared the area, he saw the brown hair of Beau's head moving around a vehicle. He was still a good distance away.

"Beau!" he shouted.

The brown hair stopped, stood taller, and looked back at Dylan. Even with the distance, their eyes locked. Beau gave him a crooked smile with a helpless look that served as a warning to Dylan. It stopped him in his tracks. He begged, "DON'T DO THIS!"

Beau held the expression, but there was determination hidden behind the sadness. Dylan watched helplessly as he climbed into a fire red Mustang and sped off.

Chance spoke into his radio, "I have a visual on Rivers. He's now in a red Mustang, headed for the airport exit."

Dylan was stunned and was slow to gain his composure. Chance pulled him back toward the front of the terminal where they had initially parked.

"Come on, let's go."

Chapter 76

Beau was improvising, but with some degree of control. He smiled at the toll operator as he passed by the window. A motorist passed under the gate, and Beau slipped out before the arm came down. Befuddled, the operator watched from inside the booth. Beau gassed the accelerator and headed east on Capital Circle. Up ahead was a marked unit headed in the opposite direction, the lights and sirens blaring. Beau watched as the cop blew past him going toward the airport.

Beau neared the next intersection and slowed down for traffic, pulling in behind a minivan. The driver was clearly unaware who was in the following car.

Staying with traffic, Beau cautiously watched the rearview mirror.

Nearing the next intersection, he saw a blacked-out Chevy Tahoe speed around the corner, heading toward the airport. Beau watched as it sped past, braked hard, and skidded down the road. Blue lights lit up from behind the grill and the dashboard. The Tahoe turned around. Beau punched the gas and made a northbound turn on Highway 319. As he turned, another black Tahoe dove into his lane, nearly colliding with him at full speed.

"Holy shit!" Beau pulled right to avoid the crash. He followed the second Tahoe in the rearview mirror. It skidded to a halt, reversed, and spun out, trying to get its bearings.

Beau pushed the Mustang over a hundred miles per hour, heading north. The Chevy Tahoes followed, weaving around cars, trying to gain ground. Beau led them north, attempting to anticipate their moves. Officially, he was no longer a cop, but he still thought like one, and he definitely still drove like one.

Sheepdogs don't need a badge to be a sheepdog.

The modernized muscle car purred at nearly four thousand rpms. The late afternoon traffic was sparse, soon to change with the approaching rush hour. The improvisation was working thus far. Now that he had led them away, it was time to finish.

***

"I just passed him on Capital Circle, going eastbound."

Grayton heard one of his deputy Marshals call over the radio. He was approaching the intersection where the Mustang was headed. As predicted, the Mustang sped through the intersection and turned toward Grayton. Without hesitation, he steered directly at the car, prepared to crash and spin him out, ending an inevitable pursuit before it started.

Coming within inches of the Mustang's back bumper, Grayton missed and slammed on the brakes before crashing into a high embankment. He flipped the gear shifter up, stepped on the gas pedal and popped it back into drive. He gassed the Tahoe, causing it to lunge forward.

Grayton grabbed his radio. "He's northbound on 319. Someone get on the PD channel and patch us in. We need a roadblock and a chopper, ASAP."

Gripping the steering wheel tightly, Grayton maneuvered the SUV skillfully around unsuspecting motorists, keeping the nimble Mustang in sight. A quick peek to the speedometer read 105 mph. The heavy truck floated on air and did what he commanded. A wave of confidence sharpened his focus.

You're not getting away from me, not today.

Unfamiliar voices came over the radio, urgency and panic in their tones. Their identifiers were from the police department, telling Grayton the channels had been patched. They were scrambling to the area and trying to set up a dragnet for the fugitive.

"This is U.S. Deputy Marshal Cole Grayton. To all units in the pursuit of fugitive Beau Rivers, we are headed northbound on 319 coming up on Ridge Road. Are there any units ahead to set up a roadblock or lay down some spikes?"

"There are two units setting up at Orange and Adams."

Grayton had to think then he remembered 319 turned into Adams. Orange Avenue was the next large intersection to the north. His new hometown had an odd street system where roadways were renamed at arbitrary points.

"Copy that," he replied.

Traffic broke, providing a clear shot of the Mustang. Grayton leveled the accelerator, pushing the Tahoe to its top speed. Around a bend to the right, he gained on the Mustang and was just off the back bumper. A hill approached, and he knew once crested, there was a downslope that would lead to the roadblock.

"I'm pushing him north to the roadblock. PD units, get ready we're making the top of the hill now—"

The Mustang's back end rose and jumped into the oncoming lane, cutting off Grayton in mid-sentence. Beau's tires screeched as he flipped a U-turn before the pursuing units could respond. Grayton's Tahoe failed to display the same deftness and lumbered well past where Beau turned.

"Shit, shit, shit!" Grayton cursed.

He must've seen the roadblock. Damn!

He stood on the brakes, sliding to a stop and nearly flipping the top-heavy Tahoe. His radio mic fell to the floor and out of reach from the force of the turn. He yanked on the curled cord, retracting the mic back within reach.

"Someone jump on that, he's flipped around, headed back southbound."

"I got 'em, Cole."

Another police unit chimed in as well and advised he was behind the other deputy Marshal. Grayton punched the dash, punishing the vehicle for not staying with the suspect.

"He dipped down the side street. Bragg Street headed west."

Grayton found the side road and tried to catch up to the chase. He was now out of his comfort zone of street knowledge. His incentive to keep up increased so he didn't get lost.

Leading the officers through south-side neighborhoods, with narrow streets lined with parked cars, the Mustang continued to elude. Quick turns, high speeds, and squealing tires drew the attention and horror of the residents watching a high-speed chase take place on their roads.

"He's headed back north, coming up to Orange Avenue," someone announced over the radio.

"Where the hell is he going?" Grayton asked his empty truck.

Jumping back onto Orange Avenue, the chase headed west. He weaved around slow-moving cars that had already parted for the front of the pursuit. The two-lane road kept the speeds low, but the agile Mustang managed to gain distance on the lumbering Tahoes.

"He blew through the light at Springhill, continuing westbound."

"Can we get another roadblock set up somewhere to the west?" Grayton requested.

"Ten-four, we're moving toward Capital Circle to see if we can get ahead of him."

"Hurry, we're back up to a hundred miles an hour."

Grayton watched the chase from a quarter-mile behind. The Mustang hugged the curve, making a bend to the right near the Capital Circle exchange.

Keeping the pedal floored, Grayton managed to catch up as they closed in on the intersection.

A steady flow of traffic clogged up the three-way intersection, blocking the Mustang from using either lane. A line of cars stacked the oncoming lane, waiting to congest it further.

Nowhere to go now.

Grayton's eyes were glued to the Mustang, trying to anticipate River's next move. Pulling to the right, he used the soft shoulder to navigate around the intersection. Grayton took the opportunity, kept up his breakneck speed, and cut Beau off from the shoulder, nearly squeezing him between the Tahoe and the stopped motorists. Grayton's Tahoe slid on the soft grass. He tried to come to a stop and block the Mustang from going further.

"Pin him in. Pin him in," Grayton barked over the radio.

Before the Mustang could be blocked, Beau floored it and headed straight into traffic. A car swerved before going head on with the fugitive with nothing to lose. A marked patrol car followed the Mustang, but a car from the cross street, unaware of the action unfolding, slid into the driver's door of the patrol car. Honks, squealing tires, and shouts came as the Mustang cut between the oncoming cars and darted between two trucks, making a narrow escape south on Capital Circle. The crash served as an effective plug, clogging up the entire intersection and causing it to come to a complete standstill.

Unable to process what the maniacal Mustang was trying to do, the traffic paid little attention to law enforcement vehicles giving chase and opted to stay still out of panic rather than move out of the way.

"Goddammit, move out of the way! MOVE!" Grayton laid on the horn and tried to maneuver through the congested traffic to pick up the chase. He was forced to wait. Smashing through with brute force, possibly rendering his truck disabled was the only other option. Moving inches at a time, the tightly packed cars ensnared the Marshal in a slowly unwinding trap.

What he thought would slow down his quarry, ended up being what led to his escape.

Grayton watched helplessly as the Mustang disappeared.

***

"He's headed back to the airport." Dylan called out. Chance drove the unmarked car, trying to get involved in the chase. They were too far behind and only halfway down Orange Avenue. "Cut down Lake Bradford. It'll put us right in front of the airport."

Chance agreed and made the left. He kept up an impressive speed over the giant speed bumps, catching air and scraping the undercarriage on each pass. Neither cop spoke about the dangerous action, just listened intently to the radio traffic.

"Why would he go back?" Chance asked.

"I don't know. It's like he's leading us on a wild goose chase."

"Grayton nearly had him hemmed up. You think he'll ditch the car?"

"Don't know."

As they reached Capital Circle, Chance pulled out, and both men strained to see down the road in case they missed the Mustang. They listened carefully for any updates from the pursuing units, but nothing came.

"Head back west. I don't think he made it this far."

Chance slowed down, without knowing where to look, careful not to miss him. As they passed the airport, they slowed down, scanning the parking lots for the Mustang.

"Should we go back in and check it out?"

"No, we would've seen him if he came this far. Keep heading west."

Chance continued as they anticipated a head-on meeting with Beau Rivers.

"The rental companies keep most of their fleet parked down the street. You think he'll dump it over there. Get another car?"

"Probably, let's check it—stop!"

Slamming on the brakes, the unmarked car came to halt in the middle of the road.

"What? What?" Chance hadn't caught what Dylan saw. "You see him?"

"There." He pointed through the windshield. "There, go there."

Chance looked and saw what had caught Dylan's attention and quickly turned off the road. They took a small side road that led to the old terminal. A small sign stood by the turn that read: Sheriff's Aviation Unit.

Chapter 77

"You saw the video game, too?" Dylan asked. "Back at Levine's house?"

During their search around the small house, Dylan saw a gaming console that didn't fit the décor of the old veteran. It was like having a state-of-the-art GPS system in a broken down, old jalopy. The only choice of game was a helicopter simulator. It was odd, but overlooked with the diversion of gallons of ice found in the bathtub.

"You think he can fly one of those things for real?"

"I think he's going to try. He was reassigned out here. Who knows, maybe he's had some hands-on training, too."

With everything going on in the last forty-eight hours, Dylan came to the conclusion, as he struggled to anticipate Beau's moves, that he didn't know his old friend as well as he thought. This troubled Dylan.

"Over there. There's the Mustang," Dylan shouted.

Parked obscurely in front of the old terminal, west of the main airport, the Mustang was abandoned with the driver's door left ajar. Chance parked next to it and Dylan jumped out, scanning the area. The former terminal was rarely used and looked barren. A security fence with a mechanical gate ran off the side. Through it was the way to the runways and other hangars, state-owned and private.

Chance checked out the stolen rental car.

"It's empty."

Dylan backed up, trying to see where Beau had gone. He peered down the face of the old terminal. There was nothing there, not even a car in the parking lot. Figuring the building was locked, he discounted it as an option for Beau when he didn't see any signs of forced entry. He stepped back to get a broader view of the area.

The gradual roar of a jet engine grew louder as a MD-88 passenger jet lifted off the ground on the westbound runway. As it nosed toward the sky, climbing toward the heavens, the engine's deafening rumble echoed over the grounds. Dylan watched, wondering if Beau had managed to sneak aboard before takeoff.

Off in the distance, movement caught his eye. Beau Rivers was running toward the main terminal. Even with the plane at cloud level, he was still out of earshot. Dylan noticed he carried a backpack and was headed toward the cockpit of the Sheriff's helicopter.

Dylan ran to the security gate and grabbed hold of it, trying to get a better view. He tested it and found it sturdy enough to scale over.

"C'mon, we need to get to him before he kills himself."

***

Captain Jared Sullivan rushed back to the hangar. After hearing the car chase involving the fugitive cop, Beau Rivers, he and his crew had to get to work. As the supervisor of the Sheriff's Aviation Unit, he had more flight time cataloged than the rest of the crew. Recently, he had taken a back seat to allow the younger guys to get more air time, but this was too important, and he wanted the action. Following the chase on the radio, he donned his flight suit, ready to get involved.

The familiar whine of the rotor engine spinning to life caught Sullivan's attention, breaking his concentration. Figuring his crew members were warming up the helicopter for him, he finished zipping up his suit.

"Make sure the oil levels are full. I want to make sure that leak on Bird One doesn't ground us," Sullivan shouted to his flight crew. "I don't want to have to come back before we catch this guy because we ran low on oil."

Sullivan removed a Smith and Wesson nine millimeter from a lockbox, inserted a full mag, racked the slide, and slid it inside his shoulder holster.

Stepping back from his locker, he noticed activity in the front of the hangar. The door opened and two of his crewmembers walked through the door. Sullivan spun his head to look into the far right corner of the hangar and saw the fourth and last crewmember at a computer, getting weather and wind conditions for the flight.

"Wait?" Sullivan asked. He looked back at the other two standing at the door, just as everyone else took inventory of the personnel. "Who the fuck started the Bird?"

Breaking into a simultaneous sprint through the office and out the door, the crew paused at the blades of the helicopter slicing through the air, nearing takeoff speed. The man in the cockpit looked up, locking eyes with Sullivan. Staring back with intensity, Sullivan couldn't gauge the man's intentions so he reached for his weapon.

The cockpit door shut and the engine was revved up, primed for takeoff. Sullivan took aim and yelled futilely through the whirlwind of the rotor wash. The man clicked the four-point harness over his shoulder in a sign of defiance.

"Stop, Sheriff's Office!"

The Bird lifted and hovered inches over the ground, unsteadily moving to the side. Sullivan yelled again. The chopper tilted toward the neighboring hanger, the blades chopped dangerously close to the awning where a large banner flapped furiously. After the hovering machine wobbled in place, the helicopter righted and slowly titled back toward the landing pad.

Sullivan weighed the danger of shooting the rogue aviator and stopping him from taking the Bird versus the potential damage a wounded or dead pilot could cause in an unmanned helicopter at full power. Then it clicked, the man in the cockpit was the fugitive they were chasing. Another reason to take the shot. He steadied his aim as the Bird rose. The downdraft whipped around Sullivan, making it hard to stabilize the gun.

"Don't shoot!" A strange voice shouted above the chaos. "Captain Sullivan, it's Dylan Akers. Please, don't shoot."

Sullivan looked back at Akers as he carefully lowered the gun.

The tornadic winds pushed them back as the helicopter lifted higher. The Bird rose and rotated to the west away from the main terminal, gaining altitude and speed. Although it wasn't smooth, Sullivan noted, the pilot was managing remarkably.

"What the fuck is going on, Lieutenant? Is that the fugitive who just stole my Bird?"

"Yes, it was."

"Well, shit."

"Don't you have another helicopter?"

Sullivan didn't answer, but barked orders to his crew to prep Bird Two, parked fifty yards away. They scattered as Sullivan turned to address Dylan.

"What the hell is he doing with my chopper?"

"I don't know, Captain. I wish I knew."

A minute later one of Sullivan's crewmembers ran up to him with urgency. "Bird 2's grounded, Cap."

"What the fuck? Why?"

"The guy must've thrown shit all over the landing pad. It'll take us forever to clean it up."

"What kind of shit?"

"Nuts, bolts, tiny metal things. They're everywhere. This guy found whatever he could that would tear up the engine and tossed it all over the landing pad."

"Hmmm." Sullivan was in awe of the bold helicopter thief.

He steals a helicopter then ensures he can't be chased by grounding the backup.

"That's probably what was in his backpack," Dylan stated. "What does that mean? Can you not take off?"

"Not until we get that pad cleared."

***

"Captain, come with us. We'll follow him. We could probably use you, too," Dylan said, urging the Aviation Captain. Sullivan told his crew to clean up the pad and get in the air, as soon as possible.

"Okay, let's go," Sullivan said.

Chance Parker waited with his unmarked car. As Dylan came running up with Captain Sullivan, he said, "I guess he does know how to fly that thing, huh?"

"Looks that way." Dylan jumped in the passenger seat. "C'mon, Chance, let's go!"

Speeding away from the hangar, they drove back up the private drive and through the gate. Restricted to the roads instead of the open air, they tried to follow. Dylan kept his nose against the windshield, straining to keep an eye on the fleeing chopper. Beau was keeping it on a heading toward the east side of town.

One of Sullivan's crew had already reported the theft over the radio.

"He's headed east toward the prison," someone offered over the radio.

Another chimed up, "Get me a sniper down here. I want that chopper shot down before he reaches the prison."

Chance and Dylan turned to each other, exchanging concerned looks. After the shock of the order sank in, Dylan realized it was Cole Grayton giving the deadly force order.

"Hand me your radio," Sullivan demanded from the back seat. Chance passed his back.

"This is Captain Sullivan with the Aviation Unit. If you're going to shoot at the helicopter, aim for the tail rotor first. That should take it out of trim and give him a chance to land it."

"Copy that," someone answered.

Dylan turned, giving the Captain a sideways look. "Hey, it's better than shooting him. That'll give him a chance to land it and could save my chopper."

"How the hell are we going to keep up with him?"

"He's not pushing the speed too much, so just roll down the windows and listen for the blades thumping."

Agreeing, Chance hit the window controls, rolling down the windows and letting in a rush of air. The whomps of the helicopter blades could be heard over the wind noise.

Over the next few minutes, units called on scene around the prison by the droves, ready to take a shot at the fugitive. Chance kept the unmarked around eighty-five miles an hour down Capital Circle, racing to keep the elusive helicopter in sight. Dylan pestered him to go faster.

Suddenly someone yelped on the radio, "He's turning back to the northwest, I repeat, he's headed back to the northwest."

***

"He hijacked a goddam chopper?" Grayton heard the radio traffic from the Aviation Unit. "Wow, this guy's got a pair on him."

"They're saying their backup chopper can't lift off, something about the landing pad was contaminated," another deputy advised on their private channel.

"I have no idea what that means."

"Means we have to chase him on the ground until they get someone from Florida Wildlife Commission in the air."

"Damn. They're stationed over in Panama City." Grayton thought about how to deal with the brazen fugitive. "He's headed east, isn't he?"

"That's ten-four, Cole."

"Then he's headed for the prison. Easiest way to get over those walls, I guess. He's going to try to take out Toombs with that thing somehow."

Grayton reached for the radio dial and switched back to the main channel. He keyed up. "Get me a sniper down here. I want that chopper shot down before he reaches the prison."

Back on the private channel, Grayton's deputy spoke up, "I'm right underneath of him, Cole. He's flying low, I can make that shot."

Considering what his deputy was offering against the intended outcome, Grayton gave in. "Take it," he ordered.

As he sped to his deputy's location, he waited anxiously for the results to be relayed. He leaned forward in his seat as the rotor thumps became audible. He was getting close.

"I missed, Cole. I missed." The excitement elevated the deputy Marshal's voice an octave higher. "But now he's turning back to the northwest."

"Shit!" Grayton spat.

***

The outside drone of the engine was much louder, flying the real thing. Beau held a firm grip on the cyclic and steadied his feet on the tail rotor pedals, keeping the chopper balanced. He had set the collective a little on the slow side, knowing average speed was at the top threshold of his abilities. Taking off was an adventure and the added pressure of having a gun pointed in his direction did not help his inexperience.

Beau saw Dylan running up and talking to the pilot with the gun. He didn't want Dylan to be there or involved in this at all. He had to ignore his concern and put it away for now. He needed to concentrate.

Pulling away from the airport, Beau glanced down to the ground and watched several cars scurry after him. The law enforcement cars were easy to spot with their flashing lights.

Peering out over the horizon, a sense of euphoria came over Beau. Controlling a machine that flew was awesome and liberating. It gave him freedom. Especially freedom from all the bad shit. Now he knew why Gary had loved flying so much.

Beau snapped out of his reverie and checked his gauges. The oil pressure was low, but not low enough to begin worrying. Holding strong, he was in perfect trim. He checked the road below. A black SUV was stopped, blocking traffic. The driver stepped out and froze. Beau checked the horizon and then looked back down.

"Shit!" Beau saw several flashes of fire in the man's hands. "They're already shooting at me."

Pulling the cyclic to the left, he banked to the north and held it until he was headed away from the gunfire. As he steadied back out, he pushed the collective forward upping his speed.

Flying over the southwest side of the county, he kept his heading to the north. He wrenched his neck around, trying to see the body of the helicopter. He didn't see any holes or noticeable damage.

"Damn, that was close," Beau said to himself. He sucked in a deep breath to calm down after realizing his heart was beating rapidly.

Sticking to the airspace over residential neighborhoods, Beau hovered just out of the reach of the trees and away from the main roadways. He didn't want to get too high, figuring being closer to the ground meant less of an impact if he crashed, but as he continued, he got the hang of flying. The hundreds of hours he had spent in Gary Levine's living room paid off; however, the slightest touch registered when the virtual version hadn't.

Over the horizon, far to the north, he saw it. He tilted the aircraft slightly turning due north. He was nearly there.

***

Dylan searched the sky to the north.
"Why did he turn?" Dylan asked.

"Probably because he heard they were going to shoot him down," Sullivan answered. "Only thing scarier to a pilot than a crash is a crash you can't control."

"There he is. Turn and head north," he ordered.

Dylan spotted the helicopter just over the treetops. It tilted left and right, giving the impression Beau was struggling to get his bearings.

"How long has he flown?" Sullivan asked.

"I have no idea. Best guess…, this is the first."

Sullivan shook his head in disbelief.

"He's keeping this heading. Where's he going?" Chance asked.

"I don't know. Just stay with him."

Chance carved his way from the south side of town to the west, battling thicker traffic from the university. Marked units from both the Tallahassee Police Department and Leon County Sheriff's Office jockeyed for position, vying for the lead pursuer of the fleeing helicopter. Through the urban sprawl of the city over residential neighborhoods of the northwest side it was a spectacle to be seen. Word had spread fast, and nearly every law enforcer was in the hunt. Continuing north, Chance raced up North Mission Road.

"He's just steadily moving over the houses." Dylan grew angry and exploded. "What the hell are you doing, Beau?"

Chance and Sullivan let the question go unanswered, sensing his frustration. The helicopter banked north and away from the trail of police cars.

"He's banking north. Turn up here on Fred George."

Like clockwork, the change in direction was updated over the radio. Someone mentioned over the air that a small private airport was a few miles north, just over the county line. Dylan, having grown up in Tallahassee, knew about the tiny airport. Located on Highway 27, it was a single grass landing strip, with one closed hangar and several open hangars with rented space for private planes.

"Get me units to that airport, now." Again, Grayton barked orders over the radio.

"Want to head that way?"

"Yeah, that makes sense, I guess," Dylan said. "But sounds like they're ahead of us."

As Chance reached Highway 27, the helicopter flew directly over the intersection, enthralling drivers in stopped traffic by how low the chopper was flying. Chance followed through the intersection and sprinted north on the two-lane highway. Dylan craned his neck outside the window, noticing Beau was holding the northerly heading.

***

"Stop here. Stop here," Grayton shouted on the radio, stopping his Chevy Tahoe in the middle of Highway 27. He waved on the civilian traffic and ran over to a boat landing that offered a huge window to Lake Jackson. Assessing the openness, he felt an opportunity brewing.

This is perfect. This is where it stops.

As his deputy Marshals pulled up, he directed them where to park and to clog up the roadway. He ordered several marked units to block the road, stopping all other traffic from passing through.

"Set up over here," he yelled to the sniper jogging up with his long rifle. "He's coming north and should pass over the lake. Take the shot when he's directly over the water."

"Copy that," the sniper acknowledged.

The blades beating against the summer air grew louder and louder. Grayton spied movement through the treetops and saw the helicopter emerge over the lake. He patted the sniper on the shoulder, giving him the green light.

***

"Isn't Lake Jackson up that way?" Chance asked.

"Yeah."

"Dylan, look!"

Turning that direction, he saw it and instantly felt numb with fear. Any chance Dylan had to control the situation was gone.

A quarter mile away, a line of law enforcement vehicles were stopped in the middle of the road, wagon's drawn and circled poised to defend against the raiding savages. In the epicenter, sat a black Chevy Tahoe. Nearing the roadblock, Dylan saw a deputy bent over a car trunk, aiming a sniper rifle out over the lake.

"Shit!"

The thump of the rotor grew softer but didn't disappear. Dylan knew he was just on the other side of the tree line. Pulling up to the vehicle barricade, Dylan jumped out and ran toward Grayton and the sniper.

The boom of the Remington 700 LTR assaulted Dylan's ears with a thunderous clap. He flinched, not ready for the shot to break. Realizing he was too late, he scanned the east, looking to see if it registered. Barely climbing over the treetops, the helicopter sputtered as smoke came from the tail. It began to rotate in a circle as it continued out over the lake.

From just over a hundred yards away, Dylan focused on the cockpit, hoping to catch a glimpse of his friend, hoping he would surrender before it was too late. As the helicopter steadied, Dylan saw the face of Beau Rivers looking down from the helm of the aircraft. Although he was far away, he swore the man smiled at him.

"Put one in the engine," Grayton ordered.

Dylan screamed out, but it was too late. The sniper was already dialed in, and the second shot cracked. It registered somewhere in the engine compartment, causing more smoke to billow out. Immediately, the helicopter turned back toward the tree line and dipped out of view. As they waited for an impact on the other side of the trees, the copter suddenly roared up and flew toward the middle of the lake. It looked like a giant mechanical insect, wounded and struggling to fly. The engine choked and coughed as it labored slowly away from danger.

"One more," Grayton said as he plugged his ears.

The rifle round ripped through a blade on the tail rotor, rendering it useless and sending the chopper into a tailspin, slow at first, but as it gained momentum, it twirled uncontrollably.

Dylan watched helplessly as his friend was met with certain death. Time slowed to a crawl. Trapped a quarter-mile away on the roadside, he watched as Beau lost control. The contraption that he tried to escape in would soon entomb him if he didn't act fast. Dylan strained his eyes, watching for any signs of escape, willing his friend to fight. Flames erupted from the engine, just above the cockpit, as the helicopter descended toward the water. Plummeting from the sky, the crash caused a huge splash as the rotor blade slapped the water surface. The resistance snapped the blades, causing them to fly off wildly as the fresh water lake absorbed the rest of the burning aircraft.

Dylan did not blink. The peripeteia was too hard to comprehend. He watched in disbelief as the lake swallowed the helicopter whole. Before it was totally submerged, erasing any hope for survival, an explosion erupted from the water's surface, sending a fiery ball into the sky followed by a thick plume of smoke. Dylan winced as the blast sent a shockwave through his heart. He clenched his fists in anger as he stood helpless, watching from the road.

Chapter 78

What started out as an exciting manhunt was now a water recovery operation. Boats and other marine salvage equipment were called in to set up around the surface where the helicopter crashed. With the amount of manpower and gear out on the water, it gave the appearance they were drilling for oil instead of investigating a crash. Floodlights, powered by generators on small rafts, sat around the marine salvage boats and were fit for a Hollywood production rather than a crime scene.

Forensic specialists trained in disaster recovery as well as the Sheriff's Office Dive Unit assisted in the operation. It was going on four hours since the helicopter had been shot down. A command post was set up on the Crowder Road boat landing after it was determined to be the closest land point to the crash site. The small landing was bustling with activity. Representatives from nearly every law enforcement agency in the county were present, dealing with the unprecedented event, trying to contain the aftermath. The overall mood was positive, given that the fugitive and the helicopter were the only casualties.

The setting sun hovered just above the western tree line of the vast lake, ready to set for the day. Despite many orders to go home, Dylan remained on scene. Standing on the grassy bank of the lake, he waited for them to pull Beau's body from the wreckage.

Brennan Headley, a Jill of all forensic trades, rode on the front of a shuttle boat from the small city that floated in the middle of the lake back to the landing. As she got close, she noticed Dylan waiting. She bowed her head, avoiding eye contact. A white body bag was laid out across the bow. A chill seized him.

"You don't have to be here for this." Chance stood behind him, noticing Brennan approaching with the body bag. Dylan didn't respond. Chance offered a consoling squeeze of the shoulder. "Yeah, I didn't think so."

Several of the Sheriff's Office detectives greeted Brennan at the water's edge and helped carry the body bag up the ramp and underneath a tent. Dylan noticed the bag was not full and appeared extremely light.

"Damn," he said. Tears welled in his eyes and his voice wavered.

"What?"

"They only found a part of him."

"Shit."

After getting the body bag under the tent, the detectives examined the contents with puzzled looks. Sergeant Polk stepped up to the other agency's detective in charge and inquired something. The detectives listened, looked at Dylan and then nodded to Polk.

"Dylan?" Polk called. "Can you come here?"

With a slow, hesitant stroll, Dylan stepped over to the tent. As he did, Dylan saw Cole Grayton and his men huddled around a black Tahoe parked near the road. Grayton took several steps closer to the tent, waiting on confirmation that his fugitive was dead. Dylan withheld his anger and distaste for the Marshal and ducked under the tent.

"You up for this?" Polk asked.

With heavy, tear-soaked eyes, Dylan studied the white plastic coffin. It was abnormally thin to hold an adult human body, and for an instant, he hoped it was empty.

Brennan Headley stood off to the side. It was she who had worked Caitlin's crime scene and pulled back the sheet revealing her lifeless body in the watery culvert. Dylan's heart sank, wondering how many times in life he was going to have to do this. Once had been enough.

Dylan nodded to Polk who then peeled back the zippered flap of the body bag to reveal its contents.

There was no head or body, only an arm. Specifically, a right arm. Burnt and singed in several places, most notably the fingers, but no doubt an adult male arm. Dylan let his eyes absorb the lifeless limb and they soon were fixed on the middle of the bicep. Etched in the skin was a fuzzy green image, and he knew exactly what it was.

"What is that?" asked one of the detectives looking on from an angle.

"It's a tattoo," Dylan answered quietly. "Of a sheepdog. He had just gotten one about a week ago." His head hung low and he wanted to be anywhere else but in the tent with the detached arm of Beau Rivers. He spun around and walked back to the road.

***

News of Beau Rivers's death reached Wendy Akers before Dylan could make it home. Baby Phoenix was sound asleep in his crib, and she sat and cried. Deep sobs came for a troubled friend who had lost his life.

As Dylan came walking through the door, Wendy was curled up on the couch. Her tear-streaked face managed a half-smile for a greeting.

"Hey," her voice was hushed.

"Hey." He joined her on the couch and immediately broke down, letting the tidal wave of emotions, pent up from the tumultuous day, loose. Wendy put her arm around him, commiserating on the loss of Beau Rivers. He sat and cried until he was out of tears.

"Why, Wendy? Why the hell would he do that?"

"I don't know."

"I mean…, I can't figure out why he escaped. I can't even fathom why he'd steal a goddam helicopter."

Silence took a hold on the room. Dylan stood up in anger, ripping away from his wife.

"I just don't get it."

"Dylan, he was a grown man. I don't think you could've stopped him, and there's no doubt you tried. Don't blame yourself."

"It's hard not to. I mean, I'm the reason he went to jail in the first place."

Wendy backed down, knowing he was right. She also had a hand in Beau's incarceration.

"It has something to do with a letter, Chance said. But I can't, for the life of me, figure that part out. What letter?"

Wendy shook her head, clueless. Dylan explained that Antonio Toombs told Chance about the existence of a letter, and no more than twelve hours later, Beau had escaped from jail.

"It must've had something in it. Something damaging to him or us."

"I wish I knew."

Dylan paced around for a minute and then sat back down next to Wendy. He leaned back on the sofa and rubbed his face with both hands, exhausted.

Dylan was suddenly reminded that Beau had come to the house to say good-bye to Wendy.

"When he came here this morning, did he say anything else?"

"Basically, he just came here to say good-bye. That's it."

"And he didn't let on about any of this? The helicopter, an escape plan?"

"Well." She paused to replay the conversation in her mind. "He said things like 'It'll be over soon,' and when I told him whatever he was doing wasn't worth his life, he said, 'I think it is.'"

Dylan shook his head.

"Nothing about a plan, though," Dylan thought aloud. "Dammit!"

"Shhhh, c'mon. I know you're hurting, but the baby is sleeping."

"I'm sorry, it's just that I never got to say good-bye, and now he's gone."

Chapter 79

Dylan walked out of the city commission chambers, unable to take pride in what he had accomplished. A review board had been put together to review the Antonio Toombs case and they hailed his extraordinary efforts to combat crime, calling it "innovative and creative." A local attorney sat on the panel and agreed that, although there were some legal issues to consider in the case, those issues were for a jury to decide at trial. Everything was admissible. The attorney used the term "unorthodox" but maintained, despite appearances, that Dylan and his squad operated on the legitimate side of the law.

Chief Shaw caught up to Dylan outside the chambers.

"Dylan, you're leaving already?"

He returned a flat look. "Not really in the mood, Chief."

"I know. I'm sorry about Beau, but to be honest, he kind of put himself in that situation."

Dylan looked away, scowling. "Is there something you want, Robert?"

"I'm sorry, Dylan. That was insensitive. I just want to focus on the positive here."

"We did good police work, that's all. Why this case needed a panel review is rather insulting, but whatever."

"It was more than that, Dylan. It was innovative, like they said."

"Whatever." Dylan shrugged his shoulders.

"They want me to promote you to Captain."

"Promote me? You're kidding?"

"No, Pritchard is retiring, and you'd be backfilling whoever takes the major spot."

"Not interested. Sorry, Robert."

"I thought so."

Confused, Dylan tried to gauge where Shaw was going with the conversation.

"In light of everything that's happened in the last few months, I was thinking of creating a new squad. I have the commission's approval and blessing to move forward with it."

"Another secret squad? Didn't you learn your lesson, Robert?"

"No." He chuckled with humility. "This is your idea, remember?"

"Not really."

"Well, you suggested it and I'm following up with it. It's official and on the books. They will target specifically violent crimes and gun violence. I want you to head that squad. I'll give you free rein on who you pick and how you operate. You've earned it."

Dylan admitted that he liked the idea of having a squad of highly motivated cops out to clean up the streets. It would be an opportunity to right the wrong he committed by exacting revenge for his slain daughter. A chance to prove he was a worthy police officer.

"Let me talk to Wendy about it first."

"Sure, sure. Let me know soon, okay. I'd love to get started."

"Okay." Dylan started to walk away.

"And Dylan?"

He turned back to Shaw.

"Thank you, again."

Dylan didn't answer, letting the Chief's guilt hang in the air. He wanted to leave it there as a reminder that when it comes to police work, there is always a right way to do things, something he had forgotten with the death of his daughter.

***

Male inmates at the federal prison were held in a smaller holding facility in the front of the campus. The prison housed female inmates, but they were convicted and serving their sentences. The men were awaiting trial, normally in federal court, but given the circumstances, Antonio Toombs was the exception. Isolated by design, it was difficult to get in and out of the prison, but news, especially sensational news, always managed to get in.

Antonio Toombs had just received word that Beau Rivers was killed in a helicopter crash after a daring escape from the county jail. Amazed at the lengths the fugitive cop would go to get to him, he reveled in the failure.

"That shit's crazy, man," another inmate said, hearing the story from Antonio's perspective. They sat in the common area, playing cards, one of the few sanctioned activities.

"Yes, but I'll take it. Another cop dead is one less I have to worry about."

"Damn dawg, that's cold."

"When it's the cop responsible for taking away ten years of my life, excuse me if I don't shed a tear."

"Oh, shit. That's the cop who put you in?"

"Yep, Rivers," Antonio snarled and sucked his teeth.

"How's that play out with your case now?"

"I've already got my get-out-of-jail-free card. I just need to cash it in. His death only makes it better. 'Cause in the slight chance my play is contested, he's the only one that could testify. But he's dead now, so it's smooth sailing from this point."

The other inmate considered what Antonio said.

"What's your get-out-of-jail-free card?"

Antonio laughed. He felt sorry for the other inmate, unprepared and destined to remain incarcerated while he would go free.

"C'mon, dawg. Help a brother out?"

"Not a chance! I tell you and next thing I know, you use my information to your own benefit."

The inmate searched for a response, unable to come up with a valid counterpoint. He resorted back to his pathetic plea. "C'mon?"

Antonio looked at his hand, two pair of spades and diamonds, and tossed one of them down on the table. "There's your get-out-of-jail free card."

Crime Stoppers started a campaign to help solve cold case murders and missing persons cases, knowing the prisons not only held prisoners, they held secrets as well. Some genius, aware that playing cards was a preferred pastime inside the walls, created decks of cards that contained summaries of unsolved murders. Along with the victim's picture and a brief about the case, the idea was to disseminate enough cards into the prison population to generate leads when one convict bragged to another.

"I don't get it?" the inmate said, clueless as to who the slain woman on the card was.

Antonio continued to laugh.

Chapter 80

The smell of death always lingered. Only a hint of an ammonia-pine mix could be detected in the astringent aroma of the morgue. Bright lighting and drab tile walls, the room was purposeful and clinical, far from inviting.

Dylan stood patiently waiting for the funeral home representative to meet him and take custody of Beau's remains. He had already made the arrangements for his friend to be buried in a plot near where Caitlin had been laid to rest.

His eyes bounced around the room, avoiding the large industrial aluminum door on the far side. The metal table, scale, surgical tools, and even the tissue sample collection were more tolerable than what was known as the "meat locker." Through the door was where the bodies were kept, waiting for dissection or release. Needing a distraction from the thought of Beau's lifeless body, or what was left of it, lying in there, he welcomed anything. The medical charts on the wall, safety instructions in case of an emergency, even the instrument cleaning protocol pulled his thoughts away from the reminder that Beau was dead.

The sound of the door opening brought relief.

"Hi. I'm Doctor Rogers."

"Lieutenant Akers. Nice to meet you, Doc." He extended a hand and they shook.

Rogers stepped over to a counter and picked up a clipboard to read something. "Are you here to take custody of someone?"

Dylan nodded. "Yes, Beau Rivers. The funeral home people should be here soon."

"Rivers, yes. He was from the helicopter crash."

"That's right. Did you…?" Dylan had seen his share of autopsies and immediately regretted asking anything. Images of Beau's body being cut open made his stomach turn. "Were you the doctor who did the examination?"

"Yes."

"Anything you can tell me?"

Dr. Rogers lowered the clipboard and studied Dylan. He was unable to hide the pain and the pathologist picked up on it.

"What do you want to know, Lieutenant?"

"I don't know. Is there anything you can tell me?"

"There's not much to tell. Like with any explosion or aircraft death, there isn't much to work with." The doctor gave his best empathetic expression. "So, we were lucky to get what we did."

"Was there more found than just his arm?"

"Yes, but that was really the most intact part that was found. They managed to recover a few more parts, but not much."

Dylan shook his head, not wanting to know more.

"So, as far as an autopsy, there wasn't much to do. The trauma was all consistent with a crash and explosion, so I just took pictures and some muscle tissue samples. The fingers were badly burned so we couldn't get any comparable fingerprints, but I collected some blood and a few DNA swabs."

"Okay, thank you, doctor."

Dr. Rogers nodded and went back to his clipboard. A knock wrapped at the door, and it cracked open. It was the funeral home rep.

He and a partner, dressed in black suits, rolled in a felt-covered gurney. One signed the logbook, taking custody of the body while the other positioned the gurney outside the industrial cooler door. Unable to watch the process, Dylan looked away, busying himself with the logbook.

Non-committedly, Dylan read the names down the logbook as the funeral home workers loaded up Beau's remains. None of the names registered and he was about to look away when one name, three spots above Beau's jumped out.

Gary Levine.

The old man Beau told me about. The one with the Vietnam era machine gun.

Dylan remembered the neighbor mentioning Levine had passed away when they were looking for Beau. He didn't know much about Levine, only that Beau liked him and trusted him. It was a connection to Beau that was foreign.

Scanning the rest of the entry, Dylan read the name of the officer who brought him in, then the funeral home rep who picked him up. The scribble of the second name looked familiar.

"Oh, one strange thing I did notice about the limb recovered, Lieutenant."

"What's that?"

"Well, it's just one of those rare things we come across, but you never know how the body will react to trauma or intense heat found in explosions; the limb had the appearance of being aged."

Dylan heard the doctor, however confusion silenced any response. He wanted to ask a multitude of questions, but needed more time to process the information and the overwhelming fact that his friend was dead.

"We're ready, Lieutenant," the funeral home rep notified him, poised to push Beau's remains outside to the hearse.

"Yeah, okay." Dylan followed the black suits out of the morgue, unable to move past the information bouncing around in his head. After the gurney was loaded and the hearse door shut, Dylan stood outside in the parking lot, working out something in his mind.

It couldn't be possible, could it?

Chapter 81

An unfathomable theory bounced around in his head. An odd feeling beckoned from the deep recesses of his mind, but Dylan forced himself to hold onto reality as he relived the horrendous crash he watched with his own eyes.

He's dead; I just don't want to believe it.

After making a few phones calls finalizing the funeral plans for Beau, he walked into the police station. He sat down at his desk, trying to bear the weight of everything. Taking down a dangerous drug lord with the perception of crossing the line, but keeping everything legitimate was a gamble, but it took its toll. Its purpose, Dylan hoped, was to achieve atonement for his past sins. Built on a lie, he narrowly escaped a guaranteed prison sentence that would have kept him from his family. A family which now included a beautiful baby boy. The thought of missing any part of his life was unbearable, but freedom came at a price: the price of losing a friend who had proved loyal through the toughest of situations and who sacrificed everything. Beau's shared indiscretion with Wendy had already lessened in importance, to the point of being inconsequential. The heaviest burden in the pile was helplessly watching his friend crash and die in an exploding ball of fire. It was too much.

A Property and Evidence employee walked past his office. "Oh, hey, Lieutenant. I heard you were moving on?"

He had already forgotten he accepted the Chief's offer to lead the new violent crime squad, a call he had made after leaving City Hall and after giving the proposal more thought. He shook the thoughts out of his head and refocused on the question.

"Um, yes. Yes, it looks that way."

"Well, I know you coming down here was under weird circumstances, but I've always enjoyed working with you and wish you luck."

Dylan smiled. The sentiment was sweet. "Thank you."

The employee moved on, and Dylan turned back to his computer. He scrolled down through a litany of emails. There were over eighty stacked in the queue.

At the top was the transfer order that reassigned him to the head of the violent crime suppression squad. This time Chief Shaw followed the accepted protocols of reassignment. He opened the file and glanced at it. He forwarded the email to Chance Parker, begging him to join the squad. Working with Parker was enjoyable. Beau would have been his first choice, but he was no longer an option.

Sifting through the rest of the emails, he saw one that didn't have a subject line. The void caught his attention, and then he read the sender. It appeared he had sent it to himself.

"What the—?"

Clicking open the email, he read the contents.

> *If something happened to me, and you know what I mean, please go and talk to my son for me. Tell him that I love him.*
>
> *Thanks, Ace.*
>
> Beau

Dylan reread the brief email over and over, hoping to get some kind of hidden message buried within the text. But nothing came. He applied every inside joke or meaning they shared and nothing popped up. Anger erupted.

That's it? That's all I get for a good-bye or an explanation?

Letting the fury subside, Dylan clicked on the properties of the email and saw that it was sent the night Beau broke out of jail and took something from the evidence lock-up. That also reminded him he had never heard back about was taken.

He picked up his phone and dialed a number from memory.

"Hello?"

"Hey, it's Akers. Anything come back on that inventory search I asked you to do?"

"Well..., kind of."

"Kind of? I don't understand."

"Well, we did it one time and didn't find anything, so we did it again. Still nothing, so we're doing a hand search, and it's taking a long time. There's over a quarter million pieces of evidence back here."

"How much do you have left?"

"A lot, but should be done sometime today."

"Did he take something or not?"

"I watched that video several times, and he definitely took something, but how we haven't deduced what it was, I can't explain."

"Okay, call me back first, please."

"Yes, sir."

Dylan hung up and opened Beau's email again, hoping somehow to read it differently. Still nothing. He took the message for what it was. Beau was asking him for a favor. To go talk to his son and help answer any questions. Dylan felt the honor Beau bestowed upon him and decided to leave first thing in the morning.

Chapter 82

The sense of accomplishment was there, but it was different from the other cases he had closed. Being close to this case, Chance Parker knew the Beau Rivers saga was over, ending with his dramatic death in the middle of Lake Jackson. Still, something was dissatisfying. It felt unfinished.

Chance gave himself the morning, so it was a few hours past normal starting time. Walking up the back staircase and into the Criminal Investigations Division, he was greeted with silence and indifference. Everyone had already moved on. His squad mates were busy working their cases, something that never slowed, even after a major case was done.

"Hey, Chance," Dani Del Rio offered from behind her cubicle wall.

"Hey, Dani."

Chance slowed, expecting more conversation, but the brief welcome was followed by more silence. He walked to his office and sat down. A pile of paperwork sat on his desk, begging for attention. He leaned back in his chair and just let his thoughts wander. From the chase of Beau Rivers to the intricate case built against Antonio Toombs to the relationship with his daughter, life was simply complicated.

He swiveled in his chair, purposely ignoring work but noticed a manila folder atop the pile. It had been left there to be dealt with later.

I guess later is now.

Inside the folder was the paperwork accumulated from the brief fugitive hunt for Beau. It contained a work-up on Gary Levine and Beau's ex-wife, Paige. There was no one else in Beau's life, at least not according to the information databases.

Flipping open the folder, glossy photographs stuffed in the middle caught his attention. He pulled them out to take another look at them.

The pictures showed Beau Rivers walking out of the evidence vault. Studying each picture, he moved them around like they were three dimensional, but nothing new stood out.

"Hey!" Del Rio poked her head in. Chance lowered the pictures. "You listening to the radio?"

"No, why?"

"House explosion and fire just got dispatched off Richmond Street. They think a body is inside. Didn't your guy Toombs get picked up over there?"

Chance immediately grew invested. This didn't sound like coincidence.

"Uh, yeah. It was the green house at the dead end. Why?"

"I think that's it. Weird, huh?"

Chance powered up his computer and opened a program that mirrored the dispatcher's screen. He confirmed the address of the fire was the same house where the arrest had been made. He tried to connect the Toombs case to the explosion, and although it felt connected, nothing fit.

Reading the dispatch notes of the call, the listed victim was a Neville Banks. It was believed that another subject was still inside the blaze. Further notes added later stated the fire was out and gave confirmation that the body of a very large man was found.

"Wanna go with?" Chance asked Del Rio.

"Sure. I'm not on your secret squad or anything. You sure it's allowed?"

"Smartass."

"Let me grab my stuff real quick."

"Okay."

Chance stood up in preparation to leave and glanced down at the surveillance picture, starting to close up the file. But something odd caught his attention. Something previously missed despite the scrutiny. Chance credited the odd angle from standing off to the side. He picked up the picture again. Just over Beau's left shoulder was a small, narrow cylinder sticking out a few inches. He had passed it off before as a weird shadow in the dark room, but now it was clear.

"It's the barrel of a rifle." The empty office didn't respond. The shadow of a thin cylinder stuck up past his shoulder giving him recognition, reminding him of a hunter toting a gun into the woods.

Further confirming his belief, he noticed the shoulder strap of the duffel bag was wider at the top. It was actually two straps overlapping, one for the rifle, the other for the bag.

Why did you need a rifle?

"Hey! You comin' or not?" Dani Del Rio barked.

"Huh? Oh, sorry. It's just that...." Chance paused and for some inexplicable reason, decided to keep what he saw in the picture to himself. He closed the folder and tossed it back on his desk. "Nothing, let's go."

***

Pulling off the main road that ran through Tom Brown Park, a small work truck traversed the dirt track around the outside of the baseball field. Past foul territory and squeezing past two wooden pylons, it continued up a small grassy hill that overlooked the field. Just past a clearing to the right was a cell phone tower, positioned on top of the hill for premium range.

The worker parked the truck at the base of the tower that was encapsulated by a chain-link fence. He looked up to the top of the tower stretched high into the sky. It looked infinite from this angle, a direct link to the heavens. He visually inspected the lights positioned at various heights of the tower and made a plan for where to start. Removing a bag of his tools from the front seat, he adjusted his hard hat and climbed the perimeter, starting his ascent of the tower.

At the first platform, he was at treetop level. Continuing, he reached the next platform and stood for a minute, taking in the view. The park stretched for several acres. A clover of softball fields was to the north, and beyond that, an open field for concerts and outside gatherings. A couple casually batted a ball back and forth on the tennis courts to the east. Taking in the panoramic view, he stopped when he peered to the west. He strained his eyes and saw the vantage was suitable for the mission. He could see straight down into the courtyard of the federal prison.

Chapter 83

The smell of smoke hung heavy in the air. Dani Del Rio parked behind all the fire trucks and emergency crews working the house fire. The flames were put out, and a three-man hose team worked the rubble, ensuring nothing was left smoldering. EMS workers at the back of an ambulance talked to an elderly black man with blank, cloudy gray eyes. His shirt was singed, and his face was covered in black soot. Chance pegged him as the victim, Neville Banks. Huddled off to the side, behind the crime scene tape were distraught neighbors watching with intense faces.

Chance tried Dylan's number one more time. He wanted to mention the rifle barrel he saw in the picture, but on the second try, there was no answer. Spying the Battalion Chief walking between the house and trucks, Chance got out and caught up to him.

"Hey Chief, Parker from TPD Homicide. I heard you had a body inside?"

"You heard right," he said, while still walking. Chance kept up.

"Can you tell me anything about the fire? How it started? Arson or accidental?"

"Too early to tell right now, but my guess is that it was intentional."

"So arson, then?"

The Battalion Chief gave him a confirming look, but didn't verbalize it. It was too early in the process, so he couldn't blame him for not committing, but if the fire was set intentionally and there was a body inside, this case would become a homicide. If that determination was made, he wanted to get started and not waste any time.

"The arson investigator is on the way. Should be here in the next minute or so. I'll make sure he hooks up with you to work the scene."

The Battalion Chief excused himself and walked over to one of the water trucks, giving the crew additional directions. Chance turned back to the house, a charred skeleton of what it was.

"What did he say?" Del Rio asked.

"Didn't really, but it's arson. That's what my gut tells me anyway."

"Well, shit. No rest for the weary, huh?"

"Not in homicide there isn't."

Within the next hour, the arson investigator arrived and walked the scene with Chance and Dani Del Rio. The dead body was in the living room. Although in life he was huge and muscular, the fire reduced him to charred flesh curled up in a small, fetal position. Chance recognized the pugilistic pose common to burn victims. The body retracts as the muscle loses all its water, a reaction to the intense heat of the fire, also an obvious sign he was overcome with smoke inhalation before the fire consumed him.

After the body, they focused on the back room of the house with the most damage. The floor had a gaping hole with blast and fire marks leaping up what was left of the walls. Standing amidst the soggy dirt and ash, Chance looked down through the hole.

"That'd do it," he said, catching the attention of the arson investigator and Del Rio.

"What?"

"The busted out hulls of three propane tanks. Something must've ignited them."

The arson investigator stepped to the edge of the hole and squatted down to get a better look. "Caps were removed."

"So, definitely arson."

"Oh, for sure."

Chance stepped away from the room and through to where the back door had been. It led to a small, cement porch and a barren patch of earth that was the backyard. Visually searching the area, he was looking for something, but it wasn't there. The only things that registered as odd were multiple piles of plastic pots, the kind used for houseplants.

"Dani, go find out if they used natural gas for cooking or anything like that. I don't see any grills or heaters that would require propane."

"There's an electric stove in the kitchen, well..., what's left of it, and I saw a kerosene heater stored in the corner."

"So, someone brought those tanks here, put them under the house, and somehow managed to ignite them."

"Looks that way."

The arson investigator chimed in, "Wouldn't have been hard with those caps off. Just needed a spark to kick those bad boys off."

"Gunna be hard to trace those tanks back to anywhere," Chance added.

Dani nodded in agreement.

"So, Mr. Banks was targeted. We need to find out why."

"This may be why," offered the arson investigator.

Parker and Del Rio turned to see the arson investigator arm deep in some sort of large metal box, burned and melted into a droopy resemblance of something once rigid. It was lying in a pile of rubble a few feet away from the giant hole in the floor caused by the propane tanks.

Looking closer, Chance saw the combination dial and a handle.

"It's a safe."

"Was a safe."

"What's in it?"

"Look for yourself."

Parker leaned over and peered inside. Reduced to wet, emulsified chunks was what he guessed was several million dollars in cash and a few handguns.

"That'll do it."

Chance's mind raced. This house was somehow connected with Antonio Toombs, but there was something else he was missing. Banks was obviously involved in Toombs's business, most likely safeguarding his money, but was there anything else?

"You think Toombs had anything to do with this? Or is it some kind of rival?"

"Could be a rival trying to take over what Toombs built, to send a message, but I don't think Toombs would have done this. I think he was keeping his money here."

"Money and guns," Dani added.

"Yeah, anything valuable—" Chance froze, as a thought snapped.

The letter.

Chance dug into the safe, sifting through the destroyed money, looking deep within. But everything was too badly burned to determine what was what. Pulling out wet mush, burnt and torn, it would be impossible to find remnants of a letter. He stood up looking around.

"You got something, Chance?" Dani asked.

"Umm, maybe. You see another safe or anything like that?"

Dani began searching along with Chance. After a thorough ten minutes of looking through the charred remains of the old house, nothing close to a safe was found.

Must've been in the safe with the money and guns.

"Want to let me in on what you're thinking?"

Chance instantly thought of Beau, but that didn't make sense either. His mind continued to race.

"Hello, earth to Chance. What are you thinking? Why were we looking for another safe?"

His eyebrow cocked, he looked at Dani and decided to keep it to himself. It sounded too crazy to repeat.

"Nothing. Just a hunch."

Chapter 84

Standing outside of Paige Rivers's home, apprehension stopped Dylan from ringing the doorbell. Facing Beau's family, however estranged, meant acceptance that he was gone. On the three-hour drive, he had dismissed all of the strange coincidences like the bathtub full of ice, the Medical Examiner's mention that the arm looked aged, and something he hung on to for a bit: Beau's use of the present tense in his email. Tell him that I love him, not loved. He allowed these anomalies to fester based on his own denial.

His phone buzzed in his pocket. Caller ID said it was Chance Parker. He needed to get through this before talking to Chance. He silenced the call and pocketed the phone.

After a deep breath and knuckles poised to knock, the door suddenly opened.

Paige waited on the inside with a somber expression.

"Hey, Paige. It's been a long time."

"Dylan Akers. Yes, it has."

"I'm sorry for just showing up like this, but I found an email from Beau asking me to come talk to Scotty, if that's okay?"

"I don't know, Dylan. He's pretty broken up."

Dylan frowned, knowing the pain of losing a loved one. He gave her a look, reminding her of his experience. "I'm sure he is. I just want to help."

"Okay, sure. Come in."

Dylan walked through the door and looked around. Memories of the house she shared with Beau seemed distant as he took in her current house. A portrait of her next to another man sat above the mantle of a white brick fireplace. They looked happy.

"I forgot you remarried."

"For about six years now. Phil is a good man, good husband, and a stable influence on Scotty. He's someone who's not going to have U.S. Marshal's kicking down my door!"

"Yeah, I heard about that. Sorry."

"So, can you tell me what happened? All I got was the notification from someone at the Sheriff's Office. Well, that and what we saw on the news."

"There's really nothing else to tell. Honestly, I have no know idea what he was trying to do. Everyone was speculating that he was going after Antonio Toombs before he got shot down."

"Why would he do that?"

Dylan recalled Chance mentioning the existence of a letter that was somehow relevant to Beau, but without anything else, he didn't want to burden her with more questions.

"I don't know."

"Uncle Dylan?"

The young voice came from the kitchen. Dylan stood up and saw Scotty staring back. For an instant, he was staring at a smaller version of Beau.

"Hey, Scotty. How are you?"

"Ehh, okay. I guess."

"You've gotten big my friend. How old are you now?"

"Twelve."

"Twelve? Almost a teenager. Well, I wanted to come see you. Check on you and tell you how sorry I am for what happened."

Scotty lowered his head. "That's okay."

"Well, I promised your dad I would come."

Paige stepped over to her son and hugged his shoulders. His head sank against her, hiding his emotion.

"He's just trying to help, son."

"Maybe I should go," Dylan said.

"Want to see my room?" the boy asked.

Caught off guard by the invite, Dylan was slow to accept. "Sure." He looked at Paige for explanation, but she had nothing to offer.

Scotty led the way upstairs and into his room. In it was a collection of baseball memorabilia, equipment, and spaceship models, including the

Millennium Falcon. He directed Dylan to sit down at a small desk where a computer sat next to the window. Scotty took a comfortable seat on the bed. His mood changed now that he was upstairs.

He smiled at Dylan.

Confused, he asked. "What?"

Scotty held his finger to his mouth. "Shhh."

Dylan hushed.

Scotty jumped from the bed and called out for his mom. She answered and he told her to never mind. "Just making sure she's downstairs." Scotty shut his door and walked over to the computer. Dylan saw a smile on his face.

"What's going on, Scotty?"

"About time you got here. I got something to show you." His demeanor was not that of a child in mourning.

He powered up his computer and directed the mouse to an icon, clicked it open, and typed in a password. It was for an email account. Watching the kid move with purpose gave Dylan an odd sensation that began to grow. It was hope.

Once the password was accepted, Scotty stood back, relinquishing control of the computer.

"Go ahead."

"What? I don't understand."

"Click on drafts. He left you a message."

Since Dylan had heard of Beau's escape, he had longed for a good-bye from his friend. He clicked the mouse, and the unsent email popped open.

Dear Dylan…

Chapter 85

The outside air was a welcomed change from the stuffy conditions inside the holding cells. Antonio stood in line as the guards opened the gate, letting the inmates file into the yard. Thirty minutes of rec time was short, but coveted. As soon as Antonio broke the threshold, he looked up into the blue sky, sucked in the warm summer air, and smiled. It was the highlight of his day, however, the thought of being out soon gave him the most comfort.

The plan was simple. Present the letter from Beau Rivers to the State Attorney in addition to truthful testimony that he saw the dirty cop pen the message. If he testified about the letter and how it detailed Rivers was taking the fall for both of the murders, it would guarantee he would walk. It would read great for the jury. In exchange for taking out a dirty cop, he sought immunity for his current charges. His crew had already taken the fall for those crimes. Sparing him wasn't too much to ask.

He couldn't help but smile.

His card-playing friend approached him with urgency.

"Hey Tony. Did you hear about Mr. Banks? You know, The Bank?"

There wasn't much that would reverse his mood, but the mention of where Antonio kept his money as well as his prized possession, the letter, caused him concern.

"Yes, yes. I know who you are talking about, and no, what happened?"

"My homeboy just said his house got blown up."

Panic seized Antonio's insides. He couldn't move and his mind went blank.

"You hear what I said, Tony Toombs?"

"What the fuck you mean blown up?" he shouted.

"They said someone put a bomb or something under the house. Blew that shit to hell. Killed his man Tiny and everything."

Antonio stood there, incredulous and unable to process what he was being told.

"What?" he asked in disbelief.

The card player began to repeat his statement but was met with a ferocious slap across the face.

"I heard what you said!"

"Sorry, Tony."

"Who'd you hear this from?"

He slowly raised his hand and pointed to another inmate standing on the side of the basketball court. Antonio found him with his eyes and walked straight over.

"Who told you about The Bank blowing up?"

Leary of the interruption, the inmate didn't answer right away, assessing Antonio.

"I said, who told you?" Antonio was seething.

"I gots people on that street. They know the old man. They told me."

It was the calm delivery from the inmate that seemed to confirm and verify the news. It was true.

"Fuck!" Antonio grabbed for more information. "Did they take the money inside, the guns, anything else?"

"No, they said the police found his safe full of burnt up money and shit."

A blinding pain seared in Antonio's brain. His foolproof plan had gone up in smoke along with Mr. Banks's house.

Antonio stormed off, feeling powerless. Who could have done this? Antonio searched the far reaches of his mind, trying to figure out who knew about the location of the letter and just how important it was.

Relocating to the corner of the yard, he needed to be alone. He needed time to think. *An up and coming rival*? But to torch The Bank, a neutral site where not only his money was kept, but also most of the Tallahassee underworld's was career suicide for anyone making a move. It didn't make sense. He thought about potential enemies of the old man, but he'd been in business for decades. That was unlikely. It had to be someone with no interest in the bank or the money inside. If it had been the cops, they would have just raided the place and seized the money as evidence, not torched the place.

Only one name remained. Beau Rivers. But how? That doesn't make any sense. He's dead.

Antonio let out a frustrated groan. His testimony would be suspicious without corroboration, but he was hoping it was still enough for immunity. He would summon his lawyer as soon as rec time was over. He needed to salvage this.

He turned his back to the courtyard, needing to look beyond the fence for a glimpse of what was outside the walls. Behind the courtyard, several of the female inmates walked between their dorms. Dressed in plain blue scrubs, they held no appeal and only reminded him of prison. In the distance, he saw the towering lights that hovered over the ballfields from the neighboring city park. Scanning the tree line, he noticed the evergreen pines were a soothing contrast to the azure sky. A moment of peace eased his anxiety.

A glint of metal pulled his attention further off in the distance. He squinted, catching the reflection again. It was coming from about halfway up a cell phone tower that sat on a small hill. Antonio made out a dark lump, the size of a man, on the tower. He stared for a moment as an uneasy feeling grew in the pit of his stomach. He sensed that the devil had finally caught up to him and wanted to collect his debt.

Suddenly, a flash of fire spat from the dark lump.

***

Waiting all morning on the second landing of the cell tower, he watched as the inmates were finally allowed recreational time in the yard. He opened up his tool bag and removed the lower part of a rifle, the stock and trigger housing. He set it to the side, removed the barrel, and screwed it into the lower. Next, he attached a magnifying optic to the top of the rifle. Lastly, he removed a single .308 rifle round and inserted it into the open bolt. Lying prone on the small landing, he pulled the stock tight against his shoulder, setting it deep into the pocket. He folded his left hand underneath his right elbow, steadying the gun. Placing his right cheek on the stock, he found a clear sight picture through the scope. Making adjustments for the distance and windage, he peered back through the scope. Moving the crosshairs across the yard, he found his target amongst the crowd. He was animated and upset about something, even slapping another inmate. After a moment, the inmate moved to the corner of the yard, giving the shooter a perfect line of sight. He inhaled, held the breath and let it out slowly. He could feel his heartbeat slowing. He did it again.

Without removing his aim from the optic, he reached up and closed the bolt, chambering the round. The target was standing still. Right hand back on the grip, he moved his finger into the trigger guard feeling it primed and ready. He flipped the safety off with his thumb and adjusted his left hand again under his right elbow. Pulling the rifle tighter against his shoulder, he took one last breath. The target turned and faced him, squinting. The reticle moved down across his chest and then slowly rose over the target's face. Letting his breath out slowly, he squeezed the trigger. With a hefty kick, the rifle sent the round hurtling four hundred yards into the forehead of his target. Blood sprayed out the back of his skull. As his life blinked off, the man fell lifeless to the ground. A pool of blood seeped from the back of his head. The other inmates scattered, followed by hysteria from the guards. Moments later, sirens wailed as everyone in the prison took shelter.

After disassembling the rifle and placing the parts back in the bag, he quickly descended the tower and returned to the truck. He removed his hard hat and tossed it on the front seat. He cranked up the engine, but before pulling back down the hill and blending in, he looked at himself in the rearview mirror. There was satisfaction and a sense of completion staring back. The job was now done. Beau Rivers left the park, knowing Antonio Toombs was no longer a threat to Dylan Akers and his family.

***

Chance Parker was covered in sweat and stank of smoke and ash. He was finalizing the on-scene duties of the Richmond Street arson, getting all the valuable evidence collected. His hunch was nagging, and he hated keeping it to himself. But working with Beau Rivers and Dylan Akers changed the way he saw law enforcement. There was right and wrong, and sometimes the law was incapable of determining which was which. It was up to the sheepdog to protect the flock, plain and simple.

Stepping away from the crime scene, he grabbed a bottle of water from the forensic van. He chugged it, thinking about his newfound philosophy.

I am a sheepdog.

Dani Del Rio hopped out of her car and, for the second time that day, delivered news to Chance Parker.

"Holy shit, you're not going to believe this, Chance."

"What?"

"A shooting just went down at the federal prison."

Chance didn't react, only absorbed the information. He let his mind consider the morning's events and why he had waded through soggy soot and ash. It was all connected to Tony Toombs. He rattled off, "It was Toombs. He's dead, isn't he?"

Amazed, Dani's eyes bulged. "How'd you know that?"

Chance shrugged.

"The guards said the shot came from Tom Brown Park, like four hundred yards away. Dropped Toombs in the yard with one shot."

Only a rifle was capable of that distance. The nagging from earlier returned. "Was he the only target?"

"Yeah, just him."

"They get the shooter?"

"No, they have the park surrounded, and they are calling in TAC to come in and search, but I'm betting that guy is long gone."

"Yeah, I don't think they'll find him."

"You think this fire and the shooting are connected?"

Chance gave her a feigned look and shrugged again, hiding his true thoughts. It was no coincidence if Antonio Toombs left the mystery letter in the safekeeping of Neville Banks that his house was burned down, and hours later, he was assassinated.

Of course they're connected.

The nagging pestering Chance turned into full-blown suspicion. All the facts smashed together in a loud collision of certainty. Chance smiled in admiration and chuckled to himself.

He walked out of earshot from Del Rio and looked up in the sky, addressing an unseen being. "I don't know how you did it, but I'm impressed, Beau. I'm impressed."

409

Chapter 86

Dylan hung on every word of the email.

Dear Dylan,

I am alive and well. I think it's best if I don't tell you where I'm at or where I'm going. I'm sorry I did not get a chance to say good-bye in person, but I think you may realize that wasn't quite possible given the circumstances. It was not my intention to hurt you further, only to protect you the only way I knew how. I decided to confess to the murders and claim full responsibility so you could return to your life with your beautiful family. I wrote you a letter detailing this, but it somehow fell into the hands of Antonio Toombs. He was planning on using it to his benefit, and I couldn't let it happen, so I broke out of jail. I hope that deputy is okay.

After taking care of a few things, I needed to create a large-scale diversion. Without it, I feared my plan wouldn't work. I thought stealing a helicopter was a pretty good attention getter. What did you think of my flying? When I led everyone near the lake, I counted on them trying to shoot me down, figuring I was going after Toombs. When they hit the rotor engine, I knew I was going to go down and the timing was perfect. When I dipped below the tree line, I tied the controls together and jumped out. The chopper continued longer than I thought and made a spectacular crash. The jump nearly knocked me out, and I laid there for a bit before dragging myself out of the area.

I know what you're thinking. The body parts. Obviously, they aren't mine. They belong to Gary Levine. His parting words to me were that he'd help me any way possible. I don't think he meant using his limbs to help fake my own death, so I hope he'll forgive me. I pretended I was from the funeral home and took his body from the morgue. I kept him on ice at his house. I removed a few parts and delivered the rest to the mortuary for him to be cremated. I left the remains in the chopper, hoping they would survive the crash. He would be happy, knowing at least part of him went on one last flight.

With everyone thinking I'm dead, I have one more thing to accomplish. I will ensure that the letter I wrote never surfaces and its existence dies with Antonio Toombs. After that's done, I will disappear. You will never see me again. This deeply saddens me, but it is what has to happen. You've been the best friend I've ever had, and I will cherish our friendship forever.

Scotty should have explained how to communicate with me, but use it sparingly. That US Marshal is resourceful and crafty. Do not tangle with him. Keep an eye on Chance. He's one of the good guys. He's one of us, a true sheepdog.

Please forgive Wendy. She loves you. You have a beautiful son who needs to know joy and love from a father like you.

Thank you for being my friend. Take care, Ace.

-Beau

Dylan wiped away a tear and reread the letter. He could hear Beau's voice as if he were sitting next to him, delivering the message in person. He nearly cried out with joy at hearing that he was alive, validating the crazy hunch that came to him at the morgue, but he quelled any reaction knowing it would be ill-received by Paige.

Scotty Rivers explained that his father opened up an email account so they could communicate with each other. Given very explicit instructions, Beau told Scotty that Dylan was the only person who he could share this information with. To talk back and forth, Scotty would draft an email but not send it. That way it refrained from leaving an imprint on the virtual world. Having the same log in and password, Beau, from a remote location, could open the account, read the draft, and reply in another draft without actually sending an email. After a month, they would switch the email to another domain to avoid detection. It was simple and effective.

"Thank you, Scotty. Your dad is a special man."

Scotty beamed with pride. "I wish he didn't have to go, though."

"Oh, I'm sure he's not too far away."

Hiding the knowledge that Beau was still alive and had faked his own death, Dylan walked downstairs to say good-bye to Paige and apologized for interrupting. She was still bitter at what she thought were Beau's selfish actions toward their son, but Dylan didn't correct her, knowing it was for the best.

Walking from the house to the car, the phone buzzed in his pocket. It was Chance Parker again.

"Hey, Chance. Sorry I didn't answer earlier. I was in the middle of something."

"You weren't over by the prison, were you?"

"Huh? No, I'm out of town actually. Why?"

"Oh, well. Antonio Toombs was just shot and killed."

"Really? How'd someone get a gun inside the prison?"

"They didn't. The shooter used a rifle from four hundred yards away."

"A rifle shot? Did they catch him?"

"No, not yet."

"Any leads?"

"Not yet, but guess what else? Guess what I've been doing all day?"

"What?"

"Working an arson-slash-homicide off Richmond Street. I'm pretty sure it was where Toombs was keeping his money and the letter, his get-out-of-jail-free card. Also, I was looking at the pictures from the evidence vault earlier, and I'm pretty sure Beau was carrying out a rifle with that duffle bag."

"Hmmm." Dylan recalled that Beau mentioned taking care of those two things in his email.

"Something you need to tell me, Lieutenant?"

"I got nothing, Detective Parker. Nothing at all."

Dylan ended the phone call and continued to his car. As he reached out for the door handle, the phone buzzed again.

He answered, "Parker, I don't have anything for you. I told you that already."

"Huh?" a female voice said.

"Oh, sorry. I thought you were someone else calling back. Hello?"

"That's okay. This is Gretchen from Property and Evidence. We've figured out what Rivers took from the vault."

"Oh, what was it?"

"It was from the Internal Affairs evidence. They keep all their evidence separate from ours. That's why it took forever for us to figure out."

"What did he take, Gretchen?"

"Well, it was two-hundred thousand dollars. The money was originally seized by Rivers during some drug raid, like, ten years ago, but then it was re-logged in by Inspector Trek as evidence in an IA case. For whatever reason, there was never a disposition for that case so it was just sitting there for years."

Dylan was speechless. Humored, but speechless at the irony. Gretchen noticed the silence.

"Hello, Lieutenant? Are you still there?"

"Um, yes. Sorry. Anything else?"

"No, nothing else."

"What about a rifle. Could he have taken a rifle from storage?"

"Oh, well. We didn't have any missing, but…,"

"But, what?"

"Well, since he was in here for at least a few minutes, he could have taken a rifle from the destroyed gun pile. We wouldn't have a record of it which would explain why we couldn't find that either."

"What do you mean?"

"All guns seized and sent off for destruction are taken out of our system and put in a large bin. When the bin is filled it is sent off to a factory that melts them down into reusable metals. If he took a rifle or anything from that bin and closed it back, it could certainly go unnoticed."

"I see. So it's possible."

"Yes. It's possible."

"Thank you, Gretchen."

Dylan hung up and sat in his car. He envisioned Beau starting a new life somewhere with money he had stolen. Thinking back, taking that money was the start of Beau's downward spiral. It was almost poetic that he reclaimed it for a fresh start.

Dylan laughed. He had been so worried about his friend he failed to realize he had been in control the entire time. He laughed until his sides hurt while tears leaked out from the corners of his eyes.

Clever, hillbilly. Clever.

***

One month later……

The rhythmic laps of the ocean waves falling on the beach were melodic and soothing. The natural sounds of the water instilled something primal, bringing a sense of peace. Peering out across the horizon from the wooden deck, Beau Rivers had found his refuge, although he still sought peace. Loneliness and isolation surrounded him, two things that were abundant when changing an identity.

It was just after sun up, and he had the boat ready. The ropes were double-checked, the oil to the engines full, gas topped off, and he ensured the instruments were all working and calibrated.

"All set down there?" a gruff voice asked from the top of the pier.

"Yes, sir. All set." Beau answered.

"Good deal."

"Anything else?"

"No, that'll be it for now. Maybe soon, I'll take you out on an excursion, let you work with Dave as the first mate."

He nodded. "That'd be great. Thanks."

"That'd let you earn a little more money. How's that sound?"

"That always sounds nice."

"Hey!" the salty captain snapped. "Captain Charlie will take care of you if you take care of him." He winked for emphasis and gave a hearty laugh to follow.

A boat motor gurgled slowly from around the corner of the marina. Turning to see the incoming boat, Beau's body tensed as he saw the distinctive blue and red light bar fixed to the top of the roof. The twenty-five-foot Nautica trolled past the sloop where Captain Charlie had moored his boat. Beau nervously coiled a rope with his back turned to the Marine Patrol boat.

As it pushed past the wake zone, beginning the day's patrol, Beau relaxed.

"We all make mistakes, son," Captain Charlie said, his voice sincere. "But sooner or later, we all have to face the music."

Beau feigned a smile. Charlie was intuitive, but Beau was confident his real identity wasn't known.

"Don't worry," Charlie added. "The sound of the ocean is my music."

Beau nodded back and stepped off the charter boat. Customers walked down the pier. He helped them load as the Captain welcomed them onboard. They were a well-to-do family down from the Midwest somewhere, Ohio, was Beau's best guess based on the accents.

After loading the boat and helping the Captain shove off, Beau walked down the pier to the warehouse where Captain Charlie kept a maintenance hangar. A small apartment, no more than five-hundred square feet, was in the corner of the hangar. Beau worked off the rent by prepping the charter boats for fishing and party excursions. The space was just enough for a bed, dresser, and television. A stand-up shower took up one corner, and a small sink and mirror sat next to it. It was plenty and all Beau needed.

Standing in front of the sink, he lowered his head and closed his eyes. He removed a dingy ball cap and slowly lifted his head to face the man in the mirror. Staring back was a man with a tanned face, thick beard, and long tousled hair. It was still him, somewhere in there, he convinced himself, just a new version hidden behind a natural veil of facial hair.

He sat down on the tiny bed. Looking around the cramped living space, there wasn't much to look at. At his feet was the black duffel bag that contained the stolen money. It was the second time he had taken it; the first was for the wrong reason. This time he would use it to jumpstart a life worth living. He kicked at it with his heels, making sure it was still there.

Nothing hung on the walls, no personal touches from his past life, making it hard to call this place home. Beau reached between his legs, underneath the mattress and pulled something out. Aside from his scars and memories, it was the only reminder of his past life. He'd left the frame, but grabbed the picture. The image of him and Dylan, arm-in-arm in their academy uniforms ready to take on the world, always gave Beau hope.

The version he left behind had set things in motion to allow a better life for Dylan Akers and his family. This gave him contentment knowing Dylan and Wendy had nothing to worry about except how to spend their future together.

This life was simple. Bad guys were replaced with bait and tackle, a friendly harbor master was substituted for a hateful IA commander, and the quaint marina took the place of a police department that didn't care. Instead of patrolling a beat, Beau took barefoot walks on the beach. There were no more carnage-filled crime scenes to work, domestic dramas to unravel, or collisions to sort through. The people he dealt with now genuinely wanted to see him and did not detest his presence because something had gone wrong. It was refreshing at times.

But with the simplicity came the silence of the sheepdog. It's hard to ignore what you are.

On the other side, Beau wondered how things would have been if everything played out differently. Prison was a stark possibility. As he looked around the dusty hangar, with the permanent smell of salt-water, he decided that with either outcome, he was destined to live in isolation and never return to his loved ones.

He wasn't sure if he had found redemption or hell. Maybe it was both.

The End

About the Author

William Mark grew up and currently lives in Tallahassee, Florida with his family. He attended the Tallahassee Community College where he graduated with an AA degree and the Florida State University where he graduated with a BS degree in Criminology and a minor in Psychology.

After college he attended the Pat Thomas Law Enforcement Academy in Midway, Florida. William has fourteen years of police experience, including assignments in Homicide and working as a member of the departments Tactical Apprehension and Control (TAC) team.

William and his family, a wife and three beautiful children, are active members in their church, avid Florida State Seminole fans, and enthusiastic travelers.

See the latest from William Mark at:

www.williammarkbooks.com